THINGS WE LEFT BEHIND

Center Point
Large Print

Also by Lucy Score and available from
Center Point Large Print:

Things We Never Got Over
Things We Hide from the Light

**This Large Print Book carries the
Seal of Approval of N.A.V.H.**

THINGS WE LEFT BEHIND

LUCY SCORE

CENTER POINT LARGE PRINT
THORNDIKE, MAINE

To 12-year-old, 17-year-old, 21-year-old, and 30-year-old me. You were never the disaster you thought you were. It's all going to work out.

1

Funeral Burrito

Sloane

The swing creaked rhythmically under me as I used a toe to push off against the porch floorboards. The chilly fingers of January slipped their way under the blanket and through the layers of my clothes. But the joke was on them because I was already frozen inside.

The droopy Christmas wreath on the proudly purple front door drew my eye.

I needed to take it down.

I needed to go back to work.

I needed to go back upstairs and put on the deodorant I'd forgotten.

Apparently, I needed to do a lot of things. All of them felt monumental, as if going back inside and climbing the stairs to my bedroom required the same amount of energy as trekking to the top of Everest.

Sorry, Knockemout. You're just going to have to deal with a librarian with body odor.

I sucked a breath of razor-sharp air into my lungs. It was funny how I needed to remind myself to do something as automatic as breathing. Grief had a way of infiltrating everything, even when you were prepared for it.

7

I lifted my dad's OPPOSING COUNSEL'S TEARS mug and took a fortifying sip of breakfast wine.

I would be spending the rest of the day in the cloying heat of Knock 'Em Stiff, Knockemout's irreverently named funeral home. The funeral home's thermostat never budged below seventy-five degrees to accommodate the thinner blood of the elderly crowds it usually entertained.

My breath left me in a silver cloud. When it dissipated, my view of the house next door was restored.

It was a nondescript two-story with beige siding and utilitarian landscaping.

To be fair, my whimsical Victorian made most homes look dull in comparison with its wrap-around porch and unsubtle turret. But there was an emptiness to the place next door that made the contrast more notable. The only signs of life for more than a decade had been limited to the crew that came to maintain the yard and sporadic visits by its obnoxious owner.

I wondered why he hadn't just sold it or burned it to the ground. Or whatever ridiculously wealthy men did to places that held shadows and secrets.

It annoyed me that he still owned it. That he still stayed there on occasion. Neither one of us wanted to be saddled with those memories. Neither one of us wanted to share a property line.

My front door opened, and out stepped my mother.

Karen Walton had always been beautiful to me.

Even today, even with fresh grief painted on her face, she was still lovely.

"What do you think? Is it too much?" she asked, doing a slow twirl in her new little black dress. The dignified boatneck and long sleeves gave way to a flirty party skirt with dark tulle that sparkled. Her sleek blond bob was held back with a velvet headband.

My friend Lina had taken us shopping a few days ago to help us find our funeral outfits. My dress was a short, fitted ebony knit with pockets hidden in the seams of the skirt. It was beautiful and I was never going to wear it again.

"You look great. It's perfect," I assured her, lifting up a corner of the blanket in invitation.

She sat and patted my knee as I covered us both.

This swing had been at the center of our family forever. We'd congregated here for after-school snacks and gossip. My parents met on this swing for a weekly year-round happy hour. After the Thanksgiving dishes were done, we'd all lounge out here with our favorite books and cozy blankets.

I'd inherited the ridiculous beast of a home with its olive-green, purple, and navy paint two years ago when my parents moved to DC to be closer to Dad's doctors. I had always loved it. There was no other place on earth that would ever feel like home. But it was moments like this that made me realize that instead of growing, our family was getting smaller.

Mom blew out a breath. "Well, this sucks."

"At least we look good *while* it sucks," I pointed out.

"It's the Walton way," she agreed.

The front door opened again and my sister, Maeve, joined us. She wore a no-nonsense black pantsuit and a wool coat, and she clutched a steaming mug of tea. She looked pretty as always, but tired. I made a mental note to harass her after the funeral to make sure nothing else was going on with her.

"Where's Chloe?" Mom asked.

Maeve rolled her eyes. "She's got it narrowed down to two outfits and told me she needed some time with each one before she could make her final decision," she said, squeezing herself onto the cushion next to our mother.

My niece was a fashionista of the highest caliber. At least the highest caliber a twelve-year-old on a limited allowance in rural Virginia could achieve.

We rocked in silence for a few moments, each lost in our own memories.

"Remember when your father bought the Christmas tree that was so fat it couldn't fit through the front door?" Mom asked, a smile in her tone.

"The beginning of our porch tree tradition," Maeve recalled.

I felt a stab of guilt. I hadn't put up a porch tree this Christmas. I hadn't even put up an indoor tree. Just the now-dead wreath I'd bought from Chloe's school fundraiser. Cancer had made other plans for our family.

I would make up for it next Christmas, I decided. There would be life here. Family here. Laughter and cookies and alcohol and badly wrapped gifts.

That was what Dad had wanted. To know that life would go on even though we missed him terribly.

"I know your father was the pep talk giver," Mom began. "But I promised him I'd do my best. So this is how it's gonna go. We're going to march into that funeral home and give him the best damn funeral this town has ever seen. We're going to laugh and cry and remember how lucky we were to have had him for as long as we did."

Maeve and I nodded, tears already welling in our eyes. I blinked them back. The last thing my mom or sister needed was to deal with a volcano of sad from me.

"Can I get a hell yeah?" Mom said.

"Hell yeah," we answered in quavering voices.

Mom looked back and forth between us. "That was pathetic."

"Geez. Sorry we're not chipper enough about Dad's funeral," I said dryly.

Mom reached into a pocket in the skirt of her dress and produced a pink stainless-steel flask. "This should help."

"It's 9:32 A.M.," Maeve said.

"I'm drinking wine," I countered, holding up my mug.

Mom handed my sister the ladylike flask. "As your father liked to say, 'We can't drink all day if we don't start now.' "

Maeve sighed. "Fine. But if we're going to start drinking now, we're taking a Lyft to the funeral."

"I'll drink to that," I agreed.

"Cheers, Dad," she said and took a nip from the flask, wincing almost immediately.

Maeve handed back the flask, and Mom raised it in a silent toast.

The front door banged open again, and Chloe vaulted onto the porch. My niece was wearing patterned tights, purple satin shorts, and a ribbed turtleneck. Her hair was styled in two black puffs on top of her head. Maeve must have lost the makeup battle today, because Chloe's eyelids were a deep shade of purple. "Do you think this will take too much attention away from Gramps?" she asked, striking a pose with her hands on her hips.

"Dear lord," my sister muttered under her breath and stole the flask again.

"You look beautiful, sweetheart," Mom said, grinning at her only grandchild.

Chloe executed a spin. "Thank you and I know."

The pudgy, grumpy cat I'd inherited along with the house slunk onto the porch looking judgmental as always. The half-feral fleabag had been given the regal name Lady Mildred Meowington. Over time, it had been shortened to Milly Meow Meow. Nowadays, when I had to yell at her for the eighteenth time not to claw the back of the couch, it was just Meow Meow or Hey, Asshole.

"Go inside, Meow Meow, or you'll be left out all day," I warned.

The cat didn't dignify my warning with a response. Instead she brushed against Chloe's black tights and then sat at her feet to lavish her feline butthole with attention.

"Gross," Maeve noted.

"Great. Now I have to de-fur my tights," Chloe complained with a stamp of one booted foot.

"I'll find the lint roller," I volunteered, rising from the swing and nudging the cat with my foot until she flopped over on her back to bare her tubby tummy. "Who wants breakfast wine?"

"You know what they say," Mom said, tugging my sister to her feet. "Chardonnay is the most important meal of the day."

The warm, fuzzy, alcohol blur began to wane around hour two of the visitation. I didn't want to be here standing in front of a stainless-steel urn in a room with moody peacock wallpaper, accepting condolences and listening to stories of what a great man Simon Walton was.

There would be no new stories now, I realized. My sweet, brilliant, kindhearted, uncoordinated dad was gone. And all we were left with were memories that would never come close to filling the hole his absence left behind.

"I just don't know what we're going to do without Uncle Simon," my cousin Nessa said, juggling a chubby baby on her hip while her husband wrangled their bow tie–wearing three-year-old. My dad had always worn bow ties. "He and your mom came over once a month to babysit so Will and I could have a date night."

"He loved spending time with your kids," I assured her.

My parents had made no secret about wanting a house full of family. That was the reason they'd bought an eighteen-room rambling Victorian with a formal dining room big enough to seat twenty. Maeve had dutifully coughed up one grandkid, but divorce and a high-powered legal career had temporarily shuttered plans for a second.

And then there was me. I was head librarian of the best damn public library in the tricounty area, working my ass off to expand our catalog, programs, and services. But I was no closer to marriage and babies now than I'd been at thirty. Which was . . . hell. A while ago.

Nessa's baby blew a raspberry at me and looked exceedingly pleased with herself.

"Uh-oh," my cousin said.

I followed her gaze to the toddler who was evading his father by running circles around the urn's pedestal.

"Hold this," Nessa said, handing me the baby. "Mama needs to quietly and gracefully save the day."

"You know," I said to the baby, "my dad would probably love it if your brother accidentally dumped his ashes today. He'd think it was hilarious."

She looked at me with owlish curiosity from the biggest, bluest eyes I'd ever seen. She was mostly bald with wispy blond hair carefully tucked under a sassy pink bow. One drool-soaked fist reached out, and she traced her finger over my cheek.

The gummy smile took me by surprise as did the delighted giggle that emanated somewhere from her round belly. Happiness—the effervescent kind—bubbled up inside me.

"Crisis averted," Nessa said, reappearing. "Aww, she likes you!"

My cousin took her daughter from me, and I was surprised when I instantly missed the warm, giggly weight in my arms. Feeling dazed, I watched the little family move down the line to greet my mother and sister.

I'd heard of women's biological clocks kicking in with one whiff of a baby's head, but a countdown kicked off at a funeral? That had to be a first.

Of course I wanted a family. I'd always assumed I'd make time . . . after college, then after I landed my first job, then after I landed my dream job in my hometown, then after I got the library moved into its new building.

I wasn't getting younger. My eggs weren't miraculously getting fresher. If I wanted a family of my own, I needed to start now.

Well, shit.

Evolutionary instincts took over, and I sized up Bud Nickelbee as he stepped in front of me and offered his condolences. Bud's thin, reedy frame was always clad in overalls. A glasses wearer myself, I didn't mind his Lennon-style spectacles. But the long, silver ponytail and his plans to retire and build an off-the-grid bunker in Montana were deal-breakers.

I needed a man young enough to *want* to suffer through babies with me. Preferably here, with a Costco and Target nearby.

My biological clock epiphany was interrupted by the arrival of Knox and Naomi Morgan. The bearded bad boy of Knockemout had fallen hard for the runaway bride when she'd swept into town last year. Together, they'd managed to build the kind of swoony happily ever after I'd devoured on the page as a teen . . . and a young adult . . . and as recently as last week.

Speaking of evolutionary instincts, the grumpy Knox in a suit—tie askew as if he couldn't be bothered to tie it correctly—was definitely fatherhood material. His broad-shouldered brother, Nash, appeared in full police uniform behind him. He possessively gripped the hand of his fiancée, the beautiful and fashionable Lina. Both men were stellar sperm material.

I shook myself out of my reproductive reverie. "Thank you guys for coming," I said.

Naomi looked feminine and soft in a navy wool dress, her hair styled in bouncy brunette waves. Her hug smelled vaguely of lemon Pledge, which made me smile. When she was stressed or bored or happy, Naomi cleaned. It was her love language. The library had never been cleaner since she took on the role of community outreach coordinator.

"We're so sorry about Simon. He was such a

16

wonderful man," she said. "I'm glad I got to meet him at Thanksgiving."

"Me too," I agreed.

It had been the last official Walton holiday in the family home. The house had been bursting at the seams with friends and family and food. So. Much. Food. Despite his illness, Dad had been deliriously happy.

The memory had a fresh wave of grief slamming into me, and it took everything I had not to give in to the ugly cry that I managed to disguise as a hiccup as I pulled free of Naomi's embrace.

"Sorry. Too much breakfast wine," I fibbed.

Our friend Lina stepped up. She was long-legged and edgy even in a sexy pantsuit and mouth-watering stilettos. She grimaced, then leaned in for an awkward hug. Lina wasn't the touchy-feely type with anyone other than Nash. It made me appreciate the gesture even more.

Although if people didn't stop being nice to me, the dam holding back the endless reservoir of grief was going to crack.

"This sucks," she whispered before releasing me.

"Yeah. It really does," I agreed, clearing my throat and forcing the emotions back down. I could do anger. Anger was easy and clean and transformative, powerful even. But the messier emotions I wasn't comfortable sharing with others.

Lina stepped back and slid neatly under Nash's arm. "What are you doing after this . . . shindig?" she asked.

I knew exactly why she was asking. They would show up for me if I asked. Hell, even if I didn't ask. If they thought for one second that I needed a shoulder to cry on, a well-made cocktail, or my floors mopped, Naomi and Lina would be there.

"Mom booked an overnight stay at a spa with some friends, and Maeve is doing a family dinner tonight for out-of-town guests," I said. It wasn't a lie. My sister *was* hosting our aunts and uncles and cousins. But I had already planned to feign a migraine and spend the night letting out my sloppy torrent of sad in the privacy of my own home.

"Let's get together soon. But not at work," Naomi added sternly. "You take as much time off as you need."

"Yeah. Definitely. Thanks," I said.

My friends moved on down the receiving line to my mom, leaving their future baby daddies with me.

"This fucking blows," Knox said gruffly when he hugged me.

I smiled against his chest. "You're not wrong."

"If you need anything, Sloaney Baloney," Nash said, stepping in to deliver his hug. He didn't need to finish the sentence. We'd grown up together. I knew I could depend on him for anything. The same with Knox, even though Knox wouldn't actually offer. He'd just show up and grumpily perform some thoughtful act of service and then get mad if I tried to thank him.

"Thank you, guys."

Nash pulled back and scanned the crowd that

spilled out of the room and into the foyer. Even at a funeral, our chief of police was like a guard dog making sure his flock was safe. "We never forgot what your dad did for Lucian," he said.

I tensed. Every time someone mentioned the man's name, it felt like a bell rung in my skull, resonating in my bones as if it was supposed to mean something. But it didn't. Not anymore. Unless "I hate that guy" counted as "something."

"Yeah, well, Dad helped a lot of people in his life," I said awkwardly.

It was true. Simon Walton had given back as an attorney, a coach, a mentor, and a father. Come to think of it, he and his greatness were probably to blame for my current marriage-less, baby-less existence. After all, how was I supposed to find a partner in life when no one measured up to what my parents had found in each other?

"Speak of the devil," Knox said.

We all looked to the doorway at the back of the room that suddenly seemed dwarfed by the brooding man in an expensive-ass suit.

Lucian Rollins. Luce or Lucy to his friends, of whom he had few. Lucifer to me and the rest of his legion of enemies.

I *hated* how my body reacted to the man every time he walked into a room. That tingling awareness like every nerve in my body just got the same message at the same time.

I could deal with that innate, biological warning that danger was near. After all, there was nothing safe about the man. What I couldn't handle was how the tingling turned immediately into a warm, happy, reflexive *There you are,* as if I'd been holding my breath for him to appear.

I considered myself to be an open-minded, live-and-let-live, reasonably mature adult. Yet I couldn't stand Lucian. His very existence pushed every button I had. Which was exactly what I reminded myself every damn time he appeared as if conjured from some stupid, desperate place in my psyche. Until I reminded myself that he wasn't the beautiful, rakish boy of my teenage bookworm dreams anymore.

That Lucian, the dreamy, hopeful boy who carried a burden much too heavy, was gone. In his place was a cold, ruthless man who hated me as much as I hated him.

"I trusted you, Sloane. And you broke that trust. You did more damage than he ever could."

We were different people now. Our gazes locked in that familiar, uncomfortable recognition.

It was strange, having a secret with the boy I'd once loved and now sharing it with the man I couldn't stand. There was a subtext to every interaction. A meaning no one but the two of us could decipher. And maybe there was a small, stupid, dark corner inside me that felt a thrill every time our eyes locked. As if that secret had bonded us in a way that could never be undone.

He was moving forward, the crowd parting around him as power and wealth blazed their own trail.

But he didn't come to me. He went straight to my mother.

"My sweet boy." Mom opened her arms, and Lucian stepped into them, wrapping her up in a hug that displayed a disconcerting familiarity.

Her sweet boy? Lucian was a forty-year-old megalomaniac.

The Morgan brothers moved on to join their friend with my mom.

"How are you all doing, Sloane?" Mrs. Tweedy, Nash's elderly, gym-going neighbor demanded as she took their place. She was wearing an all-black velour tracksuit, and her hair was pushed back from her face with a somber-looking sweatband.

"We're doing okay. Thank you so much for coming," I said, taking her callused hand.

Out of the corner of my eye, I saw Mom pull back slightly from her embrace with Lucian. "I can't thank you enough. I'll never be able to repay you for what you did for Simon. For me. For our family," she said to him tearfully.

Uh, what? My eyeballs had no choice but to fly to Lucian's devilishly handsome face.

God, he was beautiful. Supernaturally molded by the gods beautiful. He would make gorgeous little demon babies.

No. No. Nope. Absolutely not. My biological downward spiral was not going to make me look at Lucian Rollins as a potential mate.

"You know, they say weight lifting is good for grief. You should come on down to the gym this

21

week. My crew will take good care of you," Mrs. Tweedy squawked as I strained to eavesdrop on my mother and Lucian.

"I'm the one who owes you both," he said, his voice husky.

What in the hell were they talking about? Sure, my parents and Lucian had been close when he was the wayward teen next door. But this sounded like something deeper, more recent. What was happening, and why didn't I know about it?

Fingers snapped in my face, jolting me out of my head.

"You okay, kiddo? You look pale. You want a snack? I got a protein bar and a flask in here," Mrs. Tweedy said, digging into her gym bag.

"Are you all right, Sloane?" Mom asked, noticing our kerfuffle.

Both she and Lucian were looking at me now.

"I'm fine," I assured her quickly.

"She zoned out," Mrs. Tweedy tattled.

"Really, I'm fine," I insisted, refusing to meet Lucian's gaze.

"You've been up here for over two hours straight. Why don't you get some fresh air?" Mom suggested. I was about to point out that she'd been standing there just as long as I had when she turned to Lucian. "Would you mind?"

He nodded, and then suddenly he was in my space. "I'll take her."

"I'm fine," I said again, taking a panicky step back. My escape was blocked by a large display

22

of funeral flowers. My butt rammed the stand, and the arrangement from the Knockemout Fire Department wobbled precariously.

Lucian steadied the flowers and then placed a big, warm hand on my lower back. It felt like getting struck by lightning directly on the spine.

I was careful about never touching him. Strange things happened inside me when we did.

I didn't make the conscious decision to let him guide me out of the receiving line. But there I was, moving along like an obedient golden retriever.

Naomi and Lina were halfway out of their seats, looking concerned. But I shook my head. I could handle this.

He led me out of the sweltering room to the coat check, and in less than a minute, I found myself standing on the sidewalk in front of the funeral home, the overwhelming press of bodies, the hum of conversation left behind us. It was a bleak, wintery Wednesday. My glasses fogged up at the change in temperature. The swollen, slate-gray clouds hung pendulously above, promising snow by the day's end.

Dad loved snow.

"Here," Lucian said irritably, shoving a coat at me.

He was tall, dark, and evil.

I was short, fair, and awesome.

"That's not mine," I said.

"It's mine. Put it on before you freeze to death."

"If I put it on, will you go away?" I asked.

I wanted to be alone. To catch my breath. To

glare up at the clouds and tell my father I missed him, that I hated cancer, that if it snowed, I would lay on my back in it and make him a snow angel. Maybe I'd have time to let out a few of the tears I'd dammed up inside me.

"No." He took matters into his own hands and draped the coat over my shoulders.

It was a thick, dark cashmere-like material with a smooth satin lining. Rich. Sexy. It hung heavy on me like a weighted blanket. It smelled . . . Heavenly wasn't the right word. Delectably dangerous. The man's scent was an aphrodisiac.

"Did you eat today?"

I blinked. "What?"

"Did you eat today?" He enunciated each word with irritation.

"You don't get to be snappy with me today, Lucifer." But my words lacked their usual heat.

"That's a no then."

"Excuse us for having a breakfast of whiskey and wine."

"Christ," he muttered. Then he reached for me.

Rather than jumping back or karate chopping him in the throat, I stood dumbfounded. Was he making a clumsy attempt to hug me? Feel me up? "What are you doing?" I squeaked.

"Hold still," he ordered. His hands disappeared into the pockets of his coat.

He was exactly a foot taller than me. I knew because we'd measured once. His pencil line was still in the doorway of my kitchen. Part of the history we both pretended not to acknowledge.

He produced a single cigarette and a sleek silver lighter.

Even bad habits couldn't control Lucian Rollins. The man allowed himself one single cigarette a day. I found his self-control annoying.

"You sure you want to use up your one smoke break now? It's barely noon," I pointed out.

Glaring at me, he lit the cigarette, pocketed the lighter, and then pulled out his phone. His thumbs flew over the screen before he stowed it back in his jacket. He yanked the cigarette out of his mouth and exhaled blue smoke while glaring at me.

Every move was predatory, economic, and pissy.

"You don't need to babysit me. You've made your appearance. You're free to go. I'm sure you have more important things to do on a Wednesday than hang out in Knockemout," I told him.

He eyed me over the end of his cigarette and said nothing. The man had a habit of studying me like I was fascinatingly abhorrent. Like the way I looked at garden slugs in my backyard.

I crossed my arms. "Fine. If you're hell-bent on staying, why did my mom say she owes you?" I asked.

He continued to stare silently at me.

"Lucian."

"Sloane." He rasped my name like a warning. And despite the icy fingers of cold trailing up my spine, I felt something warm and dangerous uncurling inside me.

"Do you have to be so obnoxious all the time?"
I asked.

"I don't want to fight with you today. Not here."

In a humiliating turn of events, my eyes instantaneously welled with hot tears.

Another dizzying wave of grief crashed into me, and I fought to push it back.

"There won't be any new stories," I murmured.

"What?" he snapped.

I shook my head. "Nothing."

"You said there won't be any new stories," he prompted.

"I was talking to myself. I'll never have another new memory of my dad." To my undying embarrassment, my voice broke.

"Fuck," Lucian muttered. "Sit down."

I was so busy trying not to show my worst enemy my sloppy tears that I barely registered him shoving me none too gently to the curb. His hands rummaged through the coat pockets again, and a handkerchief appeared in front of my face.

I hesitated.

"If you use my coat to wipe your nose, I'll make you buy me a new one, and you can't afford it," he warned, brandishing the handkerchief.

I snatched it out of his hand.

He sat next to me, careful to keep several inches between us.

"I don't want to hear you whining about getting dirt on your fancy suit," I grumbled then noisily blew my nose in his ridiculous handkerchief. Who

26

carried reusable snot rags with them these days?

"I'll try to control myself," he said mildly.

We sat in silence as I did my best to get myself back under control. I tilted my head and looked up at the heavy clouds, willing the tears to dry up. Lucian was the last person on earth I wanted to see me vulnerable.

"You could have distracted me with a nice, normal fight, you know," I accused.

On a sigh, he exhaled another cloud of smoke. "Fine. It was stupid and selfish of you not to eat this morning. Now your mother is inside worrying about you, making a bad day even worse for her. Your sister and friends are concerned you're not handling things. And I'm out here making sure you don't pass out so they can keep grieving."

My spine straightened. "Thanks so much for your *concern*."

"You have one job today. Hold your mother up. Support her. Share her grief. Do whatever it takes to be what *she* needs today. You lost your dad, but she lost her partner. You can mourn your own way later. But today is about her, and making her worry about you is fucking selfish."

"You are such an ass, Lucifer." An astute, not exactly wrong ass.

"Get your shit together, Pixie."

The old nickname did the trick, blocking out the unrelenting sadness with a feisty bout of fury. "You are the most arrogant, opinionated—"

A dented pickup truck with Knockemout Diner

decals on the doors screeched to a stop in front of us, and Lucian handed me his cigarette.

He rose as the window rolled down.

"Here you go, Mr. Rollins." Bean Taylor, the scrawny, frenetic manager of the diner leaned out and handed Lucian a paper bag. Bean spent all day every day eating deep-fried diner delights and never gained an ounce. The second a salad touched his lips, he packed on the pounds.

Lucian handed him a fifty-dollar bill. "Keep the change."

"Thanks, man! Real sorry to hear about your dad, Sloane," he called out the window.

I smiled weakly. "Thanks, Bean."

"Gotta get back. I left the wife in charge, and she burns the hash browns."

He drove off, and Lucian dropped the bag in my lap.

"Eat."

With that order, he turned on his heel and strode back to the entrance of the funeral home.

"I guess I'm keeping the coat," I called after him.

I watched him go, and then when I was certain he was inside, I opened the bag to find my favorite breakfast burrito wrapped tight in foil. The diner didn't deliver. And Lucian shouldn't have known my favorite breakfast.

"Infuriating," I muttered under my breath before briefly bringing the filtered tip of his cigarette to my lips where I could almost taste him.

2

Keep the Coat and Leave Me Alone

Lucian

By the time I pulled into the driveway of the house I hated, fat flakes had been falling for nearly an hour. I exhaled slowly and slumped against the heated leather of my Range Rover's driver's seat. Shania Twain crooned softly from the speakers. The windshield wipers groaned across the glass swiping away the snow.

It looked as though I'd be spending the night here, I told myself, as if that hadn't been the plan all along.

As if I didn't have an overnight bag on the back seat.

As if I didn't have this cloying need to stay close. Just in case.

I punched the button on the remote for the garage and watched the door silently rise before me in the headlights. The services and meal had eaten up the remaining daylight hours. Friends and loved ones had lingered over Simon's favorite dishes and drinks, reminiscing while I'd avoided Sloane. I didn't trust myself to keep her at the necessary distance when she was wounded like this, so I'd relied on physical distance.

29

I dismissed all thoughts of the blond pixie from my mind and focused on other more important, less annoying things. Tonight, Karen Walton and a few of her local friends were safely ensconced in suites at a spa just outside DC where they would enjoy a day of pampering tomorrow.

It was the least I could do for the neighbors who had given me everything.

The caller ID on my dashboard screen lit up.

Special Agent Idler.

"Yes?" I answered, pinching the bridge of my nose.

"I thought you'd be interested to know that no one has seen or heard from Felix Metzer since September," she said without preamble. The FBI agent had even less enthusiasm than I did for wasting time with unnecessary small talk.

"That's inconvenient." Inconvenient and not entirely unexpected.

"Let's skip to the part where you assure me you had nothing to do with his disappearance," she said pointedly.

"I'd think my cooperation in this investigation should at least buy me the benefit of the doubt."

"We both know you have the means to disappear just about anyone who annoys you."

I glanced again at the fanciful house next door. There were exceptions.

I heard the snick of a lighter and an indrawn breath and wished I hadn't already smoked my only cigarette of the day. I blamed Sloane. My self-control wavered around her.

"Look, I know you probably didn't dismember Metzer and feed him to your school of highly trained piranhas or whatever the hell aquatic life you rich guys invest in. I'm just pissed. Our useless crime boss son gave us the name, we did the legwork, but it's yet another lead that didn't pan out."

The longer my team worked with Idler's, the less annoying I found her. I admired her single-minded quest for justice, even though I preferred vengeance.

"Maybe he went underground," I suggested.

"I've got a bad feeling about it," Idler said. "Someone is cleaning up their mess. I'm gonna be pissed if this keeps me from personally slamming a cell door in Anthony Hugo's face. The only two people alive who can corroborate that Anthony commissioned a list of people for his minions to assassinate are his idiot criminal son and his idiot criminal son's ex-girlfriend. Neither is going to win any points in front of a jury."

"I'll get more," I assured her. I wasn't about to let a man like Anthony Hugo walk away unscathed from hurting the people I loved.

"Until Metzer or his body show up, we're looking at another dead end."

"My team is working on untangling Hugo's financials. We'll find what you need," I promised. Hugo was good, but I was better and more tenacious.

31

"You're awfully calm for a civilian who could become part of the mess that needs cleaning," she pointed out.

"If Hugo comes for me, he won't find an easy target," I promised grimly.

"Yeah, well, don't do anything stupid. At least not before you get me something I can use to nail the bastard with."

My team had already gotten her several small somethings. But the FBI wanted an airtight case with charges that ensured life in prison. I would see to it they had it.

"I'll do my best. As long as you don't contemplate making any deals that impact those I care about." My gaze flicked next door again. The house was still dark.

"Hugo is the big fish. There will be no deals," Idler promised.

I let myself into the mudroom, the perfect organizational space for the family that didn't live here. The furniture, the finishes, even the layout of the house had changed. But even new paint, carpet, and cabinetry weren't enough to vanquish the memories.

I still hated it here.

It made no financial sense to hang on to this godforsaken place, this reminder of a past better forgotten. Yet here I was. Once again spending the night as if I could somehow weaken the hold it had on me if I just spent enough time here.

It was smarter all around to sell the place and be done with it.

It was why I'd come back last summer. But one look at those green eyes—not a soft, mossy green. No, Sloane Walton's eyes blazed with emerald flames. One look and my best-laid plans disintegrated.

But it was time. Time to free myself from the house, the memories. From the weakness those years symbolized. I'd risen above. I'd made something of myself. And even if I was still a monster under the trappings of wealth and power, I had done some good. Wasn't that enough?

I would never be good enough. Not with this blood in my veins, on my hands.

I'd made the decision to move on in the thick heat of last August. The summer swelter had made me think I'd gotten over the painful hope of spring. Yet here I was, six months later, and the ties that had anchored me to this place felt even more restricting. I blamed Sloane for why I counted down the days until spring.

Until the trees bloomed.

I hated to think the reason for my life in DC was tied to something so pathetically fragile. That *I* was something so pathetically fragile. Yet every spring when those fragrant pink blooms exploded into being, my chest loosened. My breath relaxed. And my oldest enemy stirred.

Hope. Some of us didn't get the luxury of hope. Some of us weren't worthy of it.

Soon, I promised myself. Once I knew the Waltons were taken care of, I'd sever ties with this place. I'd give myself one last spring here and then I'd never come back.

I flipped on the lights in the kitchen, a clean space of grays and whites, and stared at the stainless steel silhouette of the refrigerator.

I wasn't hungry. The thought of food made me feel vaguely nauseated. I wanted another cigarette. A drink. But I was nothing if not disciplined. I made choices that made me stronger, smarter. I prioritized the long game over short-term fixes. Which meant ignoring my baser instincts.

I opened the freezer and grabbed a container at random. I pried off the lid of some chicken dijonnaise and threw it in the microwave to defrost. As the timer counted down, I bowed my head and let the tight leash I'd kept on my grief loosen.

I wanted to fight. To rage. To destroy.

A good man had been taken. Another one, an evil one, had escaped without suffering his full punishment. And I could do nothing about either. With all the wealth and favors I'd amassed, I was once again powerless.

My hands fisted on the counter until my knuckles went white and a memory surfaced.

"Place is looking better," Simon had told me when he wandered in through the open garage door.

I'd been covered in sweat and dust, sledge-

34

hammering my way through drywall and ghosts.

"Is it?" my twentysomething self asked. It looked like an explosion had hit the kitchen.

"Sometimes in order to build things back up, you gotta tear them down to the studs. Want some help?"

Just like that, the man who'd saved my life picked up a hammer and helped me raze the ugliest parts of my past.

The doorbell rang, and my head came up. The anger retreated dutifully back into its box. I debated ignoring whoever it was. But the bell rang several more times in rapid succession.

Irritated, I yanked open the door, and my heart stuttered. It always did when I saw her unexpectedly. Part of me, some small, weak splinter buried down deep, saw her and wanted to draw nearer. Like she was a campfire beckoning with a promise of warmth and goodness in the dark night.

But I knew better. Sloane didn't offer warmth. She promised third-degree burns.

She was still wearing the black dress and glittery belt she'd worn to the funeral, but instead of the heels that brought her higher on my chest, she had donned snow boots. And my coat.

She pushed past me carrying a paper bag.

"What are you doing?" I demanded as she ventured down the hall. "You're supposed to be at your sister's."

"Keeping tabs on me, Lucifer? I didn't feel

like company tonight," she called over her shoulder.

"Then what are you doing here?" I asked, following her toward the back of the house. I hated her here. It made my skin crawl, my stomach churn. But some sick, stupid part of me craved her proximity.

"You don't count as company," she said, tossing my coat on the counter. I wondered if it smelled like her or if, by wearing it, she now smelled like me.

Sloane opened a cabinet, then closed it and opened the next. She rose on tiptoe. The hem of her dress inched higher on her thighs, and I realized she'd also removed her tights. I wondered for one brief, moronic second if she'd taken off anything else before I forced myself to drag my attention away from her skin.

I didn't know exactly when it had happened. When the kid next door had turned into the woman I couldn't evict from my brain.

Sloane found a plate and dumped the contents of the greasy brown bag onto it with a flourish.

"There. We're even," she announced. The tiny fake diamond stud in her nose twinkled. If she were mine, it would have been a real stone.

"What is this?"

"Dinner. You made your little point with your breakfast burrito. So here's post-funeral dinner. I don't owe you anything."

There were no "thank yous" or "you're welcomes" between us. We wouldn't have meant them. What did exist was a compulsion to balance the scales, to never be in debt to the other.

I glanced down at the plate. "What is it?"

"Seriously? How rich do you have to get to not recognize a burger and fries? I didn't know what you liked, so I got what I like," she said, snatching a fry off the plate and polishing it off in two neat bites.

She looked tired and wired at the same time.

"How's Karen?" I asked.

"Mom is holding up. She's spending the night with a few friends at a spa. They're having facials tonight and the works tomorrow. It sounds like a safe space to let her feel sad and . . ." Sloane closed her eyes for a moment.

It was more words and fewer insults than I was used to from her.

"Relieved?" I guessed.

Those green eyes fluttered open and bored into me. "Maybe."

"He was suffering. It's natural to be glad that part of it is over."

She hopped up on the counter, planting herself next to my fast-food dinner. "Still seems wrong," she said.

I reached around her and snagged a French fry from the plate. It was just an excuse to get closer to her. To test myself.

"Why are you here, Sloane?"

Even as I conspired to get closer, I was still

37

pushing her away. The dynamic was taxing on a good day. On a day like today, it was fucking exhausting.

She took another fry and pointed it at me. "Because I want to know why my mom greeted you like you were a long-lost Walton today. What does she think she owes you? What were you talking about?"

I wasn't about to begin that conversation. If Sloane had any hint of what I'd done, she'd never leave me in peace again. "Look, it's late. I'm tired. You should go."

"It's 5:30 in the evening, you grumpy pain in the ass."

"I don't want you here." The truth snapped out of me in a desperate rush.

She sat up straighter on the counter but made no move to leave. She'd always been too comfortable with my temper. That was part of the problem. Either she overestimated her invincibility or she underestimated what raged beneath my surface. I wasn't going to let her stick around long enough to find out which.

She cocked her head, sending that long swing of blond hair over her shoulder. She'd changed up the tone, going from a faded raspberry to a silvery shimmer at the tips. "You know what I kept thinking about today during the services?"

She as well as her mother and sister had spoken in front of the crowd, eloquently, emotionally. But it was the single tear that slid down Sloane's cheek, the ones she dashed away with my handkerchief, that had sliced me open and left me raw.

"A dozen new ways to piss me off, starting with invading my privacy?"

"How happy Dad would have been if we'd ever pretended to get along."

It was my turn to close my eyes. She landed the strike with expert precision. Guilt was a sharp weapon.

Simon would have loved nothing more than to see his daughter and his "project" at least friendly toward each other again.

"I guess there's no reason to start now," she continued. Her eyes were locked on mine. There was nothing friendly in her gaze. Only a pain and grief that mirrored my own. But we weren't going to mourn together.

"I guess not," I agreed.

She heaved a sigh, then hopped off the counter. "Cool. I'll show myself out."

"Take the coat," I said, holding it out to her. "It's cold."

She shook her head. "If I take it, I'd have to bring it back, and I'd rather not come back here." Her gaze flicked around the space, and I knew she too had ghosts here.

"Take the fucking coat, Sloane." My voice was hoarse. I pushed it into her arms, not giving her the choice.

For a second, we were connected by cashmere.

"Are you here for me?" she asked suddenly.

"What?"

"You heard me. Are you here for me?"

"I came to pay my respects. Your father was a good man, and your mother has always been nothing but kind to me."

"Why did you come back this summer?"

"Because my oldest friends were behaving like children."

"And I didn't factor into those decisions?" she pressed.

"You never do."

She nodded briskly. There was no hint of emotion on her lovely face. "Good." She took the coat from me and slid her arms through the too-long sleeves. "When are you going to sell this place?" she asked, fluffing that silvery blond hair out of the collar.

"Spring," I said.

"Good," she said again. "It'll be nice having decent neighbors for a change," she said.

Then Sloane Walton walked out of my house without looking back.

I ate the cold burger and fries instead of the chicken, then washed the plate and returned it to the cabinet. The counters and floors were next as I wiped away any trace my unwanted visitor may have left behind.

I was tired. That hadn't been a lie. I wanted nothing more than to take a hot shower and go to bed with a book. But I wouldn't sleep. Not until she did. Besides, there was work to be done. I headed upstairs to my old bedroom, a space I now used primarily as an office.

I sat down at the desk under the large bay window that overlooked the backyard and offered a view of Sloane's. My phone signaled a text.

> **Karen:** We're having a wonderful time. Just what the soul needed today. Thank you again for being so thoughtful and generous! P.S. My friend has a daughter she wants you to meet.

She included a winking smiley face and a selfie of her and her friends in matching robes, all with green goop on their faces. Their eyes were red and swollen, but the smiles looked genuine. Some people could withstand the worst without it damaging their souls. The Waltons were those people. I, on the other hand, had been born damaged.

> **Me:** You're welcome. No daughters.

I scrolled through the rest of my text messages until I found the thread I was looking for.

> **Simon:** If I could have chosen a son in this lifetime, it would have been you. Take care of my girls.

It was the last text I'd ever receive from the man I'd admired. The man who had so foolishly believed I could be saved. I dropped the phone, my fingers flexing, and once again I wished I'd saved the day's cigarette for now. Instead, I pressed the heels of my hands to my eyes, willing away the burn I felt there.

I tamped it down, picked up the phone again, and scrolled through my contacts. She shouldn't be alone, I rationalized.

> **Me:** Sloane isn't at her sister's. She's home alone.
>
> **Naomi:** Thanks for the heads-up. I had a feeling she was going to try to wrangle some sneaky alone time. Lina and I will handle it.

Duty performed, I booted up my laptop and opened the first of eight reports that required my attention. I'd barely made it through the financials on the first when my phone vibrated on the desk. This time, it was a call.

Emry Sadik.

Deciding to wallow in my misery instead of discussing it, I let it go to voicemail.

A text arrived moments later.

> **Emry:** I'll just keep calling. You might as well save us both the time and answer.

I had barely finished rolling my eyes when the next call came through.

"Yes?" I answered dryly.

"Oh good. You're not completely spiraling into self-destruction." Dr. Emry Sadik was a psychologist, elite performance coach, and—worst of all—an accidental friend. The man knew most of my deepest, darkest secrets. I'd given up trying to disabuse him of the belief that I was worth saving.

"Did you call for a specific reason or just to annoy me?" I asked.

I heard the unmistakable crack and clink of his predinner pistachios shells as they hit the bowl. I could picture him at the table in his study, a basketball game on mute, the day's crossword in front of him. Emry was a man who believed in routine and efficiency . . . and being there for his friends even when they didn't want him.

"How did it go today?"

"Fine. Depressing. Sad."

Crack. Clink.

"How are you feeling?"

"Infuriated," I answered. "A man like that could be doing more good. He should have had more time. His family still needs him." I still needed him.

"Nothing rocks our foundations like an unexpected death," Emry empathized. He would know. His wife had passed away after a car accident four years ago. "If the world was a fair and just place, would your father have had more time?"

Crack. Clink.

In a fair and just world, Ansel Rollins would

have lived out his full sentence, and the day of his release, he would have suffered a painful and traumatic death. Instead, he'd managed to escape his punishment due to a stroke that had quietly ended his life in his sleep. The unfairness of it had the rage rattling that locked box inside me.

"You haven't been my therapist for fifteen years. I don't have to talk about him with you anymore."

"As one of the few people on this planet who you tolerate, I'm only pointing out that two father figures dying within six months of each other is a lot for any human."

"I believe we've established that I'm not human," I reminded him.

Emry chuckled, undisturbed. "You're more human than you think, my friend."

I scoffed. "No need to be insulting."

Crack. Clink.

"How did it go with Simon's daughter?"

"Which one?" I hedged deliberately.

Emry snorted. "Don't make me come up there in a snowstorm."

I closed my eyes so I wouldn't feel compelled to look toward Sloane's house. "It was . . . fine."

"You managed to be civil at the funeral?"

"I'm almost always civil," I snapped wearily.

Emry chuckled. "What I wouldn't give to meet the infamous Sloane Walton."

"You'd need more than one session if you wanted to get to the bottom of what's wrong with her," I told him.

"I find it fascinating how she's lodged herself so securely under your skin when you're an expert at surgically removing annoyances from your life."

Crack. Clink.

"How did Sadie's piano recital go?" I asked, changing the subject to one my friend couldn't possibly ignore: his grandchildren.

"In my humble opinion, she outperformed all the other five-year-olds with her stirring rendition of 'I'm a Little Teapot.' "

"Of course she was the best," I agreed.

"I'll send you the video as soon as I learn how to text ten minutes of shaky footage."

"I can't wait," I lied. "Have you gotten up the nerve to ask out your neighbor yet, or are you still lurking behind your curtains?"

My friend had developed a crush on the stylish divorcée across the street and, by his own account, had only managed to grunt and nod in her general direction.

"The right opportunity hasn't presented itself yet," he said. "I would also like to point out the irony of you encouraging me to start dating again."

"Marriage is right for some people. People like you who can't stop burning casseroles and need a nice woman to force you to stop dressing like a 1980s sitcom star."

Headlights next door skimmed the fence that divided my backyard from Sloane's. I got to my feet and went to the window on the other wall that overlooked the front of her house. It looked as though Sloane was getting company whether she wanted it or not.

Emry chuckled. "Leave my cardigans out of this. Are we still on for dinner next week? I think I've finally figured out an opening that will tame your infuriating knight."

Emry and I had graduated from therapy sessions to a friendship that required dinner and chess matches every two weeks. He was good. But I was always better.

"I doubt that. But I'll be there. Now if you'll excuse me, I have work to do."

"No rest for the wicked, eh?"

None.

"Goodbye, Emry."

"Good night, Lucian."

I immediately pushed the conversation out of my head and had opened another report when the doorbell rang.

"Why won't people leave me the fuck alone?" I muttered as I opened my security app and found both Morgan brothers, shoulders hunched against the cold, at my front door.

On a growl, I slammed my laptop shut.

"What?" I demanded when I opened the door a minute later.

They tromped in, stomping snow from their boots on the entryway tile. I would clean up the puddles later, I told myself. Waylon, Knox's basset hound, marched inside, headbutted me in the knees, then trotted into the living room.

Knox held up a six-pack of beer. Nash hefted a bottle of bourbon and a bag of chips. The furry white head of his dog, Piper, poked out above the zipper of his coat.

"Girls are next door," Knox said as if that explained everything and headed for the kitchen. "Told you he'd still be in a suit," he called out to his brother.

I ran a hand down my tie, noting that they'd both changed into the standard Knockemout winter uniform of jeans, thermal, and flannel.

"Figured we'd stick around to keep an eye on them to prevent another last time," Nash said, putting Piper down on the floor and following his brother. The dog was wearing a red sweater with white snowflakes. She cast an anxious look at me and then trotted down the hall after Nash.

I closed the door and resisted the urge to knock my head against it. I didn't want company. And I didn't want to be drawn into whatever drunken escapades Sloane and her friends got themselves into. "Last time" had involved Naomi and Sloane getting heroically drunk and "helping" Lina catch a bail jumper with their wits. Well, with Naomi's wits and Sloane's spectacular tits.

I was still furious I'd missed that.

"I have work to do," I said.

"Then we'll just watch a movie with explosions quietly while you run your evil empire," Nash said cheerfully.

They helped themselves to paper towels and

glasses, then wandered into the living room, more comfortable here than I had ever been.

The room was staged with a family in mind. There was a deep sectional couch and an upholstered ottoman facing a large flat-screen TV. The white bookshelves that lined one wall had plenty of space for books, games, and photos.

There hadn't been any family photos here when I was growing up. At least none past my midteens when everything had gone to hell.

"Your security cameras get any good angles on Sloane's place?" Knox asked.

"I don't know," I hedged. "Why?"

"Wouldn't put it past them to sneak out to build an army of snowmen in the middle of the highway," Nash explained.

"I'll see what I can do."

I headed back upstairs and grabbed my laptop, but not before peering out the window into the gloomy winter night. Sloane's bedroom lights were off. I'd spent too many nights wondering why she'd kept the room she'd grown up in instead of moving into her parents' room. I hated how many questions I had about the woman I didn't want to care about.

On a testy sigh, I cued up the security feed that I staunchly refused to open. The one that angled toward Sloane's front door and driveway. It was a point of pride that I never looked at it, even when I felt homesick for a home that had never been mine.

Hearing the brotherly banter in the living room, I reluctantly changed into sweats and a T-shirt, then shoved my feet into the sherpa-lined house slippers Karen had given me two Christmases ago. I clomped back downstairs where I found my friends and their dogs lounging comfortably on the sectional.

"He's human," Nash observed when I walked in.

"Only on the outside," I assured him.

He had taken two bullets this summer when his name had landed on that list of obstacles for Anthony Hugo's crime syndicate in the DC area. After a few hairy months, Nash had managed to pull himself out of a downward spiral with the help of the stunning, monogamy-averse Lina.

While he'd convinced her to let him put a ring on her finger, I was still attempting to convince her to work full-time for me. She was smart, devious, and better at managing people than she gave herself credit for. I'd win eventually. I always did.

I dropped down on the couch and opened the laptop to the camera footage. "Here," I said, angling it toward the brothers.

"Perfect," Knox said.

"What are we watching?" I asked.

"Narrowed it down to *Shawshank* or *Boondock Saints*. Your choice," Nash said.

"*Boondock*," I answered automatically.

Knox cued it up while Nash poured the bourbon. He distributed the glasses and held his aloft. "To Simon. The man all men should aspire to be."

"To Simon," I echoed, keenly aware of a fresh stab of grief.

"Think Sloane will be okay?" Nash asked.

I crossed my arms and pretended I didn't get that nagging little rush whenever someone mentioned her name in my presence.

Knox shook his head. "It's a tough loss. She held up today after Luce here force-fed her a burrito."

Nash's eyebrows rose as he cut a look in my direction.

"Not a euphemism. It was a literal burrito," I explained.

"Sloane would break his euphemistic burrito in half," Knox predicted with a smirk. It disappeared quickly. "Naomi thinks she's gonna have a rough time and try to hide it."

"And Naomi is usually right," Nash pointed out.

"Let me know if there's anything she needs," I said, automatically distancing myself from the responsibility of looking after her.

Knox smirked. "Like a burrito?"

I glared at him. "Like moral or financial support that can be provided from a distance. My burrito wants nothing to do with Sloane Walton."

"Yeah. Keep telling your burrito that," Nash said, picking up his phone. He winced. "Great. Lina just texted. The girls are making margaritas."

Knox put down his bourbon. "Fuck."

3

Margarita Talk

Sloane

I stomped through the snow, cutting across Lucian's driveway and then my own. As always, conversations with the infuriating man left me eternally irritated. Over the years, we'd done whatever necessary to avoid each other. Yet today of all days, I'd ended up alone with the man not once, but twice. It was amazing we'd both survived.

I let myself in the front door and shrugged out of Lucian's glorious coat. I hung it in the entryway closet and kicked off my boots while thinking about a shower and pajamas. I didn't want company. I wanted a quiet night during which I could let out all the messy emotions I'd managed to—mostly—keep locked down all day long.

I opened the glass doors of the study just off the foyer. For years, it had served as Dad's office. I'd intended to turn it into a library or reading room when I moved in but hadn't gotten around to it yet. There were a lot of things I hadn't gotten around to doing.

It was a cozy space with a coffered ceiling and large bow window that protruded out onto the front porch. There was a freestanding desk and rickety set of box store bookshelves behind it. The room still felt like him. There were still a handful of photos and awards on the shelves along with a dusty set of law journals.

I sat down in the chair behind his desk and managed a watery smile at the familiar squeak. I could always tell when a case was bothering him. He'd lock himself in here after dinner to pore over files and think while rocking back and forth, back and forth.

I switched on the desk lamp. It was a hideous yard sale find featuring a faded woven shade that was constantly shedding threads and a heavy brass base etched with fanged merpeople. My mother insisted it was a travesty of interior lighting. Dad insisted it cast adequate light and was therefore perfect.

That was my father. Always finding the good in even the ugliest places.

The rest of the desk was bare except for an outdated calendar blotter and an empty pen holder. There were colorful sticky notes dotting the calendar page.

Pick up dry cleaning.

Order anniversary flowers! Bigger this year!

Tell Sloane about that book.

I skimmed the tips of my fingers over his choppy handwriting. Grief was a thousand tiny knives behind my eyes. Tears welled, and this time, in this safe space, I didn't fight it when they began to fall.

"I miss you, Dad," I whispered.

My heart ached with the knowledge that my father would never again sit in this chair. He'd never again make a ridiculous dad joke that would have Mom collapsing with giggles. He wouldn't be here to watch Chloe tear through her presents next Christmas. He wouldn't meet any new members of the family.

If I got married and had kids, how would I ever share with them what he meant to me?

Great, I thought as I dragged Lucian's stupid, still soggy handkerchief out of the pocket of my dress. Now my heart was breaking into tinier, sharper pieces, and my misery was illuminated by this god-awful lamp.

The sob I'd held in all day wrenched its way out of my throat. I took off my glasses and let it well up inside me.

I'd lost the greatest man I'd ever known.

Everyone needed me to be strong, to be okay. My mother and sister, my friends, my town. They didn't need to be worried about how deep this chasm of grief went. But tonight, right now, I could allow myself to be what I was. Devastated.

Tears spilled hot and fast down my cheeks. I hugged myself around the middle and just let them come. Like a volcano erupting, I cried as if I were splitting in two.

I was supposed to feel some measure of relief. Dad's suffering was over. He wasn't in pain anymore. His consciousness wasn't being stolen from us minute by minute by cancer and drugs. He was free of suffering. But I didn't see an end to my own. Because I would miss my dad for the rest of my life.

I blew my nose noisily.

I'd felt like this only once before. When I'd lost another man—a boy really.

Lucian.

His name floated to me over my own snotty sniffles. Despite our differences, he'd shown up today. He'd stayed throughout the services and the luncheon, saying all the right things to my mother and sister. He'd also bizarrely forced a burrito on me, then picked a fight. Fights, I corrected.

The doorbell rang.

"Dammit," I muttered.

I wanted to be alone. Maybe they would go away. I could just sit here in the dark and wait them out.

But a nudge wouldn't let me. Someone might need something. Or maybe my garage was on fire and someone was trying to save me but I was too busy crying my face off to notice.

I blew my nose again, then sniffed the air.

The bell rang again, and I swore under my breath. Scrubbing a fresh tissue over my makeup smeared face, I made my way to the door and put my glasses back on.

I found a stranger standing on the front porch, hands in the pockets of his jeans. He was mid-twenties at best guess with tight curly hair. He wore an earring, a Georgetown Law sweatshirt under a wool coat, and an apologetic half smile.

"I'm so sorry to bother you. Are you Sloane?" he asked.

"Yeah," I rasped, then cleared the messy emotions out of my throat. "Yes."

"Your dad told me a lot about you and your sister," he said, bobbing his head and swallowing hard. "I probably should have called first, but I had an exam I couldn't miss and drove straight here afterward. I feel terrible for missing the funeral." He shoved a hand through those short curls.

I stared dumbly at him. "Do I know you?"

"Uh, no. You don't. I'm Allen. Allen Upshaw."

"Were you a friend of my father's?"

"No. I mean, I like to think we would have been. He was actually a mentor. The reason I got into law school . . ." Allen trailed off, looking about as miserable as I felt.

I took pity on him. "Would you like to come in? I was just going to make some coffee or tea."

"Sure. Thanks."

I led the way down the hall, through the atrium, and past the dining room to the cavernous kitchen. The previous owners had combined the main kitchen and catering kitchen into one huge room with more cabinets and countertops than I would ever know what to do with. The walls were papered in an old-fashioned but charming plaid and adorned with solemn gold-framed still lifes of food.

"It looks the same but different," he observed. "I was here a few years ago before your parents moved to DC."

"None of us was ready to let go of the house so I moved in," I explained, turning on the coffee maker. I gestured for him to take a seat at the turquoise breakfast nook table my sister and I had helped my mom paint one summer weekend a thousand years ago.

Allen shook his head. "I can't believe he's gone. I mean, I feel bad feeling bad when you must feel a thousand times worse. But he was such an important part of my life these past few years."

"It makes me feel better knowing that he mattered to so many people," I assured him. "Cream? Sugar?"

"Both, please. Is Mrs. Walton here?"

"She's spending the night with friends." I put a mug that said I PUT THE LIT IN LITERATURE under the spout and opened the fridge.

He blew out a breath. "I'll catch up with her next week. I just can't believe he's gone." He winced. "Sorry. I feel like I'm appropriating your grief."

"It's our grief," I assured him, putting his coffee in front of him and making one of my own even though I didn't really want it.

"I don't know if you know, but he came into my life when I needed him most."

"How did he do that?" I asked as the coffee maker spit out another cup.

"I used to want to be an architect, and then when I hit fifteen, I did some dumb stuff," he said, cupping the mug with both hands.

"We all do dumb things as teenagers," I assured

him, taking the chair across from him. I had done a few spectacularly stupid things myself.

His lips quirked. "That's what your dad said too. But my dumb stuff had consequences. Consequences my mom paid for. That's when I decided I was going to be a lawyer."

"Good for you," I commended.

"I met your dad at a community job fair. I was on my own after high school, sleeping in my aunt's basement, and was working two jobs trying to save up for law school. Simon made me feel like it was possible, that I could do it. He gave me his card and told me to give him a call if I needed any help. I called him that night." Allen paused and smiled wryly.

My heart squeezed.

"I blurted it all out. How I'd screwed up, how my mom paid the price, how I wanted to make it right. Simon listened to my story and didn't judge me. Not once. And when I got done telling him why I was such a mess, he told me he could help me. And he did."

It was so exactly like my father. The lump in my throat was back. I took a sip of coffee to loosen it. "Wow," I said.

Allen rubbed his eyes with his fingers. "Yeah. He changed my life. He invested hours in me. Helping with scholarship and grant applications. He introduced me to his favorite professor at Georgetown. He was the first person I called when I got accepted. And when I still came up short, after my savings and all those grants and scholarships, your dad made up the difference for the first year." He stopped, his eyes going damp.

Pride filled my chest, wrapping itself around the pieces of my broken heart. My father wasn't just a good man. He was the best. "When do you graduate?" I asked.

"May," Allen said proudly. Then his face fell. "Since my mom couldn't be there, your parents were going to go."

My heart hurt for him.

For my mom.

For me.

There would be a Dad-shaped hole in every event from now on.

I reached across the table and squeezed his hand. "I'm sure my mom is still planning to go. She loves graduations and weddings and baby showers. Anything with a party really."

"My mom was like that too," he said with a sad smile. "Someday I'm gonna throw her a huge surprise party for everything she did for me."

He talked about his mother in an interesting mix of past and present tense that made me curious. "Is your mom still . . . around?"

He looked down at his coffee. "She's in prison."

"I'm sorry to hear that."

"It's my fault. But I'm gonna make it right."

"I'm sure she's really proud of you," I said.

His smile was stronger now. "She is. She really is."

I knew firsthand how good that parental pride felt and felt another pang.

Allen glanced at his watch and grimaced. "I should be getting back. I have another exam tomorrow morning."

"Are you sure? The snow looks like it's really starting to come down."

"The highways are clear and I've got four-wheel drive," he assured me.

I walked him to the door. "It was really nice to meet you, Allen."

"You too, Sloane."

I waved Allen off and had just enough time to clean up the coffee mugs and start crying before the doorbell rang again. It was still echoing throughout the house when a barrage of fists banged cheerfully against the wood.

"Seriously? Can't a girl have an emotional breakdown in some peace and quiet?" I muttered into a soggy tissue.

"Let us in before we freeze our asses off," Lina yelled through the front door.

"We brought hugs and tequila," Naomi called.

"Naomi brought hugs. I brought tequila," Lina corrected.

"Shit," I murmured under my breath before sticking my head under the faucet in the kitchen and washing away all signs of my crying jags.

They entered the house like two beautiful, energetic whirlwinds toting grocery bags and pitying looks. Lina looked glamorous in a royal-blue parka and fur-trimmed boots. Naomi was pretty in a pink puffy jacket and earmuffs.

"Why are you here?" I asked as they shed their winter layers.

"Lucian tattled and said you were spending the evening alone instead of at your sister's," Naomi announced cheerfully, her perky ponytail bouncing.

"That interfering son of a bitch."

"Don't worry. Naomi retaliated by unleashing the Morgan boys on him to ruin his solitude," Lina assured me.

"I didn't *ruin* his solitude. I made sure that he had the emotional support he might need," Naomi corrected.

"You have to have emotions to require emotional support," I pointed out.

"Lucian is pretty upset about your dad's death. They were close," Naomi said.

I wanted to argue, to question her. But I didn't have the energy. I changed the subject instead. "Where's Waylay?"

"My little tech genius is sleeping over at Liza J's to fix her smart TV again," Naomi announced.

Double shit. If overnight child care arrangements had been made, I wasn't getting rid of them that easily.

Naomi slid her arm around my shoulders and steered me toward the staircase. "Why don't you go upstairs and take a shower? We'll get dinner started."

Forcibly shooed upstairs, I slunk down the wood-paneled hallway on the second floor to my bedroom where I proceeded to take the longest shower in the history of indoor plumbing. I spent the first half of the shower passive-aggressively taking my time in hopes my friends would get bored and leave. When it became clear from the scents of garlic that wafted into the bathroom that this was not going to be the case, I spent the second half crying quietly until I felt as if I'd washed enough emotion down the drain to appear normal for a few hours.

I combed my wet hair and entered my bedroom, crawling onto the window seat. Outside, the snow continued to fall. Knox's pickup was parked in Lucian's driveway. I hoped he was having a miserable time with his retaliatory forced socialization.

My stomach growled and I realized I hadn't eaten since Lucian's burrito delivery that morning. Except for the French fries I'd stolen off his plate . . . and out of the bag in the car.

I returned to the bathroom, slapped on some moisturizer, then reluctantly headed downstairs to the kitchen.

My friends had topped store-bought pizzas with hot sauce and banana peppers—my favorite. There were two packs of cookie dough on the counter as well as three bags of chips with an assortment of dips. It looked as though Naomi had brought all the fixings for Honky Tonk margaritas, which she was pouring into five bucket-sized glasses.

"Nothing says mourning like post-funeral margaritas," I observed.

"Mourning looks like whatever you want it to look like," Naomi insisted. She had changed out of her clothes and was wearing red thermal pajama shorts with a matching long-sleeve shirt and fuzzy, knee-high socks.

"It can be getting drunk and going sledding at 1:00 a.m. Or it can be pizza, cookies, and a binge watch of *Cougar Town*," Lina said. She too had changed into pajamas, but hers were silky and black. Her fuzzy flip-flops had delicate puffs of fake fur that Meow Meow was glaring at from the center of the breakfast nook table. I wandered over and stroked a hand down the cat's back. She flipped over onto her side with a grumpy grunt and grudgingly accepted my affection.

"You're not seriously abandoning snowstorm sex with your men just to spend the night with me, are you?" I asked my friends.

"You shouldn't be alone tonight," Naomi insisted, nudging a margarita in my direction.

"I *like* being alone," I argued. Being alone meant not having to pretend to be okay. Being alone meant not having to be messy and emotional in front of any witnesses.

"You're welcome to be alone *with* us," Lina announced.

"I thought you'd be on my side."

Her smile was sharp and her eyes sparkled. "You

have no one to blame but yourself. You and Naomi forced me to give up my lone she-wolf ways."

"Technically, first prize in that endeavor goes to Nash. But Sloane and I *did* earn the silver medal," Naomi agreed.

"So you're saying I'm trapped in this codependent circle?" I asked, picking up the proffered margarita.

Lina nodded. "Pretty much. You might as well surrender now."

The pizza *did* smell good. And it would probably be rude if I didn't have at least a little tequila.

"Well, since you're already here . . ."

Lina dumped two slices onto a paper plate and held it out. I took it and sneaked a warm, cheesy bite while my friends plated their own meals.

The doorbell chimed again.

"Go away," I called.

But I was drowned out by Naomi and Lina cheerfully yelling, "Come in!"

We were all halfway to the door when it opened and Naomi's best friend, Stefan Liao, and his biker barber boyfriend, Jeremiah, strolled inside. With his sweater and blazer, Stef looked as if he'd just finished a photo shoot for a New England old-money fashion label. Jeremiah, on the other hand, looked more like a hot, hipster biker with a man bun, scarred boots, tight denim, and a David Bowie T-shirt.

"Ladies. I see you've started without us," Stef said.

63

"I told you the dress code was casual," Naomi teased.

"You look like your rich uncle Bartholomew has a yacht docked in Martha's Vineyard," I observed.

"You know Stef. He doesn't do casual," Jeremiah said with affection as they both shrugged out of their coats.

"There's nothing wrong with looking good. Now, I believe I was promised a margarita the size of my face," Stef said.

"Someone's got good taste," Jeremiah said, plucking Lucian's coat from the closet.

"Well, well, well. Who does *this* beauty belong to?" Stef demanded, stroking a hand over the cashmere.

Shit.

"No one," I said quickly.

"Is that Burberry?" Lina asked, reaching for the label. "Please tell me you're sleeping with someone who has really good taste."

I should have just left his damn coat on his damn kitchen counter.

Naomi buried her face in the fabric. "So soft! And it smells amazing." Her head came up, a frown pinching her mouth. "And familiar."

Stef, Jeremiah, and Lina each took a whiff.

"Lucian," they said together.

All eyes returned to me.

I turned my back on them and took my margarita and pizza into the living room, a space crowded with mismatched furniture, a six-foot fireplace with

His wife shrieked and tried to make a break for it, but Knox vaulted into the back of the truck and wrapped her in a snowy embrace. He rubbed his face against her bare neck, making her scream louder.

"That's definitely a framer," Jeremiah claimed as he snapped away.

Nash tugged the still laughing Lina to her feet. "You smell like tequila and bad decisions," he said.

She wrapped her arms around his neck and gave him a noisy kiss on the mouth. "And *you* smell like we should have sex."

Sloane, on the ground, mimed a fit of vomiting.

I tossed the bucket aside and held out a hand to her.

She eyed it for a beat too long, so I reached down and hauled her to her feet.

Her mitten-clad hands gripped my forearms as she regained her balance. She was still laughing. Her lovely face was the picture of joy. Up close, I zeroed in on the darker smudge of forest green around the iris of her left eye.

"Not down my shirt," Naomi screeched from the back of the truck.

"These shenanigans better not ruin my boots," Stef complained, looking at his feet.

Sloane was grinning, her emerald-green eyes clear and bright.

"You're not drunk," I observed.

"None of us are. It's the snow. It turns us into fourth graders. Case in point," she said and waved both magenta mittens at me. "When's the last time you did something as undignified as playing in the snow?"

"You can take the man out of Knockemout, but you can't take Knockemout out of the man," I quipped.

She frowned. "Wait. I forgot. I'm mad at you again."

"With us, I think that's always safe to assume," I said dryly.

She bent at the waist and picked up the scruffy Piper, who was going to need a new sweater since this one was covered in clumps of snow. "I'm *extra* mad because you ratted me out to Naomi when all I wanted was a quiet evening at home by myself."

"As you can see, I too am suffering the consequences of my actions," I said, gesturing in the direction of Knox and Nash.

Sloane buried her face in Piper's wet, wiry fur. "For some ridiculous reason, Naomi felt the tattler shouldn't be alone tonight either. My suffering is almost worth knowing that you have to entertain your pals instead of figuring out how to drive up the cost of blood pressure medicines or whatever it is you do to entertain yourself."

"I entertain myself by binge-watching *Ted Lasso* and cheering for Rupert the villain."

Sloane tried and failed to smother her laugh. "Damn it."

It was a headier thrill than anything I could recall in recent history. That was pathetic.

"Hold up. Are those two *actually smiling* at each other?" Lina demanded.

"My God. It's a snowstorm miracle," Stef said, making the sign of the cross as Jeremiah slung an arm around his waist.

"I better call into the station and see if some kind of asteroid is about to hit us," Nash joked.

"I don't like this," Knox said, giving me the evil, snowy eye.

"I love it," Naomi insisted, hooking her arm through his.

"Har har. You guys are *hilarious,*" Sloane said, taking a deliberate step back. She turned her back on me and took that warm feeling with her.

Knox and Nash insisted on spending the night after the girls had commandeered the dogs and taken them next door for the night.

It was midnight. Knox was passed out on the twin bed in the bedroom staged for a boy while Nash slept on the pullout couch in my office.

Anyone would have thought from the long, impassioned goodbyes they shared with Naomi and Lina that they were going off to war.

What was it about love that turned men into simpering idiots?

I considered myself lucky that it was at least one thing I didn't have to worry about.

I turned my attention back to the financial records in front of me. The digital fundraising platform would make an interesting addition to my "evil corporate empire." I saved my notes to the cloud and fired off an email to my assistant to add a meeting with the platform partners to my calendar.

I took off my glasses and rubbed my bleary eyes with both hands.

I wanted to go to bed. To fall, exhausted, into a dreamless sleep. But I couldn't. Not yet. Not with Sloane's bedroom lights still on, glowing warm and gold like a beacon as the snow continued to fall.

It was a habit worse than smoking in my opinion, not going to bed until Sloane's lights went dark. It was a compulsion that did me no favors, considering the woman was a bookworm who read past midnight most nights. I glanced down at my copy of *The Midnight Library* near my elbow and wondered if that was something else I'd give up once I finally sold this place.

I was pathetic, secretly sharing a bedtime as if timing my lights-out with hers somehow ensured that she was safe. The sooner I sold this house and cut ties, the sooner we'd both be free.

The floodlight in Sloane's backyard lit up the winter wonderland, and I was on full alert as I leaned forward to peer out the window.

There she was.

She'd changed into yet another pair of pajamas and topped them with a dark, bulky coat and bright red snow boots. I watched as she trudged purposefully out into the yard, willing her to stop before she was lost to me behind the hemlock and clump of arborvitaes.

I rose from my chair and held my breath. She paused, still in view, and I relaxed.

Sloane tilted her head to the sky and spread her arms wide. Then she pitched backward, falling flat on her back. My muscles coiled reflexively, ready to run downstairs and out the door until I realized she was moving. Her arms and legs were working in a sweeping motion. In and out. In and out.

I watched mesmerized as Sloane Walton made a snow angel.

I pressed my palm to the cool glass.

Take care of my girls. I heard Simon's words as clearly as if he'd spoken them aloud.

It wasn't his fault. He didn't know the effect his daughter had on me. How dangerous she was to me. How fatal I could be to her.

She was sitting up now, head tipped back. I wondered if she was thinking of Simon too. If that was yet another tie that unfairly bound us together. In a moment of weakness, I brought my hand to the window and traced her figure with my fingers on the glass.

I saw it before she did, the distant orange streak of light in the sky. A shooting star.

Sloane brought a hand to her face, then sat there in stillness.

She moved suddenly, done with her own stillness. I watched captivated as she carefully worked her way to her feet before jumping clear of her snowy creation.

Hands on hips, she stared down at it and nodded. Then she looked up. Not at the sky, this time, but directly at me.

My desk light was off. There was no way she could see me in the window, I told myself as I pulled my hand away from the glass. Still, I stood in the shadows and watched her stare up at my window.

After an agonizing minute, she looked away and slowly made her way back to the house.

It wasn't until she'd disappeared from view and the lights in her bedroom finally went out that I realized something.

She'd been wearing my coat.

5

Hot Guy in My Bedroom

Sloane

Twenty-three years ago

I should have been finishing my trigonometry homework or at least showering after softball practice. But to be fair, I hated math, and I didn't allow myself to shower until I'd finished my homework. So really my only option was to take a book break.

There was a tiny possibility that my frustrations might have been motivated by the fact that I was exactly one chapter away from the *really* good stuff in my pilfered copy of Kathleen E. Woodiwiss's *Shanna*.

It was my third reread of Mom's tattered paperback, and I was besotted with the mercurial Ruark Beauchamp. Even though his—and Shanna's—behavior would totally have been problematic in real life, I still liked the underlying idea that a secret torrid affair could somehow provide a safe space where you could be yourself.

I climbed onto the window seat cushion and built a mound of pillows behind me. A whiff of armpit caught me. I winced and shoved the middle window open to let in the fresh spring air. My team was on track to make the district playoffs this year, and the coaches pushed us harder every practice. I wanted it. It was all part of Sloane's Awesome Life Plan, which I was fully dedicated to. But right now, all I wanted to do was lose myself in a sexy Caribbean love story. In seconds, concerns about my dried sweat and lame homework disappeared, and I was transported into the book.

I was midway through the good stuff when my attention was ripped from the page by our next-door neighbor Mr. Rollins reversing his pickup truck out of the driveway much too fast. He shifted gears, and the truck launched forward, spinning the tires as it accelerated out of view.

My stomach knotted. Things hadn't been good next door since Mr. Rollins had lost his job a year ago. Dad said he'd been some kind of foreman at the chemical plant a few towns over. But the plant had closed. After that, Mr. Rollins stopped mowing the lawn. He didn't grill burgers anymore either. Sometimes, if my bedroom window was open to the spring breeze, I could hear him yelling late at night.

My dad never yelled. He *sighed*.

He didn't get mad at me and Maeve. He got *disappointed*.

I wondered what Lucian did when his dad yelled.

A tiny thrill rolled through me just thinking about *him*.

Lucian Rollins was a junior and starting quarterback on the varsity football team. I liked to think the serious, dark-haired boy who took out the trash shirtless was the reason for my teenage sexual awakening. I'd gone from thinking boys were gross—which, at twelve and thirteen, was absolutely accurate—to wondering what it would be like to be kissed by the bad boy next door.

Lucian was gorgeous, athletic, and popular.

I, on the other hand, was a four-eyed, busty, almost sixteen-year-old who would rather spend a Friday night curled up with a good book than drink warm beer by a bonfire in the field known as Third Base. I was *not* in his league. That league was occupied by cheerleaders and class presidents and beautiful teens who somehow escaped the desperate lack of self-confidence that had been bestowed on the rest of us.

I excelled at a not-sexy sport and had spent last week in detention thanks to my "strong objections" to dress code enforcement when my friend Sherry Salama Fiasco had gotten detention over a skirt that was one inch too short.

"Instead of policing the fashion choices of girls, why don't you put that energy into teaching boys how to control themselves?" I'd argued. Loudly. I'd even earned some enthusiastic applause and a nod of approval from one of the senior cheerleaders in my study hall.

I didn't hate the street cred. And my parents had refused to ground me for standing up for what was right.

I heard a creak and a slam next door. My book

fell off my lap as I craned my neck for a better look.

My favorite thing about my room—besides the fact that it had its own bathroom, library-worthy bookshelves, and an awesome window seat for reading—was the view. From my window seat, I could see the entire side of Lucian's house, including his *bedroom window*.

There he was.

Lucian stalked into the backyard. Unfortunately, he was wearing a shirt. His shoulders were hunched, and he was absently rubbing his right arm while staring pensively at the ground.

Our backyard, thanks to Dad's green thumb, was a fenced-in wonderland of flowers and trees and shrubs. It was late March, and the cherry trees were blooming, an official announcement of the arrival of spring.

Lucian's backyard looked more like an abandoned lot. The grass was patchy, and there were tufts of knee-high weeds against their side of the fence. A rusty grill was abandoned against the side of the garage. I didn't *mean* to judge, of course. Lots of people had better things to do than play in the dirt every weekend.

Though maybe Lucian should think about helping out around the house if his dad wasn't going to take care of the yard work anymore. There was a push mower next to the grill, for gosh sakes. I didn't want to have a crush on a lazy, entitled guy.

I willed him to approach the mower.

Instead, Lucian kicked at a rock on a bare patch of lawn and sent it flying. It soared through the air before smacking against our fence with a loud crack.

"Hey!" I yelled.

His gaze instantly came to my window. I flattened myself on the seat cushion and put a pillow over my face.

"Well, that was stupid, dummy. He already saw you," I said into the pillow. I sat up again. But Lucian was nowhere to be seen.

The cherry tree outside my window shuddered, and I heard a grunt.

"What the—"

There was something in the tree. No. Not something, *someone*. I blinked several times and wondered if I needed a new glasses prescription, because it looked like Lucian Rollins was climbing my tree. He shimmied up the trunk and gave the branch that skimmed over the porch roof a testing bounce.

Oh my God. Oh my God. Oh my God. A hot, popular junior had just climbed my tree because I'd yelled at him.

It was with a heady mix of horror and excitement that I watched him scale the branch before nimbly jumping onto the roof.

I slid off the cushion and backed toward the middle of my room as Lucian Rollins threw a leg over my windowsill and climbed inside.

Oh my God. Oh my God. Oh my God. Lucian Rollins was in my bedroom. Shit! Lucian Rollins was in my *bedroom!*

I glanced around, hoping my room wasn't totally embarrassing. Thank God Mom had insisted on giving me a room makeover for my twelfth birthday. My doll house and hammock full of stuffed animals had been replaced with floor-to-ceiling bookcases my dad had installed. The pale pink walls had been covered with a moody blue paint.

But I'd just dumped two loads of clean laundry in a haphazard pile on the floor in front of the closet because Mom needed the laundry basket. I'd also emptied the contents of my backpack at the foot of my bed because I couldn't find my favorite berry-pink highlighter that I reserved for only the most important class notes.

Dear lord. I had a favorite highlighter, and this past fall, Lucian had broken the school's passing record on the football field.

My uninvited guest said nothing as I panicked silently.

Lucian picked up my book, flipped it over, and read the back. He raised a mocking eyebrow.

I crossed to him and snatched it out of his hand. "Why are you in my room?" I demanded, finally finding my voice.

"Mostly considering apologizing for the rock," he said, his voice low and smooth.

"Mostly?"

He shrugged and began to wander the room.

"I've never been inside your house before. I wanted to see what it was like."

"You could have used the front door," I pointed out. If I were a cheerleader, I'd know how to flirt. I'd have showered and be wearing matching pajamas and lip gloss. I'd toss my hair without hurting my neck, and he'd feel compelled to kiss me.

But I wasn't a cheerleader. I was me, and I had no idea how to talk to my hot neighbor crush.

He paused at my desk and flipped through my CDs. His lips curved in a smirk. "Destiny's Child and Enrique Iglesias."

"You can't just break into my house and judge my taste in music."

"I'm not judging. I'm . . . intrigued."

He was even cuter up close.

Wait. No, not cute. *Gorgeous.*

His hair was thick and dark and curled a little at the ends. He had a straight nose and high cheekbones that were so defined, Mrs. Clawser chose him as the model for portrait drawing in art class. Becky Bunton said Lucian had taken his shirt off and Mrs. Clawser had to stand in front of her hot flash fan for ten straight minutes.

Of course, Becky *also* claimed that her uncle invented JanSport book bags, so you had to take her claims with a grain of salt.

Lucian was tall with an athletic build that filled out his worn jeans and a long-sleeve Knockemout football shirt in a way that leaned more toward man than boy.

Was it getting hot in here? Did I need a hot flash fan?

I hadn't had sex yet. I wanted my first time to be with someone who made me feel like a heroine in a book. Someone who could sweep me off my feet and make me feel special and good, not sweaty and awkward in the back seat of an ancient Toyota like Becky's first time.

Lucian, with his muscly forearms and romantic hair, would make a girl feel that way. Special. Important.

How was I supposed to date boys in my own league when presented with this specimen? My dating options were restricted to the lower tier of high school guys. Like a member of the stage crew or maybe one of the slower boys on the track team.

But none of them measured up to my gorgeous next-door neighbor.

It wasn't just his looks. Lucian moved through the halls of Knockemout High with a knowing confidence that the crowds would part around him. I, on the other hand, scurried from gap to gap, staring at the backs and shoulders of the entire student body.

Lucian cleared his throat and I blinked.

I'd been staring at him for a very long time. Long enough that he'd taken a seat on the bench at the foot of my bed and was staring back. Expectantly.

"Uh, do you want a soda or something?" I asked, not sure what I'd do if he said yes. My parents were downstairs, and they would be sure to notice me sneaking two root beers upstairs. Unlike the parents on TV, mine didn't miss a thing.

"No, thanks," he said, eyeing my trig homework. He picked up the top sheet of paper, the one I'd scrawled "This is stupid. I hate math." all over.

I snatched it out of his hand and crumpled it behind my back.

I was smart. That was my thing. Put me in an English class or history or science and I was a guaranteed straight A student. But math was a different story.

"I could help you," he said, reaching behind me and taking the paper back.

"You're good at math?" I couldn't quite keep the incredulity out of my tone.

"You think just because I play football I can't be smart too?"

Actually, I'd been thinking that in this scenario, I should be the hot athlete's tutor who he couldn't help falling in love with during intimate study sessions. But this could work too.

"Of course not," I scoffed.

"Then give me a pencil." He held out a hand, and for a second, I battled the fantasy of simply putting my hand in his . . . and then jumping into his lap and kissing him.

But I wasn't confident in my balance. What if I kneed him in the crotch or knocked the wind out of him?

Good sense won out, and I picked up my pink

mechanical pencil from the carpet and handed it over.

"Come here," he said, sliding down to the floor and patting the spot next to him.

I sat obediently.

"You had the first part right," he said, retracing my steps with the pencil. "But here's where you went wrong."

I sat next to him and watched his big hand move the pink pencil over the sheet. Leave it to Lucian Rollins to make math sexy.

"Wow. You really are smart," I said when he circled the answer.

His mouth curved ever so slightly at the corners. "Don't tell anyone."

"Your secret is safe with me," I promised.

"Your turn," he said, handing me the pencil.

He smelled good. Which made me paranoid that he could smell me.

It took me three tries and an infinite amount of patience from Lucian, but I finally got it. I got the next problem on the second try. And when I nailed the right answer on the third problem in one take, I jumped up and spiked the pencil like it was a football in the end zone.

"Yes! Bite me, math!"

I was halfway through my victory dance when I remembered that I had a hot junior audience and sweaty armpits.

Lucian leaned back on his elbows on the carpet, watching in amusement. There was an actual smile on his face. One *I'd* put there. Something warm bloomed inside me. I was pretty sure it was a hot flash.

I tucked my hair behind both ears and sank back down to the floor. "Um, so thank you for that. I don't usually get that excited over math homework."

The smile was still there, and it was turning my insides to mush.

"I take it you're more into reading than trig?" He nodded toward my bookcases.

"Oh, uh, yeah. I like books. A lot."

"Are you going to write them?"

I shook my head. "Nah. Reading is just a hobby. I'm going to get a softball scholarship and go into sports medicine." I had it all figured out. I was what my coach called an "aggressively enthusiastic pitcher."

"Really?" he asked.

"You don't think I can do it?"

"It just must be nice to know what you want to do."

"You're almost a senior," I pointed out. "Where are you going to college? What are you going to major in?"

He shrugged, then winced and rubbed absently at his arm. "I don't know yet."

I frowned. "Well, what do you want to be?"

"Rich."

He sounded like he meant it. And not in a flippant teenage boy tired of Aunt Alice asking

97

him what he wanted to be when he grew up way.

"Uh, okay. And how are you going to do that?" I asked.

"I'll find a way."

I was disappointed. A guy like Lucian should have big, specific dreams. He should want to innovate hearing aids for babies or maybe run a cool dental practice like my mom. Hell, even aiming for professional football player would be better than nothing.

"Sloane! Dinner," my mother called from downstairs.

Crappity crap crap.

"Uh, okay!" I yelled back.

"I guess I should go," Lucian said.

I didn't want him to go. But I also didn't want my parents to know a really hot football player had shimmied up a tree into my bedroom. In case he did it again and I was showered and wearing matching pj's and lip gloss when he did.

"Ask the boy who climbed through your window if he wants to stay for dinner. We're having meat loaf," Mom shouted the invitation.

"Oh my God," I muttered into my hands, mortified.

I glanced up at Lucian, and he grinned. A full-on, knee-dissolving, stomach-swooping grin.

"Thanks, Mrs. Walton, but I need to get home," he called back.

"You're welcome to use the front door," Mom shouted.

I winced. "You probably should. Otherwise, they'll just come up here."

"Okay," he said, not seeming too concerned with my humiliation.

Squaring my shoulders, I marched us out of my bedroom and down the stairs, unsure of what reaction I was about to face. Standing up for women's rights was one thing in my parents' eyes. Sneaking boys into my room was an entirely different kind of rebellion.

My parents met us at the foot of the steps in the kitchen. Dad was in a frumpy beige sweater that matched his khakis too closely. Mom was still in her work scrubs. Both had glasses of wine.

"Mom, Dad, this is Lucian. He, uh, helped me with my trig homework," I said, awkwardly making the introductions.

"It's nice to meet you, Mr. and Mrs. Walton," Lucian said, shaking hands like he was an adult. I had a vision of him in a fancy suit presiding over meetings with his serious face and strong handshake. Maybe "rich" wasn't such a lame goal after all.

"It's a pleasure to meet you officially, Lucian," Mom said, shooting me a we'll-discuss-this-later look.

"You're always welcome here, especially if it keeps Sloane from hurling her math books across the room," Dad said.

My toes curled in embarrassment. "Dad," I hissed.

He reached out and ruffled my hair. I continued to die of the fatal, incurable condition of embarrassment.

"Are you sure you can't stay for dinner?" Mom offered.

Lucian hesitated for just the barest second, and my parents were on him like pugs on peanut butter.

"Join us," Dad insisted. "Karen makes a mean meat loaf, and I made the baked potatoes with horseradish sour cream."

Lucian glanced at me, then at his feet before nodding. "Uh, if you're sure you don't mind?"

"Not at all," Mom insisted, steering us toward the kitchen island where the plates were stacked.

Oh my God. I was going to have dinner with Lucian Rollins. Yay!

And my parents. Boo!

It definitely wasn't a date if chaperones were present. At least not in this century.

"Come on, you two," Mom said, leading the way. "You can set the table."

"Your parents are nice," Lucian said as I shut the front door behind us. The scent of cherry blossoms was light on the crisp evening air.

"And embarrassing," I said, cringing at some of the topics of conversation. "You really don't have to help my dad get the summer decorations down from the garage rafters this weekend."

My ladder-fearing, five-foot-seven father was

thrilled by Lucian's height. My mother was thrilled with his apparent inability to say no.

"I don't mind," he said, shoving his hands in his pockets.

"Don't let them hear you say that, or else Mom will have you moving file boxes at her office and Dad will enlist you to trim the taller branches in the backyard."

"Your house is great," Lucian said. It sounded almost like an accusation.

"I'd say thanks, but I didn't really have anything to do with it."

"Mine sucks," he said, jerking his chin in the direction of the small, beige two-story next door. I noticed that Lucian's father still hadn't returned.

"Maybe you would think it was nicer if you mowed the lawn?" I suggested helpfully.

He looked down at me, amused again. "I doubt that would make things better."

I crossed my arms over my chest to ward off the chill. "You never know. Sometimes making things nice on the outside makes them better all the way through."

It was like when I woke up early enough to slap on some mascara and lipstick before school. A bold lip and long lashes made me feel like a prettier, more put-together version of myself.

"We'll see," he said. "Thanks for dinner. I've gotta get back and do my own homework."

He backed away.

Desperate for just another minute with him, my

mind raced for something to say. "Hey! I hate to be that girl, but you still haven't apologized for the rock," I pointed out.

He flashed that little half smile, one foot on the porch, one foot on the top step. "Guess I'll have to do that next time."

Next time.

My stomach did the nervous swoopy thing again.

"I'll see you around," he said.

"Yeah. See you," I said breathlessly. I stood there like an idiot and watched him amble down the walk before cutting across the driveway to his yard.

"Next time," I whispered.

I went to bed that night with a smile on my face, Ruark and Shanna temporarily forgotten.

The next morning when I left for school, I couldn't help but notice that Lucian's dad's truck still wasn't in the driveway. But the front lawn had been mowed.

6

Breakfast Ambush

Sloane

"T hank you, Lou," I mumbled with the hair tie in my teeth.

Lou Witt, Naomi's dad, held the diner door for me as my hands were full trying to tame my hair into the semblance of a knot on top of my head.

"Looking a little frazzled this morning," noted his wife, Amanda, the new part-time counselor for the school district.

I glanced down at my oversize sweatshirt with its fresh coffee stains. Stains achieved after dumping half a mug down my front when Mom had texted to remind me I was meeting her for breakfast.

My leggings had a hole in one knee, and I'd forgotten to change out of my slippers.

Crap.

"One of those days," I said, securing my bun.

Actually, it was more like weeks.

"That's to be expected, sweetie," Amanda assured me with a sympathetic arm squeeze. "Don't forget to take care of yourself."

"I won't," I promised before waving the Witts off and heading inside. I spotted my mother in one of the back booths and hurried toward her. "Sorry

I'm late. Naomi called. She and Eric finally found the missing garter snake from the petting zoo Wednesday night. He was in the window wrapped around a pothos plant—"

I came to a screeching halt and stared open-mouthed at the man sitting opposite her.

Mom smiled up at me as if she weren't sharing a table with my mortal enemy. "I asked Lucian to join us since he was still in town."

Lucian didn't look very happy about this turn of events either, but to be fair, the man rarely looked anything other than aggressively constipated.

"Sit," Mom said, gesturing toward Lucian's side of the booth.

"You know what? I forgot I have an appointment with someone about something—"

"Sloane, sit your rear end down now."

She'd deployed the mom voice. Unfortunately, being a grown adult hadn't come with an instant immunity to that tone.

Lucian reluctantly scooted in. Great. Now I had to play along too or look like the bigger, more immature asshole. I sat gingerly with one butt cheek on the vinyl, one foot in the aisle in case I needed to make a fast escape.

Mom interlaced her fingers on the table and looked at us expectantly. She looked tired and sad, which made me feel like a petulant child. I settled more comfortably in the booth and picked up a menu.

"So what's with the breakfast meeting?" I asked.

"I'm heading back to Washington today," she announced. "I said my goodbyes to your sister and Chloe this morning. Now it's your turn."

I put down the menu and ignored the way the right side of my body seemed to be absorbing Lucian's body heat. "Mom, there's no rush. If you want some peace and quiet, you know you can stay with me." She'd split her time in Knockemout between my place and my sister's while we'd planned the services. I'd enjoyed having her as a roommate. It made the house seem less empty. Plus she bought really good snacks.

She shook her head. "I appreciate the offer, but it's time for me to get back. Your father left me a very explicit list of things I need to take care of."

"Let me help." I was suddenly desperate to keep her in town. I didn't want her dealing with everything on her own. I also didn't want to be abandoned.

"What kinds of things need taken care of?" Lucian asked.

I spared him a glance. Not that it was any of his business, but I was interested in the answer too.

"Well, for one thing, he wanted his clothes donated to a nonprofit that gives homeless men work wardrobes to make it easier for them to interview for jobs. I'm also supposed to gather and deliver all his case files to Lee V. Coops at Ellery and Hodges for any future appeals."

"I'll take care of that," Lucian offered, pulling his phone out of his pocket and opening his texts.

105

"I'll have one of my employees pick up the files at your place and courier them over to the new firm."

Why the hell was Lucian "I Own Half the World" Rollins volunteering to help my mother with errands? And why was my mother acting like this wasn't the first time he'd played helpful?

I forced a smile through clenched teeth. "I'll look around Dad's study at home to make sure he doesn't have any old files stashed there."

"Perfect. You can give whatever you find to Lucian."

I glanced at him and found him already looking at me. Together, we turned back to my mom. "What's going on, Karen?" he asked at the same time as I said, "What's going on, Mom?"

"Simon loved you both. When the cancer came back, he started thinking a lot about what was important for a good life. And the kind of grudge you both seem to be carrying isn't healthy."

I shifted uncomfortably in my seat. The idea I'd done anything in Dad's last months to make him unhappy was like fresh lemon juice being squirted onto the raw edges of my grief.

"Dad was disappointed in me?" I asked, my voice husky.

Mom reached for my hand and squeezed it. "Of course not, sweetheart. He was so proud of you. Both of you for everything you've accomplished, everything you've built, how generously you've given. But life is unbearably short. This animosity you two are hanging on to is a waste of that precious time."

"Okay. I'm sorry and no offense, but what does Lucian have to do with our family?"

Mom and Lucian shared a long look until he subtly shook his head.

"That right there," I said, pointing at his face. "What the hell is with the secret head shake?"

"Lucian has done more for this family than he'll ever let me say," Mom said finally.

"For instance?" The words came out high-pitched and panicked.

"Lucian," my mom prompted him.

"No."

She rolled her eyes at him, then looked at me. "For one thing, he sent me and my friends to the spa after the funeral."

"Karen," Lucian said, exasperated.

Mom took his hand with her free one, connecting us through her. "Lucian, honey, at some point, you're going to have to stop denying—"

"What can I get y'all today?" Bean Taylor, in suspenders and an apron smeared with breakfast foods, appeared, his grease-stained notebook at the ready. The man was an angel on the grill but one of the clumsiest servers on the planet.

"Hey, Bean. Good to see you," Mom said, releasing our hands.

What did Lucian have to stop denying?

What secrets did he and my mom share?

We Waltons were an open book. We knew

everything about each other. Well, almost every-thing.

"Listen, I need to hit the road," Mom said, grabbing her purse and throwing cash on the table. "But it would make me very happy if you two would stay and have breakfast. And I hate to pull the guilt card, but I'm hanging on to anything that makes me happy with both hands right now." Her eyes went glassy with tears.

I rose with her and wrapped my arms around her. Maybe if I held on tight enough, she wouldn't go.

"I'll give y'all another minute," Bean said, backing away from the emotional display.

"Mom. Don't go." My voice broke, and she squeezed me tighter.

"I have to. It's good for me to be productive and start thinking about what's next. I think it'll be good for you too. You need to get back to work," she whispered. "Besides, I'm only a phone call away."

I sniffled. "A phone call and some of the worst traffic in the country."

"I'm worth the traffic."

I let out a choked laugh. "Yeah. I guess you are."

"I love you, Sloane," Mom whispered. "Be happy. Do good. Don't let this derail you for too long. Dad wouldn't want that."

"Okay," I whispered as a tear escaped, streaking down the curve of my nose.

Mom released me, gave my arms a squeeze, then turned to Lucian, who was sliding out of the booth.

He stood, dwarfing us both, smoothing a hand down his probably monogrammed button-down.

"I love you," I heard Mom tell him. His reply was too soft for me to catch, but I noticed how he hugged her to him with closed fists, his knuckles going white.

"Stay. Eat," she insisted again when he'd released her.

He nodded.

"Bye, Mom," I croaked. She wiggled her fingers at me, eyes still glistening, and headed for the door. I stood there watching her leave, feeling like Anne of Green Gables before she met Marilla and Matthew Cuthbert.

"Sit."

Lucian's gruff command was accompanied by a broad hand at my back, guiding me back to the booth. I slid onto the bench my mother had vacated and stared unseeingly at the menu in front of me.

"She's going to be all right, Sloane." That raspy rumble caressed my name with irritation and something else.

"Of course she will," I said stiffly.

"So will you."

I couldn't snark back at him. All my focus was on willing the tears to be reabsorbed into my face. I would not be weak in front of him. Again.

"You don't have to stay," I said, looking everywhere but his face.

"After that guilt trip, I'd have breakfast with Rasputin."

Even through my blurred vision, I could see him shaking his head vehemently.

"What don't you want me to know?" I demanded. "Were you blackmailing my parents? Did you trick them into a cult or multi-level marketing scheme?"

"Those are the only options you can come up with?" he asked.

"Psst! Is it safe to come back and take your orders?" Bean asked, tiptoeing back to the table.

"Sure, Bean." I managed a weak smile for him. It wouldn't do me any good to have rumors circulating about the town librarian's public meltdown. I had a reputation to uphold. I was downright terrifying when the situation called for it. It kept my library and my life here in Knockemout running smoothly.

"You know you've got stains all over your shirt?" Bean pointed at my sweatshirt with his nub of a pencil.

"I had a run-in with a coffeepot this morning. I'll have the usual with a hot chocolate." I deserved a comfort beverage.

"Extra marsh, extra whip?" Bean clarified.

"You know it."

"And for you, Mr. Rollins?"

I snorted internally. This was Knockemout, for Pete's sake, and Bean was barely a year younger than me. But it was "Mr. Rollins this and Mr. Rollins that."

"Egg white omelet with spinach and vegetables," Lucian ordered.

Ugh. Even his breakfast order annoyed me. And the way the man couldn't be bothered to say please or thank you made me want to hit him in the face with the napkin dispenser. I narrowed my eyes at him.

Lucian blew out a breath through his nostrils. "Please," he added before collecting our menus and handing them over.

"Sure thing," Bean said.

"Thanks, Bean," I said before he scurried back to the kitchen. Once he was gone, I returned to glaring at Lucian. "Would it kill you to be polite every once in a while? Or do those suits leach the humanity out of you?"

"I'm surprised you didn't order the glitter pancakes off the children's menu to go with your mug of granulated sugar."

"Have you ever even had the diner's hot chocolate?" I asked. "Oh, wait. I forgot. You're violently allergic to fun and happiness. When are you flitting back to your depressing vampire lair of seriousness?"

"As soon as I make it through this breakfast with you."

Another server appeared to top off Lucian's black coffee and deliver my hot chocolate. It was a work of art. The thick-handled mug was topped with a veritable tower of whipped cream. Mini marshmallows dotted the white swirl, and Bean had topped the entire thing off with a generous dusting of pink, glittery sprinkles.

I felt a tickle in my throat, another prickle behind my eyes. I was not going to cry over a cup of hot chocolate, no matter how obvious it was that it had been made with love.

That was why I loved this damn town so much. Why I never wanted to live anywhere else. We were all intimately involved in one another's lives. Step outside your front door, and if you looked past the leather and exhaust fumes, the luxury SUVs and designer equestrian wardrobes, you'd witness a dozen small acts of kindness every day.

"You're ridiculous," Lucian said as I pulled the mug to me with both hands.

"You're jealous."

"You can't even drink that. You'll end up wearing it."

I scoffed and reached for a straw. "You're such an amateur." With precision, I inserted the straw from the top to ensure the proper cream to chocolate ratio. "Here," I said, sliding the mug toward him.

He looked at me as if I'd just suggested he stir his coffee with his penis.

"What do you expect me to do with that?"

"I expect you to taste it, make a face, and then tell me how revolting you think it is, even though deep down, you'll like it so much you'll start plotting how to order one without me noticing."

"Why?"

"Because you sent my mom to the spa with her friends when she needed to be reminded that she could grieve and laugh. Because you stayed here to suffer through a breakfast neither one of us wanted just to make her happy. So take your *one* sip, because that's all I'm willing to share, and then we can go back to ignoring each other."

To my surprise, Lucian took the mug. He raised it to eye level and examined it as if he were a scientist and the hot chocolate was some yet-to-be-discovered member of the spider family.

I tried not to focus on the way his lips closed over the tip of the straw. The way his throat worked over his single swallow. But I did notice the fact that his grimace came half a second too late. "Revolting," he said, sliding the mug back to me. "Happy now?"

"Ecstatic."

He picked up his coffee but didn't drink. Because maybe under his fifty-million-dollar suit jacket and his rich guy beard, he was just a little human after all.

I should have opened a new straw. Should have made a show of avoiding putting my mouth anywhere near where his had been. But I didn't. Instead, I plucked it out of the drink, reinserted it on the opposite side of the mug, and closed my lips over the spot his had occupied mere moments ago.

Warm, sugary goodness hit my tongue with just the slightest hint of crunch from the sprinkles.

I wrapped my hands around the mug and closed my eyes to prolong this tiny pocket of perfection.

When I opened them again, I found Lucian's eyes on me, his expression . . . complicated.

"What?" I asked, releasing the straw.

"Nothing."

"You're looking at me like it's not nothing."

"I'm looking at you and counting down the seconds until this meal is over."

And just like that, we were back on an even keel. "Bite me, Lucifer."

He pulled out his phone and ignored me while I scanned the breakfast crowd.

The diner was hopping as usual midmorning. The patrons were mostly retirees with a few horse farm folks and, of course, the usual biker crew mixed in for good measure. Knockemout was a unique melting pot of old equestrian money, freedom-seeking outlaws, and burnt-out, middle-aged Beltway bandits.

I felt the weight of Lucian's gaze on me and pointedly refused to meet it.

"You don't have to do this, you know. I'm sure you have better things to do," I said finally.

"I do. But I'm not going to be the one to disappoint your mother today," my surly table mate said.

My glare should have incinerated him. "Does it take more or less energy to be an asshole every second of the day? Because I can't figure out if it's your natural setting or if you have to put actual effort into it."

"Does it matter?"

"We used to get along." I don't know why I said it. We had a tacit agreement never to discuss that time in our lives.

His gaze slid to my right wrist peeking out of my sleeve.

I wanted to hide my hand in my lap but stubbornly kept it in plain sight on the table.

"We didn't know any better then," he said, his voice hoarse.

"You're infuriating."

"You're irritating," he shot back.

I gripped my straw like it was a weapon capable of stabbing.

"Careful, Pixie. We have an audience."

The nickname had me flinching.

I managed to tear my gaze away from his stupidly beautiful face and glanced around us. There were more than a few sets of eyes glued to our table. I couldn't blame them. It was part of town lore that Lucian and I couldn't tolerate each other. Seeing us "enjoying" a meal alone together had probably already ignited the gossip chain. Any one of those people would have no qualms about reporting back to my mother.

I carefully returned the straw to its whipped cream home base. "Look. Since you're too stubborn to leave and you're not inclined to tell me why you and my mother are besties, let's find some topic of conversation that we can both agree on to get through this interminable breakfast. How do you feel about . . . the weather?"

"The weather?" he repeated.

"Yes. Can we agree that there appears to be weather outside?"

"Yes, Sloane. We can agree that there is weather."

His tone was so condescending I wanted to take the ketchup squeeze bottle from the stainless-steel carrier and empty it all over him.

"Your turn," I said.

"Fine. I'm sure we can agree that you dress like a deranged teenager."

"Better than a moody undertaker," I shot back.

His lips quirked, and then his expression smoothed into its baseline of irritated boredom.

The bell on the diner door jingled, and Wylie Ogden lumbered in.

Conversations cut off as gazes swung away from us to Wylie.

Lucian didn't move a muscle, but I still felt a chill descend on the table.

I hadn't seen much of the former police chief since the incident when Tate Dilton, an ex-cop gone rogue, teamed up with Duncan Hugo, the mobster's son, to shoot Nash Morgan. Wylie, whose long reign as chief of police was marked with good ol' boy cronyism, had been friends with the disgraced officer but redeemed himself when he shot and killed Dilton. My opinion of Wylie had risen several points after that. I'd even almost smiled at him the one time I'd seen him in the grocery store.

The former police chief's gaze landed on our

table. He froze, except for the toothpick in the corner of his mouth, which moved up and down, then he made an abrupt about-face to find a seat at the opposite end of the diner counter.

Lucian's cool gaze remained glued to the man.

I felt something. Something that seemed suspiciously like guilt, which made me defensive.

"You know, if you had told me everything, I wouldn't have—"

"Don't," he interrupted as if he were telling a toddler to stop trying to put their finger in an electrical outlet.

"I'm just saying—"

"Leave it alone, Sloane."

That was what we did. We left things alone. The only acknowledgment of our shared past was the bitter aftertaste that colored every interaction.

Neither one of us was going to forgive or forget. We would just continue pretending it didn't still eat away at us.

"Here's your breakfast," Bean said loudly. He slid steaming plates onto the table with forced cheer and then oh so casually slid both butter knives into his apron pocket.

7

The Evil Corporate Empire

Lucian

Rollins Consulting offices occupied the top floor of a postmodern building on G Street in DC's central business district. The proximity to the White House meant that the street in front of the building was regularly closed for the motorcades of visiting dignitaries.

The elevator doors opened to sleek marble, stately gold lettering, and a dragon.

Petula "Thou Shalt Not Pass" Reubena took her role as gatekeeper seriously. No one got past her unless expressly authorized. I'd once found her performing a bag search on my own mother when she'd come to meet me for a rare lunch.

"Good afternoon, sir," Petula said, rising from her chair to stand at attention. She'd had a long, decorated army career and after one month of retirement had decided she wasn't cut out for a life of leisure.

She dressed like someone's wealthy grandmother, and while she did indeed have three grandchildren of her own, Petula spent her spare time rock climbing. This information was gleaned from the extensive background check all employees were

118

subject to. She had never once commented on her personal life and had a low tolerance for anyone else who did.

"Good afternoon, Petula. Any emergencies while I was gone?"

"Nothing I couldn't handle," she said briskly.

I held the glass door for her, and Petula marched ahead of me, rattling off the day's schedule.

"You're expected to sit in on a conference call at 2:15. You have Trip Armistead at 3:00 and Sheila Chandra scheduled for 3:15. I assume this is either another diabolical power move, or you finally made your first mistake."

Trip was a Georgia congressman and a client who was not going to enjoy our fifteen minutes together. "I never make mistakes," I said, nodding to the associate in the gray suit whose name I couldn't remember.

Petula gave me a bland look. "I'll alert security. The cleaners won't be pleased if they have to get bloodstains out of the rug again."

"I'll do my best to keep the bloodshed to a minimum," I promised.

We headed into the busy field of cubicles where phones rang and employees diligently did whatever it was I paid them to do. The starting salary at Rollins Consulting was $80,000 a year. It wasn't that I was generous. It was that I didn't want to waste time constantly filling low-paying positions. The money also helped compensate for the fact that I was a demanding boss, an asshole as it was probably whispered around the watercooler. If I paid my team members less, I'd have to be nicer. And that didn't interest me.

We strolled through the cubicles and past three occupied conference rooms. What had begun as a one-man boutique political consulting firm that was willing to get dirty for its clients had evolved into a one-hundred-and-fifteen-person organization that put people into and took them out of office when necessary. And I still didn't mind playing dirty when it suited my objectives.

A shrill whistle caught my attention. and I spied ex-U.S. Marshal Nolan Graham behind his desk in his glass-walled office, a phone pinned to his ear. He'd come on board a few months ago after he'd taken a bullet for my friend. I'd made him an offer it would be stupid to refuse, and he'd kissed his government job goodbye.

"I'll leave you to Prince Charming," Petula said with what could almost have passed for a smile in Nolan's direction. It seemed that the man's charm had managed to put a few cracks in my no-nonsense sentry's armor.

I paused in Nolan's doorway. "What?"

He hung up the phone and triumphantly riffed a few keys on his keyboard. "Cyber team got a few more suspicious money trails for you-know-who that we're unraveling. Couple of fronts that look about right for laundering. Writing up the report now in case your Bureau buddies want to take a closer look."

It was a fine line to walk. My cybersecurity analysts—colloquially known as hackers—worked their not-technically-legal magic to find threads to pull. Once we knew where to look, the rest of the team worked to confirm and pass along that information in ways that wouldn't get the case bounced out of court.

Special Agent Idler was smart enough not to ask too many questions about how information fell into my lap.

"We need something bigger. A stash house. Distribution routes. A higher-up with a grudge who can be turned." Something that would dismantle the organization from the inside out.

"What can I say? The guy's not as big a fucking idiot as his son. If you don't mind me saying, why not let Lina take a crack at some of the intel? She's in the office today. Maybe she can find an avenue we're overlooking."

"She has a personal bias," I insisted. I was not a my-door-is-always-open, here's-the-suggestion-box kind of boss. I didn't want feedback. I wanted to tell people what to do and then not have to worry about them doing it.

Besides, in addition to being royally pissed at the Hugo family for abducting her and nearly killing her fiancé, Lina also refused to fully commit to this job. At first, her part-time dabbling power play had been amusing. Now I found it irritating.

Between Petula, Nolan, and Lina all being blatantly unafraid of me, I had concerns the rest of the employees would follow suit and start doing things like knocking on my office door for "a quick chat" or suggesting I host an office holiday party.

Nolan kicked back in his chair. "Let's see. If Lina's the kettle, that would make you the pot."

"I don't have time for your nonsensical bullshit this afternoon."

"Just to be clear you're the pot calling the kettle black in that metaphor," he said.

"I don't have a personal bias," I lied.

Nolan began a dramatic search of his desk drawers.

"What are you looking for?" I asked.

He paused, then grinned. "A fire extinguisher to put out your pants fire."

"I thought you'd gotten less annoying since you shaved your mustache. I was wrong."

He'd actually become significantly more likable after he'd stopped dating Sloane, a requirement of his employment with me.

Fuck.

I glanced at my watch.

I hadn't even made it into my office before my first thought of her. I'd had breakfast with the woman. Why couldn't I just set her aside and move on to the next thing that required handling? Sloane Walton never did anything I wanted her to. I wanted a life where nothing made me feel powerless, out of control, and until I found a way to exorcise the woman, I would always be vulnerable.

"Just saying. Seems like you're waiting for her to prove her loyalty, and she's waiting for you to prove you're worth being loyal to. If you two don't try to meet in the middle, no one's getting off this fucked-up power trip merry-go-round."

It took me a moment to realize he was talking about Lina, not Sloane.

"I don't recall asking you for your opinion."

"That's what friends are for. Speaking of, you want some backup with the feds today? I can stand behind you and make menacing faces," Nolan offered.

"I don't need backup." The fewer people directly involved in the Anthony Hugo investigation, the better. When Hugo caught wind of what I was doing, I wanted his attention focused solely on me. "What I do want is the deep dive on Fund It's partners in ten minutes," I ordered.

"Already on your desk," he said, smugly tossing a peanut M&M into his mouth.

It was less fun ordering people about when they'd already predicted what I needed and delivered it.

On a grunt, I left his office and headed toward mine.

"You're welcome," Nolan called after me.

Sometimes I wondered why I'd bothered hiring employees. They were all annoying.

"Good afternoon, Mr. Rollins," chirped a perky redhead who looked more like she should be studying for her driver's license test than working

123

for one of the country's most ruthless consulting firms.

I should have worked from home.

Holly was twenty-two years old, the mother of two, and this was what she referred to as her first "grown-up" job. She acted abominably grateful toward me as if the job and salary were personal favors I'd granted her.

It made me uncomfortable and awkward.

"Your hair is . . . interesting," I said.

She turned around, giving me an unrequested view of the back of her head. Today she wore her hair in two thick braids that looked as if birds had uniformly worked their way down each one, attempting but not quite succeeding to pull them apart.

"Do you like it? It's called bubble braids. I have a YouTube channel—"

"I don't care," I said.

She let out a girlish giggle. "You're so funny, Mr. Rollins."

"No. I'm not," I insisted.

She waved away my statement. "I just wanted to let you know that I left a little something for you on your desk. You asked me about my lunch yesterday, so I brought you some to try."

I hadn't asked her about her lunch. I'd suggested she not microwave fish chowder in the break room because it made the entire office smell like the belly of a crab trawler.

"You really shouldn't have done that."

"It was the least I could do," she said cheerfully.

"How thoughtful," Petula said, reappearing at my side like an elite sniper. "Mr. Rollins will certainly enjoy your chowder for his afternoon snack."

Holly beamed sunnily at us. "Just wait until I make you my tofu curry!"

We watched her all but skip away.

"Christ, what was I thinking hiring her?" I muttered.

"You were thinking she desperately needed a job that could support two kids. She thinks you're a knight in shining armor," Petula explained, opening the door to my office.

I wasn't the knight. I was the dragon.

"Then she's either criminally misinformed or delusional," I muttered as I entered my space. It was designed to intimidate and impress. There was nothing homey or cozy about the glass desk, the stark white couch, the dark wood. It was formal, cold. It suited me.

"It's not the worst thing in the world to have employees who aren't blatantly terrified of you," Petula said, busying herself by hitting remotes to open blinds, switching on my desk monitors, and organizing paperwork by priority while I hung my coat on the rack inside the door.

"Between Nolan and Holly, you're going soft," I complained.

"I insist you take back that insult, or I'll tell everyone you cry during SPCA commercials."

The wall of windows revealed an impressive

view of DC's business district. Most of it was still blanketed in a pristine coat of white thick enough to cover the stains and sins that happened behind closed doors in the nation's capital.

"I prefer people to be terrified. Then they don't try to talk to me about whatever the hell bubble braids are. And why are you so nice to her? You're mean to everyone."

Petula huffed. "I'm not mean. I'm efficient. Niceties are a waste of time and energy."

"I wholeheartedly agree."

"What do you want me to do with this?" she asked, holding up the container of homemade fish chowder.

"Throw it out the window."

She stared me down and waited.

"Fine. Put it in my refrigerator." I'd throw it out when I was sure I wouldn't get caught.

"Don't throw out the container. She'll need it back," Petula ordered.

Damn it.

"Anything else?" I asked with irritation.

Petula aligned the folders on my desk with a sharp tap. "These are priority. You have drinks at 7:00 p.m. at the Wellesley Club with two of the vice presidents from Democracy Strategies. And that investigator will probably be here shortly. I informed her you were absolutely not available this afternoon, but she was rudely insistent."

While she talked, I walked to the wall of glass and stared out over Washington, wondering what

126

Sloane would think of this place and what I'd accomplished.

I'd become someone. Forged an empire. And I'd gotten strong enough, rich enough, powerful enough that no single threat could take what I'd built. I'd vanquished the ghosts of the past.

"Thank you, Petula. That will be all," I said, suddenly anxious to bury myself in work.

She looked down her nose at me. "I know that will be all, because that's all I had for you. I'll let you know when that investigator arrives. And I'll send Holly back with your coffee when it arrives."

"Don't—"

But she was already smugly sweeping out the door, dismissing me.

It took three excruciating minutes of small talk about the weather and her son's sudden interest in watching other kids play video games on YouTube for me to pry the coffee out of Holly's hands.

I was only on my second priority folder, a background check on a gubernatorial candidate in Pennsylvania, when "that investigator" riffed a two-fisted knock my glass door. I gestured her inside.

Nallana Jones was a private investigator whose deep pockets were lined by clients like me who could afford to pay a premium for dirty work. Today, she was dressed like a middle-aged suburban mom out for a power walk in dumpy sweats and a bulky belt bag. She was wearing a short, brown wig under a car dealer baseball cap. Her pink sweatshirt said I LOVE MAINE COON CATS.

"You look ridiculous," I said.

"That's the idea. Nobody gives Middle-Aged Maude a second look when she hits the treadmill at their mistress's gym."

"I take it this is for someone else's job?"

"Yep." She produced a flash drive from her belt bag and set it on my desk. "This came in from my girl in Atlanta yesterday. The backups are already in the cloud. I also added a little juicy footage from your guy's arrival in town this morning. Right place, right time. Whatever you plan to do with this info, it's solid. There's no way he can wiggle out of it."

"Impressive as always, Nallana."

"Yeah, well. That's why you pay me the big bucks," she said, slapping her knees. "Anyway, I gotta jet. There's a certain twenty-two-year-old who's about to meet her fifty-eight-year-old, married sugar daddy for a personal training session. I can't be late."

"I'll call you when I need you again."

She tossed me a two-finger salute and sauntered out the door.

I inserted the drive into my secure laptop and scrolled through the files. There were over two dozen pictures and a handful of video files as well. Each one was enough to destroy a man's career. I printed two of the better stills, copied the files to a new, secure folder in my own backup, then wiped the drive.

I picked up the phone and dialed Lina's extension.

"What's up, boss?" she asked with a hint of sarcasm so subtle I wasn't sure it was actually there.

"I might have a job for you," I said.

"A real one or another gopher task?"

"Just get in here."

Seconds later, she appeared at my door. I waved her in and gestured for her to take a seat.

Her long legs ate up the space between the door and my desk. She sank into the chair and crossed one neatly over the other. "How do you not get fingerprints all over all that glass?" she asked, staring at the pristine surface of my desk.

"I refrain from getting sloppy. Which is what I'll need you to do." I slid the two photos across the desk to her. "Do you know who this man is?"

She studied the pictures. "The guy who looks like he was born in an ascot is Trip Armistead, our client and current member of the House of Representatives. I have no idea who the topless dancer is, but I'll shave my head if she's eighteen."

I glanced at my watch. "You have twenty-three minutes to take these photos and the information in the secure folder to build a compelling anonymous tip to be sent to the reputable news organizations of your choice."

"Are we actually pressing Send, or are we using it to scare the shit out of our old buddy Trip?"

"The latter."

The man had the backbone of a crustacean. One quick snap was all it would take.

"Fun. I'm in," she said, rising from her seat.

"Why haven't you accepted the job?" I asked.

She paused, then lowered herself back into the chair. "Does it matter?" she asked cagily.

"I won't know until you tell me. Is it the compensation? Does Nash have an issue with you working for me?"

"The compensation is fair. The work seems like it's interesting from the glimpses you allow. Nash is thrilled that I get to be home every day."

"Then what is it?"

"Sloane."

My grip tightened on the pen in my hand. "You don't seem like the type of woman to let other people call the shots in your life," I said evenly.

Lina scoffed. "Sloane didn't tell me not to take the job. My hesitation lies in the fact that you're an asshole to one of my only friends for vague reasons that you both refuse to explain."

I said nothing and Lina continued.

"Maybe you're carrying some multi-decade grudge about something that happened when you were practically children, which would be pathetic. Or maybe you had a secret torrid affair that went south and now you can't stand her, which would be immature. Maybe she ran over your pet tarantula

130

when she was learning to drive. I honestly don't care about the why. The bottom line is I don't want to dedicate my working life to a man who treats my friend badly. Now, if you'll excuse me, I have a politician to blackmail."

Trip Armistead was a blond-haired, blue-eyed southerner who prided himself on his charm and pedigree.

He was also an asshole who had officially outlived his usefulness.

He entered my office, arms spread, palms up, a man certain of his importance. I looked forward to ruining that.

"Lucian, old friend. We should have done this in Atlanta. I was in my shirtsleeves on the golf course two days ago," Trip said, heading straight for the decanter of bourbon I kept on a side table. He poured himself a glass and gestured toward me with it. "Want one?"

"No thanks, Trip. I'm afraid our meeting won't last long enough for you to finish that."

"Now what's this all about?" he asked affably as he took a seat in one of the chairs in front of my desk.

"You're not going to run for the Senate. In fact, you're not going to run for reelection. You're going to resign your position and scurry out of the spotlight like a cockroach on a kitchen floor."

"I beg your pardon?" His knuckles whitened against the glass.

I got out of my chair and rounded my desk. "When we came on board, you assured me there weren't going to be any problems, any dirty little secrets. Do you remember that?"

Trip swallowed reflexively. "Of course. I gave you my word. I don't know what you've heard, but I've been nothing but—"

"I'm going to stop you there, Trip, because if you lie to my face, this will get ugly. And I don't have time for ugly." I handed over the folder Lina had prepared in record time.

The glass slid from Trip's hand.

I caught it before it hit the ground and placed it on my desk with a hard *clink*. "I see I have your attention."

"How . . . Why?"

The bravado, the confidence was unraveling faster and faster now.

"You do know who I am, don't you, Trip? You understand how serious I am about protecting my clients while paving their way into history. Can you really be that stupid to think I would take you at your word? I protect my investments . . . even from themselves."

"I have a wife, daughters."

"You should have thought of them before you hired two sex workers in less than twenty-four hours."

He was visibly shaking now.

"I warned you what would happen if you crossed me," I reminded him.

132

"I didn't cross you. This isn't what it looks like," he sputtered.

"The girl you hired this morning? She turned eighteen last week. Your oldest daughter is what? Sixteen?" I asked.

"I-It's a sex addiction. I'll get help," Trip decided. "We'll keep it quiet, I'll get treatment, and everything will be fine."

I shook my head. "I see it's not sinking in yet. You're finished. There's no way for you to throw yourself on the mercy of the court of public opinion, because they'll eat you alive. Especially seeing as how you missed the vote on veterans benefits because you were paying to have your cock sucked."

Little beads of sweat dotted his forehead.

"You threw it all away because you couldn't keep your dick in your pants. Your career, your future. Your family. Your wife will leave you. Your daughters are old enough that they'll hear every salacious detail of Daddy's extracurricular sex life. They'll never look at you the same again." I nodded at the open folder in his lap. "I've already had a press release drafted about how my firm was forced to sever ties with you after learning about your sexual exploits."

He closed his eyes, and I had to turn away when his lip began to tremble.

"Please. Don't do this. I'll do anything," he begged.

He was yet another weak, pathetic addition to the

long list of men who risked everything just to get off.

"I'll give you a choice. You'll resign from Congress immediately. You'll go home and tell your wife and daughters that you had an epiphany and that your time together is precious. You don't want to work a job that keeps you away from them so much anymore. You'll go to fucking therapy. Or you won't. You'll save your marriage or you won't. One thing you won't do is ever cheat on your wife again. Because if you do, I'll deliver copies of every photo and every video to your wife, your parents, your church, and every member of the media between here and fucking Atlanta."

Trip put his head in his hands and let out a broken moan.

I almost wished he'd put up more of a fight, then smothered that feeling.

"Get out. Go home, and don't ever give me a reason to share the information I've collected."

"I can be better. I can do better," he said, rising from the chair like a puppet on strings.

"I don't give a fuck," I said, leading the way to the door.

He was weak. No one could build a foundation on weakness.

I opened the door and held it. Trip walked through, eyes down.

"I was just bringing Ms. Chandra to you, sir," Petula said.

Trip looked up, defeat fully settling over him as his shoulders hunched.

"What a small world, Trip," Sheila Chandra said with the honeyed tones of Georgia. She looked back and forth between me and my ex-client.

"Sheila is going to be running for the seat you're so graciously vacating, Trip," I said. "I'm glad we can count on your support."

Trip shot me a parting look with red-rimmed eyes and said nothing as he marched out of my office.

Sheila turned to me, eyebrows high. "I think I'm gonna need an explanation . . . and a drink."

A knock at my office door dragged me out of my never-ending inbox. I looked up to see Lina on the other side of the glass. It was after six. The city outside my windows lit up the night sky. Most of the staff had gone home for the day, but I still had hours of catching up thanks to my time in Knockemout.

I gestured her inside.

"Is it done?" I asked, firing off the reply and opening the next message.

"Yes."

"Good. Get out. I'm busy."

She ignored the command and dropped down in the chair across from me. "How did it go with Chandra?"

I took off my reading glasses, resigning myself to an unwanted conversation.

"Fine." The woman had accused me of Machiavellian-level manipulations, which I took as a compliment. Then she'd insisted on taking some time to consider my proposal that would have her taking Trip's seat before making the run for higher office. The fact that she didn't immediately jump at my offer assured me I'd made the right decision. She'd poll higher with younger voters, do more for her constituents, and wouldn't fuck around with a golden opportunity like her predecessor had.

She would see my offer for what it was: a chance to finally do the work she'd always wanted.

"What's your end game?" Lina demanded.

"That's an awfully personal question for someone who doesn't officially work for me."

"Humor me. Today alone, you forced one of your own clients to resign the seat that you won him and made him do the walk of shame past the replacement you personally chose. Then you had me deliver an envelope full of cash to a sex worker who looks like she's barely old enough to vote and opened the door of a very expensive, gated home in Georgetown."

"Is there a question in there?"

"I ran the address," she said, pausing to admire the engagement ring on her left hand.

Of course she had. "Is there a point to this?"

"It took quite a bit of digging. But it appears that that big, beautiful brick house in the nice, quiet neighborhood is a halfway house for victims of

136

domestic abuse and sex trafficking. It also appears to be owned by Yoshino Holdings, a subsidiary of a subsidiary of a subsidiary of this very consulting group."

It was annoying how good she was at her job.

"I'm still waiting for your point," I said.

"I can't tell if you're a good guy or a bad guy."

"Does it matter?"

She looked me straight in the eye. "I think it does to both of us. Are you just making power moves to remind people you're a big, strong man who needs to be feared? Or are you moving pieces around on the world's biggest chess board for the greater good?"

"I attempted to hire you for your brain. Why don't you use it and tell me what you think?"

She leaned forward, resting her elbows on her knees. "I think you are putting friendly people in positions of power and not just because they pay you to. Sheila Chandra is an elementary school principal. She doesn't have pockets deep enough to pay your fees. You don't just give Trip and his fat wallet the boot, you destroy the man's career, citing the fact that he lied to you. But I think it's more than that. I think you don't like bad men in positions of power. Which goes against the reputation you've built for being terrifying, ruthless, and maybe even a little evil."

I opened my hands. "What can I say? I'm a complicated man. You should go home to Nash."

"He's working late tonight. If I'm going to come

137

on board, I want to know what you want out of all this. Are you hoping to get a U.S. President in your pocket?"

"Is that what you think?"

"On the surface, that's what it looks like. But I wonder if you're on some solitary quest to force the world to become a better place."

"Don't mistake me for some kind of hero."

"Oh, I'm not. Let's not forget the trail of ruined lives you leave behind you."

I crossed my arms over my chest. "I don't ruin any life that doesn't deserve to be ruined." At least I tried not to.

"But you take great pleasure in ruining the ones that do."

"I do."

Lina cocked her head and grinned. "Guess I kind of like that about you."

"I'm delighted you approve," I said dryly.

She gave me another long, assessing look and then nodded. "Fine. I'll take the job at ten percent more than you offered since Nash and I are building a house and I want a closet the size of a basketball court. But if you start turning toward the dark side or whatever, I'm out of here."

"Fine. Ten percent. No dark side. I'll talk to HR. Now leave so I can focus on ruining more lives."

"There's something else I want."

"What?" I asked, exasperated.

"I want in on the secret Hugo investigation."

"What secret Hugo investigation?" I hedged.

"The one I'm not supposed to know about. Because of Hugo, I almost lost Nash, and he almost lost me. I want that man in a cell or a box. I'm not picky. But I do want to help put him there."

"Deal. Now leave me alone."

"One more question. Why are you such a dick to Sloane?"

"Go away."

"And why is she a dick to you?" she asked, cocking her head.

"Goodbye, Lina."

"If one of you doesn't tell me, I'll just have to start digging on my own."

"And then I'll rescind my offer and fire you."

She rose and flashed me a grin. "I think it's going to be fun working with you."

"How's Nash?" I asked as she headed for the door.

Lina turned, eyebrow arched. "Shouldn't you be asking him that?"

"I'm asking you."

Nash had gone through a dark period after being shot, one Lina helped pull him out of.

Her expression softened as it always did when she talked about her fiancé. I doubted she was aware of it and doubted more that she'd like attention drawn to that fact.

"He's good. His shoulder is almost back to one hundred percent, and he hasn't had a panic attack since the fall."

"Good."

"Speaking of Nash. I'm going to need to start my official full-time employment Tuesday. Because Monday is wedding dress shopping day."

"If you're looking for someone to ask you why you sound like wedding dress shopping is torture, you came to the wrong man."

She scoffed. "I don't sound like wedding dress shopping is torture."

"I don't care whether you do or you don't."

"I'm just not into the girly, fluffy bridal thing, and Naomi and Sloane took the day off to drive down here and watch me parade around like Bridal Barbie."

Sloane. My heartbeat picked up.

Despite my best efforts, my brain cataloged each and every time the woman's name came up in conversation.

Sloane would be in *my* city.

"Bring them by the office," I said.

Lina looked as if she thought I'd lost my mind. "Why?"

"They're your friends. I'm sure they'd like to see where you officially work as of two minutes ago."

She narrowed her eyes and brought a manicured finger to her jaw. "Hmm. It's almost like you want me to bring Sloane into your inner sanctum."

"You're annoying me. Go home before I fire you."

"Be nicer to her," she ordered.

"Or else what?"

140

"Or else I'll make your work life as miserable as possible while still doing my job. And I'm really, really good at miserable."

• • •

Emry: Is the pair of symphony tickets you had delivered to my house your way of asking me out on a date?

Me: Take them across the street. Knock on the door. And ASK. HER. OUT. But change your shirt first. You're going for "dateable man," not "cuddly grandfather."

Emry: There's nothing wrong with cuddly.

8

Wedding Dress Hives

Sloane

For the first time since my dad passed away, I was up, showered, dressed, and ready to go earlier than necessary. It was day one of my official comeback. Mom was right. I couldn't wallow forever. I wasn't good at it anyway. So today, I'd slap on some lipstick and a smile and go wedding dress shopping. Tomorrow, I'd officially go back to work.

I carted my breakfast dishes from the nook to the sink and grimaced when I found it already piled high with dirty plates and bowls. An oppressive weighted blanket of doom settled over my shoulders.

Energy was a precious commodity, and I'd already used all mine up putting my hair in a ponytail.

I had thirty minutes before I had to leave. I *could* do the dishes, but did I really have the mental energy for strategic dishwasher loading? I peeked inside and groaned. It was already full, and judging from the smell, the dishes on the racks were *not* clean.

Muttering to myself, I opened the cabinet under the sink and found the bottle of detergent. It was empty.

Irritated, I hurled it into the sink. The ensuing rattle and crash of dishes collapsing on themselves had the cat galloping into the room like an investigative pony.

"You know, you could help out around the house. Earn your keep," I told her.

Meow Meow sneezed disdainfully and waddled past me.

I looked at the fork and knife clock on the wall next to the portrait of a fruit bowl.

If I left now, I could stop at one of those hip DC coffee shops where power-suited coffee aficionados began their day and treat myself to an expensive, unnecessary high-calorie drink.

Or I could cross something simple off my to-do list.

I blew out a breath, ruffling the hair that framed my face. There was one thing I could tackle now that would save me considerable trouble: My dating app profile. If I filled it out now, I wouldn't have to lie when Lina and Naomi asked me about it.

I left the chaos of the kitchen behind me and drifted into the mulberry-wallpapered dining room with its heavy antique furniture. There, I flopped down in the velvet wingback chair between the built-in china cabinet that housed more liquor than china and the stained glass window.

Meow Meow launched herself onto the table, draping her considerable girth over the runner.

There was already a sizable ring of cat hair visible on the russet table silk. The dull morning sunlight cast a judgmental spotlight on the dusty table surface. I blew out a breath. Lethargic moping hadn't done me *or* my house any favors.

"I put mascara and cute clothes on this morning. It's a start. Tonight, I'll dust and vacuum," I said conversationally to the cat as I opened the app Stef had forced me to download. "Ugh. It's called Singlez with a *z*."

The pictures of "sexy singlez near me" had me perking up.

"You know, it's been a while since I've had sex. Maybe I'll match with my perfect future husband right away, and then I can get laid and snap out of this funk." Good sex, whether from a relationship or a flirtation turned hookup, had always been a nice reset for me. Like a spa day, only with more coed nudity.

Meow Meow didn't seem impressed. She continued to lavish her front paws with her pink tongue.

I turned my attention back to the screen. Username.

I probably didn't have to get too creative here. After all, I had a one hundred percent success rate when it came to walking into a bar on the prowl. It wasn't going to be *that* hard to find someone suitable on an app designed to match people up.

I glanced around the room, looking for inspiration. Books. Booze. Dust. Cat.

My thumbs flew over the keys.

"Look at that," I said. "Four-EyedCatLibrarian isn't taken."

Meow Meow shot me a disgruntled look, then yawned, baring her teeth.

Likes? That was easy. "Bad tempered cats, books, and comfy pants," I muttered as I typed.

Looking for? The standard options weren't very specific. There was a lot of mileage between companionship and marriage. I decided to go with "other" and typed in my best approximation.

"Okay. Now all we need are a couple of pictures, and we're good to go."

I scrolled through my camera roll and selected a handful of cute selfies.

"Boom! Done," I announced, dropping my phone in my lap like it was a microphone.

It had only taken me four minutes, and now I wouldn't have to lie to my friends. I was starting to impress myself with this comeback.

I glanced around the room for another easy task to cross off and remembered that I'd promised Mom I would gather up any of Dad's old files. Since I was seeing Lina today, I could give them to her instead of paying a personal visit to Suited Satan.

I marched out of the dining room, looped through the living room—man, I really needed to dust—and entered the study. The cabinet behind the desk held a collection of old ballpoint pens, broken pencils, change, and rubber bands.

In the second drawer of the desk, behind a stack of legal pads, I found Dad's candy stash. Pronounced prediabetic a few years before his first cancer diagnosis, he'd taken it upon himself to ration his candy to one piece per day.

I pocketed a mini Kit Kat that was definitely too old to eat and moved on to the bottom drawer.

It was a deep pullout with tabbed hanging folders. Most of them were empty, though their labels remained. *Property Taxes. Gift Ideas. Fantasy Football. Kids Drawings. Recipes.*

I paged through them, smiling at the ripped-out catalog pages filed under gift ideas and the stack of crayon drawings he'd collected over the years of being a father, an uncle, a grandfather, and a neighborhood favorite.

Toward the back of the drawer were a few fat files. These I liberated and piled on top of the desk as the cat pranced into the room. She jumped onto the desk and placed her front paws on the stack of folders.

"Excuse me. Do you mind?"

Meow Meow blinked at me and slowly deflated on top of the paperwork.

I ruffled her ears and then marched into the hallway to grab my coat and tote bag.

Just as I closed the closet door, I heard the frenetic skitter of claws followed by a series of thumps coming from the study. There was a final, louder thud, and then Meow Meow careened into the hall and galloped off in the direction of the staircase.

Back in the office, I discovered my neat stack of folders had exploded everywhere.

"Freaking cat," I muttered.

I sank to the floor and began gathering the jumble of paperwork. Mr. I Can Be of Assistance to You could put them back in their rightful order, I decided.

A series of now mangled printouts of newspaper stories caught my eye.

Upshaw sentenced to twenty years for drug arrest

Judge makes example of first-time drug offender

Defendant's family suggests Upshaw's sentence too harsh

I skimmed the headlines, but it was the picture of a devastated young man leaving a courthouse that caught my attention. The image was grainy and crumpled by cat feet, but I still recognized him. It was my father's law student protégé, Allen.

After an interminable amount of time spent suffering in northern Virginia traffic, I slid out from behind the wheel of my Jeep with my phone pinned between my ear and shoulder.

"Yeah, hey, Maeve. I have a question for you. It's about Dad. Give me a call when you get a chance," I said to my sister's voicemail before disconnecting the call. If Dad had been interested in Allen's mother's case, he probably would have discussed it at some point with my sister.

I reached back inside to drag my tote across the console.

I was five minutes late, which annoyed me. But I filed away the annoyance, straightened my shoulders, and pasted a cheerful smile on my face as I engaged bridesmaid mode.

I plugged in the parking info on my app and marched the two blocks to the bridal shop. Rather than a bell tinkling when I opened the front door, angelic harp music announced my arrival. I found Naomi, Lina, and Stef seated on a pink velvet banquette, each holding a tall flute of champagne, surrounded by an explosion of underskirts, lace, and every tone of white identifiable by the naked eye.

Naomi looked as though she was having the time of her life.

Lina looked like she was about to vomit.

"And how does our bride feel about one dress for the ceremony and a second dress for the reception?" asked a bald man rocking blue velvet loafers and matching cobalt glasses.

Lina choked on her champagne. "One dress is more than enough," she insisted. Her eyes darted to me. "Oh! Look! Sloane is here. I'd better go greet her." Her long legs wrapped in designer denim ate up the pink carpet between us. "Help me. I feel like I'm suffocating in taffeta," she hissed, pulling me in for an awkward and unexpected hug.

"You must be terrified. You're voluntarily hugging me."

"I'll voluntarily make out with you if you help me pick a dress in the next ten minutes so we can get out of here. I'm breaking out in hives."

"I thought you liked fashion?"

"I like clothes I'm going to wear every day. I like badass heels and designer suits and luxury gym apparel. But apparently I don't like wedding dress shopping. It reminds me that . . ." She looked over her shoulder. "It reminds me that I'm *getting married.*"

Prior to the appearance of the broody, wounded Nash Morgan, Lina had been more love 'em and leave 'em than "get engaged and build a house together." She was still finding her way as a soon-to-be married woman.

I took her by the shoulders and squeezed. "You still want to marry Nash, right?"

She rolled her eyes. "Of *course* I do. But not dressed as some virginal princess!"

"Lina, what do you think about a veil?" Naomi called from the girlie couch where Stef was modeling an eight-foot-long veil with seed pearls.

"Oh God," Lina squeaked. "I'm either not going to survive this, or I'm going to pick a dress that I hate just to get it over with."

"Oh boy," I whispered as she towed me toward our friends.

● ● ●

Ahmad, the dress shop employee with great shoes and a surprisingly thick southern drawl, led Lina back to a dressing room while a series of unsmiling assistants paraded after them carrying five gowns that looked increasingly princessy.

Naomi sat back on the couch and took a satisfied sip of champagne.

"Why do you look so smug? She's going to hate every single one of those dresses," I asked, accepting the glass Stef poured me.

"I know," Naomi said gleefully.

"Witty here has a plan," Stef explained.

"What kind of plan?"

"The kind of plan that ends with our friend getting her perfect wedding dress," Naomi declared.

"You're either being cocky or diabolical," I mused. "I can't wait to see which one."

"So. Hook up with any baby daddies yet?" Stef asked me.

"Geez. I literally just set up my profile. Give me a day or two to find the perfect man. Did you ask Jeremiah about moving in together yet?"

Naomi hid her smile behind a delicate cough.

Stef glared at her over the rim of his champagne.

"Oh, come on," Naomi teased. "Tell her your latest excuse."

"It's not an excuse. Closet space is very important to a relationship, and the man just doesn't have enough. It would never work. My wardrobe and I have been through a lot together. It deserves a beautiful, spacious home. Not a few rolling racks next to pieces of an actual motorcycle that he took apart in the living room," he said with a shudder.

"You're right," I agreed. "Closet space is definitely more important than being in love and sharing your life with someone. I'm sure you can cuddle up to those suede leopard loafers at night just as easily as you can Jeremiah. You probably won't even notice the difference."

Naomi grinned. "See? I told you."

Stef sniffed. "Wedding dress shopping makes you two mean."

"Here comes our beautiful bride," Ahmad called.

"Showtime," Naomi said, clapping her hands.

I hit the video call button on Lina's phone, and her mother immediately appeared on-screen.

"It's time!" I told her.

Bonnie Solavita was seated behind an executive desk and holding a mimosa. "I'm ready!"

Lina slunk out in an ivory ballgown so wide she had to turn sideways to squeeze between two mannequins. The spaghetti straps glittered with rhinestones. The corset was tied with a pink satin ribbon. There were so many layers of tulle I had to press my lips together in order not to make a Scarlett O'Hara joke.

The bride didn't look like she was in the mood for jokes. She looked downright miserable.

"Oh my gosh! That dress was made for you," Naomi crooned.

151

"You look . . . amazing." I managed to choke the words out.

"I'm . . . speechless," Stef said before turning to me and mouthing "What the fuck?"

"Wow! That is some dress, sweetie," Bonnie piped up on-screen.

Ahmad rested his chin on his knuckles and studied her while his assistants fluttered around Lina, fluffing the skirt until it seemed to double in size. "Do you love it?" he demanded.

"There aren't words that properly describe how much I hate this dress," Lina said through clenched teeth.

Ahmad clapped his hands. "To the dressing room."

Lina practically ran.

"That dress was . . . something, wasn't it?" Bonnie asked nervously.

I flipped the phone around so I could see her. "Naomi says she has a plan," I explained.

"What kind of plan?"

"I don't know. She won't tell me."

Naomi leaned over Stef to see Lina's mom. "Don't worry, Bonnie. We're going to make sure Lina goes home with the perfect dress. I promise you."

"Well, that definitely wasn't it," Bonnie said, taking a gulp of mimosa. "It looked like a white haystack."

"Here she comes again," Stef said, shoving Naomi back into position.

We repeated the process four more times with

each dress outdoing the awfulness of the one before it.

"You're looking a little flushed, sweetheart. Maybe you should take a break and do some deep breathing," Bonnie suggested from the screen.

"I'm fine, Mom," Lina said, sounding anything but fine. "My heart is fine. I'm just breaking out from neck-to-toe lace."

"That's very common for brides," Ahmad spoke up. "We suggest slathering yourself in antihistamine cream if you're going to wear something that irritates the skin."

"You look beautiful," Naomi assured her.

"Itchy but beautiful," I agreed.

"You know what? I think I've had enough trying on dresses for one day," Lina said, already unbuckling the crystal belt one of the assistants had lassoed around her waist. "Someone get me out of this thing before my skin peels off."

"Oh boy. She's gonna blow," Stef predicted under his breath.

As Lina danced in place while an assistant began to work on the first of seventy thousand buttons running down her back, Naomi gave Ahmad a nod. He turned toward the back of the store and made a series of elaborate swooping gestures.

Two employees appeared, lugging a mannequin between them. The mannequin was already dressed in a strapless gown with black floral appliqués that began at the fitted bodice and spilled down over the full skirt.

"That goes in the window display, ladies," Ahmad said to the women.

Lina glanced up in the mirror and froze.

"What's she looking at?" Bonnie demanded from the phone.

I angled the screen so she could see the dress.

"That one," Lina said, pointing at the gown.

"This? It just arrived this morning. No one's even tried it on yet," Ahmad said coyly.

"It's a beautiful gown," Bonnie prompted.

"I don't know," Stef mused. "How many brides could get away with wearing black on their wedding day?"

"I'll try that one on, but after that, we're leaving," Lina announced, shoving herself out of the dress. She flounced away from the three-way mirror in a strapless bra and underwear.

Ahmad snapped his fingers at the women, who made quick work of disrobing the mannequin.

"Oh my God. That's the dress," I said.

"I know," Naomi agreed.

"It's freaking fabulous," Stef said.

"I know," Naomi said again with a smug smile.

"And so is Lina," Bonnie agreed.

"Exactly," Naomi said, perching on the edge of the cushion, eagerly watching the dressing rooms.

"You're diabolical," I told her.

"I only use my powers for good," she explained.

"Here she comes," Stef said, sounding excited for the first time.

Lina swept into view like a queen. I gasped.

Naomi was already fanning her hands in front of her face to ward off tears. Stef's hands shot out to grip my knee and Naomi's.

Lina ascended the pedestal, dropped the skirts, and struck a regal pose.

"Dead. I'm dead," Ahmad said, clutching his chest theatrically.

"Nash is going to be when he takes one look at her," I predicted.

Bonnie let out a choked sob from the phone.

Lina whirled around, the skirt floating around her like it was alive. "Mom! Don't cry. You have a meeting in twenty minutes," Lina insisted.

"I can't help it. It's so perfect for you. Just like Nash. It just makes me so . . . happy," Bonnie wailed.

I wondered for the briefest of seconds what it felt like to be standing there wearing a beautiful dress knowing that I was going to marry the man of my dreams. Would I have that moment? And if I did, would it be dimmer because I knew my father wouldn't be here to walk me down the aisle?

Tears prickled behind my eyes. Damn it! No crying. No self-pity. I was Comeback Sloane, Truly Excellent Bridesmaid. Not Debbie Downer of the Whomp-Whomp Family.

"It is beautiful, and it is me," Lina conceded. "But what shoes would I wear?"

"Your black lace-up Jimmy Choo boots with the crystal bands," Stef said.

"Ooh, edgy, comfortable, *and* regal," I said.

"Shit. They would be perfect with this," Lina said, fingering one of the black appliqués.

"This dress was made for you," Ahmad decided. "It would be an absolute travesty to let anyone else even try her on." His minions bobbed their heads in agreement.

Lina spun back around to study herself in the mirror. Her eyes met mine. "What do you think, Sloane?"

"It's so perfect I can barely look at you," I admitted.

"It is, isn't it?" She brought her hand to her chest.

"Are you having premature ventricular contractions?" Bonnie demanded.

Lina rolled her eyes. "No, Mom. I'm falling in love with a damn wedding dress."

All the occupants of the little pink couch erupted in cheers.

"Now, let's talk about bridesmaid dresses," Lina said.

"I can't believe I found a dress." Lina pushed her plate away with a gusty, satisfied sigh. "No one else had even tried it on. It's like fate or whatever you weirdo romantics believe in."

We were squeezed into a small booth in the back of a trendy bistro. Stef had skipped lunch under the guise of having a conference call. Personally, I thought he was just avoiding being heckled about his lack of movement on the moving-in-together front.

I shot a glance at Naomi over my fancy-ass grilled cheese. She beamed all her happy newlywed vibes in Lina's direction as they dissected every detail of the dress.

A good friend called the bridal shop and pre-ordered the perfect gown. A great friend pretended like fate was the real hero.

My phone vibrated on the table, and I picked it up. It was a call from my sister.

"Hey, Maeve," I answered, plugging my ear with my finger and sliding out of the booth.

"Hey, I got your message, but I was stuck in court. What's up?" she asked.

I ducked behind a large potted plant next to the host stand. "Did Dad ever mention a Mary Louise Upshaw to you?"

"Dad mentioned a lot of people to me. Is she from Knockemout?"

"She was local-ish. She worked at the post office. I didn't have much time to do any digging, but it looks like she was convicted of drug charges. I think she's the mother of Dad's law school protégé Allen."

"It's ringing a vague bell. But this was probably a few years ago. Before the cancer and the move," Maeve said.

Before the beginning of the end.

"Yeah. That's probably the right timeline," I agreed.

"He wasn't her attorney, was he?" Maeve asked.

157

"No. I think she had a public defender. She got twenty years. First-time offender."

"For possession? That's excessive even for Virginia."

"I thought so too. It turns out his mother's case is why Allen went to law school in the first place. Would you mind looking into it? You know, in the spare time you don't actually have."

"Yeah. I'll do some digging and get back to you."

"In return, I'll take Chloe to play rehearsal for the next two nights," I volunteered.

"Best aunt ever," Maeve said, affection in her voice. "What am I going to do when you have kids of your own?"

"Ha. It's just me and the cat for now. I've gotta go. I'm with Lina and Naomi. I'll pick up Chloe tonight. Love you."

"Love you. Bye."

I disconnected.

"What was that about?" Lina asked when I returned to the table.

"Just some papers of Dad's I found. Get this. My mom wants me to give them to Lucian."

Naomi's brows winged up in surprise. "Is your mom unaware of the mutual animosity?"

"Oh, she's aware. I think she just wants us to find a way to be friends, but we can't be in the same room without trying to tear each other limb from limb, so I made the executive decision to dump them on Lina here since she'll be more likely to see Lucifer."

"Speaking of Suit Daddy," Lina said, running her finger around the lip of her glass of scotch. "I officially accepted his job offer after demanding more money and a few other perks."

"That's wonderful news," Naomi said.

"Congratulations?" I said. I didn't mean to make it sound like a question, but that was how it came out.

Lina laughed. "Thanks. I'm excited. I finally get to pull back the curtain and get my hands dirty."

"What perks did you hold out for?" I asked.

"He has to be nicer to you."

"Oh my God. You did *not* negotiate me into your employment contract. Did you?" I didn't want Lucian Rollins thinking I needed someone to stand up for me.

"It was more a passing comment than a demand," Lina assured me. "Interestingly enough, when he found out that you two were going to be in town today, he said I should invite you to the office."

Naomi turned to me, looking like she was about to implode with happiness.

"What?" I demanded defensively.

"He finds out that you're going to be in town with Lina and invites you to the office. You don't think that sounds like the *exact opposite* thing a man would do for his sworn enemy?" she said pointedly.

"Sworn enemy is a little harsh," I said, thinking of the breakfast burrito and my mother's spa day. "And he invited *us,* not me."

"I don't know. My instincts tell me he wants *you* there," Lina insisted.

"He does not. Maybe he was just pretending to be human to his new employee. Or maybe he has a crush on Naomi like all men with a penis and half a brain do."

Naomi tossed her hair and pouted like a supermodel. "It's true. Six men fell into manholes so far today," she said breathily.

I snorted.

Lina held up her hands. "Okay. Fine. Full disclosure. He's not even supposed to be in the office this afternoon. So maybe he offered it up knowing he wouldn't be around to fight with you."

I was not about to think about recognizing the tiny sliver of disappointment that news brought on.

Naomi, on the other hand, looked fully deflated.

"But seriously. Aren't you the least bit curious why he'd extend the invitation?" Lina pressed.

"Nope," I lied.

"Well, I've always wanted to see where he works. Does he really have a throne made out of the bones of his enemies?" Naomi asked.

"I *was* just going to give you the files to give to him next time you were in the office," I told Lina.

"Yeah, but aren't you just the least bit curious to see behind the frowny, rich guy curtain? I have to admit it's pretty impressive," she prodded. "You could deliver the files straight to his very expensive desk so you can tell your mom that you tried to give them to him personally. Maybe we could even use his in-office espresso machine."

Naomi clapped her hands. "Ooh! Espresso! Please, please, please, Sloane."

It wasn't smart, but part of me really wanted to see where Lucian Rollins ran his evil empire.

Besides, the longer I stayed down here, the higher the chances a hot, local guy on the app would slide into my DMs. There was a possibility that I could help Lina find a dress, tour Lucian's evil empire, *and* get laid all in the same day.

"I guess we could stop by and see your new office," I mused. "Since we're here and all."

Naomi and Lina shared a triumphant match-maker-y look.

"Stop making that face or I'll change my mind."

9

Canoodling with the Devil

Sloane

The offices of Rollins Consulting took up the entire fourteenth floor of a pricey-looking building with a pricey-looking view. Everything from the marble floor of the reception area to the dark, wood-paneled walls whispered wealth and power.

There was fancy art on the walls and real plants in gold pots.

"I need to see your IDs," said the woman behind the front desk.

She was somewhere in her midfifties to early sixties and had the ramrod posture of a career military woman. She was looking at Naomi and me like she thought we might try to steal a painting off the wall or stuff our purses full of espresso pods. The nameplate indicated that her name was Petula.

I found her both terrifying and fascinating.

"They're friends of mine and Lucian's," Lina insisted.

Well, *that* was a blatant lie.

Petula didn't appear to be impressed. "Just because they're friends now doesn't mean they won't be enemies later," she said. "I will accept a driver's license, military ID, or passport."

Naomi raced to comply, digging through her purse like it was a scavenger hunt.

I pulled my driver's license out of my wallet and was just handing it over when ex-U.S. Marshal Nolan Graham entered the lobby space through a pair of smoked-glass doors.

"Blondie!"

"Nolan!"

He looked good. Healthy and happy. And that made me happy.

I opened my arms for a hug. He wrapped me up and plucked me off the floor, leaving my feet dangling. We had dated. Barely. Not even long enough for more than a very nice kiss or two before his heroic injury changed the trajectory of his career and personal life.

Lucian, for reasons that remained shrouded in mystery, offered Nolan a job with his firm. A position that made it possible to win back his ex-wife, Callie.

I may not have ended up with a hot U.S. marshal boyfriend, but at least I'd gotten a new friend out of the deal.

"How's the bullet hole?" My question ended in a gasping giggle when he gave me a tight squeeze before setting me on my feet again.

His answer was interrupted by the sound of multiple throats clearing. I glanced around and spotted Lina, Naomi, and even Petula looking as wide-eyed as Taylor Swift's front row audience.

"Oh, hey, boss," Nolan said, taking his time releasing me from his embrace.

Shit.

A familiar blaze of heat swept my back from head to heel. It always made me wonder if the man commanded the powers of actual hellfire.

"So how are you doing?" I asked Nolan again, determined not to address the threat behind me.

"All healed up," he said.

"Don't listen to him. The big baby was just whining Friday about the winter wind making his bullet hole ache," Lina interjected.

"I'm a hero. Heroes are allowed to whine," Nolan insisted with a smirk.

"How is the soon-to-be missus? I heard you're eloping," I said, ignoring the fact that my back was bathed in flames.

Nolan's grin showed every tooth in his mouth. "She's great. We're great. Heading to St. Croix in a few weeks to make things official . . . again."

His happiness was palpable.

I squeezed his arm. "Congratulations. I'm so happy for you two."

I really was. Everyone around me was falling in love and getting married and starting—or growing—families. It was making me acutely aware of my current single status.

"Ladies."

The deep rumble of Lucian's voice vibrated its way up my spine.

I turned slowly and drank in the godlike hotness of Lucifer himself. It was impossible not to. It was like standing in a room with a great work of art and trying *not* to memorize every masterful brushstroke.

Lucian was annoyingly attractive in yet another impeccable dark suit with a crisp Oxford and a gray-and-blue-striped tie. I wanted to grab that tie and yank on it until that perfect facade cracked. His thick dark hair waved away from his face in a too-perfect style that begged for someone to mess it up. He was too perfect. It was unnatural.

He scanned me as he always did. And for once, I wondered what he was seeing. In contrast to his perfectly polished exterior, I was wearing snug, army-green cargo pants and a lightweight violet turtleneck. My hair was in a high ponytail, and my lips were a murderous red.

Was it my imagination, or did his gaze linger a little longer than necessary on my mouth?

Why the hell did I feel so alive when we locked gazes?

Was someone going to say something, or were we just going to stare eyeball flames at each other all day?

"I hope you don't mind that we're here," Naomi said, breaking our staring contest with her polite people-pleasing.

I looked away when she greeted him with a friendly hug. Petula, I noticed, was watching me with a calculating expression.

"Lina told us the good news, and we wanted to come see where she'll be officially working," Naomi continued as if it were her job to smooth over the awkwardness that happened whenever Lucian and I had the misfortune of being in a room together.

Lina narrowed her eyes. "I thought you were supposed to be out for the afternoon," she said to her new, official boss.

"I was," Lucian said, curtly cutting her off. "My schedule was rearranged due to unforeseen circumstances." Those deep sterling eyes came back to me.

The man probably had security alert him the moment I stepped in the building. And he'd returned . . . Why? To make sure I didn't set his office on fire?

"You're supposed to alert me to any and all schedule changes when they occur," Petula reminded him.

I smirked, entertained by the big, powerful egomaniac being chastised by the no-nonsense admin.

"I'll try to remember that in the future, Petula," he said dryly.

Lucian was still watching me, and I felt capable of doing nothing but staring back.

Lina snapped her fingers and bobbed her head. "Sooo . . ."

It looked as though we were back to awkward.

"Find a dress?" Nolan asked her.

Lina nearly sprained an elbow reaching for her phone. "I did. And bridesmaid dresses. What's Callie wearing for your beach ceremony?"

Nolan reached for his phone, and the two of them put their heads together over wedding dresses.

"You're giving me regrets about hiring you both," Lucian said irritably.

Lina looked at Nolan. "I think he's feeling left out."

"You're right," Nolan agreed.

They sandwiched their grumpy boss between them and began scrolling through their photos, explaining each in excruciating detail.

"You're fired," he said as he extricated himself from the huddle. "Enjoy your visit," he told Naomi, then headed for the glass doors without sparing me another glance.

Lina gave a satisfied sigh. "That was fun."

"Your guests are cleared for their visit," Petula said, returning our IDs. She looked disappointed as if she'd been hoping for a security breach.

"Did she just run a background check on us?" I whispered to Nolan.

"Yep. And a credit check."

"Wow."

"Enjoy your tour. I've gotta go meet an anonymous source about a top secret thing," he said.

I couldn't tell if he was kidding or not. Knowing Lucian's shadowy business dealings, anything was possible. "Good to see you, Nolan."

"You too, Blondie. Don't be a stranger."

Lina buzzed us through the double glass doors with a key card. I blinked in surprise.

I'd spent years fantasizing that Lucian ran his empire of evil from a dungeon-like lair with sweaty stone walls and a sulfuric scented fog. But this was not that. There was an acre of trendy cubicles inhabited by dozens of employees, none of whom looked like they were here against their will. Employees of all ages, races, and fashion senses congregated at communal tables and in glass-walled conference rooms.

It was busy but not chaotic. Some people were *actually laughing.*

"Wow," Naomi said.

"Where are all the instruments of torture?" I asked.

"He keeps those in a separate location. Bloodstains on the carpet and all," Lina said breezily.

"Wait up, Lina." A freckled redhead who looked like the perfect combination of dazed and happy came to a screeching halt in front of us. "Petula sent me to see if you'd like any coffee or water or tea."

Her hair was pulled back from her face in an intricate half updo. She had stickers on her fingernails. And beneath her plaid blazer, she wore a Selena Gomez T-shirt.

"This is Holly. She's a new hire like me," Lina said, introducing the woman.

Two spots of pink bloomed on Holly's cheeks, and she looked as if she were going to burst into tears or song. "This job is a dream come true. Mr. Rollins hired me as an administrative assistant.

168

It's my first real job. My kids are so proud of me they pack my lunch every morning and I have to wait until they're off to school and daycare before I can pack something besides animal crackers and string cheese," she explained to us in a rush.

"That's so sweet of them," Naomi said.

"Congratulations," I said, hoping that Lucian wouldn't turn his dragon fire on the poor girl and reduce her to ash.

"Did you say something about coffee?" Naomi asked hopefully. "Because I would love one."

It had been almost thirty minutes since her last hit of caffeine.

"How do you take it?" Holly asked with an eager smile.

"Any way I can get it," Naomi joked.

"I'll bring you my specialty then. Can I get anything for you?" Holly asked, turning to me.

"I'm fine, thanks." With my luck, I'd spill an entire mug of coffee all over Lucian's fancy-ass office and he'd sue me for damages.

"I'll catch up with you on your tour," she promised and darted off.

"She's sweet," I said.

"She really is. Two weeks ago, she and her two kids were homeless. They left an abusive home and ended up in a shelter. Word is Lucian hired her on the spot. She started the next day and moved into an apartment last week."

"That's amazing," Naomi said, clasping her hands to her chest.

"Why was he there to hire her?"

"Apparently your archnemesis is a major sponsor of the program," Lina explained.

"Yeah, well, I guess even ogres can do something good for a tax write-off," I muttered.

I didn't enjoy stumbling onto evidence that contradicted everything I believed about the man. I liked having him well defined. For years, heck *decades,* he'd been nothing but a two-dimensional caricature of a villain. Now, however, I was beginning to wonder what other signs of humanity I'd missed beneath those custom suits and heart-breaker cheekbones.

If there was a hypothetical heart that beat somewhere inside that broad, wealthy chest, what did it mean that he still hated me?

Lina continued our tour, showing us an impressive array of break rooms, conference rooms, and offices.

Hers was a light-filled, minimalist space with a desk, a couch, and a great view. There was a picture on her desk of her and Nash strapped to a parachute.

"So what exactly do you do here?" I asked, trying out the couch.

"The firm's primary purpose is to support candidates as they run for and hold office."

"So you dig up dirt on political rivals, blackmail them, and if that doesn't work, have them 'disappeared?' " I guessed. "Do you hide the bodies, or are you further up the chain?"

"Sloane," Naomi hissed.

"There's an entire supply closet dedicated to corpse disposal down the hall," Lina joked, spinning around in her ergonomic desk chair.

"Everyone here seems so happy," Naomi said, trying to switch to a more positive subject.

"It's hard not to be," Lina said. "The pay is well above fair. The benefits are generous. And the boss is a beautiful beast of a man who no one wants to disappoint."

I sniffed. "I guess if you're into the whole fire and brimstone thing."

Both women eyed me. "Even *you* have to admit that Lucian is unnaturally good-looking," Naomi prodded.

"Good-looking?" Lina snorted. "The man looks like the hottest gods in the universe got together and made the hottest baby in the universe. I'm not convinced that he's mortal. Has anyone ever seen him sleep?"

I had.

Those inky lashes against bronze skin. The slow and steady cycle of breaths that made his chest rise and fall. But even sleep couldn't steal the tension from that marble jaw.

I hated that I had those memories in my head waiting to sneak up and punch me in the feels. Guilt. Fear. Fiery, righteous anger.

"Vampires don't need sleep," I said. "Which way is the restroom?"

The bathroom was like the rest of the office,

sedately fabulous and stupidly luxurious. The backlit granite vanities held baskets of high-end hand lotions, glasses cleaner, and tidy selections of feminine products.

There was even a makeup mirror and counter built into an alcove.

I dampened a towel so soft it had to be cashmere and held it to my cheeks.

The past few weeks had made me question everything I'd been so sure of. Things I believed in like they were immutable laws of nature.

I could always count on my parents.

There was no rush to start my own family.

Lucian Rollins was a horrible troll of a human being.

Now I felt . . . lost. Like I had somehow stepped into an alternate dimension where up was down and down was purple. I couldn't handle any more change at the moment.

I patted my face dry. Then, because the supplies were there, I cleaned my glasses.

"This is all just part of the grieving process," I told my reflection. "You don't really care if Lucian is human or not. Your brain is just trying to find something else to obsess over. Things will get better. Eventually. Probably."

Half-assed pep talk complete, I exited the restroom and ran smack into a hot, hard chest.

My tote hit the floor with a thump as big, warm hands steadied me.

I knew who it was without looking at his face. I

knew it from the electrifying current that streaked through my body.

"Is looking where you're going too much to ask from you?" Lucian said gruffly.

"You're the one plowing past the ladies' restroom at a hundred miles an hour," I pointed out, giving him a shove. He didn't budge, and that irritated me.

I was the one who conceded and took a step backward. I reached down for the straps of my bag, but he got there first.

"Jesus, what are you carrying in here? A dismembered body?"

"Why do men always feel the need to comment on the weight and contents of a woman's purse?" I asked, lunging for the straps.

He held the bag out of my reach. "Curiosity. We can only carry what fits in a wallet or a briefcase. This feels like an entire set of encyclopedias."

"If you must know, they're Dad's files. I found them this morning and was going to give them to Lina to give to you."

"You were going to give them to Lina," he repeated, his voice dangerously calm.

"Yes," I confirmed.

"Rather than me."

Something prickled at the back of my neck. Danger. Beware. Proceed with caution.

I ignored the warning. "Yep."

"Why?"

"Why?" It was apparently my turn to play parrot. "You know why."

173

"Elaborate," he insisted.

"No."

He fixed me with a glare, then turned on the heels of his very expensive loafers and marched down the hall with my bag.

"Hey!" I had to jog to keep up with his long, well-dressed legs. That bag didn't just have files. It had all my essentials like car keys, lipstick, tablet, pepper spray, and snacks.

He stepped through a doorway, and I followed him inside, not realizing until he was closing the glass door behind me that I'd just voluntarily entered the devil's den.

Lucian's office.

Of *course* it was in a corner. And of course it was huge with breathtaking views. It was cold, formal, impressive. I thought of my own cozy, chaotic office.

"Weird. I expected it to smell like brimstone, but I'm catching whiffs of . . . fish," I said, sniffing the air.

Lucian swore under his breath.

"Okay. *What* is your problem, Lucifer?" I demanded.

"You. Once again, it's you."

"Give me my bag back."

Instead of handing it to me like an adult, he set it on the very expensive-looking coffee table in front of a pricy-looking white sofa. Had the guy never heard of IKEA? He pointed toward my tote bag. "Give me the files."

I sat with a huff on the silk upholstery and pulled the tote across the coffee table's marble surface.

"I don't know why you're getting so pissed off when you're proving my point. This is exactly the reason I was going to give the files to Lina in the first place," I grumbled.

"Do you think I want to dislike you?"

I looked up, startled by the sharpness of his tone. He was dragging one hand through those dark polished waves of hair while patting his pockets with the other.

"If you even *think* about lighting up a cigarette in here—"

"Don't even pretend you didn't help yourself to a drag of the last one I had in your presence," he said.

I felt color flood my cheeks. "Oh, shut up." I yanked the files free, and out came two library books, my cosmetics bag, and half of my snack stash. "And yes. I do think you want to dislike me. I think you love to hate me."

He stood, legs braced, hands on hips like he was preparing for battle. I pretended not to notice the clench of his already well-defined jaw under the perfection of his beard.

The guy had been a gorgeous teenager, and Lina was right. He'd grown up to be a damn god. Sometimes life just wasn't fair.

"Here are the damn files that you can give to the damn attorney so you can keep looking like a damn hero to my mother."

I shoved the stack toward him, then spied the Mary Louise Upshaw news clippings in the pile and snatched them back.

Quickly, I returned the clippings and the rest of the spillage to the bag and stood. Slinging the straps over my shoulder, I made a move for the door.

"I don't love to hate you."

The words, spoken softly, brought me to a halt.

I turned to face him, and then because I was feeling temperamental, I closed the distance between us. "What *do* you want, Lucian?" I demanded, looking up at him.

He said nothing. I knew there were feelings and ideas and a freaking personality beneath that beautiful surface, but he'd cut me off from it all.

"You treat me like I'm the worst person on the planet, and then you do sneaky nice things for my parents. You hire homeless single mothers. You pick fights with me, and then you have my favorite burrito delivered. How in the hell do you know what my favorite burrito is anyway?"

He took a step toward me. But I held up a hand before he could answer.

"You know what? Never mind. I don't want to know. The only thing I do want to know is *what do you want from me?*"

For one brief, shining moment, the man looming over me like a pissed-off vampire about to take a bite looked as miserable as I felt.

"I want you not to matter at all," he said. His

tone was calm, but there was heat, a silvery fire in those gray eyes.

It was rude, I'd give him that. But it felt like a damn victory. A heady one. I was tired of being the temperamental one. Of feeling like I was the only one driven to distraction by our mean-spirited back-and-forths.

I *mattered* to him, and he hated that.

"Back at you, big guy."

"You should go," he said suddenly.

"Why? Don't you like having me here in this very nice office?" I wandered over to his desk. It was a huge pane of glass with sharp corners, empty except for a keyboard, mouse, and two monitors.

I wondered if he liked order or just hated chaos.

I trailed my fingers along the beveled edge, knowing full well I was leaving smudges. "You seem upset," I said, pausing and locking eyes with him. "Want to talk about it?" I offered before hopping up to perch on the glass surface.

His gaze darkened dangerously, and he took a few steps in my direction before stopping. My heart rate kicked up. "I don't like who either of us becomes when we're together," he said.

I scoffed. "You think *I* like this?"

"I think you love it."

Had he moved closer? Or was I leaning toward him? My knees were almost close enough to brush the sharp creases of his trousers. We were magnetized to each other. Enemies drawn together again and again.

I was so damn tired of it.

There was an electric tension growing in the space between us. Like when the hair on your arms stands up just before a lightning strike.

"I don't," I insisted huffily.

Then my knees were brushing his legs, and he was stepping between them, parting my thighs as I craned my neck to look at him.

My breath caught.

His fingers flexed at his sides, and then they ghosted over the tops of my thighs before he planted his hands on either side of my hips. God. He even *smelled* gorgeous.

Lucian dominated my senses. The subtle gray stripes in his tie matched his eyes exactly. The heat pumping off his body felt like I'd entered a sauna. His scent was crisp, clean, deadly. I could hear a heart beat, and it was loud enough to think maybe it belonged to both of us.

"You do. You think that one of these days, you'll land exactly the right insult, and you'll be able to see through my cracks."

His voice was barely above a threatening whisper. His gaze was locked on mine. It created a strange gravity. As if I couldn't look away or I'd somehow just float off without that anchor.

I didn't know what was happening here. But I did know I didn't want him to stop talking. I didn't want him to step back.

"What would I see beneath those cracks?" I asked.

He closed his eyes and shook his head, trying to break the spell. But I wasn't going to let him. Not this time. I reached out and did what I'd fantasized about for years. I grabbed his perfect tie and yanked him closer.

"Do *not* play with me, Pixie," he growled. His words were a warning, but those eyes were open now, and I saw something else in them. Something fiery.

My biological instincts were scrambled. Instead of fight or flight, my body seemed to have added a third option: fuck.

"Don't call me that," I breathed.

"Then stop looking at me like that."

"Like what?" I whispered. His thumbs simultaneously brushed the outer curve of my rear end where it met his desk, and I absolutely almost lost consciousness.

This didn't feel like hate. This felt like something much more dangerous.

"Like you want me to . . ." The unflappable Lucian Rollins lost his train of thought as he looked at my mouth. The rawness I saw on that gorgeous face both terrified and fascinated me.

I wondered briefly if Lina's heart condition was contagious, because my heart seemed to be limping along like it forgot how to beat properly.

"This is a horrible idea," I said in a near whisper.

"Worst I've ever had," he agreed.

Neither of us moved. Neither of us came to our senses.

"I'm exhausted by us," I admitted.

"I *hate* us," he countered.

My fingers began to ache, and I realized I still had them locked around his tie.

His mouth hovered over mine, not quite touching. We were breathing the same air as our bodies caught fire. My head was spinning, flinging away all logic as I clung to the one thing that felt right. Him. I wanted this. I wanted him.

"Excuse me, sir."

Lucian didn't move. But I sure as hell did.

"It's time to unhand the librarian. Her friends are waiting, and you have an emergency call from Boston on the line," Petula announced briskly from somewhere behind Lucian's broad chest.

With a yelp, I launched myself forward in a panicked attempt to slide off the desk. But instead of dismounting, I only managed to crash my crotch into Lucian's.

I was sandwiched, suspended in the canyon of space between the edge of his desk and what could only be described as a mega erection. My legs were draped over his thighs in what would have been the perfect position for getting railed.

"Oh God," I squeaked.

If I could feel how hard he was, did that mean he could feel how wet I was? This was knowledge neither of us needed the other to have.

Lucian's nostrils flared, and his hands were now gripping me by the hips. Hard.

"Out," he snapped without looking away from me.

"No," Petula decreed. "You pay me to maintain order, not to tolerate your blatant disregard of your schedule. You do not have time to canoodle with Ms. Walton. It will have to wait."

"Canoodle?" There was a hysterical edge to my tone, and for one fleeting moment, I thought I caught the flash of amusement on Lucian's face, but it was gone as quickly.

"Ms. Walton was just leaving," Lucian said coldly.

He gripped my hips with powerful fingers and placed me firmly on the floor. He gritted his teeth and took a step back. The silk of his tie, the only thing that still tethered us to each other, slid through my fingers.

Feeling petty, I grabbed the tail end of his tie and flipped it saucily over his shoulder.

"See you around, *Lucifer*."

10

Annoyed and Hungry

Lucian

"You seem tense," Emry observed.

"Tense? Why would I be tense? Just because I've got clients to deal with, the FBI moving at a snail's pace, an exasperating woman interrupting my schedule, a tail that smells like the Hugo crime organization. There's no reason to be tense," I snapped.

The city streets were always bumper to bumper in black luxury SUVs. But I'd still made the tail when I'd been alerted to Sloane's arrival.

I hadn't been able to deal with the security issue because I'd needed to see *her*. I'd been compelled to ignore the situation I could have easily dealt with because I wanted to see her in my offices. I wanted to be there when she saw what I'd built.

And then I'd gone and lost every shred of discipline. I'd forgotten the most basic of lessons. Sloane's proximity to me brought her too close to danger. It always had.

My friend steepled his fingers over his rounded belly and waited expectantly.

I realized I hadn't even taken a seat. I'd been

pacing in front of the man's fireplace since the minute I arrived. We were meant to be having dinner tonight. But one look at me when he opened the door and he'd shed the apron and waved me into his home office.

I brought my fingertips to my forehead. "Sorry, Emry. I'm ruining our dinner."

It had been a long time since I'd felt this out of control. I needed to lock down my feelings to put a stop to the images that played incessantly in my head. Those green eyes at half-mast. The red lips parting.

He waved away my apology. "It's a casserole. It'll keep."

"You burnt it, didn't you?"

He grinned ruefully. "I'm surprised you didn't notice the charcoal smell."

I hadn't noticed anything. I needed to calm the fuck down. "She's infuriating," I said, resuming my pacing.

"The FBI agent?"

"No! Sloane."

Chuckling, he heaved himself out of his leather recliner and crossed to the brass bar cart he kept under a painting of stormy seas challenging a wooden ship.

I leaned against the mantel and willed myself to stop thinking about how it had felt to have Sloane pinned between me and my desk.

Emry poured two glasses of wine from a shapely decanter. He was wearing a black wool sweater covered in neon fish over a checkered button-down.

"That sweater deserves to be set on fire," I observed when he handed me one of the glasses. He looked like someone's kindly, hapless grandfather.

I wondered briefly what he thought of when he looked at me. Did I look like the CEO of a multimillion-dollar company? Did I look like I could be someone's husband, someone's father? Or did I look like the villain I was?

"Let's table the subject of the exasperating Sloane—temporarily—and go back to the part about you being followed by an organized crime syndicate," he suggested, indicating the second chair.

"I didn't lead them here if that's what you're worried about," I said as I reluctantly sat.

"Hmm," came the pointed reply.

I blew out a breath. I was, as Emry would have said in our therapy days, "coloring others' words with my ego's definitions." Nowadays, he only had to hum for me to get the message.

"I know you well enough to understand you take every precaution to protect those you care about. My concern is for *you*. Do you give yourself the same care?"

"Can't you just tell me how to stop feeling all these feelings so I can focus on what needs to be accomplished?" I asked, staring into the glass.

"If we were in a session, I'd say something thought-provoking about how sometimes the feelings we resist the most are the ones that have the most to teach us. Then we could discuss why, in an itemized list of situations anyone would find challenging, you're most concerned with a woman from your past. One you claim to have nothing but animosity toward. But we're just two friends about to order pizza so we don't have to eat the smoking meteor in my kitchen. As a friend, I'll ask this. Why is a visit from a public librarian more disconcerting to you than the fact that a mob boss might be aware you're helping the FBI build a case against him?"

Because I was in control when it came to Anthony Hugo.

Because I knew how to deal with men like that.

Because I savored their ruin.

"Because she reminds me of a past I'd rather forget," I said out loud. "She betrayed me when I was vulnerable."

And today she'd spread her thighs for me, perched on my desk like she belonged there. Like she wanted to be there. Like she wanted *me* there.

I shook the images out of my head and replaced them with another older, darker memory.

Sloane looking brokenhearted and brave, her arm in a sling, those emerald eyes glittering with defiant tears.

"What did you do?" I'd shouted at her. What I'd meant but hadn't said was, *"What did he do?"*

"Lucian, you're a smart man," Emry stated as he peered at me over the rim of his glass.

I already didn't like where this was going.

"What are you getting at?"

"As a reasonably intelligent man, I'm going to assume that you know you can't just forget the past or pretend it doesn't exist. And as you've spent significant time in therapy with a brilliant therapist, I'll remind you that the only way out is through. You can't just keep putting your emotions in a box with a lid and expecting them to stay there. That's not what feelings do."

"Then I'll remind you that we both know why letting those emotions out of their box is dangerous."

"You have a lot more control than you give yourself credit for," he pointed out.

"That control hinges on not letting my emotions get the better of me."

"There's a difference between quelling impulses that everyone has and refusing to acknowledge any feeling at all."

I scoffed. "I have feelings that I acknowledge all the time."

"For instance?" Emry prompted.

"For instance, I'm hungry and annoyed right now."

My friend chuckled. "Pepperoni and sausage?"

"Fine."

"Lucian, I don't pity you for what you went through as a child any more than I excuse you from doing the hard work of realizing you are a whole, complicated man capable of not only experiencing happiness but sustaining it."

"Why is everyone so obsessed with happiness? There are other aims a bit more worthy than walking around with an idiotic grin on my face."

"Let me say this. You're a grown man who has achieved wild levels of success, which in itself is impressive. But when you factor in your upbringing, it's downright miraculous. Trust yourself to handle having feelings. Even the uncomfortable ones."

The man gave me too much credit. He didn't know what I was capable of. But I did.

I exhaled slowly.

"Out of curiosity, what did she do this time that aggravated you?" Emry asked, his eyes dancing behind his half-moon spectacles.

"She got fingerprints on my desk," I said testily.

Our bickering had always turned me on. It was a weakness that made me feel pathetic. But today she'd taunted me on my own turf, and my cock had risen to the occasion so swiftly I'd gone light-headed.

I'd wanted her. I'd craved her. And I would have had her right there on that desk.

Maybe that was the answer. Maybe this torturous tension between us would finally vanish if we gave in, just once.

Emry chuckled. "Sooner or later, my friend, you'll learn that embracing the messiness of life is where you find its greatest treasures."

"I prefer my orderly piles of money, thank you." But I wasn't thinking about bank balances. I was thinking about Sloane, thighs spread, red lips parted as I finally thrust home.

"Come on. Let's order our dinner, and then I'll let you trounce me at a game of chess."

11

Shania Twain Is a Beautiful Badass

Lucian

Twenty-three years ago

Here we go," Simon Walton said as he set a Garfield coffee mug that said I WISH THIS WERE LASAGNA at my elbow.

We were facing off in the breakfast nook in the Waltons' kitchen, a room that was almost the size of the entire first floor of my house. Leaves of orange and rust whispered on the other side of the angular windows above the banquette.

On the freshly painted turquoise table between us sat a worn chessboard midbattle.

"Thanks," I said, still frowning at the board. I liked that he didn't question me or make fun of me for asking for coffee. Men drank coffee. I was learning to like it.

I closed my fingers around the knight's head and moved it deeper into enemy territory.

"Remember, you can't just go on the attack willy-nilly," Mr. Walton explained. "You need to have a plan. A strategy. You can't just think about what you're going to do. You have to predict what your opponent is going to do."

With that advice, his bishop neatly destroyed my knight.

"Damn it," I muttered, picking up the coffee.

Mr. Walton grinned. "No quitting. See it through."

Annoyed, I sacrificed a pawn.

"And that's checkmate," Mr. Walton said, nudging his glasses up his nose.

I slouched against the yellow patterned cushion. "I don't think I like this game."

"I have a feeling with a little more practice you'll find your stride. It's just like what you do on the football field from inside the pocket."

It was a November Sunday afternoon. Which meant no game, no practice, no escape from the hell I lived next door.

Dad was out fishing with friends. Mom was where she spent most of her free time when my father wasn't around: alone in her bedroom. I'd spotted Mr. Walton in his backyard deadheading flowers and volunteered to help.

"How are the chess lessons going?" Karen Walton asked, sweeping into the room with two bags of groceries.

"Great," Mr. Walton insisted.

"Terrible," I said.

We both rose from the table and each relieved her of a bag. While Mr. Walton laid a loud kiss on his wife, I busied myself with delivering the bag to the huge central island. There were small messes and chaos here. A haphazard stack of cookbooks, a flour spill next to the porcelain container that no one had gotten around to cleaning up. The bowl of apples sat half on and half off a magazine open to an article about sending kids to college.

Messes weren't tolerated in my house. Anything that might be a trigger had to be avoided at all costs.

"There's more in the car," Mrs. Walton announced, giving Mr. Walton an embarrassing pat on the ass. Affection was something else that didn't exist at my place.

"We'll get them," Mr. Walton insisted. "Treat yourself to a cup of coffee while my protégé and I unload."

"What would I do without you two? And I think I'll have wine instead," Mrs. Walton said, giving me an affectionate pat on the arm as she headed toward the large built-in china cabinet that housed a menagerie of mismatched bar glasses.

I didn't quite manage to hide the wince when her fingers accidentally came in contact with my latest bruise. The Waltons drank. There was wine at the dinner table, and I saw Mr. and Mrs. Walton sometimes enjoying cocktails on the front porch. But I never saw either of them drunk.

That was the difference between Mr. Walton and my father. Self-control.

Maybe that was what he was trying to teach me on the chessboard.

"Football injury?" Mr. Walton asked, looking at my arm.

"Yeah," I said, tugging the sleeve of my shirt

down to cover the bruise. The lie stuck in my throat.

Mrs. Walton crooked her finger at me and pointed up. I hid my smile. I liked being needed even if it was just for my height. I found her favorite long-stemmed wineglass with flowers etched on it on the top shelf and handed it to her. She wiggled it in her husband's direction, asking a silent question. Mr. Walton gave her a geeky thumbs-up, and I pulled a second glass off the shelf.

"Lucian, I don't like you playing that game," she lectured, taking the second glass and heading to the counter. She put the glasses down, rummaged through one of the bags, and produced a bottle of wine. "There are too many ways to get hurt. And yes, young bodies heal faster, but you don't know what that kind of damage can add up to later in life."

"The boy is starting quarterback in his senior year, love," Mr. Walton pointed out. "He's not quitting the team and taking up knitting."

"Nobody said knitting," she said. "What about softball? Sloane hardly ever gets hurt. Where is our daughter, by the way?"

I'd been wondering the same thing for the last two hours but had refused to ask.

"On a date with the Bluth boy," Mr. Walton said with an exaggerated eyebrow wiggle.

I stiffened. This was news to me. We'd talked about it. Not at school because we never talked at school. It was some unspoken rule between the two of us. She probably thought I was an asshole. The popular quarterback who thought he was too good to be seen talking to the sophomore book-worm.

"I forget. Do we like him or not?" Mrs. Walton asked, inserting the corkscrew.

Jonah Bluth was a punk-ass junior defensive tackle who'd made the mistake of running his mouth in the locker room about Sloane Walton's tits that he was going to get his hands on. I'd waited until we'd gotten out on the practice field before I hit him hard enough to knock some sense into him. Unfortunately for him, that sense didn't tell him to stay down, and Nash had been the one to pry us apart.

I'd told Sloane in no uncertain terms to dump Jonah's ass. She'd demanded to know why. For some reason, she felt like she had the right to know everything about everything. It was infuriating and endearing at the same time.

I told her he was an asshole and that she deserved better. Both truths.

She said she'd think about it, which apparently meant she was going to do what she damn well pleased no matter what.

"I think we're withholding judgment to see if our daughter likes him," Mr. Walton said. Then he beckoned to me. "Come on, Lucian. I'll tell you about the Scandinavian defense while we cart in the groceries."

"I'm making your second favorite for dinner

tonight, Lucian. Frozen ravioli with store-bought sauce," Mrs. Walton called after us.

I didn't recognize the warm feeling in my chest, but I liked it.

The metallic tang of blood filled my mouth. My arms and shoulders sang from the half dozen bruises I'd have to hide. My jaw ached from his fist. And for once, the knuckles of my right hand were bruised and split.

The blow had surprised us both.

Worse.

He was getting worse.

And so was I.

"Your father didn't mean it," Mom said in her whisper of a voice. She always whispered. "He's got a lot on his mind."

We were sitting side by side on the worn linoleum of the kitchen floor in the middle of the mess like we were two pieces of trash waiting to be scooped up and disposed of.

"That's no fucking excuse, Mom. Mr. Walton next door—"

She flinched. That was what had started it this time when Dad came home stinking of booze.

It was always something. Dinner was cold. I'd parked my fourth-hand car wrong. A tone of voice wasn't respectful enough. Tonight, it had been the chess book Simon Walton had given me.

"You think you're better than me?" Dad had growled. "You think that fucking pussy next door is better than me? You think you can read a fucking book and forget where you came from?"

There were nights that I prayed to a deity I didn't fully believe in, begging the divine to have him arrested for drunk driving or something worse.

It was the only way we were going to survive.

Though part of me worried that it was already too late. I was filled with the kind of anger that festered deep down, that never found a release, that changed who you were as a person.

As hard as I tried, I couldn't seem to unfist my hands.

He had done this to me.

It wasn't so much the pain. At least not anymore. It was the humiliation. His demands that Mom and I both cater to his every whim. His belief that he was the center of our universe. That our needs were secondary to his own.

I was big enough, strong enough that I could fight him if I had to. He realized that now. He realized it and hated me even more for holding back from doing just that.

I didn't want to be him, and he knew it. So he was going to do his best to break me. And if I wasn't there, he continued to break my mother.

Broken men broke women.

That refrain echoed in my head as I got to my feet, helped my mother to hers, and then slipped out into the backyard.

The autumn chill cooled my skin. Dead leaves crunched softly under my feet.

I wanted to run. To leave this place far behind and never look back. But without me, it would only be a matter of time before he killed her. Before he pushed her too hard or lost control and couldn't stop swinging.

I was the only thing keeping her alive.

I didn't know why the three of us continued to pretend that college was an option. That I'd actually take the football scholarship I'd worked so fucking hard for. We all knew what would happen if I left. Yet we never spoke about it. We never talked about the dirty secret we shared.

I spit out the blood and bitterness into the dark and started to work out the pain in my right shoulder with arm circles. He always knew just where to hurt me. Just enough to remind me he could but not enough for anyone else to take notice.

Until tonight, I reminded myself, flexing my jaw. There would be no hiding the bruise on my face.

"Psst!"

I stopped circling my arm and peered around the side of my house, beyond the dingy beige siding, past the patches of weeds to the fence that divided good from bad in my life.

And there she was in the window beyond the cherry tree. The good.

"What are you doing up? It's late," I scolded in a whisper.

"Couldn't sleep," Sloane called back.

I wouldn't be able to now either. He wasn't

coming back. Not tonight. He'd go to a buddy's house and drink until he passed out. I, on the other hand, would lie there awake, staring at the ceiling, wishing he'd never come back. That he'd drive that truck off a bridge and put us all out of our misery.

I looked back at my house. The lights in Mom's bedroom were on. She'd be curling up in that tight ball like she always did after. She used to curl up around me. When times weren't quite as bad. When he wasn't quite as vicious. But somewhere along the way, she'd started curling in on herself, and I became the protector.

I should stay. I shouldn't taint Sloane's life with the ugliness of my own.

"I got a new CD. Wanna listen?" she hissed in the dark.

"Fuck it," I murmured to myself and entered her yard.

The gnarled bark of the cherry tree abraded my hands as I climbed to her.

"Hi," Sloane said, pretty and perky in a pair of pajama pants and a David Bowie tank top when I climbed through her window.

"Hi," I said, carefully stepping over the books littering her window seat.

She had a pillow crease on her cheek under her glasses. Her hair was piled on top of her head in a knot so messy it was clear she'd been sleeping at some point.

She was . . . cute. Adorable even. I was drawn to her, but in a way that wasn't what I was used to.

"What woke you up?" I asked uneasily.

Her gaze darted to the window and then back again. She raised her chin. "I don't know."

She was a good liar, but I could still tell. "Did you hear something?" I pressed.

"You're bleeding," she said, ignoring my question and jumping into action.

My fingers found the corner of my mouth and came away red. "Shit."

She grabbed a box of tissues and yanked several free. "Here. Sit."

"No, it's fine. I should go," I said, starting for the window. I should have known better than to bring this here. Just because I was feeling sorry for myself didn't give me the right to bleed all over her room.

"Hey. You can't go. You still haven't apologized for the rock last spring."

"Next time," I said briskly. It was our refrain. Our promise that I'd be back. A promise I needed to give serious thought to breaking.

I got one foot up on the window seat when she grabbed me by the back of my sweatpants. "Seriously, Sloane?"

"Let me look at your mouth. I mean the blood on your mouth," she insisted.

She clung to me like one of those fucking burrs you got stuck to your socks after a walk in the woods.

"Fine," I muttered. I sat on the cushion between a John Grisham and an Octavia Butler.

"Stay," Sloane ordered.

"You're bossy for a pixie," I complained.

She snorted as she collected the clump of tissues and a glass of water from her nightstand. Her bottle-green eyes were solemn as she approached me. And I knew then that she knew.

She knew and she felt sorry for me. My hands closed into fists again.

"So are you ready for your chem test tomorrow?" she asked.

She knew my secret, knew I didn't want to talk about it, so she was just going to clean me up and pretend everything was normal. I didn't deserve her.

"Sorry for never . . . you know . . ." I gestured helplessly.

"Acknowledging me at school?" Sloane guessed, filling in the blank for me. She had an uncanny knack for knowing what I wanted to say even when I didn't have the words to say it.

"Yeah."

She shrugged those dainty shoulders and flashed me a smirk. "Eh. It's fine. It would ruin my street cred if the captain of the football team started paying attention to me."

"Your street cred?" I scoffed.

She dunked the tissues into the water and began to gently dab at the corner of my mouth. It felt . . . nice to have someone care.

"People would start expecting me to try out for the cheerleading squad and go to the bonfires at

Third Base. It would cut into my reading time. Plus, I'd have to give up my secret crush on Philip."

"Stage Crew Phil is your secret crush?" I teased.

Stage Crew Phil's claims to fame were his perfect grades in calculus and the headset he got to wear backstage during school productions because he was in charge of the curtain. He gave zero shits about what anyone thought of him and went to school in the same jeans and black T-shirt outfit every single day. Except for Picture Day when he wore a bow tie over the T-shirt.

"I can't help it. I'm a sucker for a guy with power. Every time I think of him hissing 'curtain up,' I get weak in the knees."

I was smiling in spite of . . . everything. That was the effect she had on me. She was good. Everything about her seemed to sparkle. Good people got good things.

Then I remembered Jonah.

"Your dad said you were on a date tonight." It sounded accusatory, but I couldn't help it.

"Relax. I went out with Jonah so I could dump him in person."

I straightened. "You broke up?"

"Mm-hmm," she said, her gaze glued to my mouth. "He was kind of an ass. You were right."

"Say that part again," I insisted.

Her lips quirked as she worked. "No."

"Come on," I wheedled.

"No. And shut up. But seriously," she continued,

pressing the wet wad of tissues to the corner of my mouth, "I understand."

"You understand what?"

"You can't be seen being friendly to a four-eyed sophomore nerd. It would tear a hole in the space-time continuum of high school society."

She didn't know the real reason why I didn't want anyone to know about us. If my father had an inkling that something mattered to me, he destroyed it or ruined it in whatever way he could. The only thing he "allowed" me to have was football because it meant something to him to have a son who excelled on the field.

But if he ever had a hint that Sloane meant something to me, that I valued her, he would inflict damage. And if he did, if he managed to hurt her in some way, I didn't think I could live with that . . . or let him live.

"Nerd," I said lightly.

"Does it hurt?" she asked me, changing the subject again. Her voice was husky and serious now.

"It's fine," I lied.

"Lucian—"

"Don't," I said.

"You don't even know what I was going to say."

"Yes, I do. And it's none of your business."

"But—"

"Not everyone has the family you do. Okay?" She had no idea what I dealt with on a daily basis.

Not when she'd been raised by Simon and Karen Walton.

"But why can't we go to the cops?" she pressed.

The idea of picking up the phone and calling the cops on my father was laughable.

Police Chief Wylie Ogden was one of Dad's best friends. I was ten years old when Wylie had pulled my father over for speeding and swerving between the lines. He was drunk. He'd handed me his open beer can when he pulled over onto the shoulder.

The nerves in my belly had just started to unclench. The police would help. We watched videos about this in school. Don't drink and drive. But my dad did.

I'd thought the police would stop my dad from making this mistake, from scaring me, from hurting someone.

"Someone started early today," Wylie had cackled when he walked up to my father's window.

The chief had let him off without even a warning. They'd shot the shit about a fishing boat and made plans to meet up at the bar later that evening. And then Wylie had waved my father back onto the road as if bestowing some kind of special privilege on him.

"I just can't," I said tightly.

"Yes, we can," she insisted.

She kept saying "we." As if she was in this too when that was the *last* thing I wanted. If she got too close . . . If she got hurt . . . I wouldn't be able to hold back. I wouldn't be able to stick to defense. I would end him, and in doing so, I would become him.

"If he's hurting you, Lucian—" Sloane's voice broke, and so did a piece of my heart.

"Stop," I whispered, gathering her into my arms as I stood.

She wrapped her arms around my waist and held on tight. Her face pressed against my chest. I hated how good this physical affection from her felt.

It wasn't the way I felt about Brandy Kleinbauer when I'd lost my virginity to her at barely sixteen. Or the hormonal longing I'd felt for Cindy Crawford all through junior high. And it wasn't what I felt for Addie, my on-again, off-again weekend hookup.

This was . . . more complicated. I liked Sloane. I wanted to keep her safe. And every time we touched, no matter how innocently, part of me wished for more. But that wasn't an option. I was broken and she was beautiful.

I didn't know what we were to each other beyond the fact that she was important to me. More important than anyone.

"What CD did you get?" I asked.

She pulled back from our embrace, and I was both relieved and regretful. Her glasses were askew. Her hair was even more of a wreck. I felt something warm and tender slide through my chest. Like I was absorbing her goodness. But it wasn't mine to take.

"Shania Twain."

I smirked. "You're kidding right?"

"What's the matter? Aren't you man enough to listen to girl country?" She bounced over to her bed and picked up her headphones with a challenge in her eyes. "Shania Twain is a beautiful badass. Wanna listen?"

She looked so sweet and hopeful, her hair lopsided, eyes wide. I wanted nothing more than to lie next to her in that soft bed, in this nice room, in this big house, and be part of it all. And that was exactly why I couldn't.

I brought darkness with me. My bruises were contagious.

"I should get back and . . ." And what? What was left for me at home?

Sloane cocked her head. "Please?"

"It's not a good idea, Pix. What if your parents come in? I shouldn't be here." I shouldn't be anywhere near her.

"They're asleep on the other side of the house. And honestly, if you leave right now, I'm just going to spend the whole night worrying about you. I won't be able to sleep. And I'll be so tired tomorrow that I'll fail my trig test. Come on, big guy. Do you really want that on your conscience?"

"You're ridiculous."

"Three songs," Sloane bargained, hopping onto her bed and patting the mattress next to her.

I sighed. She sensed victory and grinned. "One song," I countered.

"Two," she insisted.

It was selfish and absolutely stupid, I thought, as I toed off my shoes. If Sloane's dad were to come in here and find me in his daughter's bed, he'd never forgive me. Even if I tried to explain. He knew how special she was, and he could sense how damaged I was. That was why they were so nice. Because they felt sorry for me.

"It's *Come on Over*, not advanced calculus," Sloane teased.

I climbed onto the bed next to her and resolutely stayed above the duvet cover. But I did let her pile her insane pillow collection around us. "What are you doing?" I asked as she tucked a pillow under my arm.

"I'm building a nest. This is how I sleep," she explained, fluffing the two behind me.

"You sleep with forty-two pillows every night?"

"It's six, smarty-pants. And don't judge me until you've tried it."

I had one pillow and a mattress on the floor after Dad had splintered my bed frame throwing me on it last summer. I relaxed against the mound of pillows and tried not to think about how good it felt being surrounded by softness.

Sloane cuddled up against my side. It was just the two of us supported by a soft U of pillows.

"Is he like this all the time?" she asked softly.

I looked down at my hands in my lap. They were balled into fists again. "Only when he drinks. He just drinks more often now. He still acts normal some of the time." And it was that act, that pretense that I hated more. I preferred the monster to the man pretending to care by showing up to football games or taking us out to dinner.

"I hate him." Her voice quivered. "I really hate him."

I slid my arm around her shoulders and cautiously drew her closer. It felt so good that I knew it was wrong. "I don't want you thinking about him."

"Why can't we tell the cops?" she asked.

I shook my head. "It's complicated, okay? Just trust me."

"Promise me you'll take care of yourself, Lucian? Like if he gets too out of control, you won't let him . . . you know."

Kill me. Kill my mother.

I would kill him first. Even if it sealed my fate as a monster. *Like father, like son,* I thought. "I promise if you promise me you won't call the cops. Ever. No matter what."

She took a deep breath and blew it out.

"Pixie," I prompted. "You have to trust me. Cops would just make it worse."

Her silence lasted too long, and I squeezed her shoulder.

"Ugh. Fine. But I'm not happy about it."

"Promise me," I insisted. She was the daughter of a lawyer. I knew better than to accept "Ugh. Fine," as an answer.

"I promise," she said miserably.

Some of the tension drained out of me with at her assurance.

Sloane looked up at me with those forest-green eyes. "You're not going to college, are you? You can't leave her alone with him."

I looked away. "No. I can't."

She sat up next to me, her small body tight with indignation at the injustice of it. "That sucks. You have to sacrifice your entire future because your dad is a monster and your mom won't leave? It's not fair."

"Life's not fair, Pix."

"What if I looked out for her?" she offered hopefully.

"No." The word came out so loud it seemed to echo around the room.

We both froze and listened for the telltale sounds of waking parents.

I grasped her by both shoulders and made her look me in the eye. "You're not to ever get involved. Do you hear me? You don't ever go over there. You don't speak to them. You don't ever draw any attention to yourself. And you don't ever stand between him and someone else when he's been drinking. Okay?"

She was wide-eyed and scared. But I needed her to be. I needed to ensure she never went near my father.

"Okay. Geez. Chill out. It was only a suggestion," she said, looking like I'd just asked her to set her favorite book on fire.

I heaved a sigh. "I'm sorry for scaring you."

"You didn't scare me. You *annoyed* me with your intensity."

"Three songs," I conceded.

She brightened and crawled over me to reach for the earbuds on her nightstand. This time when I fisted my hands in the bedspread, it had nothing to do with fear or anger. I was having . . . feelings. Normal teenage guy feelings. But I wasn't allowed to have those with Sloane. Mr. Walton trusted me. And I needed that trust. Sometimes the Waltons felt like the only anchor I had.

She crawled back across me and handed me an earbud before settling into my side again.

"Does Addie know that we do this?" she asked.

"What?"

"Addie. Your *girlfriend.*"

"She's not my girlfriend." Not exactly. She was a girl I'd spent time with in the past few weeks. Some of that time was spent partially naked. But that was because I was seventeen and she was trying to make her ex-boyfriend jealous. It wasn't like I talked on the phone with her or had dinner with her parents . . . or climbed a tree and crawled through her window at night to hang out.

"Does your not girlfriend know about any of this?" she pressed.

"No. And we're not seeing each other anymore." She'd gotten a little too demanding. Wanting to make plans, wanting to meet my parents. I couldn't give her any of that. And I didn't want to either after I'd overheard her telling one of her friends that the busty Sloane Walton was definitely a slut.

"Oh?" she said innocently.

"You don't look broken up about it," I observed.

She shrugged. "She just wasn't very nice. You could do better. But if you did do better and you were with someone nice, I guess we wouldn't get to hang out like this. And I kind of like our secret little friendship or . . . whatever."

Friendship didn't describe what I felt for her. I was friends with Knox and Nash Morgan. But I sure as hell wouldn't curl up with them in a pillow nest to listen to music. Hell, I wouldn't do that with Addie either. Maybe Cindy Crawford.

"I like us too," I told her.

I caught a glimpse of the bright smile she couldn't quite hide as she ducked her head and reached for the CD player.

I slid my arm around her shoulder and guided her head to rest on my chest. Between the pillows, Shania Twain's "From This Moment On," and the soft, warm heat of Sloane pressed up against me, I felt almost happy. I could nearly pretend that this was my life. Here in this house. With the good, sweet girl in my arms.

The song was over too quickly, changing to a country anthem. Something about black eyes and blue tears. She was never going back. It must have been the exhaustion that painted the story in my head. Walking away. Moving on. Growing up.

For a second, I wanted it so badly that I didn't

realize how tight I was clinging to Sloane until my fingers started to ache.

Wincing, I relaxed my grip on her. She tilted her head to look up at me. "It's okay. You can hang on to me. I won't break."

I pushed her face back down and resumed my hold on her, keeping it gentle this time.

The track changed again. The third song was the ballad "I Won't Leave You Lonely," and despite my best efforts, the words got in my head and tattooed themselves on my soul. I'd never be able to hear this song and not think about Sloane and how safe she made me feel. I wanted to hear it again, but I wasn't about to ask her to replay it. Maybe I'd buy the album myself . . . and hide it in my car.

When the final chords of the song played in my ear, Sloane slid a slim arm over my stomach and clung to me. I'd fulfilled my promise of three songs. But there was nothing for me at home. And there was everything for me here.

She didn't say anything when the next song began. Neither did I.

12

Livin' La Vida Library

Sloane

The library was my happy place, *not* my horny place.

Despite the action my vibrator had seen last night, I still unlocked the door feeling edgy and unsatisfied. And I blamed *him*.

I relocked the door and flicked on the first-floor lights. My shoulders instantly relaxed as the quiet and natural order soothed me.

I loved being the first person here in the mornings. Loved soaking up these precious moments of silence while gearing up for another day. Despite the stereotypes, the library was rarely quiet. There were two quiet rooms tucked away at the back of the first floor for studying or reading or the weekly meditation class. But there was life in these walls.

When I'd first become head librarian, we'd been crammed into a musty municipal building with peeling linoleum floors, flickering fluorescent lights, and creaky metal shelves. The entire catalog was about a decade out of date, and the staff and patrons had to share two eight-year-old laptops.

Now, the citizens of Knockemout entered

a bright, airy space with cozy seating nooks, lightning fast Wi-Fi, two entire floors of books and media, and all the technology a reader could want.

Books on every subject sat neatly on the white oak shelves lined up like a precision marching band. The long, low circulation desk was clutter-free and ready for business. We'd gone with a wheelchair-friendly low-pile carpet in a soft green that made me think of grassy pastures. Tuesday morning sunlight slanted in through the generous windows, bathing several varieties of houseplants in its beams.

Dumping my tote on the circulation desk, I cued up a fun playlist of instrumental versions of pop songs over the sound system and booted up the two desktop computers.

I checked the events calendar posted on the wall against the internal calendar to make sure the listings were up-to-date and made mental notes to send a confirmation email to the animal rescue for our Caturday event and order extra cookies for Drag Queen Story Hour since we'd run out early last month.

Two organizations had the upstairs conference rooms booked for meetings today, which meant I needed to make sure the tables were configured correctly and the whiteboards were free of teenage graffiti.

The fish girl was coming to rebalance the water in the children's section fish tank. I fired off a quick text to Jamal, the youth services librarian, to ask him if he'd run the UV wand over the floor cushions since the elementary school had reported an outbreak of pink eye yesterday.

Coffee came next.

I stowed my bag under the desk and headed for the coffee counter. We'd sprung for one of those fancy instant espresso machines and a dishwasher to deal with the mugs. Not only did patrons enjoy the step up from regular drip coffee, it was just another experience that encouraged them to stay a little longer. To take a breath and enjoy themselves with a book or socialize with staff and patrons.

Machine levels checked and coffee condiments restocked, I unloaded the previous day's mugs from the dishwasher and organized them on their hooks.

I wondered if Lucian felt like this when he strode into his offices every morning. Was it pride like I felt?

Not that I was thinking about him again, because I *definitely* wasn't.

Except now I definitely was. Had he even thought about me after I'd left his office yesterday?

"Oh my God. Stop!" I said to myself out loud.

"Stop what?"

"Mother of dragons! Where did you come from?" I demanded, immediately dropping the hands I'd raised in a protective stance.

Naomi, pretty in a long-sleeve ribbed dress and tights, stood clutching a gallon-sized to-go coffee.

"That depends on how far back you want to go. I woke up to my naked husband—"

I held up a hand. "New rule in our friendship. No bragging about your stellar sex life when your friend is in the middle of a dry spell."

"That's fair," Naomi agreed. Despite the fact that she already had a cup of coffee in hand, she headed straight for the espresso maker. A swing of chestnut hair fell over her face in a perfect wave.

"Your hair looks good," I noted.

"Thanks. Waylay did it. Jeremiah got her an astronomically expensive curling iron for Christmas, and she's already mastered it. So what are we stopping?"

"Hmm?" I feigned innocence.

"You were standing there lost in some sort of reverie and then ordered yourself to stop."

I hadn't mentioned yesterday's "unfortunate incident" with Lucian to Naomi and Lina. Mainly because I didn't want to deal with their demands for a play-by-play or their misguided hopes that this was the beginning of the end of our feud. I also didn't want to admit to anyone that Lucian Rollins had made my lady parts feel things they had no business feeling where he was concerned.

"Oh, I'm just all up in my head about . . . stuff when I really need to be concentrating on . . . other stuff." Smooth. Real smooth.

"Yeah. You know I know you're lying, right? I have a twelve-year-old at home."

"Pfft. I'm not lying," I lied.

She pinned me with an earnest look. "You also know I'm here for you whenever you're ready to talk about whatever it is you're lying about, right?"

"Yeah. I know." I said it mostly to my sneakers. I wasn't required to tell my friends every single thing. I didn't expect that of them. I did expect them to tell me the big, important things though. Whatever the hell Lucian and I had done yesterday didn't qualify as big or important.

We'd *barely* touched. And whatever grazes or brushes or intense looks of fiery longing had passed between us before Petula came barreling in all meant nothing. Absolutely nothing at all.

Great. Now I was thinking about it again, and Naomi was looking at me expectantly as if she was waiting for an answer.

"Hey, do you know if Jamal disinfected the kids' section last night?" I asked.

"A subject change. Not at all suspicious," she teased. "You're still coming to dinner tonight, right? Nash and Lina will be there."

My social life consisted of me being the fifth wheel tagging along with two couples with smoldering hot sex lives.

Ugh. I really needed to make some changes in my life. I wanted to be the one making my friends uncomfortable with over-the-top PDA. I wanted to be making plans for the future with my hot life partner with a large penis.

A salacious memory of Lucian's trouser-covered erection immediately appeared in my mind. *No!*

215

Bad, brain! Bad. Lucian was not life partner material.

"I'll be there," I said grimly.

The day was busy enough that I managed to table all thoughts of Lucian, except for the particularly steamy ones that popped into my head every ten to twelve minutes. By the time I called the afternoon staff meeting to order, I'd already tackled all my to-do list, plus dealt with the elevator maintenance people for the annual inspection, the fish girl, and a hysterical toddler who refused to come out of the pillow fort. Her dad was recovering from knee surgery, which meant I was the one who had to crawl in after her. It had taken one bag of goldfish crackers and the promise that she could scan all the books at checkout to negotiate her surrender.

"Those are some great ideas on fundraisers for our free breakfast summer program," I said, scribbling down the last suggestion on my iPad, then scrolling back to the agenda. "Let's see. Ah. Book club. I heard back from Matt Haig's agent. She said he's happy to answer our five-question Q and A for book club."

The news was met with enthusiastic mumbles around the table. Everyone had their mouths full of baked goods, a staff meeting requirement.

"What's next?" I asked.

Kristin, the adult services librarian, waved her cheese Danish in my direction. She was a curvy woman in her midfifties who had taken up dating bikers and pole dancing after her divorce. "I ordered the new Cecelia Blatch romance novel for the catalog, and my clever social media stalking of her reveals that she lives about an hour from here. What if we hosted a signing for her? Maybe something on Valentine's Day."

"I like it. She could give a reading and then sign copies of her books," I mused.

I had read three of the author's titles. The growly, alpha heroes were just overprotective enough without being assholey. The heroines were the perfect balance of feisty and endangered. And the sex on the page was straight up fire.

I wondered what Lucian was like in bed. Would he be as restrained as he was in everyday life, or did he let go of all pretenses between the sheets?

Oh, for fuck's sake!

I brought a hand to my cheek. My skin felt like the surface of the sun. I needed to deal with this. I needed sex with someone who was not He Who Shall Not Be Named.

I forcefully evicted all thoughts of the man from my brain and focused on the last few agenda items.

"Good meeting," I said, closing the cover of my tablet. "If anyone comes up with anything else—"

"Your door is always open," they said in unison.

"One more thing," Jamal said. At twenty-six, the youth services librarian was our youngest employee. The kids adored him. Not just because he wore cool baseball hats to work and played ultimate Frisbee. He was also a talented amateur artist whose sketches and caricatures entertained patrons of all ages. "We received Marjorie Ronsanto's weekly email complaint—"

Our collective groan interrupted him.

"About the LGBTQ+ books in the children's section being 'dangerously inclusive,'" he continued, glancing down at the printout. "Actually we received the complaint meant for us *and* one she wrote to Target for using an interracial couple in their TV commercial. She also reminded us of her 'generous donation' of the break room trash can."

"I hate that thing," Kristin said.

It was one of those smart trash cans that wasn't quite smart enough to open when it was supposed to. Six months ago, I had lost my temper and finally pried the lid off it.

"Can't she take a week off from hating everything?" Naomi asked.

"Marjorie's on a one-woman crusade to be a gigantic pain in the ass," Blaze said, crossing her tattooed arms over her chest. Blaze was one of our board members and volunteers. She also put the L in LGBTQ+.

"Her mother clearly didn't love her enough when she was a child," I said dryly. "All in favor of doing what we always do with Marjorie's complaints?"

Everyone around the table raised their hands.

"I'll send her the canned response," Agatha, Blaze's wife and fellow board member, volunteered.

"When you do, tell her that her copy of *The*

Witch's Mountain Lovers: A Dubious Consent Paranormal Reverse Harem was due back two days ago," Kristin said smugly.

Agatha grinned and mimed dropping a microphone.

Back in the safety of my office, I cracked open my afternoon root beer and flopped down behind my desk.

It wasn't shiny, sterile glass like Lucian's. My office was furnished with what I liked to think of as generic administrator furniture: sturdy budget pieces that lacked personality. I made up for it by painting the walls a hunter green and cramming the shelves full of personal memorabilia. It was cluttered, colorful, and chaotic. Just like me.

A delightful hot mess such as myself did not belong with an emotionally stunted neat freak. Not even between the sheets.

No, if I was serious about finding my life partner, I needed to focus on that. Not the potential of really hot sex with a guy I didn't actually like.

I remembered the dating app and perked up immediately. Perhaps my future husband was already in my inbox.

I pounced on my phone like my cat on her chicken-and-waffle-flavored treats . . . and immediately deflated.

No notifications. How was that possible?

I checked my inbox and found it empty.

"This can't be right," I mumbled to myself. I

scrolled through the history of male profiles I'd hearted. Seriously? How was a girl supposed to get laid, let alone fall in love, when none of the men I'd hearted had hearted me back?

Maybe the app was broken. I'd probably missed a button to publish my profile. I'd have to ask Stef or Lina and soon, seeing as how my "quivering sex" was so ready for action it was starting to consider Lucian Rollins as a potential candidate.

"When you're finished scowling at your screen, I have something for you."

I backhanded my tumbler off the desk and hurled my phone in a wide arc. I was halfway out of my chair before I came to my senses.

And my senses told me that Lucian Freaking Rollins was standing in the doorway of my office.

"What . . . why . . . er, how?" I croaked as I came to my feet.

He crouched down smoothly and picked up the water bottle I'd accidentally assaulted. "Funny, I remember you being more eloquent than this."

"Don't start with me, Lucifer," I warned, snatching the tumbler out of his manly hand. "Why are you haunting my office instead of purchasing blood diamonds and selling stolen internal organs on the black market?"

He tossed a manga novel onto my desk. My manga novel. Well, technically the library's.

"You left this in my office. I heard the librarian here is a stickler for late fees."

"You know there's this thing called the postal

service," I said, liberating my phone from the floor.

"Unfortunately for you, I was already going to be in town." He tucked his hands into his pockets and prowled my office in a slow circuit, pausing to look more closely at my personal effects.

He was too big to be in here. He seemed to suck all the oxygen and color out of the room until the only thing I was aware of was his presence.

"What has you spoiling for a fight, Pixie? Did another squirrel get stuck in the book return?"

"You're hilarious. So funny. I'm so glad we had this time together. Why don't I open this second-story window and assist you out of it?" I offered, rubbing the wrist that had connected with my water bottle.

"Interesting reading material," he said, tilting his head at the book on my desk.

"It's for a teenage boy with dyslexia. I figured he'd like all the fight scenes, but I wanted to read it first before I recommended it to him." I didn't know why I was explaining myself to him. It wasn't like he actually cared what I read, and I certainly didn't put any stock in his opinion of me or my reading habits.

"Nearly every memory I have of you involves books."

It came out of him sounding like a confession. We stared at each other for a long, silent thirty seconds.

I shook my head. "You know, sometimes I think I imagined it all."

He put down the framed photo of me and my parents at the ribbon cutting for the library and fixed those assessing gray eyes on me.

"Imagined what?"

"You. Me. The cherry tree. I thought we were friends."

"We were. Once."

He layered blame on top of that one syllable until it was all I heard.

"I don't get you. I didn't get you as a high school senior, and I don't get you as a business mogul. And I sure as hell don't get what happened yesterday."

His eyes changed. It was an almost imperceptible shift, but I'd spent a lifetime studying him and didn't miss the glint of silver.

"Let's add yesterday to the long list of mistakes better left in the past," he suggested.

"I've already forgotten it," I boasted.

"Which is why you were the one to bring it up five seconds ago," he pointed out.

I'd forgotten how deftly he played his enemies. He and my father had spent countless hours with a chessboard between them.

"I may have brought it up, but we both know it's no coincidence that yesterday happened and now here you are, paying me a visit in a place you've never once set foot in."

The air in the room was electric. I could practically see the sparks flying between us. But they weren't the romantic, will-they-won't-they sparks.

These were the kind that burned things to the ground. The kind that destroyed everything in their wake.

Through my window, the late afternoon sun bathed his face in golden glow and shadows.

"How's your mother?" he asked before turning back to the next piece of me that caught his eye.

"She's fine."

His expression shifted to irritated patience.

"She's okay," I amended. "I helped her go through some of Dad's things yesterday after dress shopping and it was . . ." What? Excruciating? Heartbreaking? Even though we each set aside favorite pieces, boxing up his clothes added another layer of pain to our goodbye. "Difficult," I decided.

"I was thinking the other day about Simon's gardening T-shirt," Lucian said. "From the one and only 5K he ever completed."

I was relieved he was looking away from me because I had to bring my fingers to my mouth to keep the unexpected sob inside.

"Knockemout Runs for Breast Cancer," I said when I'd regained my composure.

It was a hot-pink, double extra-large freebie T-shirt with cartoon breasts emblazoned across the chest. My father's medium frame swam in it. But he'd been so proud of his accomplishment and the money he'd raised that he turned it into his gardening shirt, knotting it on his hip like he was a teenage girl. I'd spent years in agonized humiliation because of that shirt. It was the only item of his clothing I'd kept.

"The first time I saw him in it, he was attacking that bush in your backyard—the one with the red berries—with electric hedge trimmers and telling your mother that he was Simon Scissorhands."

My laugh, watery though it was, surprised us both.

His lips curved, and for a moment, it felt like there was no desk between us, no ugly history. He used to make me laugh, and I used to make him smile.

"I don't know how to react when you're nice to me," I announced.

"If you didn't make it so difficult, I'd be civil more often," he said dryly.

"It's probably better this way. You might sprain something pretending to be human."

The ghost of a smile remained on his mouth.

"About yesterday," I prompted.

What about yesterday? What the hell was I thinking bringing it up? *Again.*

"What about it?" There was a dare in his question.

"I met Holly," I blurted out, going for the first topic that didn't involve us touching each other. "She seemed very grateful for the job. Lina told us how you hired her. Maybe you're not a complete asshole."

"No one gives a compliment like you, Pixie."

I rolled my eyes. "Oh, shut up. I'm trying to be nice."

"The only nice thing you can say about me is that I hired someone to do a job?"

"Maybe I'd have more to say if you'd tell me why my mother is so grateful to you," I reminded him.

"Leave it alone, Sloane," he said wearily.

The awkward truce between us was cracking, crumbling. I didn't know if I was relieved or disappointed.

Lucian turned his attention to the contents of the bookcase.

His gaze landed on the display case containing a bronzed softball. Those lips went flat again.

"What's this?" he asked, eyeing the acrylic case.

"It's the ball from my last game. Maeve had it bronzed as a joke." It had been my first real, fall-on-the-floor, couldn't-catch-my-breath laugh after my injury. After finding out that my plans for a softball scholarship were officially over.

I didn't know if the twinge in my wrist was real or just the echo of a memory. And I didn't realize I was massaging it until Lucian looked down.

His eyes went storm cloud gray. He opened his mouth, then closed it with a snap.

"What?" I asked, not bothering to keep the annoyance out of my tone.

"I don't have time for this. For you."

"Like I said, no one asked you to play delivery boy."

225

"And *I* didn't ask you to get involved and end your softball career," he said.

"Clearly, we're even then," I joked.

"As always, you're infuriating, irresponsible, and immature." His tone was flippant, as if I were barely worth the effort to insult.

"And you're a mercurial pain in my ass," I pointed out, feeling the sting.

"Always so charming. It's such a mystery why you're still single."

The man wielded sarcasm with the dexterity of a master manipulator. I had the urge to pat myself down and search for physical wounds.

"You're late for your next ritual sacrifice, Lucifer. You'd better be going."

He smirked. "Thank you for reminding me why our relationship is what it is. Every once in a while, I manage to forget what you really are."

"Is that so? And just what do you think I am?" I asked.

"Dangerous."

I flashed him a saccharine-sweet smile. "Do you think you can find your way out, or do you want me to help you down the stairs face-first?"

"I think I can manage. Keep your things out of my life."

"Yeah? Well, keep your life out of my work," I shot back, crossing the room and gesturing toward the open door.

"Hey, Uncle Lucian," Waylay called from behind the community desk where she was working on

226

a laptop. The two teenage boys leaning against the desk looked at Lucian with wide eyes.

"Hey, Way," Lucian said, stalking toward the stairs.

"Do you need us to escort him out, Ms. Walton?" Lonnie Potter offered, hooking his thumb in the direction of Lucian's retreating back.

His friend's eyeballs doubled in size behind his glasses.

I would have laughed if I hadn't been too busy breathing flames.

"No. But thank you, Lonnie. That's very gentlemanly of you."

I stomped back to my desk and pressed the heels of my hands to my eyes.

"What the hell does mercurial mean?" I heard Lonnie whisper to his friend.

"For fuck's sake," I muttered.

I needed a meditation class. Or hypnotherapy. Or some kind of drug that rendered me immune to Lucian Rollins. So what if he hated me? So what if he went out of his way to piss me off? Every time I reacted, I was giving him what he wanted. That alone should be enough to stop me.

"Knock knock?" The tentative greeting came from Naomi, who entered my office with my sister. "I was bringing Maeve up to you, and we ran into Lucian on the stairs," Naomi said. "I think he actually snarled when I said hello."

"Please don't speak that name in my presence ever again," I begged.

"Wow. You two really can't stand each other, can you?" Maeve observed. "You guys used to be so tight."

"They did? When?" Naomi pounced on the information like a cat with a catnip taco.

"I'm going to ask you both a huge favor that involves changing the subject immediately," I interrupted.

"She doesn't like to talk about whatever it is that happened with Lu—that guy," Naomi whispered to my sister.

"I just so happen to have the perfect subject change," Maeve said, eyeing the visitors' chairs that were buried under books and the remains of a children's diorama of the first public library in Knockemout.

"Let's take this to the conference room," I suggested, wanting to get away from the Lucian-y vibe of my office.

"I need to get back downstairs," Naomi said. "Neecey's coming in when she finishes her shift at Dino's, and I'm helping her find some Medicare information for her dad."

"Thanks for bringing me up," Maeve called after her.

"Yeah, thanks," I said belatedly. "Come on." I led the way to the conference room and settled in at the table with my sister. "Okay. Lay it on me."

"Mary Louise Upshaw," Maeve said, removing a file from her slim, snazzy briefcase. "She was arrested for possession and transporting a controlled substance. She was sentenced to twenty years in prison. She's eleven years into her sentence in Fraus Correctional Center about an hour south of here."

"That seems unusually harsh," I noted.

"It is," my sister agreed. "The average sentence for similar charges is usually closer to three to five years."

"Why would her case warrant such an excessive sentence? It was her first offense."

"The judge hearing the case made a career out of being tough on drugs. He could have been making some kind of statement."

I picked up the folder and looked at Mary Louise's mug shot. She looked like a scared suburban mom who had no idea how she'd gotten herself into a predicament that involved a mug shot. "She doesn't look like someone who would traffic a few pounds of weed and a couple tabs of ecstasy."

"From what I could gather, Mary Louise claimed the drugs weren't hers and initially pleaded not guilty. But a few weeks later, she changed her plea to no contest."

I thought about what Allen had told me the day of Dad's funeral. *My dumb stuff had consequences. Consequences my mom paid for.*

"Oh, Allen," I sighed. "Why didn't she appeal?"

"She has. Or at least she's tried. She's been through four public defenders since her arrest.

I have the contact info for her current representation," Maeve said.

I knew from my sister and my father that public defenders were notoriously overworked and the turnover was brisk.

"I'm sorry it's not a deeper dive. I've been in court, and there were some other things demanding my attention, so I didn't have as much time to dig into the case as I would have liked."

I flipped through the paperwork. "I appreciate you doing this. I know you've got a lot going on."

"Never too much for family," she said.

There was that flare of guilt again. I had been too busy for family. Too busy to start one.

"Hey. How are you doing with everything?" I asked, reaching across the table and squeezing her hand.

She squeezed back. "I'm doing okay. Chloe is a good distraction. That girl can suck all the attention out of a room and leave its occupants too exhausted to think after she leaves. But I really miss him."

"Me too," I said.

I felt like there was more to the sad shrug, the forced smile. Something she wasn't telling me.

"What else is going on?" I pressed.

An uninitiated observer would have missed the flicker in her eyes, but I was a nosy little sister. I saw it all.

"Nothing," she said innocently.

"Liar. You've been off since before Dad died.

What's going on? You might as well spill it because you know I won't leave you alone."

She rolled her eyes. "Ugh. Fine. I was seeing this guy, and it didn't work out. It was nothing. No dramatic breakup. No tearful confrontation."

My eyebrows winged up. "You were seeing someone and managed to keep it a secret in this town?"

"It wasn't exactly a relationship I wanted broadcast to the world."

"You had a secret, taboo affair and managed to keep it quiet? I'm impressed. Why did you dump him?"

"How did you—never mind. I'm too busy for a relationship. He wanted serious, and I didn't—don't—have the time for serious."

My sister was the calm, collected person you'd want on your side in the middle of an emergency. She never let emotions get the best of her. The fact that she was pretending not to be upset about the breakup told me it was more than "nothing."

"I'm sorry it didn't work out," I said, treading lightly.

"It's fine. Thanks again for play rehearsal pickup. That's been helpful," Maeve said, reeling in her emotions.

I studied her for a moment, then decided to let it go . . . for now.

"Hey, do you and Chloe want to come over Sunday? We'll make Dad's chili and Mom's cornbread and watch *Erin Brockovich*." And I could sneakily work more information out of her about this mystery man.

"The Simon Walton Memorial Trifecta," Maeve said with a smile. "Count us in."

"Great."

My sister packed up her tidy briefcase and got to her feet. "Listen. If you decide to dig into this Mary Louise case, let me know. I'm interested."

"Thanks, Maevey Gravy," I said wrapping her in a hug.

"Anytime, Sloaney Baloney."

13

An Electrifying Dinner

Lucian

I pulled my Range Rover into Knox's driveway behind his truck. The lights were on in the big house, casting a glow that cut through the winter gloom. I'd loved coming here as a boy. The freedom Liza J and her husband, Pop, had allowed. Entire summers were spent here swimming in the creek, sleeping under the stars, climbing trees, daring each other to do the stupid shit of boyhood.

Of course, once we discovered girls, our priorities had changed.

The old timber house had changed as well. Since Knox and Naomi had moved in, there was a tidy order that had never existed before. There were candles in the windows and boughs of pine looped through the porch railing.

They'd gone all out for Christmas, their first as a family. It had been admittedly spectacular. I couldn't blame Knox for the sleigh and reindeer on the roof. If I'd had a chance at a family like that, I'd probably go crazy overcompensating for all the holidays I hadn't had as a kid too.

I got out of the car and debated smoking my cigarette now. Grabbing a last few quiet moments before going inside. It had been a feat of sheer willpower not to smoke it after leaving the library. The odds were I'd need it after dinner.

Sometimes I enjoyed these loud, casual gatherings, and other times I felt like a ghost haunting a happy family. As boys, Knox and Nash had accepted me for who I was. As men, we could pick up and put down our friendship at any time without consequences or hurt feelings.

But with Naomi and Lina now added to the mix, the relationship seemed to take on more responsibilities. If I disappeared to Washington or New York or Atlanta for weeks without contact, I had no doubt Naomi would track me down, demanding to know if everything was okay and when she could expect me back. Lina would, at the very least, expect a heads-up on my departure and a general timeline for my return. Both would take it personally if I went weeks or months without reaching out.

Women complicated things. And not just for the partners they chose. For everyone connected to their partners.

The front door banged open, and Knox ambled out just as headlights cut across the driveway. Muted music filled the night air over the rumble of engine.

Sloane's Jeep pulled in behind my vehicle. The lights and engine cut out, but the music continued. It was "Man! I Feel Like a Woman." I sighed. Some things never changed.

Knox reached me. He was wearing jeans and a thermal shirt in charcoal gray with one chewed-up sleeve.

"You didn't tell me she was coming," I said, hooking a thumb in the direction of the Jeep.

The song ended and the driver's side door opened. Sloane slid to the ground, her cowboy boots landing with a clomp.

"Whose Rover?" she called out to Knox.

I stepped around the hood and watched her recoil.

"You didn't tell me he was coming," she snapped.

"This is exactly why I'm standing out here instead of opening my goddamn front door to you two," Knox announced.

"What are you grumbling about now?" Sloane demanded, storming toward us. She was wearing leggings and an oversize ruby-red sweater that matched her lipstick. Her hair was half up and half down, with the length of it hanging in thick, careless waves. Casual. Touchable.

"Waylay and I had to listen to Naomi talk to herself for an hour about which one of you to uninvite tonight," Knox explained.

"I believe the term is disinvite," I said.

"Fuck you," Knox replied.

"I don't understand the conflict. I'm Naomi's friend and her boss. Ergo, I win," Sloane said testily.

"Yeah, well, Luce here is *my* friend. And apparently Naomi is worried about him," Knox added.

I ignored the smug look on Sloane's face.

"There's nothing to worry about," I insisted, both annoyed and oddly comforted that someone out there was worried for me.

"Besides being a soulless cadaver hell-bent on bringing misery to all," Sloane added.

"Just you, Pixie. I only live to destroy your happiness," I said.

"That right there is the reason I'm freezin' my ass off in my driveway instead of making out with my wife. So this is what's going to happen. The three of us are going to go inside, and you two are going to behave like adult humans with impulse control. Or else . . ."

Sloane's eyes narrowed. "Or else what?"

She always had the wrong reaction to challenges like that.

Knox's grin was wicked. "I'm glad you asked. Since I don't want Naomi to know about this and since I can only punch one of you in the face and since I'm a little bit afraid of you"—he pointed at Sloane—"I had to get creative."

He held up two small boxes with wires running out of them.

Sloane was already shaking her head. "No. Nope. No freaking way."

"Oh, yes freaking way," he insisted.

"What are those?" I asked.

"Well, Lucy," Knox continued conversationally. "These here are transcutaneous electrical nerve stimulation machines, a.k.a. TENS, a.k.a. period cramp torture devices the girls at Honky Tonk deploy during their Code Reds every month. They tape these sticky pad things onto a guy's stomach and proceed to shock the shit out of him to show him what they go through on a monthly basis."

Sloane scoffed and crossed her arms. "You're not seriously saying you plan to electrocute your dinner guests."

"I'll be honest. I don't care about dinner or our friendship that much," I said, pulling my car keys out of my pocket.

Sloane put her hands on her hips in triumph. "Good riddance."

Knox snatched the keys from me. "I don't think you're hearing me. Naomi has decided you both can't be invited to the same social shit. Which means she'll schedule twice as much social shit to make sure both of you pains in the ass get the same amount of quality fucking time with us. And I don't want more social shit. I don't want more quality fucking time. I want you two to put aside your petty 'we have a secret feud that we won't talk about' bullshit and make my wife forget that you can't stand each other."

"This is ridiculous," I insisted.

"No. You're fucking ridiculous for making me do this. So either you both go in there strapped up to these toys, pretend to be adults for the evening, and make my wife happy, or you both go the hell home and think about how stupid you must be for making me the fucking voice of reason in this scenario."

I glanced down at Sloane, who seemed to be weighing the ridiculous options.

"What's for dinner?" she asked, eyes narrowed in calculation.

"Tacos."

"Dammit," she muttered and grabbed one of the TENS units.

"You're joking."

"I'm hungry, and I'm proving to the bearded barber here that I'm a better friend than you are," Sloane announced. She pulled up the hem of her turtleneck, baring her smooth stomach.

"I'm not doing this," I told Knox.

"I'm not forcing you. You know the choices and the consequences. But I meant what I said. It's both of you or neither. And if I go back in there and have to tell my wife that you two couldn't even agree to not be assholes for however long it takes to shove a bunch of tacos into your face, she's gonna be upset, and that'll make me fucking furious. I'll have no choice but to make it my mission in life to destroy you both," Knox threatened.

"What's the matter, Lucifer? Afraid of a little pain or afraid you won't be able to control yourself?" Sloane taunted with a challenge in her eyes.

Swearing, I yanked my belt free and untucked my shirt. "For the record, these better be the best tacos I've ever had, because I'm not convinced this friendship is worth it."

Sloane's green eyes skimmed over the skin I was baring as I slapped the two adhesive pads to my abdomen.

"Get it out of your system now, 'cause Waylay is sitting between you two. If my girl catches you being dicks to each other, she gets to shock the shit out of you."

As we marched toward the house, I comforted myself with the fact that it would be Waylay, not Knox, behind the controls. Besides, how bad could period pain be?

Lightning bolts of agony raced across my abdomen and down my legs. I slapped a palm to the table, rattling glasses and silverware.

Piper yipped and Waylon grumbled about their exile on the other side of the dog gate.

Waylay snickered, and all conversations ceased as everyone turned to look at me.

Knox looked smug. Sloane's shoulders were shaking with silent laughter on the other side of Waylay's blond head. Everyone else looked concerned.

"You okay there, Lucy?" Nash asked from across the table.

"Fine," I rasped as the pain dissipated.

Sloane dabbed at the corners of her eyes with her napkin. "I believe you were saying my voice reminded you of a rabid chihuahua. Did you want to continue that thought or—"

Her napkin and salsa spoon fell to the floor as

Sloane's entire body tensed. She let out a high-pitched squeak.

"What's going on?" Naomi asked from Knox's right.

"Nothing," Waylay, Knox, Sloane, and I announced at the same time.

We all managed innocent smiles that didn't seem to be fooling anyone.

"Naomi, what did you say our reception colors are?" Lina asked, drawing her attention to the other side of the table.

"I didn't insult him, you little punk," Sloane hissed to Waylay.

"You were baiting him. That's just as bad. Trust me. I'm basically the queen of trash talking on the soccer field," Waylay informed her.

"You have to have my unit dialed up higher," I accused. It had felt as if my insides were in danger of exiting my body.

"Actually you're only at an eight. Knox and me figured Sloane had an advantage seein' as how she's a girl and has had her period for a few decades."

"Exactly how old do you think I am?" Sloane asked, then shook her head. "Never mind. Just tell me what mine is set at."

"You're a nine."

Sloane punched the air in victory. "Yes!"

Naomi was watching us again. I held up a taco and gave her a friendly nod. "Take me to a ten," I told Waylay when Naomi looked away.

"I don't know. Knox said the girls aren't allowed to use level ten at the bar anymore since Garth Lipton almost pooped his pants."

"Take me to ten," I insisted tersely.

"There's nothing heroic about shitting your pants, Rollins," Sloane said under her breath. Her body went rigid again, and the taco she was holding exploded when it hit her plate. "Gah! Waylay, I wasn't insulting him. I was giving him advice."

"It sounded like an insult to me. Besides, you swore, and that's a dollar for the swear jar, which means Aunt Naomi gets to spend extra time in the stupid produce aisle."

"Waylay, how are your tacos?" Naomi called.

"They're good. They'd be better without all the slimy weird vegetables in them, but I guess I can suffer through that part," the kid said.

"Garth Lipton is forty years older than me," I said to Sloane over the top of Waylay's head.

"I'm just looking out for you. You could barely handle an eight. I'd hate to see what a ten would do to you. I mean, I'd love it. But I'm being the bigger, more mature adult here," she whispered back.

"Just because you can't handle a ten has no bearing on my endurance. I'll be fine."

"I am a woman. Two weeks ago, I had cramps so bad I had to lie down on the floor of the public restroom *at the mechanic's garage*. And *then* I had to get back up and go do my job for eight hours. I was born to handle a ten."

"You two aren't saying mean things, but your tones are getting kinda snippy," Waylay warned.

"Take me to a ten," I ordered.

"Fine. Tens all around. I'll show you how to handle it," Sloane snapped.

"I hate to point this out because I'm definitely having fun here, but I think you guys are losing sight of the reason Knox is letting me electrocute you."

First Knox, now Waylay. The voices of reason were getting less likely as the evening wore on.

Sloane glared at me over Waylay's head. I glared back.

"Bite me," she mouthed at me.

"You're not my type," I mouthed back.

"Is everything okay down there?" Naomi asked, sounding nervous.

"Fine except for Lucian scowling at me like a—" Sloane grunted, her face contorting in pain. "Worth it," she wheezed.

"You're such an idiot," I told her. And then I was doubling over, my face hovering over my plate of tacos as an excruciating current of pain tore through me. "It's in my kidneys."

Waylon and Piper were barking frantically now.

"Knox Morgan! Why is our daughter electrocuting our guests?" Naomi shrieked.

My friend held up his hands. "Daze, there's a perfectly logical explanation for this."

"Jesus," Nash muttered. "I don't know which one to arrest first."

"You know what? I think I'll go get the cobbler . . . and more alcohol," Lina said, getting up from the table.

"I'll help," Waylay said, escaping the room before a punishment could be dealt out.

"I'll supervise," Nash volunteered.

We got to our feet and began ripping off electrodes. My legs felt like they were made of brittle wood. One wrong step and I'd collapse. There was an echo of pain in my lower back.

I took Sloane by the upper arm and steered her toward the back door. "Outside," I said tersely.

"But I want to watch Naomi tear Knox a new one," she complained.

"You have a lifetime of opportunities for that." I dragged her outside onto the deck and shut the door. It was cold and dark. The naked trees cast skeletal shadows over the snow from the stingy light of the crescent moon.

"Did level ten fry your brain?" Sloane asked, slipping out of my grip.

"We're calling a truce," I announced.

"That's not how that works."

"I'm forty years old. I run a multimillion-dollar business. I own property. I pay taxes. I vote. I cook. I get the goddamn flu shot every year."

"Congratulations. Where can I send your gold star?"

"We're adults," I said, pointing to the window where it appeared chaos was still reigning. "And that in there was the latest performance in a long

243

line of immature shit shows that we've starred in together."

Sloane crossed her arms and looked down at her feet. Her boots were brown with purple stitching. "I'm not saying you're right. But you're not exactly wrong."

"This has to stop."

She puffed out her cheeks. The light from inside made the stud in her nose twinkle. She looked like a mischievous forest fairy. "I know." She turned away from me and moved to the railing. "I hate that every conversation with you has me regressing to a teenager with no impulse control. It's embarrassing."

"I hate that I let you get under my skin. It's infuriating," I admitted.

She gave the night sky a small smile. "So you admit to being partially human."

"I'll deny it if you repeat it."

She hugged her arms tighter around her and hunched her shoulders against the cold. Slowly, I moved closer until my arm brushed her shoulder, lending her some of my heat.

"What are we supposed to do? Just forgive and forget?" she asked.

"That's not possible," I said dryly.

She let out a short, bitter laugh. "Tell me about it."

"We have to come up with some sort of solution. For them."

We both glanced over our shoulders to the

kitchen where everyone was gathered around the island with coffee and cobbler.

"They look really happy without us," Sloane observed.

"Then we'll find a way to keep them happy with us."

"Let's start with no interaction between us when we're in the group," she suggested. "I don't think we're ready for polite small talk."

I hated to admit it, but she was right. It was safer to just avoid each other until we developed a tolerance.

"Fine. And if for whatever reason one of us doesn't feel they can stand the sight of the other for a particular event, we make prior arrangements to stagger our attendance."

"That is such a rich-person-fancy-dinner-gala thing to say. No offense," she added quickly, then winced. "This is going to be harder than I thought."

"It's a habit. Nothing more," I insisted.

I wasn't about to allow a habit to control me. Unironically, I pulled my daily cigarette from the breast pocket of my shirt and produced my lighter.

Sloane looked pointedly at the cigarette as I lit it. "Some habits are harder to break than others."

She had no idea the struggle I'd endured that afternoon after our exchange in her office. I'd wanted nothing more than to soothe away the flood of anger with my daily dose of nicotine. My fingers had itched to hold the filter between them; my ears longed for the scratch of the lighter.

But I'd refused to give in.

A reward. Not a crutch.

A reward was a marker for an accomplishment. A crutch was a symbol of weakness. And I had no tolerance for weakness, especially not within myself.

"In the future, if you feel you can't control yourself and the need to insult me is too overwhelming, we'll deal with it privately," I suggested, exhaling smoke toward the moon.

"Me?" She turned and looked up at me. "You didn't even make it through your first taco tonight before cracking like an egg."

"Yes, well. It's over now." I both loved and hated it when I had her undivided attention. I forced myself to look away from her.

"From now on, to me you'll just be the vaguely racist, misogynistic, hard of hearing uncle everyone avoids engaging with at Thanksgiving."

"And *you* are nothing more than Naomi and Lina's annoying invisible friend I pretend to acknowledge when they insist on setting a place at the table for you," I said.

Sloane stepped away from the railing and held out her hand. "Deal?"

I covered her hand with mine. It was so small, and delicate in my grip. "Deal."

It would be so easy to break something so fragile. It *had* been so easy to break. I hated that we both had that knowledge.

Snap.

Her red lips curved wickedly as we shook. "I'd say it was nice knowing you, but we both know that's a lie."

I dropped her hand and turned my back on her, willing her and the sound that haunted me to disappear.

I waited until I heard the door open and close, leaving me alone in the dark on the deck, before I took a long drag on my cigarette.

14

Red Flags

Sloane

"Did you at least hide the body, Sloaney?" Nash asked when I entered the kitchen. He was rubbing Lina's shoulders while she topped off glasses of wine.

"He's still breathing. I see you two made up," I said to Knox, who had Naomi caged between the counter and his chest. His hands were tucked into the back pockets of her jeans, an expression of wolfish anticipation on his handsome face.

"I'm impossible to stay mad at," Knox said.

"All it takes is for him to load the dishwasher the right way and I'm a puddle of forgiveness," Naomi said. Her engagement ring and wedding band winked in the light.

"Do you two have a minute to talk about something?" I asked Naomi and Lina.

Both women extracted themselves from their men and followed me into the living room on the other side of the kitchen.

"I don't like the sound of this," Knox grumbled as we left.

"They're absolutely going to eavesdrop on us," Lina warned, dropping into a chair and swinging her legs over the arm.

Naomi perched on the couch and patted the cushion next to her. "Is this about the mercurial pain in your ass?"

Lina choked on her wine.

I shook my head. "We've called a truce, and no, before you ask, I don't wish to discuss the terms of said truce." I heard the back door open and close, followed by the low rumble of male conversation. "This is about what we were talking about regarding legal aid. I wanted to run something by you two."

I gave them the bare bones of the Mary Louise case.

"I think Allen did something stupid or got caught up in the wrong crowd and his mom protected him. And no one deserves twenty years for protecting their kid. Obviously, I wouldn't just go and commit your money to anything without discussing it with you first. It might not be the right fit for what we want to do, but I'd at least like to go talk to her and get some more details about her case and her sentencing." I took a breath and scrubbed my hands over my knees. "So what do you think?"

"I think this is an amazing idea and your dad would be so proud," Naomi said, squeezing my hand.

"Agreed," Lina said.

"It could cost a lot. Like more than we have. There wouldn't be anything leftover for anyone else," I warned.

"It's a woman's life," Naomi said. "Of course it's worth it."

"If you're sure, then I'd like to meet with her and hear her side of the story if she's willing to share it."

"Where is she incarcerated? I'll go with you," Lina volunteered.

"Me too," Naomi agreed. "I'd like to meet her."

"The fuck you three are." Knox stomped into the room followed by Nash. Lucian lingered in the doorway.

"Now, Viking—" Naomi began.

"Don't you, 'now, Viking' me, Daze," her husband shot back. "You're not going to prison, even if it is just to have a chat."

Nash had his arms crossed over his chest and his gaze locked on Lina. She shook a finger at him. "Don't you even try the bossy-pants, alpha-male routine, hotshot. I've interviewed prisoners before."

"Oh, I'm not siding with my dumbass brother. But if you're goin', I'm goin', Angel," Nash said amicably.

"How about I save everyone a whole lot of marital strife? I'll go by myself and—"

There was a resounding "No!" From everyone. Everyone including Lucian.

A flare of temper winked into existence. "To be fair, none of you have any right to tell me what I can and can't do. I understand the intricacies of relationships, and you all can deal with that

250

yourselves. But I don't owe that consideration to any of you."

"You're not going," Lucian said as if he had any right whatsoever to make such a decree.

"Can I speak to you outside?" I said through clenched teeth.

"I'll go with you," Nash interrupted.

"Well, if you two are going, I'm definitely going," Lina argued.

"Ahem! This is *our* money for *our* initiative," Naomi reminded the men. "Ergo, we are the ones who get to make the decisions."

Knox held up a finger like he was about to start yelling and then left the room instead.

His booted footsteps echoed through the house as he stomped away and then back again.

He returned with a checkbook and a pen in hand, Waylon and Piper dancing at his heels.

Knox scrawled ink violently across a check, then ripped it free. "Here. Now I get a say, and you're not going."

"You can't just throw money at everything, Knox," Naomi pointed out, getting to her feet. "This woman deserves a real second chance."

"She probably does," Knox agreed aggressively.

I held up a finger. "Wait. I'm confused."

"No one's arguin' that this isn't a good cause. But *I* don't want to deal with the fallout of you three going in there and getting your hearts broken over some sad story about how life ain't fair."

251

Knox Morgan couldn't stand tears and broken-hearted females. They were his kryptonite.

"You don't want us try to do something good because you'll be inconvenienced by our feelings?" Naomi looked as if she'd forgotten all about Knox's dishwasher-loading prowess.

"That's not what I said, Daze."

"Actually," Lina interjected, "it kind of is."

"Not helping, Solavita," Knox said under his breath.

"Don't take a tone with her, or I'll kick your ass and then arrest it," Nash warned his brother.

I stood up on the ottoman and whistled. "Everyone shut up!"

They all shut their mouths and looked at me.

"Obviously, this is a hot-button issue. Let me do a little more research, and then we can discuss this like rational adults."

There was a grumbling chorus of "fines" and "okays."

"Hey, what do you guys like to take for cramps?" Lina asked me suddenly.

Knox and Lucian vanished from the room like someone had just suggested we form a trust circle.

Nash ran his hands over Lina's hips. "You okay, Angel?"

She winked at him. "Yeah. I just wanted to get the testosterone out of here so I can interrogate Sloane about her dating app."

"On that note, I'm out." But he didn't leave before planting a steamy kiss on his fiancée.

"Wow," I said, fanning myself.

"Yeah. Wow," Lina said dreamily as we all watched Nash leave. He really did have a butt that didn't quit.

The haze disappeared when Nash's ass did. I flopped back down on the couch. Waylon the basset hound hurled himself into my lap, pinning me to the cushion. He let out a snorty sigh as I played with his silky ears.

"So how's the app going? How many men are you talking to? Any dates lined up?" Lina asked.

"I think I might not have completed the profile correctly. I haven't matched with anyone. No messages, no matches, no unsolicited dick pics."

"You must have just missed a step in the setup process," Naomi said loyally.

"Lemme see," Lina said.

I opened the app and tossed my phone to her.

Lina's eyebrows arched. "I'm sorry. Are you trying not to get laid?" she asked.

"What are you talking about?" Had I accidentally uploaded the wrong picture? Maybe someone had hacked my account and said I was into ritual sacrifice and attending spelling bees.

"It can't be that bad," Naomi insisted. Lina turned the screen in her direction, and my friend winced. "Okay. She's definitely self-sabotaging."

"What exactly is so wrong with my profile?" I demanded, struggling with the dead weight of the snoring basset hound.

"Let's ask the experts," Lina suggested.

"Don't you dare!"

But it was too late. The men, who had obviously been eavesdropping again, appeared in the doorway.

"Someone say experts?" Nash asked with a charming grin.

Lina held up my phone. "Tell me why you wouldn't click on this profile."

The Morgans leaned in and then out again in unison.

"Jesus, Sloaney. What are you trying to do, repel dicks?" Knox said.

I withered in embarrassment as Lucian glanced at the screen. Unlike his friends, he didn't flinch. He smirked.

"What's the first problem?" Lina asked as if she were instructing a class.

"Cat," the brothers said together.

"Wait. What about the cat? Cats are cute," I argued.

"A cat in the profile picture says crazy cat lady," Nash explained.

"And cat in the username screams it," Knox added, stroking his beard. "Then there's the hair color."

Waylon snorted out another snore, vibrating my lap. "It was Santa Story Hour. The red and green were temporary," I said defensively.

"Wild hair colors in the main profile picture is a clue that the woman could be high-maintenance and—" Nash said.

"Attention whorey," Knox added.

I grabbed my dyed ends. "That's rude."

"I'm not sayin' it's true. I'm sayin' what you put in a dating profile is what you think are your best qualities. And all your ass is sayin' is that you like cats and weird hair."

"Then there's the fact that you're dressed in an elf costume," Lina piled on. "Sloane, you're a smart girl. Why in the hell would you ever pick this picture?"

"The lighting was great. I liked my smile. And the angle made my cheekbones look more defined. Besides, I thought showing me with a cat would tell guys that I'm nurturing."

"Why the fuck do you want to look nurturing?" Knox asked, horrified.

"Because she's ready to settle down and start a family," Naomi told her husband.

"I need a drink," Lucian muttered under his breath. He left the room.

"No offense, Sloaney, but this profile doesn't make you look like marriage material. It makes you look like a human red flag," Nash said.

"Are these rules written down somewhere?"

"Yeah, on a place called the internet," Knox shot back.

"Great," I muttered. "So how do I fix this?"

"Now, that we can help you with," Lina announced.

By the time Lucian returned to the room with a tumbler of liquor, I was standing against the stone fireplace holding a glass of wine—which according to Naomi said responsible but fun—with my hand on my hip, pretending to laugh at something self-appointed art director Knox was saying while Lina took pictures.

Nash had removed a lampshade from a floor lamp and was angling the light bulb in my face.

"I'm hilarious and you're having the best fucking time," Knox insisted on a near snarl.

"Maybe if you'd tell me a joke," I suggested, wondering if I should have just skipped over dating and gone straight to the sperm bank instead.

"Hmm. Do you think we should show more boob or more stomach?" Lina asked, cocking her head and studying me.

"Boob," the Morgan men said in unison.

Lucian was looking at me with a strangely murderous expression on his face. I stared back.

"Oh, I think we've got one. You look all smoldery and sexy," Lina said, studying the phone screen.

Naomi peeked over her shoulder. "Yet approachable and interesting."

Knox and Nash leaned in to give their opinions.

"Hot, but not too hot," Knox decided.

"You'll land a husband in no time," Nash agreed. "And we'll make sure he's worthy when you do."

"Let me see," I demanded.

I glanced at the screen when they held it up and felt heat rise in my cheeks. I'd been giving Lucian the side-eye. That was how I looked when I looked at him? My chin was jutted out, lips parted, eyes smoldering. I looked hot . . . and horny.

Damn. I actually looked good.

Lucian approached and, to my humiliation, peered at the photo. His gaze returned to me, and I knew he got it. He knew that I'd been looking at him. That that look had been just for him. What was one more secret between the two of us?

"I need a real drink," I muttered, putting my untouched wine down on the coffee table.

Wordlessly, Lucian handed me his glass and walked out again. I gawked down at it in surprise.

Naomi nudged me. "Look at you two playing nice."

"Told you electrocuting them wasn't stupid," Knox said.

"It's just a truce," I said. Then I helped myself to a slug of what turned out to be very nice bourbon.

Waylay sauntered into the room and threw her arm around Naomi's waist. "What's going on in here?"

"I thought you were fixing your teacher's laptop," Naomi said, brushing Waylay's hair out of her face.

The girl shrugged. "I finished that in, like, ten minutes. People really need to pay attention to their virus software. Easiest thirty bucks I made all week. Anyway, you guys sounded like you were having more fun than I was. I came to snoop."

"We're helping Sloane with her dating profile," Naomi explained.

"Cool. Can I have more cobbler?" Waylay asked.

"Only if you get me a second helping," Nash called from where he was putting the shade back on the lamp.

Naomi opened her mouth, but Waylay held up a hand. "Sorry, Aunt Naomi. But a grown-up already said I could and I'm not willing to wait for a second opinion."

"Fine, but I'm coming with you and making sure your second helping doesn't weigh half a ton," Naomi conceded. They headed for the kitchen just as Lucian returned with another glass.

"Let's talk about this username," Lina said, drawing my attention away from him and back to the topic at hand.

Nash peered over her shoulder, his hands settling on her hips. "Four-EyedCatLibrarian?"

I winced. Okay, even I had to admit that wasn't my finest moment of creativity. "What do I want my username to say about me?"

"That you're not crazy," Knox said, settling himself on the couch. Waylon hopped up next to him and flopped over on his back.

While my friends decided on a new username, I sipped bourbon in a wingback chair by the fire and wondered why I was so bad at this. I could rock a grant application like a boss. Put me in a social situation, and I could charm the pants off a cute, single guy in record time. But having to market myself in profile form felt overwhelming and stupid.

"You're holding your wrist," Lucian said, his voice low and grave.

I jolted. I'd been so lost in thought I hadn't felt him approach.

"What?" I glanced down and realized I was absentmindedly rubbing my right wrist with my opposite hand.

"Does it still bother you?" His voice was soft, but there was something brittle about the words.

"No. Of course not," I said, dropping my hands.

Naomi reappeared. "Did you hurt yourself?" she asked, proving that becoming Waylay's guardian had given her superhuman hearing.

"Is it carpal tunnel?" Lina asked.

"I, uh, broke my wrist in high school. It was no big deal," I added quickly.

Knox frowned. "I don't remember that."

"You had already graduated. It happened right before summer break."

"I forgot about that," Nash mused. He pinned me with a long, inscrutable look. As chief of police, Nash would have access to all those old records.

"How did you break it?" Waylay asked.

I purposely didn't look at Lucian, but I could still feel his attention on me. "The same way a teenager breaks anything. With a lot of clumsiness and a flair for drama."

"And it still bothers you?" Naomi asked me.

"No. I barely think about it anymore."

Lina hooted. "Guess who just got three matches and two DMs?"

259

"Who?" I asked, perking up.

"BlondDirtyBookReader," she said and triumphantly tossed me my phone.

Three photos of reasonably attractive, not insane men stared back at me.

"You guys are miracle workers," I told them.

"Look at that. You're practically married already," Naomi teased.

On a low growl, Lucian abruptly left the room.

"What the hell crawled up his ass?" Knox wondered as he stole Waylay's spoon and helped himself to some of her cobbler.

"Maybe he had to fart," Waylay suggested.

15

Prison Lot Strip Tease

Lucian

I started my day at 5:00 a.m. I'd worked out, had breakfast, handled three conference calls—two from the car—fired three people, and closed an eight-figure deal. All before noon.

I had two in-house meetings that couldn't be rescheduled, so I did the thing I really didn't want to do and offloaded them onto Nolan with strict instructions not to fuck anything up.

All so I could beat her here.

Sloane's little "I'll do some research" might have fooled everyone else, but not me.

Sergeant Grave Hopper was only too happy to agree to fire off a text when he saw the underhanded little librarian pulling out of the parking lot on her way to a mysterious Wednesday afternoon "meeting."

"Here she is," Hank, my driver, announced when the Jeep roared into the parking lot of the Fraus Correctional Center.

"I'll call you back, Nolan," I said and disconnected.

Sloane had her music loud and sunglasses on. Not a care in the world. Thinking she could just

261

ride to someone's rescue without bothering to think of her own safety first. I wasn't going to stand for that again.

She was frantically digging through her gigantic I'D RATHER BE READING tote on the passenger seat when I approached her Jeep window. I peered in and caught a glimpse of her phone screen in her lap. It was an internet search for "what not to bring to prison visiting hours."

With an eye roll, I rapped on her window.

Startled, Sloane jolted, and the contents of her bag exploded everywhere.

On an aggrieved sigh, I opened her door. She stared up at me, her jaw slack, her sunglasses askew.

I waited.

"What are you doing here?" she demanded, finally regaining the power of speech.

"Waiting for you."

"How—Why—"

"That innocent little librarian routine might work on your friends, but it doesn't work on me."

She scoffed and started shoveling female paraphernalia back into her bag. "I don't have an innocent little librarian routine."

"Did you tell Naomi and Lina that you were coming?"

"No. But—"

"Did you tell Nash or Knox?"

She stopped shoveling. Her chin jutted out.

"No," she said.

"You went behind everyone's backs because you decided you knew better than everyone else. Not the best way to begin your partnership."

Judging from her expression, she knew I was right and wasn't happy about it.

"Are you going to lecture me to death or leave me alone so I can continue to fuck everything up?" She tried to angrily exit the vehicle only to be held back by her seat belt.

I reached across her and released it. "Neither. Let's go."

"No freaking way, Lucifer. I'm not letting you go in there. You'll scare this poor woman out of her wits with your disapproving death glare."

"You're not going in there without me," I said succinctly.

"Yes, I am," she spat. She turned away from me and tried to wrestle her bag across the seat.

"Leave it. You can't take it in with you," I said as I pulled out my phone.

"What are you doing?" she asked.

"Calling Naomi." My thumb hovered over the Call button.

"Damn it!"

"Did you just stomp your foot?" I asked. Sloane's comfort with expressing anger had always intrigued me. But I guess one was free to express their anger when one could control it.

"I was picturing your foot under mine," she shot back.

"Either I go in there with you, or you turn around

and drive home. Those are your only two choices."

She crossed her arms over her chest and glared up at me. Her gaze slid to the prison entrance. Her lips pursed.

"You wouldn't make it," I advised.

She dropped her arms and fisted her hands at her sides. "Fine. You can come in. But you can't glare or growl or roll your eyes. And definitely no speaking."

"May I breathe?"

"I'd prefer if you didn't," she said.

"We're supposed to be in the midst of a truce," I pointed out.

"What truce involves you ambushing me in the parking lot of a women's correctional facility?"

She had a very small, practically insignificant point. "If I had called you to discuss this, would you have even answered?" I already knew the answer.

"Probably not," she admitted.

"Then let's deal with the situation at hand. I'm going in there with you. End of story," I snapped.

"Gee, maybe try to turn down the charm there, Master of the Universe. You might dazzle this woman into a faint."

I shut the door of her Jeep and gestured toward the front of the prison. "Let's go."

We crossed the asphalt side by side, heading toward the monstrous monument of security. Earth-brown sandstone and concrete formed the towering facility walls beyond the double barbed wire fences.

Women in beige jumpsuits huddled in groups in the dismal yard. The asphalt inside the fences was crumbling, dead weeds poking up through the cracks.

Sloane stopped suddenly on the sidewalk. "Why are you here?" she asked again.

"You already asked me that," I reminded her.

She shook her head, sending that thick, blond ponytail swinging. "Fine. It's Wednesday. Why aren't you ruling the corporate world? And you can't stand me, so what does it matter to you if I screw up this partnership with my friends? I'd think you'd be happy to watch me crash and burn."

"If you manage to make a mess of things, there's a chance you could be essentially setting your friends' money on fire. More importantly, there's a woman behind those walls who might suffer because of it."

She closed her eyes and took a breath. "You've buried and forgotten so many things, I just assumed you were over that as well."

She was wrong. I'd buried and forgotten nothing. Instead, I'd used it all as fuel.

"There are some things we never get over. Some things we hide from the light," I said, patting my pocket only to remember I'd left my cigarette in the car.

Sloane lifted her gaze to the heavy gray clouds and wrinkled her nose. Her stud was a pale pink today. "I take it you used your creepy spy network to dig into Mary Louise's case," she guessed.

"I may have glanced at some files."

My team had done a fast, deep dive, and I'd managed to pore over their findings between everything else I'd had to do today. By all accounts, Mary Louise Upshaw was a model prisoner who used her time inside to earn two degrees and start a creative writing program for her fellow inmates. My own legal counsel had reviewed her sentence and found it "absolute bullshit." Which meant the justice-seeking Sloane was probably about to have her heart shattered.

"So you think we might have a case," she pressed.

"I think a lot rides on what she has to say," I hedged.

The visitation room was more depressing than I'd anticipated. There were two rows of scarred folding tables sandwiched between cracked and faded vinyl chairs. The industrial tile floor was stained and peeling. Some of the ceiling tiles were missing between flickering fluorescent lights. There was something that looked suspiciously like mold climbing the walls under the glass block windows.

Sloane was clicking her pen and gnawing on her lower lip, her eyes wide behind her glasses. With a sigh, I gripped the back of her chair and pulled it and her into my side.

She stopped clicking her pen and frowned up at me. She'd always had that little line between her eyebrows that deepened when she was deep in thought . . . or pissed off at me. I wanted to run my finger over it.

"There's nothing to be afraid of," I told her.

"I'm not afraid."

I looked down pointedly at the denim-clad leg that was jiggling a mere inch from my own.

"Fine. I'm not afraid, I'm nervous. Okay?"

"What do you have to be nervous about? You get to walk out of here."

"Thank you, Captain Obvious. But what if she's wonderful? What if she really is in here based on some gross injustice? What if she's lost all these years of her life to an unfair sentence?"

"Then you'll help her."

She went back to chewing on her lower lip for a few moments and then shifted to face me. Her knee was pressing into my thigh. Those green eyes were earnest. "What if her sentence was unfairly harsh but she's a terrible person?"

I felt myself softening toward her. Just like her father, she wanted to make a difference in the lives of strangers. But Sloane didn't have Simon's unlimited capacity for forgiveness. Neither did I.

"Then we'll talk afterward and figure out the best way forward. There's no point wasting any mental energy on a scenario that hasn't played out yet."

She frowned. "You strike me as the kind of man who goes into every situation having considered every possible scenario."

My lips quirked. "It's a luxury of someone who has no human feelings."

"Lucian, I'm serious."

"As am I. You approach this conversation your way, and I'll approach it mine. We'll discuss it later. For now, all you need to do is ask questions and listen."

"I just . . . I don't want to give her false hope."

"You won't," I assured her.

It was a lie. One look at Sloane's earnest face, those eager eyes, and Mary Louise Upshaw was going to feel what I had felt at seventeen. *Hope.*

The heavy metal door on the far end of the room opened, and a woman in a beige jumpsuit entered.

My throat felt dry and tight.

She was white with thick, wavy chestnut-brown hair streaked with gray. Without the jumpsuit, she would have looked like anyone's middle-aged mom. The guard pointed to us, and a look of curiosity flitted across her features.

She headed in our direction, and I felt Sloane stop breathing.

I slid my arm around the back of her chair and gave her shoulder a squeeze. "It's just a conversation," I said, keeping my voice low.

I felt her relax infinitesimally.

"Hello," Mary Louise said, pulling out the chair across from us and sitting.

"Hi." Sloane's voice squeaked. She cleared her throat and began again. "Mary Louise, I'm Sloane Walton, and this is my . . . associate Lucian

Rollins. We had some questions about your case and sentence."

"Are you reporters?" Mary Louise asked, cocking her head.

Sloane's gaze slid to me. "No."

There was a guard stationed across the room, looking blank-faced and bored. It made my skin crawl.

"Lawyers?" Mary Louise looked hopeful.

Sloane shook her head. "No. Just . . ." She looked at me again, *help* written in those lovely green eyes.

I leaned forward. "Ms. Upshaw, we recently stumbled across a mention of your case. Did you ever meet with a Simon Walton? He was an attorney."

She shook her head slowly. "No. I've only had public defenders. Simon was my son's mentor. He helped Allen get into law school. He unfortunately passed away recently."

Sloane tensed against me as if bracing for the inevitable blow of grief.

"It looked as though Simon had taken an interest in your case, specifically your sentencing," I continued. "Can you shed any light as to why that might be?"

Mary Louise shrugged and interlaced her fingers on the table. "Maybe because it was one of the harshest sentences for possession and trafficking in the state of Virginia in the last thirty-five years."

Sloane cleared her throat. "You said initially

that the drugs found in your car during your traffic stop weren't yours. And then you changed your statement and pled guilty."

Mary Louise studied us with narrowed eyes for a beat. "Who are you? Why are you here?"

"I'm Sloane Walton. Simon was my father. I think he wanted to help you, but he got sick before he could."

Mary Louise took a breath, sympathy shining in her eyes. "Your father was a good man. He changed my son's life, so I can only imagine what he did for you. I'm so sorry for your loss."

Sloane reached across the table with one hand. Mary Louise took it and squeezed.

And there it was. That sneaky bastard that would only lead to disappointment, devastation. Hope. It bloomed over both women's faces, and I resigned myself to the fact that things were going to get messy . . . and expensive.

"I met Allen the day of my dad's funeral," Sloane told her. "You raised a great kid."

Mary Louise's face rearranged into maternal pride. "I know it. I wish I could take credit for it, but I've been in here since he was sixteen."

"What happened the night you were arrested?" Sloane asked. "We're not here to judge. We want to help if we can."

Mary Louise shook her head. "Honey, I appreciate that, but I've been in here eleven years. I don't believe in miracles anymore."

"We're not offering a miracle," I clarified.

"Anything that would get me out of this place one day early would be a miracle," she insisted.

"Then tell us what happened that night," I said.

Under the table, Sloane's hand found my thigh and squeezed. Hard.

"Please," I added briskly.

Mary Louise closed her eyes and reached up to rub the back of her neck. "My son was fifteen. His father and I had just split up, and he fell in with the wrong crowd. He had plans. He was going to be the first kid in my family to go to college."

Sloane's knee pressed more firmly against my leg. I kept my arm where it was on the back of her chair but allowed my fingers to brush her shoulder. I felt better, less anxious in here touching her.

Mary Louise locked eyes with me. "He was a good kid. A really good kid."

"Good kids can make stupid choices," I said.

Sloane tensed.

"I was working two jobs at the time. I wasn't around as much as I should have been. I missed the signs. He'd started experimenting. Nothing too crazy. But his 'friend' told Allen he had a way they could make some money. Allen being Allen knew times were tough and thought this was a way he could help out the family. They took my car from the parking lot while I was working third shift to meet some dealer somewhere."

She interlaced her fingers and rested them on the table.

"I got pulled over on the highway halfway

between work and home. I had a headlight out. It turns out they decided it was safer to keep the drugs in my car. I had no idea I was driving around with almost five pounds of marijuana in my back seat. I didn't even know what a dime bag was until I came here. I've learned a lot of things in here."

There was no blame, no malice in her tone. She was simply stating facts.

"When you found out the drugs belonged to your son, that's when you changed your plea, isn't it?" Sloane guessed.

Mary Louise nodded. "He had a whole bright future ahead of him. I wasn't going to let one mistake ruin all that."

I felt a tightness in my chest. The sacrifice this woman had willingly made for her son was unfathomable. At least in my family.

"I had a public defender. The prosecutor offered me a deal. If I pled guilty, she would recommend one year with time served and the possibility of early parole. I was only supposed to do six months max. Six months and then I would be home. I'd see my baby's high school graduation. I'd send him off to college."

"What happened to the deal?" Sloane asked, leaning forward.

Mary Louise shrugged. "The prosecutor made the recommendation. But for whatever reason, the judge didn't like the deal. He said drugs had been infiltrating his community for far too long and it was time to set an example for criminals like me."

Sloane winced.

My free hand balled into a fist in my lap. I too knew what it was like to be at the mercy of a twisted justice system.

Mary Louise held up her palms. "So here I am in year eleven of a twenty-year sentence. But I wake up every day so glad that it's me here and not my baby."

It was too warm in this room. My tie was too tight. I needed air.

"I'm so sorry this happened to you," Sloane said.

"Do you know if the drugs or bags were finger-printed?" I asked.

She shook her head. "I'm sure it wasn't. From my arrest to me changing my plea was only a few days. I doubt any evidence was processed. My second public defender recommended that we appeal. He thought we could prove I didn't do it without implicating my son. He was digging into the case, getting ready to file a motion. Then he got a job at his mother-in-law's firm and moved to New York," she said wearily. "I'm on public defender number four now, and she's so overworked it takes her a week to return my calls."

"That's really unfair. But you don't seem bitter," Sloane said, shooting me a nervous glance.

She was about to promise this woman the world. I removed my arm from the back of her chair and squeezed her leg under the table.

"Bitterness is a waste of energy. All I can do is make the best of this situation."

"It looks as if you've kept busy," I said, flipping open the file I'd brought with me.

Her eyebrows lifted. "Is that a dossier on me?"

"Where did you—never mind," Sloane said before turning back to Mary Louise. "What have you been doing since your sentence?"

"I got an associate's degree in business and one in creative writing."

"You founded a creative writing program for inmates," I added.

She smiled wryly. "I did. But that was more for me than anything. I like talking about writing, and in here, I have a captive audience."

"Your son. He's in law school now?"

A slow, proud smile spread across her face, making her look younger, lighter. "In his last year at Georgetown. He says as soon as he graduates, he's going to find a way to get me out."

"We have to help her," Sloane said as we exited the prison.

An involuntary shudder worked its way up my spine when the heavy door closed behind us. Had it not been for Sloane's father, this could have been my fate. I turned up my coat collar and sucked in a deep breath of icy winter wind.

I could breathe again. It felt miraculous.

Sloane's cheeks were flushed pink with excitement. "I mean, obviously it's going to take a lot of time and energy—"

"And money," I added. I could give it to her. But

she wouldn't take it. Not if she knew it came from me.

"And money," she agreed. "But we can't let her sit behind bars. Not for protecting her son. And certainly not for another decade."

Her eyes sparkled behind her glasses. She hadn't been this excited in my presence since we were teenagers. It was another sting of loss.

"I guess I need to talk to Naomi, Lina, and Stef first. Then I'll call Maeve. We'll have to find a lawyer. A good one."

As she babbled on, I thought about how much her energy reminded me of Simon's. Simon had loved nothing more than a challenge when justice was at stake.

It appeared the apple hadn't fallen far from the tree.

The Waltons were good people. They weren't stained with bad blood as I was.

"Your father would be . . . proud." The word lodged itself in my throat, and it took effort to let it loose. It was the greatest compliment I could think to give.

Sloane stopped her bubbly, one-sided conversation to gawk up at me.

"Thank you," she said finally. Her eyes narrowed. "Are you okay?"

"I'm fine," I said testily.

"You don't look fine. You look pale."

"I always look fine," I insisted as I guided her across the parking lot.

She glanced back at the building we'd just left. "I'm sorry. I didn't really think about it, but I guess being in a prison even as a visitor could be triggering after—"

"You aren't going to need just an attorney," I couldn't stand the pity I heard in her voice. "You'll need an entire legal team."

"That sounds expensive."

"Justice isn't cheap, Pixie."

Her chin jutted out. "I'll find a way," she said.

"I have no doubt."

She fished her car keys out of her jacket pocket when we arrived at her Jeep.

"I happen to know a few lawyers who specialize in appeals and commutations. I'll send you some names." I'd used one of them to seal my own record.

She frowned and the line between her eyes returned. "Thanks."

It sounded like a question.

"What?" I demanded.

"You liked her, didn't you?" she prompted.

"I found her story interesting."

Sloane threw her head back and let out a noise that was half groan and half snarl. "Can you just for once say what you're thinking? I'm not going to take your opinion and use it against you or try to scam you out of a kajillion dollars. I just want to know what you think."

"Why?" There were reasons I guarded my words. The same reasons I walked through life with a poker face.

She crossed her arms. "Because you're a rich megalomaniac who plays dirty with politicians all day long. I assume you see things from a different angle than a small-town librarian."

"Her story—if it's true—is compelling. Even if it's not entirely true, the sentence was excessive, and she's done nothing while serving her time to indicate she's a dangerous criminal. With the proper team, you should be able to at least shorten her sentence significantly."

Sloane smirked. "There. Was that so hard?"

"Excruciating." I had a headache forming at the back of my head. I didn't like being anywhere near prisons. Even being able to walk out didn't help shake the memories of a broken, traumatized teen.

"She did it to protect her son when he was a stupid teenager. I mean, what parent wouldn't do that for their stupid teenager?" She flinched the moment the words left her mouth. But she didn't apologize. "I mean, what good parent wouldn't do whatever it took to . . ."

She was making it worse, and she knew it.

"Shut up, Sloane."

"Shutting up," she confirmed. It lasted nearly a full five seconds before she opened her mouth again. "What would you do next if you were me?" she asked, toying with the button on her coat.

"I'd talk to the son again."

That had her perking up.

"*With* your partners," I added.

"Of *course* with my partners," she said haughtily.

277

I glanced down at my watch. I hadn't wrapped this up in time to take the call from New York. Nolan better not have fucked it up. If he hadn't fucked it up, the rest of my afternoon was open.

"Are you hungry? Do you want coffee?" I asked.

Her spine straightened. "Shit! What time is it?"

"Nearly three."

She unlocked her car. "Damn it! I'm gonna be late for my date."

"Your date," I repeated. I hadn't meant to; the words had just slipped out. They were accompanied by an irrational burst of irritation.

"Yeah," she said, turning to examine her reflection in the side mirror. "You know. Meet for food. Make awkward conversations about what you wanted to be when you grew up and what your favorite appetizers are. A date."

She yanked the tie out of her hair and bent at the waist, shaking all that silver-tipped blond out.

"Who is this date with?"

Sloane flipped right side up, looking less like an innocent librarian and more like a bed-headed vixen. "Some guy named Gary? No, wait. Gary is later. This is . . ." She opened the door of her vehicle to grab a lipstick out of her cupholder. She uncapped it. "Massimo." She slicked the red over her lips with an expert hand.

"Massimo?" He sounded like a man with a gold chain woven into his chest hair who wore sunglasses indoors. "You're meeting a stranger from the internet alone?" Irritation was giving way to a simmering panic. It was hard to breathe again.

"That's kind of how these dates work," she said, grabbing onto my arm for balance while she toed off her sneakers. The socks with cats and books came next.

She released me to toss her discarded footwear in the back seat and produce another pair of shoes. Purple ones with stick-thin heels. The coat came next. This she threw at me. I caught it despite the feeling of anxiety that was blooming like a fucking flower.

"Have you really never done the dating app thing?" she asked.

"Do I look like I use dating apps?"

"You look like you hire high-priced call girls to act out your lewd fantasies."

"And *you* look like . . ."

I lost my train of thought when she whipped her black turtleneck over her head. She was wearing a thin-strapped, lacy camisole that dipped low over the tops of her full breasts.

"I look like what?" she prodded, sliding her arms through a hunter-green cardigan in a chunky knit. There were no buttons, nothing to close the sweater over her fantasy-inducing cleavage.

"What?" I repeated. My mouth was dry, and my headache was raging in full force now.

"You were about to insult me. Hit me with it, big guy, before I go meet the future Mr. Sloane Walton."

I closed my eyes. Her nicknames for me the past several years had been limited to Lucifer and "Hey, asshole."

"You can't be serious with this emergency quest for a husband," I told her.

"Spoken like a man who has all the time in the world to decide when to start a family."

"I'm never starting a family." I blamed the dark cleft between her breasts for my uncalculated confession.

She paused, mid-tug on the hem of her tank. "Really?"

"That's not the point. You can't go meet a stranger for a date. What if he's a predator?"

She fluffed her hair out of the neck of her cardigan. It made the generous curves of her breasts threaten to spill over the top of her shirt.

Swarthy Massimo was going to take one look at her and do or say something stupid, and then I was going to have to ruin his fucking life.

"It's fine. People meet strangers on the internet all the time now, and hardly any of them end up murdered."

"Sloane," I barked.

She grinned at me. A happy, smug, full-fledged smile. Jesus, between her breasts and the smile, Too Many Gold Chains Massimo was going to feel like he'd hit the fucking lottery.

"I'll be *fine*. Geez, for someone who doesn't want a family, you're sure acting Dad-like."

"What if he doesn't like to read?"

"Then I guess I'll just have to keep shopping for a husband."

"I'm fucking serious, Sloane. What precautions are you taking? Where is this date? Who knows you'll be there?"

She gripped my coat by the lapels. "Calm the fuck down, Lucifer. It's in Lawlerville. Lina and Naomi are tracking my phone with a locater app. I sent them screenshots of his profile and our chat. I'm texting them a picture of him when I get there and proof-of-life messages every thirty minutes. If things go downhill, Stef is on deck to call me with a fake emergency forty-five minutes into the date, because I can handle pretty much anything for forty-five minutes, right? If things go *really* badly, I have pepper spray and a big, fat hardback in my bag. Is that good enough, Suit Daddy?"

"That's . . . reasonably thorough," I admitted when she released me.

"Good. Now, how do I look?" She spread her arms out wide.

She looked beautiful. Fun, spunky, smart, sweet, funny. Fucking breathtaking. I hated Massimo's fucking guts.

She rolled her eyes. "Never mind. I forgot who I was asking."

"Suit Daddy?" Her words had finally sunk into my reeling brain.

16

Crunchy Soup and Bad First Dates

Sloane

Massimo was a fraud. Instead of the six-foot-tall, glasses-wearing, gourmet cook hobbyist with a love of popular thriller authors, I was seated across the table from a five-foot-four man-child who had just ordered buttered noodles because marinara was "yucky."

"My mom makes the best buttered noodles. So if you wanna get with this," he said, gesturing at his sweater that looked as if it had been intimate with a Weedwacker, "you better learn how to melt that butter just right."

My God. What had I done to deserve this karma? All I wanted to do was meet a nice, hot guy, have kids, and get a woman out of prison. Was that too much to ask? At least the restaurant was nice. It was part café, part Italian restaurant, part wine bar with checkered tablecloths and the comforting smells of garlic and espresso. If I didn't have to drive all the way back to Knockemout, I would have been ordering the largest glass of pinot grigio they had.

"Uh, yeah," I said. "So you said you're a Grisham fan. Did you read his latest?"

"Who?"

"Grisham. John Grisham," I prompted.

He was squinting at me through bloodshot eyes.

"The famous legal thriller writer. You said *A Time to Kill* was one of your favorites."

"Ohhh!" he said a little too loudly. "That was actually my mom. I don't like to like . . . you know. Communicate? So she writes all my texts and emails for me. Sometimes she even impersonates me on the phone."

"I don't know you well enough to know if you're joking," I said.

He flailed his arms at the server. "Hey, man! I know we, like, just ordered some food, but I'm starving. Is there any way I could get, like, two baskets of bread? Oh, and some fried mushrooms. And you know what? Throw in a bowl of soup. But not, like, something mushy. I like crunchy soup."

The server's gaze slid to me.

"We met online," I explained.

"Got it," he said to me, then turned back to Massimo. "I'll be back with your bread, mushrooms, and crunchy soup."

"Cool, man. Thanks."

The server disappeared, and I was left alone with the very hungry, red-eyed mama's boy.

"Are you high?" I asked.

"You know it. Twenty-four seven, baby. Livin' the blaze life. Relaxin' with the reefer. Sparkin' up Saturday."

"It's Wednesday." I wanted to stand up and walk out, but I had actual concerns about what damage he would inflict on himself and others without any adult supervision.

"It's cool, baby. It don't matter what day it is because you're hot and I've got buttered noodles coming." He reached into his messenger bag and pulled out a half-eaten brownie. "You wanna share the rest of this edible?"

"No, I don't. Did you drive here, and if so, do you remember hitting any people-shaped objects?"

His giggle was so high-pitched I almost didn't hear the buzzing of my phone in my bag. I pounced on it, grateful that Stef was calling me early with his fake emergency.

But it wasn't a call from Stef. It was a text. From Lucian.

Lucian: Is Massimo husband material?

Massimo put his chin in his hands. "Oh, hey, listen. I, like, forgot my wallet, and my mom totally withheld my allowance this week because I accidentally set the basement on fire. You don't mind picking up the tab, do you? Oh, and I need you to drive me home."

Under normal circumstances, I wouldn't have even replied to Lucian's text, let alone allowed the man the tiniest glimpse into my personal life. But this was an emergency.

Me: He's not even adult material. Thinking about setting a fire in the ladies' restroom

and making a run for it. I'm not going to survive until Stef's fake emergency.
Lucian: Where are you?

My heart skipped a beat.

Me: Vino Italiano. Why?
Lucian: Stay there.

Stay there? As in stay here with Massimo the Mooch?

I glanced up from my phone. "Is your real name Massimo?"

He let out another guffaw. "Nah. It's actually Eugene. You can call me Euge. You know. Pronounced like the Pittsburgh 'huge'? Mom thought I'd get more chicks as a Massimo."

"Your crunchy soup, sir," the server said, setting down a bowl of soup filled with at least nine packs of crushed-up saltines.

"Cool, man. I'll make sure this pretty lady with the awesome rack tips well. What's your name again?" he asked me. "S Loan?"

"Oh my God. Okay, that's it," I said, throwing my napkin down on the table.

"If you're going to punch him, can you try not to get any blood on the tablecloth?" the server asked me. "The last couple that sat here was on a blind date too, and she dumped an entire bottle of wine over his head. I'm out of fresh linens."

The bell on the door jingled, and in strode Lucian

Rollins, looking just as beautiful as he had when I left him less than an hour ago.

Every woman in the place, including the lesbian couple and the ninety-second birthday attendees in the corner, stopped what they were doing and stared.

I too fell under his spell as he swept toward me. His eyes were all silver fire. His mouth was pressed in that mean, firm line that made women vie for a smile. His coat today was charcoal gray and billowed behind him like a superhero cape. His trousers were a lighter gray and fit extremely well in the crotch. I hadn't noticed *that* at the prison.

"Man, these guys make a good crunchy soup," Euge said through a mouthful of saltines.

"Huh?" I said, not bothering to tear my eyes away from Lucian.

"Sloane," he greeted me with that gravelly rasp.

"Hi."

Euge turned and found himself face-to-crotch with Lucian.

"Your pants look expensive," Euge announced to the entire restaurant.

Lucian shot me a smirk.

"Don't you smirk at me. Apparently his mother made his profile."

"Dude, I'm kinda in the middle of something with Rackety Ann here. We're vibing."

"Rackety Ann?" Lucian repeated.

"He's talking about her chest," the server offered helpfully.

Lucian rolled his eyes and clenched his teeth. He reached out and grabbed Euge by the collar and hauled him out of his seat.

"Don't get blood on the tablecloth," I warned.

"We're just going to take a little walk," Lucian promised. He looked at me. "Stay."

With flaming cheeks, I watched him march Euge out the door like a puppet. The rest of the diners were riveted. I was debating texting Lina and Sloane when the woman at the table next to me leaned over.

"Girl, I don't know what's happening right now, but I'm a nurse and if you don't go home with Tall, Dark, and Tight Crotch, I'm gonna check you for head trauma."

The man next to her nodded. "I'm her husband, and even I think Suit Guy is fucking hot."

"Noted," I said.

A minute later, Lucian returned alone, looking moderately cheerful.

He pulled out Euge's chair and sat.

I bit my lip. "Did you crumple him up and throw him in the gutter?"

"I arranged for my driver to take your date home in my car."

I covered my face with my hands and groaned.

"I took the liberty of canceling the stoned gentleman's noodles and brought you this," the server said.

I dropped my hands to see him handing Lucian a menu and a bottle of wine.

Lucian thanked him and the man scampered off, obviously thrilled by the lack of bloodshed.

"That was the worst first date in the history of first dates," I said.

"You'd be surprised," Lucian said.

"Oh, please. You don't date. You pick up a rich-guy-trophy-girlfriend takeout menu and place an order. This is different. This is humiliating and a total waste of time."

"What did you expect?" he asked, looking amused. "Also, where can I get a copy of the rich-guy-trophy-girlfriend takeout menu?"

"Don't be funny or nice. I don't want your pity."

"I'm not pitying you, Pixie. I'm enjoying your misery."

"Well, you're doing it too nicely. Be meaner."

"Fine. You should have walked out the door thirty seconds after your introduction. What were you thinking?"

"I was trying to give him the benefit of the doubt . . . and I was really hungry."

"What a coincidence. So am I."

"Are you seriously planning to have lunch with me right now?" I asked.

He closed the menu. "Yes. But rest assured, it's not the company I'm interested in. It's the chicken piccata."

The server reappeared with two wineglasses and took Lucian's order while he poured us each a glass.

I accepted my wine and leaned back in my chair.

288

"I can't believe I'm about to say this, but thank you for riding to my rescue . . . twice today."

He arched an eyebrow. "I'm impressed. You said that without wincing."

"I was wincing on the inside."

Was Lucian Rollins flirting with me? Or was he just being human, and it was so far from his usual icy devil asshat routine that even the most benign polite gesture felt like it was sexually charged?

"Then you're welcome," he said.

I tipped my glass toward him. He raised his at me.

"Okay. Enough of this being nice to each other. It makes my skin crawl," I said with a shudder.

Lucian chuckled and I nearly fumbled my glass. Clearly I had tumbled into an alternate reality, like *Sputnik Sweetheart* by Haruki Murakami. Was this a new world where Lucian Rollins and I got along?

"Agreed," he said.

"So, about Mary Louise. If I talk to her son and her story checks out, what would the next step be . . . hypothetically?" I asked.

"You'd need to hire an attorney with experience in cases like this. Someone who has the time to dedicate and a good rapport with both judges and juries. They'd need to build a team of associates, paralegals, and interns."

"You're saying I need a team of unicorns."

"And don't forget about the money. Appeals are expensive."

"We're sitting on a pretty nice nest egg," I bragged.

"If it's less than a seven-figure nest egg, I wouldn't be so sure," he said.

I sputtered into my wine, narrowly avoiding a spill. "A million dollars?"

"Depending on how long the appeal process lasts, it could be more."

"Are you fucking around?"

His eyes locked on mine. "I never fuck around about money."

"Shit." I put down the wine and picked up my water. "Shit."

"I could be persuaded to—"

"No!" I said.

"Definitely a concussion," the woman at the table next to us stage-whispered to her husband.

"He's, like, beautiful and handsome at the same time," her husband whispered back.

"Why wouldn't you take money when it's offered, Sloane?"

Because it was his. Because he'd hurt me. Because I'd hurt him. Because the last time our lives had gotten tangled up, neither of us had ever recovered.

"Because I said so." It was too bad Massimo turned out to be a big, stoned phony, because I was clearly ready to become a parent.

"Still unnecessarily stubborn, I see," he said.

"I think we've both proven on multiple occasions that we can't work together."

"That doesn't mean you can't take my money to do something good."

"That's exactly what it means," I said. "We don't trust each other enough for money to change hands."

"And whose fault is that?" he asked quietly.

"I think we both played a role."

Our meals arrived, and we stared down at the plates before us.

Lucian heaved a sigh. "Let's table this discussion for another time. I rarely get a Wednesday afternoon off, and I'd prefer to enjoy it."

I picked up my fork. "Don't you already own half of the Eastern Seaboard? How much money do you need before you can afford to start taking afternoons off?"

"You're awfully judgmental for someone who agreed to a date with a man-boy called Euge."

"Ugh. Naomi and Lina are going to have a field day with this," I grumbled. Though it was hard to be grumpy with a plate full of ravioli.

"What are friends for if not making fun of us when we're at our worst?" he philosophized.

"It's not that. Well, not *only* that. They're so smug about their happily ever afters."

"So are Knox and Nash," Lucian agreed. "It's annoying."

"When I meet my future husband, I'm going to have some dignity. I'm not going to get caught making out in public. And I certainly won't be shoving the joys of monogamy down the throats of my single friends," I said, plowing my way through the first pillowy, cheese-stuffed ravioli.

Though come to think of it, almost all my friends were in committed relationships. I frowned and chewed. When the hell had that happened? The endless parade of bridal showers, weddings, and baby showers had punctuated the past several years of my professional march toward library domination.

"I was supposed to meet Knox at Honky Tonk two weeks ago. I got there early and found Mr. *and* Mrs. Morgan climbing out of his pickup truck wearing only half their clothes," Lucian said as he pulled a piece of bread in half.

I hid my laugh behind my napkin.

"I FaceTimed Lina from a store to ask her opinion on a jacket. She answered the phone *from the shower*. I got an eyeful of Nash Junior in the background."

Lucian shook his head. "For future reference, when you're on a date, you should refrain from discussing other men's penises."

I choked out a laugh. "Wow. Wednesday Afternoon Lucian could almost pass for human."

His lips curved up ever so slightly. "If you spread that around, I'll deny it."

"Your secret is safe with me," I said.

My statement had the effect of a record scratch. Lucian went very still, his eyes boring into mine, telling me what I already knew.

He *had* trusted me. Once. Just like I'd trusted him. Neither one of us had any intention of making the same mistake again.

I cleared my throat and focused on my plate.

Lucian sliced through a delicate piece of chicken with surgical precision. "Why are you so intent on finding a husband? Why now?"

"Can't we just talk about the weather or something?" I asked.

"It's cold," he retorted. "Why are you hunting a husband like it's a sport?"

"Because I've spent so much time on my career I'm freaking out at how little time I have left to start a family."

"And you need a family because?"

Normally, I'd have no problem calling him an inhuman robot monster with a wallet where his heart should be. However, I was keenly aware that we'd grown up in very different homes. He wasn't asking to be an asshole—well, not *only* to be an asshole. The man across from me genuinely didn't understand the purpose a family served.

"Because I've always wanted one. I always assumed I'd have one. I want what my parents had. I want to give my mom grandkids who are so excited to see her they smash their sticky little faces up against the windows just to watch for her car. I want a house full of people."

He grimaced and helped himself to a sip of wine. "That sounds horrible."

"Which part?"

"Mostly the sticky part. But also the house full of people." He shuddered.

I couldn't help but smile. "It's definitely not

for everyone. But I'm Team Sticky Face. I love spending time with Chloe and Waylay and watching them awkwardly turn into slightly less feral, more hormonal people."

We ate in silence for a few moments, which gave me plenty of time to spiral mentally. I could not believe I was sharing a meal with Lucian Rollins. He made eating sexy. No one in the real world could do that. Everyone looked like idiots trying to cram food into their faces. But not Lucian. The way he held his fork and knife. The way he never seemed to get anything stuck between his teeth. The way his lips parted just enough for the fork to pass between them . . .

"You know, it's not too late for you," I said, interrupting my stupid train of thought. "You could start a family."

"Or I could keep doing what I've been doing."

"And what have you been doing?" I asked, trying to dislodge a piece of parsley with my tongue.

"Exactly what I want, when I want."

"You sound like an overgrown toddler," I pointed out.

"At least I don't dress like a teenager who shops at yard sales," he teased.

Before I could take offense and then tell him I'd taken offense, I heard a faint buzzing noise.

He reached inside his jacket and produced his phone to frown at the screen. "Excuse me a moment," he said as if I were some business associate he had to be polite to. "What?" he answered.

I didn't like when people couldn't be bothered with a greeting. How hard was it to say "Hi" or "Hello"? Or "Lucifer's phone, Satan speaking." My dad used to answer every call to the house with a boisterous "Yellow?"

Lucian's frown deepened. "I see. When?"

I almost felt bad for whoever was on the other end of the call, because whatever they were saying was not making him happy. He looked as if he'd just won the World Championship Glaring Contest and was pissed off about it.

"Where?" His tone was clipped. He looked over my head at some unknown spot, still frowning. "Fine. Get me in."

He hung up, still looking grumpy as hell.

"Problem?" I asked.

"You could say that." He picked up his knife and fork again. This time when he cut a bite of chicken, it was with controlled violence.

"Let me guess. The trophy girlfriend you ordered isn't available?"

"Close. The man who sold Duncan Hugo the list of law enforcement officers just turned up dead."

My fork dropped with a clatter. "What happened to him? Who was he?"

"A low-level independent contractor criminal. His body was dumped in the Potomac. He was shot twice in the head."

"Why are you getting calls about that?" I asked, my blood running cold.

"Because someone ordered a hit on my friend."

His voice was colder than the polar ice caps before global warming.

"Duncan Hugo is behind bars, and Tate Dilton is dead," I reminded him.

"Anthony Hugo is the one who commissioned that list, and he's still out there operating his business."

"Lucian, you can't just decide to go head to head with a mob boss or whatever the appropriate terminology is."

"As it happens, I'm uniquely suited to do exactly that," he said, picking up his wine.

"The FBI is investigating him. You don't need to go make yourself a target."

"It almost sounds like you care, Pixie."

"Lucian, I'm serious."

"So am I."

"What can you do that the FBI can't?" I asked.

"For one, I can expedite things. My team isn't overworked and understaffed. We have the capabilities to find the right thread to pull on and point the FBI in that direction." He looked at me, eyes narrowing. "I already regret telling you this."

"What is Anthony Hugo going to do when he finds out that you're helping the FBI build a case against him?"

"Become irritated?"

"Don't play the blasé butthead with me. This guy is dangerous. There's a three-part docuseries about him on YouTube that was never finished because the channel owners *died in a mysterious house fire.*"

"I'm perfectly capable of protecting myself," he insisted.

Now, maybe. But there had been a time when he hadn't been. When he'd been too busy protecting others to worry about himself. Old habits died hard, especially when the habit holder was a stubborn pain in the ass.

"His organization is rumored to be directly linked to a South American drug cartel, and his right-hand henchman is serving a life sentence for brutally murdering a federal witness *and his family*." My voice was getting higher pitched by the syllable.

"Someone's done her homework," he said, sounding not the least bit concerned.

"Of course I did. Nash is my friend, and Anthony Hugo is still out there walking around."

"Then you understand why I'm doing what I'm doing."

"But what if he comes after *you?*" I pressed.

He looked up at me, his eyes flat and cold. "I'll be ready."

If we were friends, I could argue with him. I could make him listen to reason. But we weren't. There was nothing I could do to make him take my opinion seriously. Nothing I could do to change his mind.

I suddenly wasn't very hungry anymore. "I don't suppose you're willing to talk about any of the precautions you're taking," I prodded.

"I don't suppose I am."

"Is he going to go after Nash again?"

Lucian sighed and put down his utensils. "I didn't come here to talk about this."

"Well, tough shit. Because you're here, and we *are* talking about this."

"All signs point to Hugo focusing on business as usual."

"That's not a no."

"I'm watching him. The FBI is watching him. His enemies are probably watching him to see if they can take advantage. It would be incredibly stupid of him to make a move right now. And Anthony Hugo might be many things, but he isn't stupid. Nash, Lina, Naomi, Waylay, they're all safe."

I crossed my arms. "Are they all safe because Nash and Knox are taking precautions that the rest of us aren't aware of?" Naomi and Lina would not be pleased when I told them. Of course, telling them would require me confessing to the worst first date of my entire life.

Lucian raised an eyebrow. "I don't know why I bother asking you to trust me to handle this. You've never done anything I wanted you to do before."

He was baiting me, distracting me. Trying to guide me away from my pointed questions with a pat on the head and a "look at something shiny" redirection.

"I just don't understand what you can do that a law enforcement agency can't."

"I have the budget and resources and technology

the government wishes it had. I'm simply sharing some of my toys. By the way," he said, buttering a piece of bread, "you'll need to drive me home since I loaned my car and driver to your date."

"Did you at least bring your wallet?" I asked, picking up my fork again.

17

Too Close for Comfort

Lucian

Duncan Hugo looked significantly the worse for wear since I'd last seen him being led in handcuffs to a police cruiser. The hair he'd died an earthy brown was showing a full inch of natural red root. He'd lost some weight, and the hunch of his shoulders hinted that his time behind bars had relieved him of some of his arrogance. The dark circles under his eyes almost made up for the fact that this was my second prison visit in two days.

This prison was in better shape than yesterday's, I noted. It wasn't winning any design awards, but the furniture wasn't disintegrating, the paint wasn't lead-based, and there was a faint scent of industrial cleaner throughout the facility. It still made my skin crawl, my tie feel too tight against my throat.

I focused on Nolan, who leaned against the wall, hands in his pockets.

He hadn't managed to run my business into the ground yesterday, so when he'd insisted on joining me for this little field trip, I hadn't said no.

I faced Duncan across the table in the interview room the FBI had arranged.

It could have been me, I thought as I studied him. If it weren't for the Waltons, I could easily have been the one on the opposite side of the table.

Duncan hadn't had a Simon or a Karen or a Sloane. He'd had a father like mine. That was why I was here.

"I said I wanted to talk to the feds, not some stuck-up dick in a suit," Duncan said, slumping in his chair like a six-year-old on the verge of a temper tantrum. His baggy orange jumpsuit accentuated the red in his hair and scraggly beard.

"I'm an ex-fed. Does that count?" Nolan asked.

"Didn't I shoot you?" Duncan asked.

"You missed, shithead. Your pal Dilton got lucky."

Duncan grunted. "Don't know which was worse. His aim or his personality."

I cleared my throat. "Do you know who I am?" I asked Duncan.

His mouth pinched, but he nodded. "Yeah, I know who the fuck you are."

"Then you can probably piece it together from there. You've already talked to the feds on several occasions. Yet you remain essentially useless."

"So they send Lucian Rollins in here to do what? Break my fucking kneecaps?" He picked up one of the loose cigarettes on the table and lit a match.

Watching Duncan's thin lips wrap around the filter was enough to make me consider skipping today's cigarette.

"I'm here to dig into the space between your ears

301

to see if there's anything useful squirreled away."

"What the hell else do you assholes want? I gave you drop locations. I gave you names. It's not my fault if you're not doing shit about it."

"The information you provided was street-level. Any gutter rat would know it. It's almost like you're holding out or your father didn't trust you."

Duncan pulled the cigarette out of his mouth. A tic appeared in his jaw. "What the fuck does it matter? I'm stuck in this shithole for a fuck ton of years."

"Felix Metzer," I said.

"Already told that FBI bitch that's who I bought the list off of."

"Did she mention that his body was fished out of the Potomac yesterday? The two slugs in his brain indicate it wasn't a boating accident."

He held up his palms. "Hey, man. Don't look at me. My ass was in here."

From his position against the wall, Nolan rolled his eyes and shook his head.

"Someone was cleaning up their mess. I'm curious who that would be," I said.

"Felix was into shit with every fucking one. What makes you think him gettin' whacked had anything to do with me?"

"He was last seen the day before you were arrested for trying to kill my friends."

"Look, man. It was nothing personal."

"You weren't even man enough to pull the trigger the first time around."

Duncan scoffed. "It's called delegating. Bosses don't do the dirty work."

"They do if they want to *earn* that title." I'd done my share of dirty work as I climbed the ladder of success. I'd earned the respect and the fear.

He crossed his arms over his chest. "This chat has been real nice and all, but I'm over it."

"What else do you have to do? Go back and stare at four walls?"

"Better than listening to this bullshit."

"If you had two brain cells in that dumbass head of yours, you'd be all ears," Nolan warned him.

"Your father doesn't see you as a threat," I said to Duncan. "Maybe you should make him reconsider that. Remind him who you are and that you're still dangerous to him."

Duncan shoved a hand through his hair. "Look, man, I tried. I lost. He won. That's the way it always goes."

Did we all have this wound from our fathers? Was it necessary for every son to challenge his father to become a man? Was there always a winner and a loser, or was there a different rite of passage, a different path to respect?

"There's still time to change that," I told him.

"He didn't fucking tell me shit, okay? He thought I was a fuckup. A loser." Duncan tapped the ash off his cigarette into the ashtray.

"So you wanted to show him that you were more," I prompted.

"Yeah, and I fucked that up too."

The woe-is-me, defeated criminal routine set my teeth on edge. "You realize if you don't give the feds something to work with, they'll transfer you out of this place to a federal facility. The kind where you're in a cell twenty-three hours a day."

I caught the nervous shift of his eyes. "They say where?" he asked, trying and failing to sound disinterested.

"I heard Lucrum. That's maximum security. It makes this place look like a day care center. I saw its sister facility, Fraus. It wasn't pretty."

The feet of Duncan's chair hit the floor. "I can't go there."

"You won't have a choice," I pointed out.

"I can't go to Lucrum. I won't last a fucking day."

"You should have thought of that before you tried to kill a law enforcement officer, kidnapped a civilian, and then turned out to be an absolute waste of time for the FBI."

"You don't understand. He's got guys on the inside there. No enemy of Anthony Fucking Hugo survives a week in that hellhole," he insisted.

I leaned forward. "Then give me something I can use. Tell me what you know about Felix. Why did your father commission the list from him?"

Duncan swiped a hand over his sweaty upper lip. "Felix is like a squirrel, you know? Always scurrying around, picking up little nuggets here and there. Storing them away for winter . . . or a payday. He is . . . fuck. He *was* a likable guy for a dirt bag. A real charmer. He was like Kevin Bacon on the streets. Everyone either knew him or knew a guy who knew him. If you needed intel, he could usually dig it up."

"Who did he work with? Who were his friends?" I asked.

"Like I said, everyone knew him. Everyone liked him."

"Then who was he closest to? Maybe someone outside the game?" Nolan prompted.

Duncan tipped his head to the ceiling. "I don't fucking know. Maybe his girl?"

"He had a woman?" I asked. Nolan and I shared a glance. This was news.

"One he paid for, if that counts. I saw him once having lunch with her. Real high-class. Way too good for him."

"What was her name?" I asked.

He took a drag and blew out a cloud of smoke that swirled lazily between us. "Maureen Fitz-gerald."

I sat back in my seat.

Duncan's smirk was back. "Huh. Maybe you're a client too? Isn't that a small, incestuous world?"

"Prisons give me the heebie-jeebies," Nolan announced when we hit the parking lot, the barbed wire and block walls behind us. "Every time I walk in, I'm worried they aren't gonna let me walk out."

I grunted and continued toward my car.

"Was it my imagination in there, or did that

305

ginger asshole insinuate that you were acquainted with Maureen Fitzgerald, DC's highest caliber madam?" Nolan wondered.

I yanked open the door of my Jaguar and grabbed my phone.

"It wasn't your imagination, and I am acquainted with Maureen," I said, thumbs flying across the screen.

Me: We need to talk. Call me.

"Huh. Didn't think a guy like you would have to buy a date. Makes me feel pretty damn good about myself."

The phone vibrated in my hand. But it wasn't Maureen. It was Special Agent Idler.

I swore under my breath, ignored the call, and slid behind the wheel. I never should have allowed Nolan to tag along. I needed to think, to plot. I didn't want the feds talking to Maureen before I did.

"Get in," I ordered.

"Hey, listen, you're the boss. You don't have to tell me anything as long as you keep paying me," Nolan said as he climbed into the passenger seat.

I waited until both doors were closed. "Maureen is a friend. She feeds me information on some of her more depraved client requests. I use that information as I see fit."

"And you don't want to give the feds a reason to look directly at her," Nolan guessed, securing his seat belt.

I nodded and started the engine.

"Seems kinda odd. Maureen Fitzgerald associating with a Felix Metzer type?" he mused. "I've seen her in person a few times. Gorgeous lady. Classy. Rich."

It wasn't just odd. It was completely implausible.

My phone vibrated again, and I fantasized about tossing it out the window and backing over it but managed to refrain.

A glance at the screen told me it wasn't Idler.

Karen: Tonight we will be dining on the finest frozen pizza and a reasonably okay-ish bottle of wine.

Fuck. I'd nearly forgotten.

"Big plans tonight?" Nolan asked.

"What?" I looked up, intending to glare him into silence.

He nodded at the screen in the dashboard where Karen's text was on display. Damn Bluetooth.

Another call from Idler appeared on the screen.

"You look like you're about to rip the wheel out of the steering column," Nolan observed mildly.

I gave him another cold glare.

"Okay, fine. You don't *look* like it, but that's the vibe you're putting off. I'm observant as fuck. Don't hate me."

"I'm fine," I insisted stiffly.

"Here's what I'm thinking. You try to get a hold of your 'business associate' Maureen and keep your dinner plans. My bride is working late tonight prepping with her team for some big meeting tomorrow morning. Why don't you let me handle updating Idler?"

I opened my mouth to give him a litany of reasons why that wouldn't be happening, but he pressed on.

"I'll keep the madam out of it for now and stick to the sweet little shell company your team of hackers untangled fifteen minutes ago."

"What shell company?" I demanded. "And for legal reasons, you can't call them hackers."

"The one digital security specialist Prairie texted me about."

"Why didn't she contact me directly?"

"Because you're a scary motherfucker, man. No one actually *likes* talking to you. You make small talk feel like a root canal without anesthesia."

"I do not," I argued, feeling surly.

"Karen is Sloane's mom, isn't she?" he asked.

"Yes."

"There are certain jobs you're uniquely suited for. Looking a politician in the eyes while you destroy his career. Forking over a few million when the situation calls for it. Calling the woman who runs the highest-priced call girl ring in the metro area. And visiting your friend while she's mourning her husband. I've got the rest of it covered."

I blew out a breath. "You aren't completely worthless as an employee."

"Thanks, boss. Those gold stars you're handing

out get me right here," he said, thumping his chest.

My phone rang again. This time it was Petula. "What?" I snapped after hitting the Answer button on the console.

Nolan looked at me pointedly. I rolled my eyes.

"Hello, Petula. What can I do for you?" I said with exaggerated politeness.

"Are you all right, sir? Are you under duress? I can have a security team to your location in minutes."

"I'm fine," I said dryly.

"Don't worry, Petula. I won't let anything happen to the boss man," Nolan announced.

"I'm delighted to hear that," she said dryly. "However, we have a problem."

"What is it?" I demanded, my mind still focused on Duncan, Felix, and now Maureen.

"When Holly went out to pick up lunch, she was chased by two men in a black Chevy Tahoe."

I accelerated out of the parking lot.

"Is she all right?" Nolan asked.

His hand closed covertly over the door handle as the car fishtailed onto the road.

"She's fine. A little shaken up. But her car wasn't so lucky," Petula reported. "She got a partial license plate."

"Run it," I said curtly. "We'll be there in half an hour."

"Black Tahoe sittin' all by her lonesome," Nolan reported. He handed me his binoculars.

309

I frowned. "Where did you get those?"

"Never leave home without binoculars, a pocket knife, and snacks," he said sagely. "Want some beef jerky?"

"What I want is payback," I muttered, peering through the binoculars and spotting the SUV in the parking lot of the luxury condo building.

The vehicle was registered to one of Hugo's corporations. According to the mortgage on the three-bedroom Alexandria condo, it was owned by one of Hugo's enforcers.

"Did you tell security to—"

"Deliver the company Escalade to Holly's place?" Nolan said. "Yeah. Lina and Petula are going along to make sure the kid isn't still freaked out. Hell of an upgrade over a twelve-year-old sedan with primer-gray trunk."

I handed the binoculars back to him and said nothing.

It was the least I could do.

I'd been prepared for Hugo's escalation, but I'd been anticipating him escalating things with me, not an employee on a salad run. He'd sent a message, made an example. I'd overestimated his sense of fair play, and one of my people paid the price. It wouldn't happen again.

"Stay here," I ordered and opened the van door.

I'd borrowed a cargo van from the security team. It was my turn to send a message.

"Sorry, boss. No can do," Nolan slipped out the passenger door. He pulled a black wool cap out of his coat pocket and yanked it down over his head.

"I'm about to break half a dozen laws," I warned before rounding the back of the vehicle.

"And here I thought you'd have minions for that," Nolan said, opening the cargo doors.

I grabbed the sledgehammer. "Sometimes it's better to get your own hands dirty. And by that I mean my hands, not yours."

He picked up the six-foot coil of material off the van floor. "Can't let you have all the fun. Besides, if we get caught, your scary lawyers will have me out before my ass touches a holding cell bench."

I was oddly touched.

I gave an exasperated sigh. "Fine. Let's go play with fire." I didn't wait for an answer and headed into the shadows.

"Never got to have fun like this in my last job," Nolan whispered gleefully behind me.

"You're late," Karen announced, opening the door with feigned motherly disappointment.

I leaned down and pressed a kiss to her cheek. I was late and exhausted, but vengeance had dulled the rage. Now I was almost cheerful. It had been a while since I'd gotten my hands dirty.

"I'm sorry. There was a situation that I needed to deal with," I explained, slipping off my coat.

"Hmm, you're late, you smell like gasoline and smoke, and your coat is torn," she noted as I hung it on the rack inside the door.

"All reasons why I could use a large glass of this mediocre wine you promised."

The explosion had happened a little earlier than anticipated. Nolan's giddy "Holy fucking shit!" still rang in my ears.

Knox would have been proud. Nash would have been furious. As for me, I was starting to appreciate Nolan as more than a minion.

"Follow me, my dear," Karen said, leading the way toward the kitchen.

The condo was nothing like the family home in Knockemout. I'd chosen it for proximity to the hospital, not personality. But in the two years that they'd lived here, Karen had managed to convert the off-white-walled, blank slate into a comfortable home.

The large, framed photo of Simon, Sloane, and me the day Sloane got her driver's license caught my attention as it always did. Though this time, it delivered a punch to the gut in addition to the twinge of regret I usually felt.

Simon wasn't waiting for me in the kitchen like he had been for so many years of my life. I didn't know how Karen managed to stay here surrounded by memories of a life she'd never get back.

She was barefoot and casually dressed in a pair of leggings and an oversize sweater. Her hair was held back from her face with a wide, paisley-patterned headband.

I liked that there was no formality among the Waltons. The women I dated—however briefly—

312

were never seen without a full face of makeup, their hair perfectly coiffed, and their wardrobes ready to be whisked away to the symphony, Paris, or a black-tie fundraiser.

"You sit. I'll pour," Karen insisted when we entered the small but efficient kitchen. She'd painted the walls a sunny yellow and swapped out the sedate white quartz countertops for terra-cotta tiles topped with cobalt-blue accessories.

I pulled out an upholstered stool in tangerine corduroy and reached for the appetizer plate. There was always a can of my favorite smoked almonds in Karen Walton's pantry. She stocked them alongside Maeve's favorite cereal and Sloane's root beer as if I too were one of the family.

"How is it being back?" I asked.

She slid a wineglass in my direction and picked up her own. "Terrible. Okay. Haunting. Comforting. A never-ending misery. A relief. You know, the usual."

"We could have rescheduled," I said.

Karen managed a small, pitying smile as she moved to the oven. "Sweetie, when will you learn that sometimes being alone is the last thing you need?"

"Never."

She snorted and opened the oven door, filling the room with the scent of store-bought pizza.

I got off my stool and rounded the island to nudge her out of the way.

"You get the salad, I'll cut the slices. You

always cut them crooked," I teased. She also never remembered to wash the cheese off the pizza cutter, which resulted in a congealed mess that required serious muscle.

She handed over the utensil. "Teamwork makes the dream work."

We both froze. I'd heard the phrase a few hundred thousand times in the Walton kitchen, mostly from Simon when he and Karen shared meal prep duties.

I didn't know where to look. The glimpse of raw grief as it flitted across her face was like a knife to my heart. I wasn't equipped to deal with emotions like that. I handled problems, presented solutions. I didn't navigate personal loss with someone, no matter how much I loved them.

Karen was more a mother to me than my own. And Simon had been the kind of father I wished I'd deserved.

She cleared her throat and pasted a cheerful look on her pretty face. "How about we just pretend everything is normal for a while?" she suggested.

"Fine. But don't think that I'll let you win at rummy just because you're a widow now," I warned.

Karen's laugh was nothing like Sloane's. It was a loud, joyous guffaw that made my chest feel warm and bright. Sloane's was a throaty chuckle that went straight to my gut.

I could picture her across the table, smiling at me as if we weren't poison to each other.

A sharp burning sensation against my thumb yanked me back to the present moment.

I adjusted my grip on the potholder.

I'd managed to set fire to a vehicle without burning myself, but give me a frozen pizza and time to think about a certain blond librarian and my guard crumbled.

I forcibly blocked the vexatious vixen from my mind and focused on the Walton woman before me.

It was late by the time I got home and showered the arson off me. I collapsed on my king-size bed and blew out a long breath.

The lamp on my nightstand cast a quiet glow on my copy of *The Midnight Library*. I wondered if she was reading right now. Or if maybe, just maybe she was lying in her bed thinking of me.

I doubted it. Every time I saw Sloane, she looked both surprised and disappointed to realize I still existed.

I shouldn't be the only one losing sleep. I picked up my phone. It took me a minute to settle on the right approach. I scrolled through my contacts, found the one I was looking for, and sent it off.

When the message wasn't immediately read, I threw the phone onto the bedspread next to me and covered my face with my hands.

I was an idiot. A weak, undisciplined idiot.

Just because we'd managed to share a civil lunch together didn't mean . . .

The phone vibrated against the plush bedspread. I dove for it.

Sloane: What did you just send me?
Me: The contact information for an attorney who specializes in appeals. She's expecting your call tomorrow. You're welcome.

I saw three dots appear, then disappear. I stared at the screen, willing them to reappear. Thirty seconds later, they did.

Sloane: Thanks.

It took that much effort for her to type one word to me?

What was I even doing? I could have had an assistant send her the information. Hell, I could have had an assistant give the information to Lina, who actually worked in my office. I didn't need to be texting Sloane at—I swiveled to glare at the clock. It was almost midnight.

Disgusted with myself, I tossed my phone on the nightstand and stacked my hands under my head.

The phone vibrated again.

I pulled a neck muscle pouncing on it.

Sloane: Lina told me what happened to Holly today. Is she okay?

Rubbing my neck, I debated waiting to respond, then decided I was too tired to play games.

Me: Everyone is fine.
Sloane: Are you okay?

Was I? I didn't *feel* okay. I felt like things were unspooling, slipping from my fingers. I'd made a career of foreseeing every contingency, every play. Yet I'd missed this one. What else was I missing? And why was I slipping now?

Me: I'm fine.
Sloane: My phone has this cool bullshit detector app, and that "sorry, wrong answer" buzzer noise just went off. It scared the cat.
Me: I'm fine. Just tired.
Sloane: You do know it's not your job to protect everyone from everything, don't you?

But it was my job to protect my people from my actions and the consequences of those actions.

Me: I saw your mother tonight.

No dots appeared. I'd pushed too far. Or she'd fallen asleep.

I was just dumping my phone on the nightstand again when it rang.

317

"What?"

"You really need to work on your phone etiquette." Sloane's voice was husky in my ear. It made me think of those fleeting perfect moments from before. Falling asleep next to her on a pile of pillows in a nice bedroom in a safe house. I hated that my body so viscerally remembered those times. "How's she doing?"

"She's holding up," I said, wincing at the pain in my neck as I adjusted the pillows behind me the way teenage Sloane had.

"Maeve and I call her every day, but it's hard to tell if she's hiding stuff from us."

"She put the ashes on top of the refrigerator," I told her.

Sloane let out a soft, sad laugh. "He'd like that."

"He would," I agreed.

She was quiet for a long beat, and I worried she was about to hang up.

"So did you go beat the crap out of whoever ran Holly off the road?" she asked.

"Now, why would I do that?"

"Because you're you."

"Let's just say they won't be running anyone off the road anytime soon," I told her.

"Nash told me that you kicked Jonah Bluth's ass at football practice because he was talking shit about me in high school."

Nash had a big mouth to go along with that shiny badge.

"I have no recollection—"

"Errr!"

Sloane's wrong answer buzzer *almost* made me smile.

"So what did you not do to these guys?"

"Nolan and I made sure they didn't have a vehicle to run anyone off the road with and that the local police knew where to look when Holly reported the incident."

"Look at you and Nolan becoming buddy guys. Did you go for a buddy guy beer afterward?"

I'd actually had a scotch to Nolan's Coors Light.

"Don't be ridiculous."

I wondered what she was wearing. If she was in bed or if she was curled up on the couch, lipstick still on, book in her lap. My cock stirred.

I pressed the palm of my hand to my groin. I didn't get spontaneous erections . . . unless I was near her. I was an adult in control of his baser instincts. The husky phone voice of the woman who had nearly destroyed me shouldn't have this effect on me.

"So you cleaned up the mess, got back at the bad guy. Now what?"

"What do you mean?" I repeated.

Was it just Sloane's voice that had me thickening with arousal? Or was this a symptom of something else? Of me losing control, my edge.

Me sending a message to Anthony Hugo wasn't going to stop him from making more moves. I wanted him to. Because sooner or later, he'd slip up, and I'd exploit that mistake to beat him.

319

"I can practically hear the fury dripping off your syllables, big guy. Someone messed with one of your employees. You handled it. But how do you blow off steam when justice doesn't take away the mad?"

I scoffed. "I don't need to blow off steam."

"Personally, I'm a fan of sweaty, dirty sex. It always seems to set the world right again," Sloane said cheerfully. "You should try it sometime."

A strangled sound tore free from my throat. My cock pulsed and I pressed my palm over it, hoping to suffocate the arousal. I wasn't going to sit here having a conversation on the phone with a woman and jerk off. Even if that woman was Sloane.

She laughed softly. "Only messing with you, Lucifer."

But I could picture her sprawled beneath me. Her hair fanned over a pillow like a halo. Those milky thighs locked around my hips. Her breasts half an inch from heaving out of one of those useless tops with the spaghetti straps.

"Oh, so you don't actually enjoy sweaty, dirty sex?" I shot back.

"Wouldn't you like to know?" She all but purred the words in my ear.

I didn't know what the right move was, what tactic I should employ. Because I couldn't have what I wanted. I didn't want what I wanted.

"Why are you still awake?" I asked gruffly.

"Some pain in the ass wouldn't stop texting me," she said lightly.

I could hear the smile in her voice, could picture it in my mind. That slow, sultry curve of her lips usually reserved for anyone who wasn't me.

This was a mistake. I was making another mistake. I couldn't stop myself. Sloane was the bad habit I couldn't quit.

"You should go to bed," I said.

"Geez. Maybe you should take a class in how to talk to people without sounding like an ass."

"I don't have time for pillow talk with you."

"That settles it. My next book club selection is going to be something about *Dr. Jekyll and Mr. Hyde*. Maybe then I'll understand why you go from almost human to Lucifer between two sentences."

It was a dance we'd been locked into for years. Every time one of us showed a side that was a little too human, the other managed to strike. Walls were rebuilt, animosity reinforced. We kept relearning the same lesson over and over again, but it never stuck. We weren't good for each other. I wasn't good for her. And I could never trust a woman who had so thoroughly betrayed me.

"Don't waste your time thinking about me. I don't waste any of mine on you," I told her.

With her gasp ringing in my ear, I disconnected the call, switched off the light, and lay in the dark hating myself.

18

Ruins of the Past

Sloane

I dragged the recycling bin up the short stretch of concrete, around Lucian's Range Rover, and plunked it down in front of his garage door. It was a dark, damp Saturday evening.

It had been one of those days where one thing went wrong followed by everything else spiraling out of control. The computers in the library had crashed for over an hour, my shipment of paperbacks for the Valentine's Day author signing arrived missing their covers, *and* I'd squeezed in a fourth blind date in hopes that BeardedByron223 would turn out to be better than my last three matches.

He was not. BeardedByron was neither bearded nor a fan of Lord Byron. He'd shown up late and drunk, and in the middle of me telling him it wasn't going to work out, he took a phone call from his current girlfriend and told her he was at the gym.

He was so not better than the last three that I had plans to curl up tonight by the fire with the sperm bank's website. If I couldn't find a date with future husband potential, maybe I'd have better luck with a child.

To add to my already bad mood, I'd spent the past few days ruminating about Lucian. Lucian having dinner with my mom. Lucian texting me from bed. Lucian generously giving his employee a brand-new SUV. Lucian almost kissing me in his office. Lucian working with the FBI to take down one of the most dangerous criminals in the Mid-Atlantic region area. Lucian naked, crooking his finger at me.

That last one hit me in the shower yesterday after I spied his Range Rover in the driveway. Then again right before bed . . . and when I woke up . . .

I liked it better when I only occasionally remembered that the man existed.

We were on a never-ending roller coaster of insults, sexual awareness, bitterness, and flirtation. And it was time to put an end to it. I wanted to get off this ride so I could focus my energy on what I actually wanted . . . which was *not* Lucian Rollins.

I marched up the walkway to his front door, finger poised to jab his doorbell, when the door swung open.

"What?" Lucian demanded.

He was missing a jacket, tie, and shoes but was still dressed in tailored trousers and an Oxford with his sleeves rolled to the elbows. His socks were a fancy plaid pattern. He looked like he'd just strolled off the pages of *Rich Guy Weekend* magazine.

He also looked annoyed, tired, and obnoxiously sexy. A woman who didn't know what a pain in the ass he was would have been tempted to shoo him back inside with promises of hot, homemade soup and a night of forgetting his troubles.

But Lucian Rollins didn't deserve homemade soup.

"I'm sure you're used to having your butler drag your trash bins back inside in the city, but around here, we do it ourselves," I announced.

"Why would I need a butler when I have an overbearing neighbor who can't seem to remember to put on a fucking coat?" he shot back.

"I don't think you should be working with the FBI," I snapped, going with the first item on my mental list of problems that I had with him. Well, the first problem that didn't involve my inconvenient physical attraction to him.

With an eye roll, he reached out, fisted his hand in the front of my sweatshirt, and pulled me inside.

"Excuse me! Didn't anyone ever tell you kidnapping women on your doorstep is rude?"

"Didn't anyone tell you screaming shrewishly about private business in public places is dangerous?"

I stuffed my hands into the pocket of my hoodie. "I'll give you the shrewish part, but I did *not* scream."

"How generous of you."

"I stand by my statement," I said, looking around.

The TV in the living room was on to some kind

of financial news report. There was an empty bowl and an open laptop on the ottoman. Flames danced cozily in the fireplace. Yet the room still managed to feel somber, lonely even. Gray walls, gray couch, scratchy-looking ivory pillows. It felt soulless. Except for the music.

I frowned. "Is that Shania Twain?"

Swearing under his breath, Lucian hit a button on his phone and the music stopped. "We're not discussing the FBI, Anthony Hugo, or my personal business. So unless there's another topic you'd care to yell at me about, you can show yourself out."

I blew out a breath. "Thank you for the referral to the attorney," I said. "I had a call with her yesterday and sent her everything I had on Mary Louise."

"So you came to yell at me *and* thank me?" he asked, sounding slightly less irritated.

I shrugged. "I'm a complicated woman."

"Noted. Now, if you're done shrewing, I'd like to enjoy my house without you in it."

"I don't think that's a word. And I'm not leaving until you hear me out. I've been thinking about this a lot—"

He smirked. "You've been thinking about me? Shouldn't you be too busy finding Mr. Right to give me a passing thought?"

I glared at him. "I've got a big brain, Lucifer. There's room for lots of stuff up there."

"Have you found him?" he asked.

325

I didn't quite suppress the shudder that rolled up my spine as my recent dating shenanigans tap-danced onto center stage in my mind.

"Not yet," I said with forced positivity. "I didn't come to talk about my dating life."

"Then why did you come?" he pressed, looking vaguely amused.

"To yell at you about the trash bins. Weren't you listening?"

"You've been on how many dates and still haven't found a suitable candidate?" he asked.

My eyes narrowed. "Listen, Rollins, this isn't hiring an employee to fetch you coffee and smoothies made from the blood of puppies. Finding your life partner should be . . ." Disheartening? Physically painful? Excruciatingly depressing? "Challenging," I said out loud.

He crossed his arms and leaned against the cased opening to the living room. "Elaborate."

"I'm not discussing my dating life with you."

"There's nothing to be ashamed of. I'm sure them not calling you back is a them thing and not a you thing."

"It's not them ghosting me! Well, except for that one guy. But that was more literal ghosting. Do you even know what ghosting is?"

"I work with a twenty-two-year-old who insists on talking all the time about things I don't care about. Not only do I know what ghosting is, I could name all the Kardashians if pressed."

"Is she okay? Holly, I mean."

"She's fine," he said curtly.

"I was thinking about it. Have you considered that the men who chased her—"

"Back to the ghosting," he insisted.

I shook my head. "Nope."

Those cool gray eyes went shrewd. "I'll give you an entire Stucky's soft pretzel if you tell me."

I scoffed. "You can't just bribe me with food."

That was a lie. Stucky's pretzels were the size of my face and irresistibly flaky.

"It's cinnamon and sugar . . . with caramel sauce," he added.

Dammit. My favorite. I glared at him. He stared back. The staring contest lasted until my stomach growled like a damn traitor. I'd missed lunch during the computer fiasco and hadn't gotten around to dinner yet.

"Fine," I conceded. "But I'm only telling you because you'll hear about it anyway in our weird little incestuous group of big mouths."

Stef, Naomi, and Lina had already been thoroughly entertained by the story.

"I'm all ears," Lucian said.

"Uh-uh. First I wanna see the pretzel."

A hint of amusement played across his lips. I wondered how he kept his beard trimmed so neatly. Did he have a special razor, or did he have a beard guy who came to his house every other day?

"Come on then," he said, heading in the direction of the kitchen, his socked feet making no noise as he walked.

I had a feeling I was going to regret this, but at least I'd get a pretzel out of it.

Just like the living room, the kitchen and dining area were ruthlessly clean. As if the rooms had just been sanitized or were only staged to make it look as if someone lived there. I wondered what the inside of his refrigerator looked like. Would I find expired jars of mustard like in everyone else's kitchen, or would there be more ruthless sterility? Did vegetables dare rot in Lucian's crisper drawer?

He flipped the lid on a pink bakery box and angled it my way.

My mouth watered.

There was only one pretzel.

"Even though you're you and I'm me, I can't take your last pretzel. Why do you even have this? Don't you subsist on a diet of egg whites and unicorn hoof?" The man took discipline to a whole new, annoying level.

"I'm willing to part with it in exchange for the story of the man who ghosted Sloane Walton."

"You make it sound like a children's book."

"You're stalling," he said, getting a plate out of the cabinet.

I really wanted that pretzel. "Fine. But let's split the pretzel. I hope to be getting naked for a stranger soon, and I need to be in decent, non-baked-good shape."

Wordlessly, he produced a second plate, then cut the doughy goodness into two equal halves.

I salivated as he put both plates in the microwave.

"Talk."

"Okay, fine." I planted myself on one of the stools he had parked under the peninsula. "So I match with this guy named Gary. According to his profile, he's a pediatric nurse who enjoys reading, hiking, and spending time with his nieces and nephews."

"Clearly he's an asshole," Lucian teased.

I ignored the jab and continued. "He sounds normal in his messages, so I agree to dinner. After the last fiasco that you had a front row seat to, Nash and Lina decided to go along as backup. They got a table near us, and small talk commences. He seems nice enough, but when I ask him about his job, he doesn't seem to know anything about hospitals or nursing or children. He keeps asking me stuff like 'How much money does a librarian make?' and what kind of car I have and do I have any retirement savings."

Lucian closed his eyes and pinched the bridge of his nose.

The microwave dinged. He opened it, releasing the smell of cinnamony deliciousness.

"I'm definitely suspicious by this point, so I give Nash and Lina the sign, and they come running up and tell me my uncle Horace just fell off a ladder, and they whisk me away."

He put one of the plates in front of me and dug two forks out of the utensil drawer.

I wasted no time yanking the lid off the caramel sauce and dipping my first bite in it. "Anyway, we're on our way home, and Gary calls. I, of course, let it go to voicemail. Oh my God, this is divine," I moaned as the flavors melted in my mouth.

Lucian took a smaller, more dignified bite of his half. "What did Gary have to say?"

I pulled out my phone. "Listen for yourself."

I scrolled through my voicemails and pushed Play.

"Hey, Sloane. This is Gary. I just wanted to check in and see how your uncle is—Oh my God! Ahhh!" His voice was replaced with the sound of a revving engine, squealing tires, and finally a spectacular crash. Then the sound of static filled the kitchen.

Lucian shook his head. "You can't be serious."

"Go on. I know you're dying to say it," I said, gesturing with my fork.

"He's scamming you."

I held up a finger and pushed Play on the next message.

"Hey, uh, this is Vick Verkman, a friend of Gary's. I don't know how to tell you this, but Gary was in a terrible accident last night. He's in a coma, and the hospital is threatening to unplug him unless someone pays his hospital bills. He keeps whispering your name."

Lucian put down his fork. "Vick Verkman's voice sounds a lot like Gary."

"Oh, just wait," I said, playing the next message.

"Sloane? This is Mercedes, Gary's mom. I'm

sorry to tell you that Gary passed away last night from injuries sustained in a car accident he had while worrying about you and your uncle. The funeral home is threatening to keep his body unless we pay them—"

I stopped the message and took another bite of soft pretzel.

Lucian rolled his eyes. "Tell me you didn't send him money."

I grinned. "I texted his 'mom' back and asked her where I could send the check. She suggested I write it out to Gary Jessup and mail it to his home address so his 'estate could handle it.' "

"He gave you his real name and address after he faked his own death?"

"Yep. It made it easy to report him to the app and track down his employment so I could send a funeral arrangement of flowers with my condolences to him there."

"Where does he work?" Lucian asked, picking up his fork again.

I swirled warm pretzel through the caramel puddle on the plate. "For one of those skeezy debt collection places. You know the kind. They buy medical or mortgage debt for pennies on the dollar and then try to collect on it by harassing people. I think it was called Morganstern Credit Corporation."

Lucian said nothing as he took another bite. He was eating standing up, leaning against the sink, the counter between us.

"What? No 'You're so undesirable men fake their own deaths to get away from you' jokes?" I asked.

"Too many punch lines. I froze," he said. "Why are you subjecting yourself to this?"

"To spending time with you?" I asked, coyly batting my eyelashes.

"I know you're only here for the baked goods."

I savored my last bite and refrained from licking the drizzle of gooey goodness from the plate. "I want a family. It's time."

I got up and rounded the peninsula. Silently, Lucian slid to the side, allowing me access to the sink. I washed the plate and fork, then left them to dry.

"You're serious about all this, aren't you?"

He sounded baffled, and I glanced up at him. There wasn't enough space between us, which created an odd, barefoot intimacy.

"I'd think you of all people would understand. Haven't you ever made up your mind about something you wanted and then gone out and got it? Or in your case, coughed up a few million and bought yourself whatever it was you wanted."

He nudged me out of the way, my body heating at the innocuous contact. I put a little distance between us and hopped up on the counter while he washed his dishes, then used the towel looped over the oven handle to dry both our plates before returning them to their respective homes.

Meticulous, I noted. The man couldn't tolerate

things out of place. He probably folded his socks before sex.

"That's very pragmatic of you," he said.

I bristled from my perch. "I can be pragmatic."

He glanced my way, and I felt the heat from those molten silver eyes.

"In many areas, yes," he conceded. "But given your usual reading material, I would have expected you to prioritize romance."

"What nonsense are you spouting now?" I demanded.

"You've been reading romance novels by the truckload since you were a teenager. You practically have 'happily ever after' tattooed on your forehead."

I crossed my arms. Did I wish I could meet someone who would sweep me off my feet like Naomi and Lina had? Yes. Was I more than a little jealous of their over-the-top sex lives and grand romances? Absolutely.

"Sometimes you have to stop waiting for something to happen and start making it happen," I said.

"I don't believe you."

"I don't care," I snapped back.

His grin was devastating and fleeting.

I examined my fingernails and feigned boredom. "Just out of curiosity, what don't you believe?"

"You're not going to settle for a man just because he ticks off the 'potential father material' box. That's not how you're wired."

"Oh, and how exactly am I wired?"

He moved quickly, like a beast lunging for its prey. I found him standing between my knees, caging me in with his hands on the counter. "You're wired to want a man who's going to live up to every one of those heroes you read about. The ones who fight for their woman, who drag her off into dark corners because they can't stand not touching her a moment longer. The ones who would do anything for her. That's what you want."

His voice was a rough rasp, an invisible caress.

Why did it feel so good, so thrilling to be this close to him?

"This is starting to feel like your office all over again," I warned.

His eyes narrowed, but he didn't budge. He stayed where he was, almost touching me in a dozen places.

"Don't settle," he said. "You'll regret it for the rest of your life."

"Are you seriously giving me love life advice right now?"

"I'm merely pointing out that you could be lining yourself up for more trouble by forcing things to happen instead of letting them unfold."

"That's easy for you to say. You can have kids when you're seventy-five."

"No. I can't. I had a vasectomy."

My mouth fell open. "What? When? *Why?*"

He pushed away from me and stood in the center

of the room, looking supremely uncomfortable. "You should go," he announced.

But I was riveted. "I mean, you don't have to tell me. Even though *I* just spilled my guts to you about my very personal, humiliating dating life. Don't feel like you owe me anything."

"I gave you a pretzel."

"Half a pretzel," I pointed out.

For a moment, I thought he was going to close down again, like he always did. Then he gritted out a sigh. "I was in my twenties. There was a pregnancy scare with a girl who didn't matter. I already knew I had no intentions of ever starting a family, so I made sure it wouldn't happen."

"Wow. That's a big decision to make when you're that young," I observed.

"I haven't changed my mind, so you can stop looking at me like that."

"Like what?"

"Like you pity me."

I snorted. "I don't pity you, you gigantic oaf. I'm just . . . surprised. I guess I always just assumed you were more calculating with your decisions. That seems like a knee-jerk reaction."

"This conversation is annoying me. You should leave," he announced.

"Lucian." All the aggravation, the frustration that roiled inside me came out in those two syllables.

"What?" he asked quietly.

"Why do we keep getting on this roller coaster?" I asked.

"I always thought of it as more of a dance," he countered.

"Roller coaster, dance, series of huge mistakes. What are we doing, Lucifer?"

He locked eyes with me, and I felt as if I was frozen to the spot.

"We're holding on to something that doesn't exist anymore," he said flatly.

I absorbed the blow and sighed out a breath.

"How do we let go of something that doesn't exist?" I asked.

"If I figure it out, I'll let you know . . . in a letter . . . from my attorney."

My lips quirked. That was the magic of Lucian. I could hate him, and he could still make me smile. "Did you ever want a family?" I asked.

"Once. A long time ago," he said, his voice low.

I bit my lip and tried to avoid the barrage of memories.

"You should go, Pix."

"You don't have to be like them," I told him. "You're already better. I mean, besides your terrible personality. You'd do it better than they did."

He was already shaking his head. "I invest my time in what matters most. I don't have any left over for a wife and kids. I'd only be putting them at risk."

I straightened. "I talked to Nash about you working with the FBI—"

"Of course you did."

The roller coaster was inching its way up that first hill.

"You told me not to worry. You didn't say 'don't talk to your friend.' "

"You haven't changed in the least," he snapped.

Actually, I'd gone up a cup size since I was sixteen. But that didn't feel relevant in this conversation.

"And *you're* a completely different person than you used to be," I pointed out.

"I have work to do, and you're annoying me," he said.

"I talked to Nash, your *friend,* and he isn't too thrilled about you becoming BFFs with the FBI." Nash's exact words had been something along the lines of "it gives me fucking heartburn."

"I don't care." Lucian's tone was just flippant enough it made me want to march into the living room, pick up one of the scratchy pillows, and hurl it at him.

"We both couldn't help but wonder if it was Anthony Hugo's men who went after Holly," I said.

"It's none of your business. But if it was Hugo's men, then I just proved my point. I do things that get people close to me hurt," he snapped, that beautiful facade cracking just enough for me to catch a glimpse beneath.

"Lucian," I said softly.

He held up his hand. "Don't. I'd like you to go."

I crossed my arms. "Not until you tell me where

the investigation stands. Are you in danger? Are the rest of your employees taking precautions?"

"I'm not discussing this with you," he said and headed out of the kitchen.

I followed him into the hall. "You said the guy who sold Hugo the list turned up dead. Felix Metzer, right?"

Lucian stopped with his hand on the doorknob. "How did you know that?"

"It's not that hard to search the news for dead bodies pulled out of the Potomac."

"The news didn't identify him," he countered.

"I'm a fucking librarian. I have literal resources."

"You're *not* getting involved in this, Sloane."

His tone was icy and hard.

"I'm not asking to be involved. All I'm asking for is answers. Is the FBI close to making an arrest? Is Hugo going to retaliate again, and if so, are Lina and Nolan targets? If the guy who sold Duncan the list is dead, does that mean it's a dead end? Is the FBI looking into financial crimes because those carry more charges? It's not as sexy as convicting him for murdering people, but it's usually easier to prove—"

"This is none of your business. *I* am none of your business."

"Just convince me that you're smarter and faster and more diabolical than some mob boss who's managed to operate the family business for forty years without getting arrested once. Then I'll leave you alone."

"I don't have to convince you of anything except getting out of my house, Sloane."

He looked like he was edging past mad straight into fury.

"Look. Since you don't seem to have a pack of family or friends giving you advice, you're stuck with me. Messing with Anthony Hugo is a bad idea. He'll retaliate. Let the FBI build their case, and stay out of it."

I didn't know why it was so important to me that he heard me. But it was.

"Your opinion is noted," he said coldly.

I stood. "Why are you doing this?"

"Why?" he scoffed. "He tried to take from me."

I planted myself in front of him. "So you're going to spend your life doing what? Taking down every single person who ever wronged you?"

"I don't have to explain myself to you."

I blew out a breath and tried a different tactic. "I get that your father made you feel powerless, but—"

"Not another word."

He used his scary voice on me. But it only succeeded in riling me.

"You can't spend your entire adult life righting the wrongs your father committed. He's already behind bars—"

"Not anymore."

"What? He got out of *prison?*" My voice escalated into dog-whistle octaves.

"No. He died."

I blinked rapidly and brought a hand to my forehead to stop the hallway from spinning. "He *died?*"

"Last summer."

"Last summer?"

"You don't need to repeat everything I say," Lucian pointed out.

I rubbed my temples. "Why wasn't I notified?"

His brow furrowed. "Why would you be notified?"

"Because as a victim of Ansel Fucking Rollins, I'm supposed to be alerted every time he's moved or up for parole or fucking dead! Because I testified before the parole board every single time he was up for release to make sure that monster stayed where he belonged." I threw my hands up in the air. "What the hell kind of justice is him just dying? Tell me it was at least horrifically painful."

"You testified?" His voice was a strangled rasp. Hands reached out and closed around my biceps in a warm, firm grip. Gone was the unflappable Lucian, and in his place was a man on fire.

"Of course I did. Dad went with me every time. I was worried about going back without him this year, but I would have done it."

"No one asked you to do that. It wasn't your responsibility to keep him in there," he said, still sounding as if he were about to erupt.

"How did it happen?" I asked.

He took a deep breath, let it out. "A stroke in his

sleep. I'm told it was painless." The words landed bitterly.

"Painless." I choked out a humorless laugh. My father had spent his last weeks on earth suffering, and Ansel Rollins escaped peacefully in his sleep.

"Your father didn't tell me you went before the parole board," Lucian said.

"Why would he?" I asked, pulling out of his grip so I could pace. I thought better when I moved. "I can't believe this. They should both be here."

"Who?"

I stopped my frenetic pacing to look up at him. "Our fathers. Mine should be here because he was good and kind and smart and wonderful. He should be here playing with his granddaughter, planning a Mediterranean cruise with Mom, and helping us get Mary Louise out of prison. And that vile excuse for a human being who called himself your father should be here suffering every minute of every day for what he did to you."

"And you," Lucian said quietly.

I ignored him and marched into the living room. There I picked up one of the scratchy throw pillows, held it against my face, and let loose the scream that had been building in my throat.

"What the hell are you doing?" he asked, having the audacity to sound almost amused.

I tossed the pillow back on the couch. "I don't know. It's something Naomi does. I thought it would help."

"Did it?"

"No. I am so enraged right now, you should probably leave."

"This is my house," he pointed out.

"Fine," I huffed. "I'll go break my own stuff until I feel better." I headed for the front door.

He caught me just as my hand closed around the doorknob and planted his palm against the door, holding it shut.

"Back off, Lucian," I hissed without turning around.

"Why are you so angry?" he asked.

I whirled around to face him. "You're kidding me, right?"

"Sloane," he said almost gently.

"I'm *angry* because he hurt you and your mother. He ruined you. And he gets to just, what? Escape it all? *Peacefully?*"

Oh, for fuck's sake. One hot, angry tear spilled over and carved a path down my face.

He took me by the shoulders. "Don't you *dare* shed a single tear over him."

"Don't you *dare* tell me how to feel about this."

"He didn't ruin me," he insisted. "I didn't let him stop me from building this life."

"Lucian, what life?" My voice cracked.

"I have more money and power than—"

"You have *things*. You have millions of dollars and acquaintances in high places. You work every waking hour of the day. But none of that made you happy. You rescued the family name so it would never be associated with him, and that's great,

342

but that name ends with you. You got a *vasectomy* because he made you believe you were damaged."

His beautiful face turned to stone. "Not everyone gets to be happy, Sloane."

"See? That right there." I shoved a finger in his face. "He ruined you. He ruined us."

For a second, Lucian looked shell-shocked. He looked as if I'd hit him. And then the mask slid into place again. He released me and took a step back.

But now that I'd gotten started, I couldn't stop. I closed the distance between us and said the words I'd been choking on since I was fifteen. "He took a sweet, smart, beautiful boy and made him feel broken. And I will never forgive him for that."

"He didn't ruin me. I am who I am in spite of him."

"No. You're who you are *to* spite him," I countered. "Every time you make a choice based on what he would or wouldn't do, you're still giving him the power. He's still ruining you. First from prison and now from the grave."

Lucian didn't look happy about my astute assessment. He looked downright pissed. His jaw worked under his pristinely trimmed beard. "Think what you will. But one thing he didn't do was ruin us. You did that on your own."

I sucked in a breath and absorbed the punch of his words.

"I apologized for that. I was sixteen."

"And how old are you now? Because once again,

343

you didn't trust me to handle my business. You couldn't be trusted then, and you certainly can't be trusted now."

My head was pounding. The pretzel sat like a brick in my stomach. "You can't forgive me for that? Well, I can't forgive you for letting Ansel win."

"Go the hell home, Sloane."

"Gladly."

I waltzed out the door and slammed it as hard as I could.

19

Mistakes Were Made

Lucian

Twenty-two years ago

I woke with a start, the echo of a sound ringing in my ears. I didn't have the luxury of holding my breath and waiting to see if it was the shadows of a dream or if it was the nightmare I actually lived. I was already pulling on a pair of shorts when I heard it again. The shrill plea drowned out by the snarled accusation.

Dinner was cold.

The house was a mess.

There were muddy footprints in the garage.

Too loud.

Too quiet.

I'd looked at him wrong.

I'd been born.

There was a crash, followed immediately by a broken cry from the first floor as my bare feet hit the stairs. They were too loud for this to have just started. I'd fallen asleep.

Stupid.

I never fell asleep before he did. It wasn't safe. I didn't trust him. But I'd been so fucking tired. Between the last weeks of my senior year, a part-

345

time job, and the pretense of college preparations, I crawled into bed, mine or Sloane's, exhausted.

Mr. Walton had done so much for me.

He'd helped me apply for and get a scholarship and two grants. I wouldn't even have to play football in college. Football had already taken a toll on my body. Football and living with my father. In public, the three of us acted out the same ridiculous farce over and over again, pretending that the darkness didn't exist behind closed doors. That we weren't living the same nightmare over and over again.

But no one can hide the truth forever. Especially not when it was this ugly. I wasn't going to leave this house, not while my parents shared it.

I couldn't. I was the only thing stopping him.

I'd been watching him closely, knowing it was going to happen again. The clock had been reset weeks ago with his last violent explosion. I still didn't have full range of motion back in my shoulder, and my mother had a new scar at the corner of her mouth. She was wasting away before my eyes as if she were erasing herself from reality.

I'd wanted to hurt him that time. Not just stop him but really hurt him that time. I'd wanted to show him what it felt like.

But I'd held myself back. Barely. I'd thought of Mr. Walton and the chessboard as red had bled in on the edges of my vision. Sometimes the best offense is a good defense.

So I'd defended. And then he'd been fine. But I

knew he couldn't stay good for long. The man was a ticking time bomb.

I knew better, yet I'd still fallen asleep. It was my fucking fault.

I flew down the stairs as the sounds of fist against flesh, the dull thud of a body crumpling, and alcohol-fueled shouts tore through the house.

I found them in the living room. He stood over her, right hand clenched in an angry fist. Bicep bulging. Jaw clenched from the rage that ruled him. He'd put on weight while my mother had lost it. Almost as if he were sucking the life out of her like one of those vampires in the books Sloane was obsessed with now.

"I'm sorry," Mom whispered brokenly. She was crumpled against the baseboard. Blood from her face smeared the drywall and floor. It soaked into the T-shirt that hung limply off her bony shoulders.

He kicked her viciously in the ribs.

"Stop!" The command ripped its way out of my throat.

He turned to stare at me with those dead, bloodshot eyes.

"It's the booze," he'd say after he'd sobered up. After Mom had bandaged the knuckles he'd bloodied on us. "It won't happen again."

I hated him. In that moment, time froze, and I was so overwhelmed with hate that my knees threatened to buckle.

"What did you say to me?" he demanded. The words were precise and loaded. He didn't slur

347

when he drank. Everything just got sharper, meaner.

"I said stop," I repeated as that familiar haze of red began to appear. My heartbeat thumped at the base of my skull, and I reveled in the adrenaline that dumped into my bloodstream.

"Lucian, go," Mom pleaded, now on her hands and knees.

He kicked her again without even looking at her. The blow of his boot knocked her back to the floor where she curled into a ball, whimpering.

That was when I saw it. The long, jagged cut on her forearm. The glint of metal in his left hand.

"You don't ever raise your fucking voice to me in my fucking house, boy," he said.

My eyes were fixed on the knife I'd washed and stowed in the block on the kitchen counter. There was blood on the blade. He'd cut her. And now he was brandishing it at me.

"Fuck you!" I shouted. The snap in my head was like a rubber band breaking. I wasn't the dutiful teenage son anymore. I wasn't the peacekeeper or the protector. I was *him*.

A fury like nothing I'd ever felt before propelled me across the room. My hands fisted in his sweaty T-shirt. They looked like his. Big, bruising, capable of destruction.

It stuck in my head, lodged there like a jagged stone.

He seemed distantly surprised. Because I knew my place. I didn't fight back. But tonight I did.

348

Tonight it ended before he ended one of us.

I used his surprise to my advantage and threw him bodily into the wall he'd pinned me and my mother against countless times. My fist flew and connected with his concrete jaw. Pain exploded distantly. I could hear my mother screaming from far away.

He was shouting now. Horrible, disgusting abuse. The kinds of things you saved up for the enemy who took everything from you. Not the son who'd once only wanted to make you proud.

He slashed at me with the blade. But I felt nothing except a burning anger that would never be quenched. A need to destroy. It felt so good to finally unleash it all back on him.

Fresh pain fueled me. I snatched the knife out of his hand and threw it to the floor. His fist caught me in the temple, and everything went sideways. But I didn't crumple. I didn't fall or beg or cry.

I snapped.

I wouldn't stop until he fell. Until *he* begged, *he* cried.

Like father, like son.

I heard it in my head like a mantra on repeat. Over and over again. Over the faraway sound of breaking glass.

Like father, like son.

Over my mother's low wail.

Like father, like son.

I kept going. Kept swinging, kept dodging his fists, kept going even as my head rang. Even as the red changed and became blue and white and then red again.

Sloane

My hands shook as I clutched the cordless phone in them. I wanted to cry or throw up, and before this was over, I was fairly sure I'd do both.

I'd made Lucian a promise. He'd been adamant. But if I didn't do something, someone was going to get hurt. Really hurt.

I'd seen Mr. Rollins come home. The fuel door on his truck still open. He'd swerved into the wrong lane then back again to avoid Mrs. Clemson walking her two Saint Bernards. Shouting profanities at the woman, he'd hit the gas too hard and then slammed on the brakes, stopping mere inches from his own garage door.

There had been so many times over the last year that I wanted to tell my parents. But Lucian had made me promise. I was to stay out of it and let him handle it.

He never talked about it. But I knew enough to watch for the signs. I always left my window unlocked, but on the bad nights, I left it open an inch or two and huddled under a blanket on the window seat, listening.

Since I couldn't stop it from happening, I could at least suffer through it with him.

We were so close in some ways and yet practically strangers in others.

There was the Lucian I saw at school. The

beautiful boy with the entourage. The one who'd wink at me or give my ponytail a tug when no one else was looking.

Then there was the Lucian who had dinner three nights a week at my parents' table. Polite, respectful, quiet. The one who'd volunteered to teach me to drive in the high school parking lot on Sundays after my mom said her blood pressure couldn't take it.

And there was the Lucian who climbed through my window. He was funny and broody and smart and interested in me. We argued for hours over music and movies and books. Sometimes he read what I was reading just so we could talk about it. He'd even coached me through my first real relationship with Trevor Whitmer, a sophomore trombone player with an in-ground pool.

It was June. Lucian's eighteenth birthday was coming up on Tuesday. The same day as his high school graduation. It felt like a ticking clock was hanging over our heads. He was going through the motions of a graduating senior. Summer plans and college T-shirts. But no matter how many times I tried to pin him down about it, he wouldn't open up. Sometimes it seemed like he wanted to know everything about me without giving up anything of himself.

I heard another faint shout carried on the night air and cringed, clutching the phone to my chest.

Lucian almost always came over after. After the fight. After his father had passed out or left again.

After his mother had been soothed. There was no one to look out for him. So I stocked bandages and Neosporin in my nightstand. Sometimes I snuck downstairs to throw ice cubes in a baggie or to forage for snacks.

He trusted me enough to tell me. Maybe that meant he also trusted me to do what was right, even if it was something he didn't want, I rationalized.

I chewed nervously on my lip. I couldn't just sit here in my pretty room with my pretty life and wait for his father to stop hurting him. That wasn't what friends did. That wasn't what you did when you loved someone, and I loved Lucian.

In what way, I wasn't sure. I just knew that I loved him and I couldn't stand to see him hurt anymore.

I shoved the window up and climbed out onto the porch roof.

It was almost midnight. My parents would have been asleep for hours, and I couldn't very well go running into their room, blurt out the whole story, and then ask them to call 911. Could I?

To be fair, my parents were pretty great. They'd call 911 and my dad would run next door and try to calm things down.

I could appreciate the need for de-escalation every once in a while. But Mr. Rollins seemed like the kind of guy who wouldn't even let you finish your first sentence before decking you. And I didn't want my dad to get hurt. Besides, he'd be crushed if he found out what was happening next door. He and Mom would feel guilty that they hadn't seen the signs. And they'd try to make up for it somehow, which would only embarrass Lucian and make him start avoiding me.

I hated Mr. Rollins with the kind of dedicated passion that only great works of fiction seemed to capture. Every time I saw him, I glared my hate into him, willing him to feel it. To turn around and find me shooting poisoned eye daggers at him. To know that he hadn't fooled everyone. That I knew his dirty little secret.

But he never noticed me. Never once glanced in my direction. It was better that way, I supposed. Then when I put my plan into action, he'd have no idea that I'd played a role in his karma.

I had a lot of plans. A whole notebook of them. WAYS TO GET MR. ROLLINS ARRESTED SO LUCIAN CAN GO TO COLLEGE. I'd written that in big, block print with my favorite purple highlighter on the first page. On the outside of the notebook, I'd scrawled GEOGRAPHY NOTES so no one would get snoopy.

The last plan I'd sketched out skipped the "get arrested" part and went straight to the "murder him" part. I'd noticed Mr. Rollins changing the brake pads on his truck in the driveway every few months—probably because he was a drunk and constantly slamming on the brakes to avoid hitting things. I'd thought about sneaking over there while he was under the vehicle and taking the parking brake off.

Then I'd wait until I was sure he'd been crushed before I'd call 911 with a quaver in my voice.

The more realistic plans that didn't involve me committing a homicide, no matter how much he deserved to have his face murdered, centered around drawing the attention of an independent witness.

Like Lucian's football coach who had to wonder about the bruises. Or maybe the neighbors who lived on the other side of the Rollins family. Except Mr. Clemson had a hearing aid that he rarely used, and Mrs. Clemson was so busy talking she never seemed to hear anyone else.

I was going to figure it out, and I was going to make him stop. Then Lucian could go to college and not have to worry about his mom, and he'd be happy. Like really happy.

A muffled shout startled me. It was followed by the sound of breaking glass. Loud breaking glass. As in their living room window, I guessed.

My thumbs punched 911 before I'd even fully made the decision.

A sob broke the eerie silence, and I realized it had come from me.

I was shaking so hard my teeth were chattering.

One of us had to end this tonight. And if it meant he'd hate me for the rest of his life, at least he'd have the rest of his life.

"911. What is your emergency?"

"There's a man hurting his wife and son. It sounds bad. Please send help before it's too late." My voice broke.

"Okay, honey," the operator said in a softer tone. "It's gonna be all right. What's the address?"

It took me two tries to get it out between sobs.

"I've got officers on the way right now."

"Tell them to hurry up and to be careful. Mr. Rollins is a big guy, and he drinks all the time and he drives drunk," I said, spewing out the list of reasons why I hated the man.

"Okay. The police will take care of this," he promised.

"Thank you," I whispered, wiping my eyes on my sleeve. It was cold up here on the roof. Cold and lonely waiting for Lucian to be okay.

"Are these your neighbors?" the operator asked.

I could hear sirens in the far-off distance and willed them closer.

"He's my friend," I whispered.

Lucian

The handcuffs bit into my wrists. Broken glass cut the soles of my feet as Wiley Ogden marched me out the front door. Blood coursed from a dozen cuts on my face and arms. My father had managed to carve a shallow slice over my ribs with the knife before I'd taken it from him. My head hurt, and I was having trouble paying attention to what people were saying. Everything was blurry and muffled.

There were two patrol cars on the street in front of the house and an ambulance parked in the driveway. All three vehicles had their lights on, alerting everyone in the neighborhood to my shame.

There was a small contingent of concerned neighbors in bathrobes.

"What are you doing?" Simon Walton marched toward me, fire in his eyes and cats on his pajama pants.

I looked away, not wanting to see the judgment in the eyes of the man I'd come to think of as a surrogate father. But it wasn't me his ire was directed at. He stepped between me and the chief of police and drilled a finger into Ogden's flabby chest.

"Just what the hell do you think you're doing, Wylie?"

"I'm arresting this punk prick for trying to cut his parents to ribbons with a chef's knife," the chief said loud enough for the neighbors to hear.

"That's not what happened!" The crowd parted, or my vision cleared long enough to bring Sloane into focus.

I looked away quickly, but not before seeing her tear-streaked face. The horror. The guilt. She was still holding the cordless phone.

It was her. She'd called them. She was the reason my life was over. The reason my mother was unprotected. My mother, who had remained silent when my father told the cops I'd attacked them unprovoked.

A wave of nausea rolled through me.

"Sloane, I'll handle this," Mr. Walton insisted. "Uncuff him now, Wylie, or we're going to have an issue."

"I don't take orders from some namby-pamby ambulance chaser," Ogden said, giving me a hard shove forward. My knees buckled, and I went down on them hard on the sidewalk.

Sloane cried out, but I refused to look up.

"Officer Winslow, will you please take care of Lucian while I talk to Chief Ogden?" Mr. Walton said through clenched teeth.

Another cop and an EMT each took an arm and helped me up.

"Hang in there, buddy," the officer said to me quietly as they guided me toward the ambulance.

"Don't bother patching him up. Let him bleed on the way to jail. See how he likes it," Ogden called after them.

I thought I heard the EMT mutter "fucker" under his breath, but I wasn't sure.

The cop eased me into the back of the patrol car, where I collapsed against the seat.

"I'll get you some water, and we'll clean you up down at the station," he promised.

I nodded but didn't open my eyes. There was no point. There was nothing left for me here. This life was over.

"Lucian."

I managed to open my eyes and found Mr. Walton leaning in the open door. "Listen to me. I'll be right behind you. Okay? Don't talk to anyone. If they try to question you, tell them you won't speak unless your lawyer is present."

His tone was calm, soothing.

"What . . ." My voice sounded rusty, and I cleared my throat. "What about my mom?" I rasped.

"They're taking her to the hospital to get her checked out," he said, keeping his voice low.

"Lucian." Sloane's panicked face appeared next to her father's earnest one.

I turned away, not wanting to see her. Not wanting to face the betrayal . . . or the shadows my family had put in those green eyes.

"Go," I said.

"What?" Mr. Walton asked, leaning closer.

"Get her out of here! Please."

"Lucian, I'm sorry—" Sloane began.

"Go stand with your mother, Sloane," Mr. Walton said using his lawyer voice.

My father was standing guard at the back of the ambulance watching me. I knew what he was really doing. Reminding my mother what happened to wives who didn't know their loyalty lay with their husbands instead of their sons.

I didn't blame her. I didn't even know if I blamed Sloane. I just knew that everything I'd fought for for so long was now over. It was all for nothing. I was going to jail. My father would kill my mother. Then he'd either go to jail or drink himself to death. No matter which way the dice landed, this was the end of the Rollins family.

"But, Dad, you can't let them take him. It wasn't him. It wasn't Lucian's fault. Mr. Rollins—"

If he heard her, if he even had an inkling that she knew . . . I wouldn't be there to stop him. I felt sick.

"Enough!" I barked sharply. I still couldn't look at her. She needed to get away from me.

"Lucian." Sloane's whisper was broken.

"Go wait with your mother," Mr. Walton ordered briskly.

I sensed her leaving. A wave of hopelessness crashed over me. "You don't want to get involved in this, Mr. Walton. It's not safe."

He reached in the car and put his hand on my shoulder. "We're not abandoning you, Lucian. You're a good kid on your way to being a good man. I'm going to fix this."

On the way to the police station, I found myself wondering why some people dedicated their lives to fixing things while others set out only to break them. Not that it mattered anymore. I was one of the broken.

20

No One Else Can Have Her

Lucian

Maureen Fitzgerald crossed her long legs at the ankles and smiled her enigmatic smile at me.

"What's so important that you insisted I cut my Parisian shopping spree short?" Her tone was well-modulated. Her posture and diction served to remind her audience of private boarding schools and summers in Europe. Not a single chestnut hair dared escape from the classic twist. Her jewelry was expensive yet tasteful, and her tailored pantsuit exuded both style and money.

But I knew better. The real Maureen was more impressive than some daddy's girl with an inheritance. Like me, she'd created herself out of the nothing she'd been given. Also like me, she'd built a safety net of money, power, and favors.

In her fifties, she managed to turn more heads walking into a room than most of her employees. Which was quite the statement, given the fact that she was in charge of a bevy of beautiful sex workers who kept the wealthy Washington, DC, elite satisfied.

I handed her an espresso on a delicate saucer and took a seat on the edge of the desk I'd commandeered. The hotel manager was outside, probably nervously pacing and wondering why the man who owned this place and signed her paycheck was using her office to meet with the most notorious madam on the East Coast.

"I need information," I said.

"Don't be greedy, Lucian. It's unbecoming."

"Don't pretend you feed me out of the generosity of your heart, Maureen. I've made your life easier in a number of ways."

It was a symbiotic relationship we shared. She divulged information on any problematic clients her workers encountered, and I used the information to make sure there were no further problems. Depending on the individual in question, my tools ran the gamut from blackmail to sometimes more creative means.

"Sooner or later, someone could draw a connection between us, and then where will we be?" she asked before taking a delicate sip of espresso.

"We're both too cagey for that."

"Hmm. How very optimistic of you. But people get distracted. They get sloppy."

"Is that why your name came up in connection to Felix Metzer's untimely demise?" I asked, dropping the information like a dead body at her feet.

Her face remained perfectly impassive, but I didn't miss the rattle of china when she set her cup down.

"Who have you been talking to?"

"Someone you're lucky enough is too stupid to connect any dots. He assumed Felix was a client."

"What a limited imagination your little birdie has," Maureen said, patting her hair.

"Why were you seen having lunch with a man who was—by all accounts—a likable, networking, criminal middleman until his body was fished out of the Potomac?"

She sighed. "First tell me why you're involved."

"Felix sold a list with my friend's name on it to Anthony Hugo. Hugo made it known that every name on the list needed to be eliminated."

"You have friends?" She arched an eyebrow, her brown eyes sparkling.

"More like family," I said.

"Then you already understand."

"Understand what?"

"Felix is . . . or was family. We were cousins in what feels like a past life. We grew up together. I went my way, he went his. But we stayed in touch, met up on occasion. Never anywhere that someone would recognize me, of course. I have a reputation to uphold."

Except someone had recognized her, and now Maureen was my only lead.

"Did Felix ever talk to you about work?"

"We thought it best not to discuss our professions. Plausible deniability and all that."

"But you would have looked out for him. You would have had an idea of the company he was keeping," I pressed. Maureen was a caretaker at heart and a guard dog when necessary.

"Why are you focusing on Felix and not Hugo? Lord knows that man has broken enough laws to earn a few lifetime sentences in prison."

"Someone who wasn't Hugo put my friend's name on that list for reasons I want to know. That person needs to pay."

"Sounds like someone had a vendetta against your friend."

"I need to know who." Even if Anthony Hugo finally went down for his crimes, there was still someone out there who thought of Nash Morgan as a threat. And I wouldn't rest until I had them.

Maureen studied her pale-pink nails. "As I said, we didn't discuss business."

"That's never stopped you from acquiring information before."

She inhaled deeply. "Fine. Not all of Felix's friends were on the wrong side of the law. Some of them at least worked on the right side."

"A cop?" I asked.

"There was a gentleman—and I use that term loosely." She glanced at her discreet Cartier timepiece. "He showed up at a family backyard cookout this summer. I wasn't there, of course. My aunt mentioned that Felix's cop acquaintance made quite the little show of introducing himself around as Felix's 'old friend.' It rattled my cousin, which was not an easy thing to accomplish."

"So you looked into him?"

"Someone gets that close to my family, and I will do what's necessary."

"Name," I demanded.

She lifted her slim shoulders. "It won't do you any good in this case. Seeing as the man was shot and killed after an abduction gone wrong last year."

I swore under my breath. "Tate Dilton."

"Very good," Maureen said, impressed.

I shoved a hand through my hair. Did it really all lead back to him? Did all these loose ends tie up with Dilton's corpse?

The man had a grudge against Nash for taking Ogden's position as chief of police. But Dilton had been the triggerman the night Nash was shot. Why would he have put Nash on an elimination list—a coward's move—if he was going to be the one to shoot him anyway?

"According to my digging, he wasn't the brightest crooked cop on the payroll," Maureen said. "I warned Felix to stay away from him. But he obviously didn't listen."

If this was true, I'd wasted the last weeks chasing down a fucking ghost.

"I see this news isn't exactly welcome," she noted. "But I'm afraid I don't have time to stick around to find out why. I have a previous engagement."

"I'm sorry for cutting your trip short," I said gruffly, walking her to the door.

She gave me a peck on the cheek. "Time spent

with you is never wasted, Lucian. But you do owe me a very nice gift. I'm thinking something from Hermès."

My lips twitched. Maureen had a maternal fondness for me.

We said our goodbyes, and Maureen left through the private elevator to the parking garage.

I thanked the manager for allowing me to commandeer her office, then headed for the marble lobby.

It was the Saturday before Valentine's Day, and the self-important murmur of DC's young and elite nearly drowned out the live piano music in the bar. I'd been one of them once. Now I was something wholly different.

Everyone was either a pawn or a king. The pawns wanted to grow up to be kings, and the kings missed the innocence of being a pawn.

He ruined you. He ruined us.

Sloane's words from the previous weekend echoed in my head.

She didn't know what she was talking about. She didn't know me. She certainly wasn't in any position to judge me. I'd meant what I said. Happiness wasn't for everyone. I preferred security. I'd built a life that was impervious to any threats.

"How did it go, boss?"

Nolan leaned casually against the concierge desk, his fingers in the bowl of mints.

"What are you doing here?" I demanded.

A raucous burst of male laughter rang out from the bar.

Nolan straightened from the desk. "A little bird of prey named Petula told me you had an important, after-hours meeting. And after that tail you had to shake and Holly's trouble, I figured you might want some backup. At least until I saw Maureen Fitzgerald walk out of here on a security monitor a minute ago."

"Spying on your employer isn't generally a smart business move," I pointed out.

"Eh. You say spying, I say having your back." He unwrapped a mint and popped it into his mouth. "Did the lovely madam have any information on our deceased pal Felix?"

I scanned the lobby. It was crowded with well-dressed, well-funded people certain of their importance. Men and women who spent their days chasing power or catering to it. I nodded in the direction of the bar.

"Don't have to ask me twice," Nolan said and followed me.

Forest-green walls, dark wood, and paintings of hunts on the English countryside made the bar feel like an old-money country estate library.

We created a space for ourselves at the end of the mahogany bar where we were sheltered from prying eyes and ears by a thickly carved column.

I caught the eye of the bartender and held up two fingers. He nodded and snagged a bottle of bourbon from the top shelf.

"She may have just closed the book on who put Nash's name on that list," I said, keeping my voice low.

"I'm all ears." Nolan looked at ease leaning against the bar, but his eyes were constantly scanning the room. You could take the man out of the marshal service, but you couldn't take the marshal out of the man, I supposed.

The bartender delivered the bottle and glasses with a hesitant fold at the waist.

"Did that guy just bow to you?" Nolan asked.

"It happens," I said.

He shook his head and sighed. "To walk in your shoes for just a day."

"It's not nearly as entertaining as it looks," I muttered.

"Oh, I'd find a way to have some fun," he insisted.

He probably would. Some people were cut out for a life like that. Each day was an endless source of entertainment and enjoyment. Sloane's life would be like that. She'd choose a man who would make her laugh. Who'd be home for dinners. Who'd wake her up on a lazy Sunday morning with an adventure planned.

My jaw clenched.

I was important, respected, and feared. Yet all I could think about for the past week was Sloane's accusation that I'd wasted my life on the wrong things.

"Tate Dilton," I said, keeping my voice low.

Nolan's gaze landed back on me. "You've got to be shitting me."

I shook my head. "She mentioned a family party of Metzer's that Dilton crashed. He made a show of getting close to his family. Probably to drive home a point of just how close he could get."

"Playing a little 'look at me eating your mom's potato salad and playing horseshoes with Uncle Joe so you better not fuck me over,'" Nolan mused.

"That's what it sounds like. And Metzer disappeared while Dilton was still alive. So it's possible he's the answer to both questions."

"That would leave only Hugo on the revenge list. And since you're already working with you-know-who on that, it sounds as if your to-do list just got a lot shorter."

I grunted. "But why would he have put Nash's name on the list and then be the one to pull the trigger?"

Nolan shrugged. "The guy was an opportunistic egomaniac. He saw a chance to take out the guy who booted his buddy from his job. Then he got the opportunity to get paid to be the one to do the taking out. Hated him enough to want him out of the picture but not enough to make it happen until someone sweetened the pot with a cash offer."

It made sense in that it was a stupid move and Tate Dilton had been full of stupid moves.

I frowned over my drink. "I don't like the

connection to Felix and the feuding Hugo father and son. How would a crooked small-town cop land on any of their radar?"

"Criminals are like one big inbred family. Dilton didn't just suddenly up and go bad like an avocado. That boy had been rotting from the inside for a long time. He could have done a favor here for Daddy Hugo and worked a job with Hugo Junior over there. Hell, you know, a bunch of bad guys sit down for a friendly poker game when one henchman says he's looking for a getaway driver, and another henchman says, 'I got a guy.' "

"That's possible," I agreed.

"You've seen Dilton's finances. That dumbass was sitting on a lot more money than just a cop's salary. It didn't all have to come from the same employer."

Raucous laughter echoed from the opposite end of the U-shaped bar where several men were gathered in a tight circle. Probably around a woman, I guessed.

Nolan sniffed the bourbon appreciatively, then sipped. "Damn, that's good. Do they just keep a bottle here for you in case you show up?"

"It pays to own the hotel," I said dryly.

Of course there were drawbacks, like the hungry eyes zeroing in on me. Some wanted to make deals. Others wanted to stand close enough for a photo op. Still others wanted to get even closer in hopes of being chosen for a more intimate kind of fun.

369

"Ever get the feeling like you're in a zoo?" Nolan asked observantly.

I smirked. "Only every day."

"You could try being less handsome. I mean, I'm a straight guy, but even I know a suit daddy when I see one. Maybe shave the beard, lose a few teeth," he suggested.

A tall blond wandered by with a seductive swing to her hips. She was dressed in Alexander McQueen, and I could smell her cloying perfume from six feet away. The hair was what caught my eye, but I immediately rejected her. She didn't have green eyes and glasses.

Damn it.

I set my glass down with a snap.

Ever since she'd shown up at my office, it felt like Sloane had infiltrated this life too. Not just the one I carried on periodically in Knockemout. I needed to get her out of my head. I'd tried everything over the years. Except one thing . . .

That one thing slammed into me like a train. The fastest way for me to get bored with a woman had always been to take her to bed. Sex always triggered a countdown clock. Once the hunt was over, so was the interest for me.

A vision of Sloane perched on my desk, her thighs and lips open for me, had my blood racing to my cock.

"So if that fuckface Dilton is the one, then it's case closed. At least on that end of things," Nolan said, oblivious to my predicament.

I gritted my teeth and willed my body to have some fucking self-respect.

"As long as Anthony Hugo doesn't get it in his head to revisit the list," I said.

"It would be stupid, not to mention pointless. The CIs who stuck around after finding out Hugo had a target on them were all shipped off courtesy of WITSEC. If anything happens to any cop on that list, Hugo knows he's the first person they'll look at," he pointed out.

"Let's make sure it was Dilton," I decided.

Nolan nodded. "I'll have one of our guys or gals pay Metzer's family a visit and see if they remember him. Maybe Metzer told one of them something about the prick."

"Do it."

There was another burst of merriment, accompanied by a flash of blond. This one did have green eyes and glasses. Sloane Walton in bloody murder red was in the center of a circle of men vying for her attention. Every muscle in my body went rigid. The erection I'd almost willed away was back in full force.

"Of all the hotels in all the capitals," Nolan muttered. "You want me to stick around and make sure you don't need help disposing of a bunch of bodies?"

"No. Go away."

"I'll have Petula ready with bail money," he said, putting his empty glass on the bar and tossing me a salute.

I was already on the move, the gravitational force of Sloane pulling me across the bar like it was an inevitable event.

Every step that brought me closer made me angrier, more frustrated. I didn't want to want her, but I didn't want anyone else wanting her either. Wading my way through her admirers set my teeth on edge. She was sitting on a bar stool in a dress and lipstick that arrested the attention of any red-blooded male within a thirty-foot radius.

"What are you doing here?" I demanded crisply.

She tilted her head back to look up at me as I loomed over her. Those red lips pinched into a disapproving frown. "Oh, no. Not today, Satan."

"Can I buy you another drink?" the guy on her right asked, trying to reclaim her attention.

"No, you can't. Go home," I snapped.

Sloane bared her teeth at me before turning to the moron hoping to get lucky. "Don't listen to him. He's permanently insufferable," she said, laying her hand on his sleeve.

Two of the younger men behind her were whispering. I heard my name mentioned.

Good. The sooner this flock of idiots realized who I was and that I didn't want them anywhere near her, the better.

"Uh, it was nice to meet you, Sloane," the blond one with too many teeth said, shooting me a nervous glance.

"Yeah, we have to . . . uh . . ." His friend in too-tight Hugo Boss hooked a thumb toward the door.

"Go," I snarled.

Most of the crowd scampered off like half-terrified squirrels.

"What is your problem, Lucifer?" Sloane demanded.

"The answer is always you."

She slid off her stool and marched up to me. "I have an idea. Why don't you go fuck yourself and leave me alone with . . . what was your name again?" she asked, looking toward the man who obviously didn't know any better.

"Porter," he said with a thick Southern accent.

Porter. I rolled my eyes. He was too eager, too "aw shucks, ma'am." And I hated the fact that he made Sloane smile.

"I'll make you a deal, Porter. I'll pay your bar tab—including the drinks you've already bought my wife—if you leave in the next ten seconds."

"Y-your wife?" he sputtered.

"I'm going to murder you with an olive skewer," Sloane hissed.

Maybe I couldn't make her smile, but *I* was the one who made the color rise in those smooth cheeks. *I* was the one who started the emerald fire in her eyes.

Porter held up both palms and took a self-preserving step back. "I'm so sorry, man. I had no idea." His eyes darted back to the impressive cleavage on display above the square neckline of Sloane's dress. "Uh, if it doesn't work out, you go on and give me a call."

The power of the woman's draw was enough to override any instincts for self-preservation. I knew the feeling.

Sloane and I were too busy scowling at each other to watch him leave.

"Lina was right. You're a cockblocker, Rollins," she said, climbing back up on her barstool. The bartender appeared eagerly in front of her.

"Can I get you something, Sloane?" he asked.

"No. The lady was just leaving," I said icily.

Sloane rested her elbows on the bar and cupped her chin. "Don't listen to the tall, dark lord of the underworld. I'd love another dirty martini."

The bartender's eyes skated to me again. I shook my head.

"Sorry, Sloane. Boss won't let me," he said and disappeared down the bar.

She spun around on her stool. "The boss? You *own* this place?"

I couldn't focus on her words. Only her mouth. Those red-slicked lips that had tortured and taunted me for years.

"Are you here with someone?" I demanded, drawing out the stool next to hers and sitting.

"I was about to be until *you* went all you on my starting line."

I closed my eyes. She wasn't here on a date. She was here to get laid. One night. One night, and we could put this all behind us finally.

"You're not picking up a stranger in my hotel."

Her spine straightened and she lifted her glass.

374

Her nails were painted a sparkly purple. She wore a trio of bracelets on her right wrist and dangling earrings that danced when she moved.

"Fine," she said. She drained the last of her martini and set the glass down on the bar. "I'll pick one up someplace else."

She shifted on her stool to turn away from me, but I was faster.

I gripped the suede cushion between her parted thighs and dragged her closer.

The little gasp that escaped her lips had my cock stirring. We both stared down at my hand she was now straddling. The hem of her dress tickled my thumb. Her smooth, bare thighs caressed the sides of my fist. I could feel the heat from her core.

I pulled the stool even closer until her legs slid between my own. An inch. Maybe two. That was all that separated the heel of my hand from the heat of her core.

"Have you lost your already addled mind?" she hissed.

But she didn't push me away, didn't slap me like I deserved. No, the woman put here on this earth with the sole purpose of irritating me spread her thighs ever so slightly wider.

It was a trap. I was sure of it.

"Probably," I admitted. I signaled the bartender for another round. The poor kid looked moderately scared.

The feel of her caged between my legs was intoxicating. It had been a stupid move designed to get a rise out of her, yet I was the one with a stone-hard erection and elevated heart rate.

"Can't you just go back to your evil lair and forget we ran into each other?" she asked.

Go home with the knowledge that she was picking out a lover and taking him back to her hotel room? That she was undressing for him, letting him see things I'd never earned the right to see? Letting him touch places I could only dream of?

Her breasts rose against the confines of her dress. There was nothing subtle about the view the square neckline provided.

"Why are you here?" I demanded again.

"To get laid, and you're really messing with my mojo."

My jaw tightened.

"Go ahead. Say something so I can give you the sex-shaming lecture before I kick you in the balls," she challenged.

It was a legitimate threat. If she moved forward, her knees would be within striking distance.

"I thought you were getting serious about . . . dating," I said.

She shrugged and the motion drew my attention back to her cleavage. My cock throbbed painfully against my zipper.

"I was. I am," she corrected. "I just haven't met anyone worth dating, let alone anyone I'd let give me a few orgasms. So here I am. Sex is a good stress reliever."

"So you're just going to pick up a complete stranger and let him touch you?"

"You do not get to judge, Rollins. I'm willing to bet you've had more than your fair share of uncomplicated one-night stands."

"I'm not judging," I lied.

She peered over my shoulder at a man ordering a beer, and my grip tightened on her stool. "No," I said.

"You need to back off or I'm going to end up wasting a night in a hotel room with my vibrator."

Spots danced before my eyes.

She squirmed almost imperceptibly on the stool. The movement brought her forward, giving my hand a brush of hot satin just as her knee settled against the ridge of my dick.

Fuck.

Those green eyes widened, her ruby lips parted, and there was no mistaking the quickening of her breath. Hot, damp flesh taunted me from the other side of her fuck-me underwear.

I was tired of fighting. Tired of fighting with her. Tired of fighting my baser desires. It was self-destructive to want the only woman who had shattered my life. Who'd broken my trust. Who had landed me behind bars and very nearly ruined my life before it had even begun.

Yet here I was, closer than I'd ever been before and still not close enough.

"What if you didn't have to pick up a stranger?" I said, shifting my hand just enough to press harder against her sex.

Her nostrils flared delicately, making the stud in her nose sparkle. But she still hadn't moved away, still hadn't threatened to rearrange my face. "What exactly are you suggesting?"

"I'm suggesting you go upstairs now. With me."

Her long lashes fluttered behind her glasses, and she shook her head. "You're fucking with me, aren't you?"

"You're here. I'm here. It's been a while for me too." I wanted to shift my hand, to hook my finger in the band of satin that stood in my way. I wanted to slide it to the side and stroke my knuckles over that soft, tempting flesh.

"We can't stand to be in the same room together. What makes you think I'd let you inside me?"

Inside her. She was teasing me now. Planting images in my mind of how she'd look the first time I drove into her.

The pulse at the base of her throat fluttered. Her breasts rose and fell as her breath came in short, delicate pants.

"It's an itch that needs scratching. Not the beginning of a relationship," I said dryly.

"Your capacity for romance knows no bounds."

"What's the one thing we haven't tried to stop whatever this is between us?" I pressed.

"Murder?"

"Sex," I countered.

She blinked and the color rose in her cheeks. "You're serious."

"One night," I offered. "We get this insanity out of our systems."

"We don't even like each other. How am I supposed to let someone I don't like do naked things to me?"

I let the heel of my hand press harder. "Because I'll make it feel so good you won't care."

Her pupils were dilated, candy-red lips parted.

Our drinks appeared on the bar, but neither of us looked at them.

"Of course, if you don't think you could control your feelings—" I began.

She tossed her head back. "You can't double-dog dare me to get into bed with you, smart-ass."

A man in Armani sidled up behind her and leaned on the bar. Sloane, sensing new quarry, peered over her shoulder. She flashed him the sunny smile that I never got out of her. The idiot looked as if he'd won the lottery, then glanced at me.

"No," I said coldly.

I held his gaze and stroked my thumb over the middle of the damp spot I found on Sloane's underwear.

She jolted, nearly knocking over her drink. To steady herself, she gripped my arms.

"You sneaky son of a bitch," she hissed. Her knee was now pressed firmly against my balls.

"Either you and I go upstairs now, or I shadow you for the rest of the night," I warned.

"You devious bastard."

"Decide."

"Fine," she said with a careless shrug. "I'll fuck your brains out for one night only. But don't think this means anything."

This victory was a sweeter, headier rush than any I could remember.

"You have five seconds to finish your drink," I told her, signaling the bartender again.

She picked up her martini, eyes narrowed.

"Five, four, three . . ."

She took one fortifying gulp, then put the glass on the bar. The look she sent my way was the definition of antagonistic.

Neither of us was walking away this time.

With a mix of reluctance and anticipation, I removed my hand from between her legs and coasted my fingertips down her thighs.

"Let's go."

I threw some cash on the bar, gripped her arm, and pulled her toward the elevators. As I did, I brushed my thumb over my lips and savored the faint flavor of Sloane Walton.

21

The Dumbest, Hottest Mistake
I Ever Made

Sloane

It was the longest elevator ride of my life, and my room was only on the fourth floor. The atmosphere between us was charged with something that felt like lightning. We didn't touch, didn't look at each other. We both just stared straight ahead at the brushed gold doors.

His stony, silent presence made it feel like the car was closing in on me.

This was a bonkers idea. It was so stupid I still wasn't sure I was going to say yes once we got to my room. Could two people who rubbed each other so wrong figure out how to rub each other the right way for just one night? Doubtful.

This was definitely a mistake. A big, dumb mistake.

But at least I'd finally know, I rationalized as the elevator doors opened and we exited.

Maybe I owed it to my teenage self. I could put the years of "what if" to rest and move on. Besides, it had been months since I'd even been kissed, let alone properly laid.

There was also the possibility that he would be terrible in bed. That thought cheered me considerably. One mediocre roll in the hay and Lucian Rollins would be out of my system forever.

381

"Never play poker."

Lucian's sudden proclamation had me blinking as I dug through my clutch for the key card.

"What? Why?"

He shook his head. "Your face broadcasts every thought like an open book."

I scoffed. "It does not."

He took the card from my hand and opened my door. "The only way sex will be disappointing is if it's your fault."

My mouth fell open. "That's *not* what I was thinking," I lied. "And if the sex is bad, it's one hundred percent *your* fault. I'm great at sex."

"We'll see," he said before pushing me across the threshold into the room.

It was a nice space chosen with the practicality of a one-night stand in mind. There was a fluffy king-size bed with the extra pillows I'd asked for. The bathroom had flattering lighting *and* a tiled walk-in shower. And best of all, there was an extensive twenty-four-hour room service menu I could order off once I'd kicked Lucian to the curb.

He shut the door and locked it, then turned to face me.

I swallowed hard, suddenly feeling like Little Red Riding Hood coming face-to-face with the big, bad wolf. He was so . . . big. So frowny. He was looking at me like I'd pissed him off somehow in the last four seconds.

Nervously, I wet my lips and caught the interest in those cold, gray eyes.

He was standing legs braced, hands fisted at his sides, staring me down like I was the enemy . . . or a conquest.

Were we really about to do this? Would this end up being just one more dirty, little secret between the two of us?

"We should discuss ground rules," I announced.

Lucian set my key card down with a snap on the table, his eyes no longer cold. Now they smoldered with a heat that licked at my skin.

What had I been saying?

Oh right. Rules. Rules were good.

"I don't think we should kiss—"

I didn't get to finish the sentence because Lucian's hand snaked out, gripped my wrist, and yanked me into him. Hard. I was off-balance and fell into his chest. My bones reverberated from the collision of our bodies.

And then his mouth crashed down on mine.

Dear God.

There was nothing icy about the man against me. He was hot and hard.

I opened my mouth to breathe or insult him, but he took advantage and his tongue swept past my lips. It plundered as it went, turning my insults into unintelligible, needy moans.

It was pure possession. With one kiss, Lucian held my body captive.

He kissed like he'd invented it. And I followed his lead as if I had no choice in the matter.

He dragged his mouth away from mine and

swore. "Fuck," he muttered, glaring down at me.

"Problem?" It came out as a breathless taunt.

"You're my problem," he growled.

I shoved at the unyielding chest beneath the crisp button-down. "If you're just going to fight with me, I'm going back to the bar."

I made it exactly two inches in the direction of the door before his hands were on me again. A delicious sense of triumph rolled up my spine. It was the biggest win I'd scored against him in years. His self-control was—in my opinion—infuriating.

This time, he didn't just pull me to him, he lifted me off the floor and pinned me against the closest wall . . . with *his body*. My feet dangled inches above the carpet as his king-size erection lodged itself against me, effectively skewering me to the wall like a butterfly in a shadow box.

I was a lust-filled rag doll, and his casual show of strength had my vagina swooning. He looked at me like he wanted to destroy me. And I loved it. There was no hiding behind a cold, calculating mask now.

The man may have had a poker face, but there was no such thing as a poker dick.

As if to demonstrate, he rolled his hips, thrusting powerfully against me.

I groaned irritably against his mouth. "Of *course* you have a big dick."

"And of *course* you're disappointed by that fact when I'm about to fuck you with it," he shot back.

I hitched my thighs around his hips as high as my

dress would allow. "I'd always thought the whole all-powerful, shadowy puppet master thing was an overcompensation for a cocktail wiener."

"Your fucking mouth," he growled. He used both hands to shove the skirt of my dress up around my hips. I gasped as his erection lodged itself against my pretty, one-night-stand panties.

"What about it?"

"It's why you have to troll bars for unsuspecting men. Why you aren't dating. Why you're not married with four kids." He punctuated each sentence with another bruising kiss.

"Yeah? Well, at least it's not my personality. You're stupidly hot and ridiculously rich, and even *that* isn't enough to keep a girlfriend for longer than a few weeks." I nipped his lower lip with my teeth and he hissed.

He pulled back a few inches, leaving us connected below the waist. "How would you know that unless you've been paying attention?"

He was teasing me, body, mind, and soul, and for the first time, it occurred to me that I might not be up to the challenge.

"I don't pay attention to anything that involves you," I insisted. "I hate being bored."

His exhale was closer to a growl than a sigh. With one hand, he took both my wrists and pinned them over my head. "Goddammit, why are you so fucking small?" He gritted out the words like they physically pained him.

His next kiss was tempered, restrained.

My eyelids popped open. Lucian Rollins was afraid of hurting me. The big, evil asshole was afraid of fucking me too hard with his giant penis.

"Jesus, big guy. I'm petite, not fragile. Get over it."

"Just because I want you out of my life doesn't mean I want to hurt you."

I gripped his waist with my thighs and squeezed. "Either fuck me hard and fast or get out of my room so I can find someone who will. I don't want to be treated like some glass figurine."

"You always think you can handle more than you can," he said, removing his hand from my wrists and curling his fingers into the neckline of my dress.

"And you always think I'm weaker than I am," I hissed.

With one sharp tug of his fingers, the fabric ripped all the way to my belly button and my breasts spilled free.

"Christ."

Lucian's nostrils flared and his gaze scored my chest, making my nipples pucker, my breasts feel swollen and heavy.

For a moment, the only sound in the room was us panting.

"Damn it, Lucifer. You owe me a new one-night-stand dress."

"Try going downstairs now." His words were a low rumble of thunder.

My nipples hardened to rosy points.

"You think I don't have a backup dress in that bag?" I taunted. I leaned forward until my lips brushed his ear. "That one shows even more cleavage." I nipped his earlobe and felt the shudder that rolled through him.

"You're not leaving this room," he vowed.

My snarky comeback was lost as he filled his hands with my breasts.

My head fell back against the wall with a thunk. His palms were warm and firm against my soft, sensitive flesh. I'd developed early and spent my teen years wishing the puberty fairy hadn't been quite so generous, but in this moment, it was all worth it.

My stoic enemy couldn't suppress a groan of satisfaction as his hot mouth closed over one needy nipple and began to suck.

I gasped. I didn't mean to. It seemed safer, smarter to control my outward reactions. But the hungry pulls of his mouth, the throb of his God-given erection between my legs had my head spinning.

His mouth was performing magic with tongue and suction. His eyes were closed, fringed with long, dark lashes. What he was doing to me didn't feel like a by-product of hate. It felt like reverence.

His beard was deliciously rough against my skin. His cologne enveloped me like a euphoric fog. I bucked against his thick, hard shaft, against the heat of his body, begging for more. Begging to be taken and used and pleasured.

Too soon, he released me from his mouth, leaving my nipple straining and wet.

"We have one night," he said.

"Then take your shirt off so we can get started."

He nuzzled his cheek against my breast, sending arrows of fire straight to my core.

"This isn't the beginning of something," he warned. His tongue darted out and danced over the other puckered peak.

I sucked in a breath. "Do you always talk your dates to death before you have sex?"

"I'm simply making sure we're on the same page."

"I can't tell if you're talking to me or my boobs, but frankly, we're all in agreement. I could never date a smoker. This is just sex. Don't make me regret choosing you tonight."

His gray eyes danced with sterling fire, the corner of his mouth lifted in a confident smirk. With an expert upthrust against me, he filled his hands with my breasts, and I lost my train of thought.

I attacked his tie, nearly choking him in an effort to loosen it, but he was too fixated on my chest to notice the lack of oxygen. The hot suction of his mouth was driving me mad, and I was already dangerously close to coming thanks to the position of his cock against me.

Tie finally freed, I shoved his jacket off his shoulders.

He abandoned my breasts with an irritable snarl that I felt in my core and shed his jacket. I managed to register the fact that he was too busy fondling me to pick up and fold his clothes as I'd assumed Sexy Time Lucian would.

"You're smiling," he said accusingly.

"No, I'm not," I snapped, forcing the corners of my mouth down.

"The only thing I want your mouth doing tonight is opening to say *my name*."

"Really? That's the *only* thing?" I smirked.

In response, Lucian pulled me away from the wall. Less than a heartbeat later, I was flat on my back on the bed and he was kneeling between my legs, his hands guiding my knees wider as he stared heavy-lidded at what was revealed to him.

"Fuck," he muttered, staring down between my legs at what I could only assume was the wettest thong in the history of thongery. His hands slid from my knees and fisted at his sides. Another display of self-control. I'd had enough of it. I wanted him off the leash.

I reached for his belt. "Lose the shirt."

He hesitated for the barest of seconds before complying.

He worked the buttons free with one hand while the other loosely collared my neck. A show of dominance I found . . . Well, honestly, I found it fucking hot.

I yanked his belt open and got to work on his fly. His erection was straining so hard against the fabric it was a damn wonder it hadn't ripped free yet. He probably had a tailor reinforce all his crotch seams.

With his zipper finally opened, the treasure I sought was barely contained by a silky pair of black boxer briefs.

Lucian ripped the shirt down his arms, baring his disgustingly awesome torso. There was muscle. A lot of it. The scars I'd known he had were gone. In their place were tattoos.

My heart lurched.

Without thinking, I ran my finger over one long, slivery imperfection over his ribs. The scar had been partially camouflaged with an inked griffin. A symbol of strength and power.

Lucian sucked in a breath as if I'd hurt him somehow, then shoved the remains of my dress up to my waist.

"That's better," I said, rewarding his show of impatience by smugly sliding my palm up the length of his shaft. He was so thick, so hard now that the blunt crown had breached the waistband of his underwear.

He towered over me, one hand behind me on the mattress. The other he used to stroke my cheek, my jaw, my neck. Our eyes met. I didn't recognize what I found in his, but it took my breath away. His gaze bored into me, an unbreakable connection.

As we stared straight into each other's souls, he released my face and trailed his fingers all the way down my torso to the naughty, red satin that covered my center.

"You're fucking soaked and I haven't even touched you yet."

He sounded annoyed by that fact.

"What's your point?" I retorted.

"Is it for me, or was it for one of them downstairs?"

"Does it matter?"

His thumb pressed against the wet spot, causing my legs to spasm around his hips. My empty channel pulsed greedily, craving more. "It matters," he gritted the words out.

Rather than answer him, I hooked my fingers in the band of his briefs and yanked the silky material away from my prize.

I barely managed to swallow my gasp. King-size didn't do it justice. Lucian Rollins was the proud owner of the biggest cock I'd ever seen in my life.

"Jesus, Lucifer. What do your dates usually do? Unhinge their jaws?" I demanded.

His eyes seemed to glow as he looked down at me. "You and your fucking mouth."

He looked like he wanted to punish me for the last two decades of misery, and some dark, depraved part of me wanted him to try.

"What are you going to do about it?" I taunted, gripping the thick base of his shaft.

His nostrils flared and a bead of moisture welled up from the slit in his crown.

My entire focus zeroed in on his thick, rigid erection. I was going to come so fucking hard.

If I could get him to fuck me from behind,

I could muffle my screams in a pillow so he wouldn't know. Women had been faking orgasms for centuries. I could fake *not* having one. And wouldn't that throw him for a loop? I liked the idea of getting off while dinging his self-confidence.

"Whatever it is you're plotting, it won't work," he said.

"I have no idea what you're talking about," I lied and began to stroke the thick column of flesh.

I saw a flash of teeth, the narrowing of his eyes, and then nothing because in one swift move, he yanked my thong to the side and thrust two fingers inside me.

"Lucian!"

So much for muffling my pleasure. I was so wet, so hot, my sex practically sucked him in deeper. The untended muscles of my inner walls spasmed around him.

He swore darkly, and his cock flexed in my hand.

"Don't come." The order was delivered through gritted teeth.

"Bite me."

"Don't tempt me, Pixie. I want to be inside you the first time you come. I want to feel you fall apart."

The first time? I scoffed. Mr. Big Dick had an ego the size of . . . well, his gargantuan penis. I was a one and done kind of gal. Multiples were for romance novel heroines . . . and Naomi and Lina.

"Then you'd better hurry the hell up," I warned. I shoved my other hand between our bodies and cupped his heavy sack and double-timed my strokes. I needed him to be as close as I was. I needed him to feel as out of control as I did.

He glared down at me, jaw tight, muscles tensed. He looked as though he were hanging on by one thin thread. I gripped harder.

His hands were in my dress again. There was a rending of fabric, and the entire thing fell open, leaving me in just my underwear and stilettos.

"Safe word," he demanded as his hand covered mine on his dick.

"You're either severely overestimating your prowess or once again underestimating what I can handle."

"Give me your safe word, Pix."

He enunciated the sentence as if I were both aggravating and stupid.

"If it'll get you to move things along, fine. Library."

"Good girl," he growled.

I didn't know what it said about me, but those two words delivered so gruffly from him had my inner walls spasming around his fingers.

"Fuck," he muttered.

"Can we get this show on the road?" I demanded. If he so much as crooked his fingers, I was going to come all over him, and I preferred to do that on his monster penis.

He glared down at me. "You're so beautiful and so goddamn irritating at the same time."

"I get that a lot. Condoms are in my clutch," I announced.

Reluctantly, Lucian withdrew his fingers. I didn't quite manage to smother my moan.

"Christ. How much sex were you expecting to have?" he demanded, dangling a roll of foil-wrapped birth control over me.

I shrugged. "There's more in the nightstand. I guess I probably won't need more than one since I ended up with you."

Lucian pushed my hands away from his dick and rolled on a condom over what had to be a *Guinness World Record* penis. "You'd be a lot more attractive if you'd shut up."

"Your dick doesn't seem to mind my mouth," I pointed out. I was going for sheer bravado at this point. Because it had suddenly occurred to me I could be on the receiving end of a serious vaginal injury from an appendage of that girth.

Would people take one look at my gait tomorrow and know that Lucian had fucked the ability to walk out of me? Would my one-night stand destroy my ability to stand?

Lucian took the long, thick shaft in one hand and guided the tip to my slick entrance. My knees shifted higher of their own accord, making the corner of his mouth curl in amusement. "Someone's eager."

"Are you gonna loom over me all night or do something interesting?" I demanded.

In response, he dragged the crown of his shaft through my slick folds, pausing to nudge my already swollen clit. The promise of it had my core contracting. I tried to bow off the bed but his hand on my chest held me in place. Again and again, he moved over my sex, spearing himself between my spread legs until my thighs trembled and he'd spread my wetness everywhere.

Jesus, I was going to have to call housekeeping for a fresh set of sheets when this was over since he'd turned my own body into one gigantic wet spot.

Neither of us could deny the attraction now. And I was one thousand percent sure he was going to make me come. I'd just have to pretend I wasn't.

Lucian paused midthrust, and my ab muscles went into spasm.

There was nothing holding him back from jamming that gigantic penis inside me. I let my knees fall open and reveled at the feel of him against my flesh. An insistent, throbbing pressure built inside me.

If either one of us moved a millimeter, he'd officially be inside me. And damn it, I *wanted* it. I wanted *him*.

"Look at me," he commanded.

I opened my eyes and tried to keep my expression neutral. "Why?"

"Because I want to see your eyes when I take you."

Gulp.

"Then hurry the hell up, because I'm about to fall asleep from boredom here."

I felt his muscles coil under my palms, against my torso and thighs. He entered me with one vicious thrust.

Time stopped.

Oxygen ceased to exist.

Everything I knew to be true flew from my head to make room for one crystal clear realization: Lucian Rollins was inside me.

"Breathe, Sloane." The command sounded pained.

I sucked in a wheezy breath.

"Christ. Baby, I need you to relax." Lucian's forehead met mine. "You don't have all of it yet."

I didn't have all of it yet? I was already stretched to max capacity. I was one tiny wiggle away from orgasming all over however many inches he'd managed to cram inside me.

"Again, Pix. Breathe for me," he ordered.

I managed a deeper breath this time and felt my muscles give ever so slightly.

"That's my girl." His voice was a rough caress. "Again."

This time, the oxygen came easier. I forced myself to relax, muscle by muscle, until I was no longer clinging to the man like a horny barnacle.

"Okay, I think I—"

Lucian fucked the thought right out of my head. I had him all. Every throbbing inch of him had invaded. I was pinned to the bed on the verge of supreme sexual satisfaction, and there was no going back.

I screamed something unintelligible.

"Fuck," he rasped.

Oh no. It was happening. I felt it building in my body. Two thrusts and Lucian Rollins was about to make me come. The early tremors began. I could feel those delicate little muscles fluttering over his hard flesh.

I had to hide it. Had to pretend it wasn't happening.

A rumble let loose in Lucian's chest. He was scowling at me, into me like he was pissed off that it felt so good. I wasn't happy about it either. And then he moved and I forgot what I was thinking because I was falling apart.

The orgasm detonated inside me, ripping through my body and annihilating everything that had ever existed before Lucian's cock entered me. I rippled, convulsed, writhed around him, clinging to him with nails and teeth as colors burst behind my eyelids like an erotic fireworks display.

Every inch of me from my glittery toenails to the roots of my hair participated in the ecstasy.

This wasn't the best orgasm of my life. Because this wasn't an orgasm. This was a life-altering religious experience. It rolled on and on, wave after wave of pleasure.

I was trembling from the aftershocks, each one more satisfying than any orgasm I'd ever had in my entire sexual career.

"You just came on my cock."

I pried one eye open to peer into his unfairly handsome face. He looked smug, as to be expected.

But there was something else there. Wonder? Awe? Possession?

"I did not. You're mistaken," I panted. My throat hurt, which I found odd. Was I coming down with something? Had Lucian's giant penis thrust so far into my body that I got a sore throat?

"You just screamed 'Lucian, I'm coming' loud enough that I'm probably going to have to call down to security to assure them everything is fine."

That explained the sore throat.

"Well, that was fun and all. I think I'll go back down to the bar and—"

Lucian showed me exactly what he thought of that empty threat by sealing his mouth over mine and driving into the very depths of me.

His long, hard body pressed mine deeper into the mattress as he thrust with expert precision. Even now, he was so controlled, and I felt like I was spinning off into space.

I dug my nails into his shoulders. "Stop treating me like I'm going to break."

He stilled, another annoying display of will-power.

"Believe it or not, I don't want to hurt you."

"Unless you hit me in the eye with that nightstick between your legs, you're not going to hurt me. You've got this one night to fuck me any way you want me. Don't waste it being some gentle giant."

"Sloane."

He packed quite the ominous warning into my name. But there was a spark, a question in those liquid silver eyes.

"Lucian." I gripped his face in my hands and dug my heels into his firm butt cheeks. "I want you to take me *hard*." It was what I needed. What he needed. If we were really going to get this out of our systems, we had to do it the right way.

I felt the involuntary twitch of his cock inside me. He wanted it too.

"I'll tell you if it's too much," I added.

"Promise?" The question was a gravelly rasp.

"I promise. Now fuck me like you mean it."

The man delivered.

He rose up on his knees, gripped my ass with his palms, and unleashed the beast within.

My body accepted his brutally beautiful thrusts with something that felt like joy, which made absolutely no sense. There was something in his eyes that didn't match the grim set of his jaw. Something softer, brighter.

I ignored it and shifted my legs restlessly as a warmth started to build in my core.

Reading my mind, Lucian hooked my ankles over his shoulders and bent me in half.

I was pinned. Conquered. Completely at his mercy. And I *loved* it.

Sweat slicked our skin as our eyes met and locked as his body pumped into mine.

The tendons in his neck stood out fiercely, and his biceps bulged as he relentlessly drove me toward heaven. Or maybe it was hell. It didn't matter.

I was quivering from the inside out.

"Lucian!" It was a low, keening wail.

His erection seemed to swell even bigger, and he gritted his teeth. "Damn you, Pixie," he snarled. He brought one hand to my jaw, holding my head still. Those beautiful storm cloud eyes went glassy as I clamped down around him.

"Please," I whispered. I didn't know what I was asking for, what I wanted from him. But Lucian understood. He gave one final vicious upthrust, and his body went rigid.

I didn't think. I just reached up and grabbed his face in my hands and we stared into each other's eyes as I experienced my first second orgasm of my life.

A shout tore loose from his throat, and I felt him ejaculate. For one stupid, fleeting moment, I wished there wasn't anything between us. No protection to stop me from experiencing every sensation of Lucian's climax.

He was moving again, short, jerky thrusts as he used my orgasm to milk his own. He used my body for his pleasure, and that made me come harder.

We kept right on coming, muscles trembling, breath panting as we stared into each other's eyes.

"This is the dumbest, hottest mistake I've ever made," I moaned.

22

Sloane to the Rescue

Sloane

Twenty-two years ago

Six days. That was how long Lucian had been behind bars. He'd turned eighteen and missed his own high school graduation because of me. Well, technically because of his horrible, disgusting monster of a father, but also because I hadn't listened to him.

I told my parents everything I knew the night Lucian was arrested. They hadn't been happy with me keeping that kind of secret from them. Their disappointment in me only made me feel worse.

My dad had put everything on hold and was fighting tooth and nail to get Lucian out of county jail. From what I'd gathered through pointed questioning and blatant eavesdropping, Chief Ogden was pushing to charge Lucian as an adult. The judge seemed amiable and set the bail at an astronomical $250,000 during the arraignment, which I hadn't been allowed to attend.

According to what Mom told Maeve over the phone, Dad had nearly had an aneurysm on the spot.

I was listening outside his office later that day when he took a call from the district attorney, who had suggested Lucian accept a plea deal for eight years in state prison. My father, one of the nicest, most polite human beings in the entire universe, told the DA to go fuck himself.

Meanwhile, Mom had visited Lucian's mom twice since she got out of the hospital with a pair of broken ribs. Both times, the woman had refused to talk about Lucian or what really happened that night. She had also declined Mom's offer to let her come stay with us "until things were sorted out."

Ansel Rollins appeared to be behaving himself, for the moment.

I'd overheard my parents talking on the front porch the night before. Dad broached the subject of a second mortgage to Mom for Lucian's bond.

"Darling, of course we'll do it. We can't leave him behind bars."

In that moment, I realized what a privilege it was to grow up with good people for parents. I'd pressed my teary face up against the inside of the window screen and scared the shit out of them by yelling, "You can have my college fund too!"

I came from a family of heroes and wasn't about to be left out. Certainly not after my mistake had caused the current situation.

I had a plan.

I'd done enough research on abusive relation-ships over the past year that the librarian was starting to give me funny looks every week when I checked out a new batch of books.

I knew I wasn't supposed to blame Mrs. Rollins.

She was a victim of domestic abuse. I was savvy enough to understand that systemic abuse did things to the psyche that other people couldn't fathom. However, even with that in mind, a very large, very loud part of me wanted to tell her exactly what I thought of her choosing her dirtbag loser husband over her son.

I felt dizzy every time I thought of the boy I adored behind bars for the crime of protecting his mother.

So while my parents decided to move forward with coming up with bail money, I decided I was going to fix the whole damn mess. I was going to make it clear to everyone, including the blind-as-a-bat Chief Ogden, that Lucian Rollins wasn't the dangerous one in the family.

I just needed the right opportunity.

I thought of going to Lucian's friends Knox and Nash Morgan for help. But I didn't know how much they knew about Lucian's situation, and they were boys. They were more likely to go off half-cocked and screw up everything. It made sense to keep it to myself.

What I needed was irrefutable proof of Ansel Rollins's villain status. To sixteen-year-old me, that meant video. After double checking that Virginia was a single-party consent jurisdiction when it came to recording conversations, I squirreled away my parents' camcorder under my bed along with a mini tape recorder I borrowed from my friend Sherry.

Every night, I stayed up late, sprawled on the window seat with my window open wide, listening.

Waiting with a sick mix of anticipation and dread churning in my stomach.

I dropped the book I'd been ignoring onto the cushion and shot my legs up in the air above me. My toenails were purple, and both pinkies had already chipped. I'd painted them the day before Lucian got arrested, and since then, everything else had seemed so frivolous.

This wasn't how the summer before my junior year was supposed to go. I was supposed to be looking forward to the summer softball league that was starting in a week. The one where I was going to get scouted by one of my dream colleges. I was supposed to be accepting invitations to Third Base and making out. Maybe even losing my virginity. I was supposed to be convincing Lucian that it was safe for him to go out into the world and live his life.

Instead, I'd been the one to ruin any chance at that future.

I sat up and peered morosely out the window. The look on his face when he'd seen me standing there as he was led to the police cruiser, when he realized I'd done the one thing he'd made me promise not to . . .

I'd begged to be allowed to visit him at the county jail. Dad had diplomatically told me it wasn't a good idea, but I knew by the shifty look behind his glasses that Lucian didn't want to see me. Because it was my fault he was there in the first place. Because I'd broken that trust.

I heard the chirp of tires, the squeal of brakes, and I popped up onto my knees. Mr. Rollins's pickup came to an abrupt stop in the driveway. He'd parked crooked, and he stumbled when he got out from behind the wheel. He slammed the door, but it bounced open again without his notice.

I scrambled off the window seat and dove for the box under my bed. I stuffed the camera and the recorder in an NPR tote bag, shoved my feet in a pair of sneakers, and let myself out into the hall. I held my breath as I tiptoed to the stairs, ears straining for any noises coming from my parents' room on the opposite side of the house.

They were going to be so pissed. I'd be grounded until I was thirty. But the end justified the means. If I could show the police department irrefutable proof that put Mr. Rollins behind bars and freed Lucian, it would all be worth it.

I detoured into my dad's office and grabbed the cordless phone off his desk. I wasn't sure if the signal would reach from next door, but I could at least run and dial 911 if necessary. Phone secured in the tote bag with the rest of my equipment, I unlocked the front door and slipped out into the night.

I stumbled twice in my haste, my heart pounding louder the closer I got.

There were lights on, upstairs and down.

"Please be downstairs," I murmured to myself, wincing when I realized I was actually hoping that a woman was about to be attacked. I felt sick to my stomach as I stayed low and made my way up to the front window.

This was going to work. It *had* to work.

I heard voices, one soft and pleading, one raised. A shadow passed by the glass, and I ducked low in the overgrown flower bed. Something with thorns bit into my forearm. Every twig snap, every breath, every beat of my heart sounded like it was amplified.

There was a dull thud inside and an angry muttering. Carefully, I reached into the bag and produced the recorder. I didn't know if it was sensitive enough to pick up what was going on inside, but it was worth a try. I hit Record and placed it on the skinny window ledge.

I hauled out the camera, took off the lens cap, and fired it up.

With a shaky breath, I stood up in the flower bed and peered through the camera lens.

They were in the kitchen, Mr. Rollins prowling back and forth. "I told you I expect dinner on the table when I get home," he barked loud enough for me to hear.

"It's almost midnight, asshole," I muttered under my breath.

I caught a glimpse of Mrs. Rollins in a nightgown as she scurried past the kitchen door, shoulders hunched.

He caught her by the elbow and slapped the plate out of her hand with a crash.

A dog barked next door, one of Mrs. and Mr. Clemson's Saint Bernards, scaring the heck out of me.

Mr. and Mrs. Rollins disappeared from view, and I used the opportunity to pull out the cordless phone. But there was no dial tone. I was too far away from the base.

He was shouting again inside, but I couldn't see anything. Shit. I needed to get a better view. Camera still rolling, I looped the bag over my shoulder and took off running around the side of the house. In the dark, I banged my hip off the rusty grill. But that pain was nothing compared to what Ansel Rollins was inflicting right now, I reminded myself.

I limped around into the backyard to the rickety, rotting deck off the back of the house, and there, through the sliding glass door, I saw them. He backhanded her across the face hard enough that I gasped. His brutal grip on her arm kept Mrs. Rollins from folding to the floor.

"You disgust me, woman," he said and hurled her into the kitchen table. "You make me fucking sick."

This had to be enough evidence, I decided, feeling pretty sick myself.

Mrs. Rollins was crumpled in a dining chair like a wadded-up piece of paper. Silent sobs shook her frail shoulders. I hated him. I hated Ansel Rollins for ever existing. For treating his wife like that, for forcing his son to stand between them. I hated the man with every fiber of my being.

"If you don't quit your bawling, I'll give you something to bawl about," he slurred.

Stop crying, Mrs. Rollins. Please stop crying.

Suddenly, the woman's head came up. I saw her mouth moving but couldn't make out what she was saying.

"What did you say?" he snarled.

"I said, I have *nothing* because of you," she said, getting to her feet on shaky legs. Tears were still streaming down her cheeks.

Oh God. I tried the phone again, but there was still no dial tone.

"The only reason you have anything is because of me." He moved into view, and every muscle in my body went tight when I saw what he was holding. He was drying a long, serrated knife on a dish towel.

I remembered Lucian's bloody arm. Assault with a deadly weapon.

I left the camcorder on the deck, angled toward the door, and ran. I was inside my house in seconds, dialing the phone and flipping light switches.

"Mom! Dad! He's hurting her again," I shrieked from the foot of the stairs. A light clicked on upstairs. "We have to stop him!"

"911, what's your emergency?"

"Ansel Rollins is attacking his wife with a knife again, and if Wylie Ogden doesn't arrest him this time, I'm going to sue the entire police department," I shouted into the phone. I had to get back. I had to stop him or bear witness.

I heard my parents' muffled voices coming from upstairs.

"Hurry!" I said before dropping the phone on the floor and bolting back out the door.

The tree frogs were still chirping outside, but I barely heard them as I sprinted across our driveway and into the Rollinses' backyard.

I landed on the deck with a flying leap. Through the glass door, I spied them. He had her pinned to the table, the knife to her throat. There was blood on the linoleum.

Dogs were barking frantically now, but the rest of the neighborhood was still.

I had no choice. He had to be stopped. I had to stop him.

I picked up an old, cracked clay pot and, with a primal scream that came from the depths of my soul, hurled it into the glass.

The door shattered, sending shards of glass and clay everywhere.

Someone was calling my name. Multiple some-ones from the sounds of it. But I couldn't scream back. I couldn't move. I was rooted to the spot as Mr. Rollins stared at me through his busted door.

We locked eyes, and I poured every ounce of hate that I carried inside into that one look.

"You're gonna pay for that, you little fucking bitch."

I was shaking with fear, with rage. "Fuck. You. You stupid, worthless piece of shit!"

He lunged for me, and I felt pain around the edges of the rage. I fought him as the shouting got closer, as the sirens finally cut through the night, as the tree frogs stopped.

Snap.

23

I'm Not Done with You Yet

Lucian

Hold your damn horses. I'm coming."

The irritated voice on the other side of the door did nothing to calm me. She was here. She was fine. Which meant she'd snuck out on me like I was some shameful one-night stand that she didn't want sticking around for breakfast.

Sloane Walton was about to learn a very serious lesson.

The front door swung open, and I enjoyed the flicker of shock on her pretty face. She was wearing a robe. Her hair was damp and her face free of last night's makeup. She looked young and fresh . . . and nervous.

Had she tried to wash away what we'd done like it had never happened?

I hadn't. I woke to a bed full of pillows and no Sloane. Five minutes later, I was in the car.

I slapped a hand to the open door in case she thought about shutting it in my face.

"What are you doing here? Did I leave something—"

"I'm not done with you yet." I'd fucked her into the early hours of the morning until neither one

411

of us could move. Then I'd fallen asleep with her back pressed to my front, my face in her hair, and slept like the dead. When I woke, there was one clear thought in my head.

Sloane wasn't out of my system.

"Excuse me?" Her squeak was indignant and accompanied by a dangerous narrowing of the eyes as she took immediate offense.

We were both poised to fight. However, our bodies seemed to have different ideas. One second, I was standing on her I'M PROBABLY READING welcome mat; the next, I was crossing the threshold and hitching her up with one hand on her curvy, little ass. She wrapped her legs around my hips and speared her fingers into my hair, pulling my head down to hers.

Her mouth found mine, and a bolt of relief sliced through me.

She still wanted me.

That was all that mattered. One more time. That was what we needed. Then it would be out of our systems.

I kicked the door closed and spun around to press her against the wall. A picture frame tilted, then smashed to the floor.

"Sorry," I muttered against her mouth and whirled us away from the wall. I needed to find a place to pin her down, hold her still. To make her stay.

But she was already frantically working the buttons of my shirt free, and I knew there was no chance in hell that I was going to make it upstairs to her bedroom. I dragged her robe open and threw it on the floor. Underneath, she was wearing one of those lacy bra tops that did nothing to hide the pucker of her nipples from my ravenous gaze.

I'd barely registered the small, purple bruise just above her nipple when she shoved a hand between us and found my belt buckle with a triumphant cry.

God, I wanted her. I craved her hands on me, her pleading whimpers of "please" and "more" in my ear. I needed to be inside her again.

I stumbled into the family room, bumping an end table and knocking over a lamp in my haste. The shade popped off and fell to the floor.

"It's fine. I hate that lamp," Sloane said against my mouth as she went to work on my fly.

I kicked the coffee table out of the way, spilling a pile of paperbacks onto the floor. My shins finally met an appropriate flat surface. The couch.

We landed like a felled tree with me barely managing to cushion our fall. Her hands abandoned my zipper and gripped my shirt. Something hissed, and a flash of gray and white fur darted over the cushion onto the console table behind the couch.

I didn't care if it was a cat, a rat, or a possum. Nothing was more important than stripping Sloane naked.

My tongue plundered while I shoved the waistband of her underwear down her legs. Her frame was so small and delicate, yet her curves were tantalizing. That smooth ivory skin begged for my hands to cruise, to stroke, to nip.

I buried one hand in that beautiful fucking hair and sent the other diving between her legs. Decadently wet. I'd touched her sixty seconds ago, and her pussy was already ready for me. My cock gave another convulsive twitch, and I felt a hot burst of moisture flow from the tip.

We were making a mistake. I knew it. But I couldn't stop myself.

She whimpered against my mouth and gripped my hair with one hand while the other one tried to shove my shirt off my shoulder.

I wanted to go slower this time. But anger and desire had blended into an adrenaline-fueled cocktail in my blood.

"You'd better have a condom somewhere on your body," she said, nipping at my lower lip.

On a growl, I reared up and reached for my wallet in my pants pocket.

"Oh, thank God," she breathed when I yanked the foil packet free and tossed the wallet in the direction of the coffee table.

She shoved my pants down to my thighs as I shredded the foil. I was on my knees between her legs, and she was spread out under me like a sacrifice.

"This is the last time," I said as much for my own benefit as hers.

"Yes, yes, yes," she chanted as I took my throbbing dick in one hand. Sloane snatched the condom from me and rolled it on, gliding it down my erection.

"So impatient," I said on a groan.

My vision started to go dark when she gripped me at the root and squeezed. "Last time," she repeated. "Might as well get it over with."

I was going to ruin her for all future partners. That was my new goal in life.

I snatched at the spaghetti straps of her top, dragging them down her shoulders, trying to restrain myself from breaking the delicate threads. Then, with one swift yank, I bared the breasts that I knew would haunt my dreams forever.

"Now, Lucian. Now! Please, baby," she demanded.

I couldn't have stopped myself even if I'd wanted to. Not after knowing what awaited me between her legs.

I guided my swollen crown to her glistening entrance, notched it into place, and with one mean thrust, I embedded myself inside her.

She screamed and I let out a guttural yell.

I hadn't prepared her for it. I hadn't softened up her sex with foreplay and teasing. I'd battered my way in. And now she was holding me in a grip so tight it stole my breath.

"Breathe, baby," I said through gritted teeth. "You need to relax." If she didn't, I was going to humiliate myself.

Her eyelids fluttered open, and jade-green eyes stared up at me. "Don't hold back on me," she said.

I pressed my lips to her throat. "You have to relax. Make room for me, Pixie."

"I hate how you feel so fucking good."

It nearly made me smile through the agony of holding still.

I pulled out a few inches, reveling in the slick, wet slide of her flesh against mine. "You'll hate it even more when you have all of me."

She hitched her thighs higher around my waist and squeezed.

Her groan was an exquisite torture to my ears. "Here I thought Lucian Rollins just took what he wanted."

"I don't want to hurt you," I reminded her.

"Then *please* me," she demanded. With that, she reached around me and sank her nails into my ass cheeks.

"Fuck."

I thrust into her, going deeper this time, gripping her hips so she couldn't wiggle away from me.

"God, yes."

"Almost," I rasped.

"More. All of it. Please," Sloane begged.

I pulled out almost to the tip and then I drove back in on a vicious upthrust. Her tight muscles fought against my invasion for an agonizing moment, and then something gave way and that final inch slid home.

It was ecstasy. I'd fucked my way into heaven again. She held me in a tight, wet clutch better than anything I'd ever experienced. Despite last night's debauchery, my balls felt so full they ached. My ass was clenched tight, ready to fuck. My entire body was rigid with the desire to move.

I managed to pry my eyes open to take it all in.

I had her pinned to the couch. Her legs spasmed restlessly around my hips. I could feel the soft buds of her nipples as they played against my chest hair. I wanted to taste them again. I wanted to taste *her* again. I wanted to bury myself in her until I didn't want her anymore.

"Are you good?" It came out as an angry growl.

"So good. So fucking good," she whimpered.

It was all I needed to hear.

"You shouldn't have left me," I said, sliding out, clenching my teeth at the delicate drag of her muscles. Her body had fought my entrance, and now it was fighting to keep me inside.

I punctuated the accusation with several hard thrusts. Those full, round breasts bounced every time I bottomed out inside her.

"We could have been doing this in a bed," I chastised.

"Your couch performance is adequate," she panted.

"You made me drive all the way here just to take you and your sweet pussy again," I growled.

"Nobody asked you to waste the gas." Her inner walls fluttered around me. My little librarian liked it when I talked dirty.

I ducked my head to lick over one nipple, then the other. She shivered under me and arched her back, putting her breasts on display for me.

I fucked into her again and again, using my foot to push off the floor to gain as much leverage as possible.

"Yes! More. Harder," she chanted.

It was like she was begging me to break her.

"God, I hate that you're so good at this," she moaned.

"Shut up and take my cock like a good girl," I ordered.

That was all it took. I felt her orgasm slam into her. It was familiar to me now. I knew I would never forget how it felt to have Sloane Walton fall apart on my cock.

Those slick, tight inner walls clamped down on my aching erection as I impaled her on it. My vision went black as her pussy milked my shaft with an explosion of ripples. I hated the latex that separated us. I hated that last barrier between us with a passion, as if it was keeping me from something I'd waited for my entire life.

I held deep and buried my face in her neck, hand gripping her hair, and willed myself not to come even as she writhed under me, undulated around me.

This was the last time. And I *still* hadn't had enough.

"Please don't come yet," she sobbed as she bucked under me, using my body to shamelessly ride out her release.

"Why?" The question was harsh. My balls were so full, so tight. I needed release.

"I want more," she confessed.

"Goddammit," I muttered. Beads of sweat broke out on my forehead and back as I fought for control. As I pushed my need down. I held there, sheathed to the hilt, as her tremors finally gentled to delicate squeezes.

She was clung to me like I was her salvation. Her entire body vibrated from the orgasm.

"Do you still want more?" I growled.

Her eyes fluttered open. "Yes," she said without hesitation.

"Then ask nicely."

Her unpainted lips curved in a knowing, female smirk. Her muscles clamped reflexively around my throbbing dick. Yes, Sloane Walton liked dirty talk.

"Please fuck me so hard and deep that I have to think about you and that magnificent cock every time I sit down at work tomorrow."

I closed my eyes and clenched my jaw. I wanted that. Wanted to know she'd be thinking about me, remembering how I'd made her feel.

I pulled out of her, the pout of her full lower lip making my dick ache.

"Hey!" she complained.

But she stopped abruptly when I manhandled her to the edge of the cushion. Wanting to feel her skin against mine, I shrugged out of my shirt and tossed her legs over my shoulders.

"Oh God." It was a whimper that ended in a muffled squeak when I dragged my tongue through her slick folds. She tasted like secrets and truth, and I was instantaneously addicted.

Her thighs trembled on either side of my ears.

"Open," I ordered, teasing her with the tips of two fingers.

"Lucian," she begged.

"Baby, open for me. Let me taste you."

Her eager compliance went straight to my head and my aching dick. She relaxed her thighs, letting her knees fall open on my shoulders.

Apparently the only way I could get Sloane Walton to do what I wanted was by keeping her on the brink of orgasm.

"Don't make me regret this," she hissed. She had her hands over her eyes so she didn't see the fiendish smile as I pushed my fingers inside her. Her body responded immediately, heels digging into my back, thighs tensing, smooth stomach tightening. Those perfect, full breasts hitched as her bare lips formed an enticing O.

"Relax," I urged, crooking my fingers in her wet channel.

A soft cry escaped her, and the tension slowly began to leave her legs again.

I took the opportunity offered and dove between her legs. My tongue laved the hard bud of her clitoris as I pumped my fingers into her precious little cunt.

She'd gone rigid again, but it didn't matter, because I had access to everything I needed. I plundered with my mouth, stroking and teasing her while I worked my fingers in and out. She was writhing beneath me, her nails digging into my biceps as I held her still.

I couldn't get enough of her flavor. I wanted to taste her as she came. I wanted to sample the flavor of her surrender.

"Come for me," I growled against her sex.

She let out a whimper and squirmed against my grip. "I don't want this to be over."

She didn't know what she was saying. She didn't mean it, I told myself. I'd just pushed her past the point where she could comfortably insult me while I fucked her. I'd pushed us both too far.

"What are you saying?" I demanded without slowing the rhythm of my fingers.

"Wh-what if I don't want it to be the last time?"

Something big and bright lodged itself in my chest. "Then I'll just keep making you come until we're tired of it." I didn't know if it was a promise or a threat, but I meant it.

"Are you just saying that? Are you fucking with me right now?"

"I'm not fucking *with* you. I'm fucking you," I pointed out.

Her hands fisted against the cushion. "Oh God, I can't fight it."

"Don't you dare fucking fight it." To ensure she couldn't, I added a third finger to her tight sheath and spread the lips of her sex with my opposite hand. My tongue found her swollen clit with laser-like precision.

She screamed my name as her body tensed. My balls tightened and my cock jutted out as the pressure built to painful heights. And then she was coming, her beautiful body using my mouth and fingers to steal every ounce of pleasure she craved. She came apart on me, and I could taste the glory of her release.

I wanted her to say my name again. I wanted to hear that broken hitch in her husky voice.

But she went limp under me as if her body were melting wax.

"You okay?" I asked, hovering over her.

"Nope. Never be okay again."

"Baby." I gave her a little shake.

She opened one mischievous green eye and arched her eyebrow. "My turn."

I had to give her credit for taking me by surprise. She had her hand on my erection before I realized she wasn't about to faint.

It was so sudden I almost came in her hand.

I gripped her wrist and could feel the pulse of my own cock. "No," I said.

"You went down on me twice now. I get to go down on you," she insisted.

"No," I said again.

"Why not?" Her hand tightened wickedly on my shaft.

To distract her and give myself what I needed, I turned her around and placed her on her knees on the floor in front of the couch. "Because you're going to be too busy getting fucked," I told her as I pushed her head and shoulders down flat on the cushion. I knelt behind her, spread her legs, and adjusted her hips until the crown of my cock was aligned with her weeping sex.

Just the barest brushes of that hot, tight little heaven that awaited me had me reaching for every iota of control.

"Please, Lucian!"

There it was. My name from her lips. Begging me to give her something only I could. I bucked forward, seating my entire shaft to the root inside her in one thrust.

Her scream was muffled by the cushion. I ran my hands up her spine, over her shoulders, and down her arms while I waited to regain control.

"Hang on tight, baby," I warned.

I eased out and then used her hips to fuck my way back into her.

Her pussy convulsed around me when I hit that secret spot. Jesus, how could she be ready to come again? Her body was a fucking miracle. My fucking miracle.

I slid my palms up to cup the heavy weight of her tits and used them for leverage as I began to thrust.

I squeezed those full, perfect breasts as I fucked into her tight, wet pussy.

"Oh my God," she chanted.

She was ready to come. All she needed was a little bit of pressure in exactly the right spot. I fucking loved being in charge of her pleasure. Deciding when and how. It was headier than any other achievement of my entire life.

I folded over her, adding my weight to her back and thrusting harder, deeper. I released one breast and brought that hand between her legs.

She went rigid under me. "Lucian, I—"

"Such a good girl," I praised. "You're so wet for my cock, aren't you?"

"What I want is that magical dick of yours in my mouth," she said, sounding adorably disgruntled.

I found her clit just as I gave her nipple a hard tug and buried my cock to the hilt, angling my hips up, up, up. She could do nothing but take what I was giving her, and it went to my head, my balls, my fucking heart.

"Come for me, Pix. Come on my cock so hard it hurts."

"Yes, Lucian. Yes," she cried brokenly.

Music to my fucking ears. And then she did exactly as I told her.

This time, when she fell apart, convulsing around my shaft, I didn't fight the overwhelming urge to let go. I let her quivering pussy pull my release from me. I ejaculated fiercely, a scorching burst that I wished she could feel. Even as the next hot rope of come wrenched free and the next, I thought about how it would feel if there were no barriers between us.

"Lucian!" She squirmed against me, coming again, or still, as if my pleasure triggered her own.

"That's my good girl," I said as I emptied myself into her, imagining a life where she was mine and I was hers.

24

Grilled Cheese Peace Talks

Sloane

I'm not cuddling with you," I murmured into Lucian's neck. "I just can't use my arms or legs."

I was sprawled naked over the man's godlike body, too many hours and orgasms beyond caring about anything except Lucian's cock and the endless pleasure it gifted me.

He landed a stinging swat to my rear end.

"Ow."

"My limbs still work," he said smugly.

His limbs *and* the superhuman dick that was still semihard and wearing the last condom in my house.

I lifted my head and looked around. "Oh good. We made it upstairs to the bedroom finally."

He pulled me back down, cradling me against his chest, but not before I caught a glimpse of an honest-to-God smile on the man's beautiful face. I decided after the seven orgasms he'd delivered, I could let him have this moment.

Teenage Lucian had been affectionate, I recalled. He'd snuggled with me in this same bed, playing with my hair, stroking my arm or back.

He'd submitted to all the hugs and back pats and shoulder squeezes from my parents with a rueful smile. Like he'd craved physical contact but didn't want to let on.

My heart clenched for the boy who'd deserved so much more.

He stroked a hand through my hair, letting the strands fall against my back, and I felt my eyes go damp.

The panic was rising again.

That was what had propelled me out of my own hotel room after four orgasms and less than two hours of sleep. The realization that I was muddling the no-strings-attached present with the feelings of the past.

Neither of us was the same person we'd been back then. I couldn't afford to let my feelings for teenage Lucian get tangled up in what was clearly just a physical thing.

A *very* physical thing.

"Are we going again?" I asked nonchalantly, hoping not to let on that my entire body was too tired and too sore.

Lucian sighed. "Much as it pains me to admit, Pixie, you've bested me. I'm going to need an ice pack, a bucket of ibuprofen, and a four-hour nap if you want one last last time."

"Loser," I muttered into his neck. "I'm ready to go again."

"Liar."

He tugged on my hair until I looked up at him.

"Okay. Fine. I'm back to being nauseated by the thought of sex with you," I teased.

"So we're officially done then?" His face was once again guarded. It was somehow worse after having seen him in so many shields-down, orgasmic moments.

I shrugged one shoulder. "I guess so. I suppose I could feed you before I send you packing."

As if on cue, Lucian's stomach rumbled.

I feigned a gasp. "I didn't know vampires got hungry."

He lunged for me, his teeth grazing my neck. "Hold still, you snack-size human."

I gasped with laughter and collapsed against him again. Playful Lucian was an entirely new creature to me. Like Edward after Bella had discovered his secret in *Twilight*. Only I hadn't discovered Lucian's secret. I'd just had a whole lot of sex with him.

His hands gentled on me. "You have a beautiful laugh."

I sat up again and frowned. "Okay. You're officially delirious. Come on. I need lunch and electrolytes since you dehydrated me via my vagina."

"My cock is sore. As in the-day-after-leg-day-at-the-gym sore," he complained as we crawled out of bed.

I pulled on a blue bathrobe with daisies while Lucian yanked on his underwear. He frowned down at his dress shirt. It was missing a few buttons and had a questionable wet spot on the sleeve.

"Hold on." I limped into my closet and found the sweatshirt I was looking for. "Here," I said, tossing it to him.

He caught it and his frown turned into a scowl. "Whose is this?" he asked, holding up the extra-extra-large Penn State hoodie.

"Mine now," I said.

"Whose *was* it?"

"An old boyfriend. We dated for a couple of months after I graduated college and was working in Hagerstown. He was a social studies teacher."

"Blake." He said the name like it was an insult.

I raised an eyebrow. "You know, Unfucked Sloane would be giving you shit for knowing my ex-boyfriend's name from fifteen years ago. But Well-Fucked Sloane is too tired and hungry to start a fight."

He threw the sweatshirt back to me. "I'm not wearing this."

"You're missing out. It's comfortable and it'll fit you."

Lucian picked up his ruined dress shirt and stubbornly shoved his arms through the sleeves. "You probably think of him every time you wear it."

"Fondly," I said, not above adding just a few drops of lighter fluid to the flames. "Come on. I'm starving."

We made quite the picture, stumbling and limping our way down the back stairs into the kitchen.

Meow Meow glared judgmentally from her perch

on a pot holder in the middle of the island. The tip of her tail twitched.

"That's incredibly unhygienic," Lucian observed.

"Good thing you don't plan to spend any time in this house, because every flat surface has probably come into contact with cat butt," I said, ruffling her ears before opening the refrigerator door.

"What's it's name?"

"Her name is Meow Meow."

"That's an unimaginative name."

"Her official name is Lady Meowington," I said, opening the cheese drawer.

"That's worse. I'm horrified. You're terrible at naming things."

"Cats name themselves. You start with an official name, and it devolves over the years until you find something they actually respond to. Lady Meowington here only responds to Meow Meow or 'Hey, asshole.' " I glanced up and found Lucian eyeing the cat while she devoted herself to cleaning her belly.

Meow Meow was a furry lump of disdain. My one-night stand, however, in his underwear and open shirt with his tousled hair and sleepy eyes, was absolutely delectable. I'd known he was good-looking. Devastatingly handsome even. But I'd never allowed myself to *really* look.

Now that I had? I was going to need some alcohol with my post-sex snack.

I held up two blocks of cheese. "How do you feel about grilled cheese?"

Lucian grimaced. "You eat like a child."

"I'm going to make you the best damned grilled cheese you've ever had, and then I'm going to allow you to rub my feet while groveling for my forgiveness."

"A little more pressure on the arch, servant," I ordered.

Lucian's strong thumbs dug deeper on the sole of my foot. "Your feet are so small. How do you walk on these things?"

"You're so weird after a sex marathon and grilled cheese." I took another victorious bite of my buffalo chicken grilled cheese sandwich of awesomeness. Lucian's plate was empty. He'd inhaled his sandwich with gusto and was shooting longing looks at my second half.

With an eye roll, I tore the half into two pieces and handed him one.

He dropped my foot in his lap and dove in.

We'd set up camp in the family room off the kitchen at the back of the house to eat and watch *Night Court* reruns. I said it was because the TV was bigger, but really it was because I didn't want anyone catching a glimpse of Lucian Rollins through my front windows and broadcasting it to the entire town. Sharing this catastrophe with anyone was not an option.

As Bull delivered a punch line to Judge Harold T. Stone, I heard a dramatic thud behind us. I tilted my head on the cushion and spied the cat's hulking fluff prance across the console table against the couch.

"What is it doing?" Lucian demanded, swiveling his head.

"*She* is trying to make you uncomfortable."

Meow Meow sat directly behind him and stared at the back of his head. "It's working."

"She doesn't really like people," I explained. "Mom and I are the only ones who can pet her. Dad was the only one she'd let pick her up, and that was only if he stood still."

"I feel her eyes boring into the back of my head," he complained, shifting closer to me on the cushion. His bare thigh rested snugly against my knee, his shoulder a comforting weight against mine. Couples did this. Had sex on a Sunday morning and then snuggled up on the couch with junk food to watch old favorites.

We were not a couple. We were a mistake. A hot, sexy, mind-melting mistake.

"Just ignore her. She's so lazy she'd never go out of her way to jump on your head just to bite and claw your face off," I promised cheerily.

"That's comforting," he said dryly.

I took Lucian's empty plate and placed it on the table behind me. Meow Meow gave the back of Lucian's head one last scowl before sauntering over to investigate the crumbs. Satisfied that what we were eating was subpar, she heaved herself to the floor and wandered off.

Lucian slung his arm over the back of the couch behind me.

Was Lucian Rollins *snuggling* with me? Had I given him a concussion when I'd accidentally banged his head against the headboard while riding him?

The studio audience dissolved into hysterics over Dan Fielding's flirtation with Christine Sullivan. This was so *normal*. So not *us*. So exactly what I wanted . . . with a different man, of course, and with a couple of kids thrown into the mix. Lucian had always wanted something different. I couldn't help but wonder if all those things he'd wanted—the wealth, the power, the ability to crush enemies with a flick of his wrist—were just a replacement for what he thought he could never have.

"Your father loved this episode," Lucian mused as I attacked the last quarter of my grilled cheese.

"He did," I agreed, stacking my empty plate on his. "Now that your penis has invaded my vagina on multiple occasions, I think you should tell me why you're so close to my parents. Oh God." I sat up straighter. "You didn't have an affair with my mom, did you?"

"I did not have an affair with your mother," he said dryly.

"Then what kind of a relationship do you have with her?"

He sighed and paused the episode. "Your parents helped me through a difficult time in my life. I owe them for that."

"So you have some kind of invisible tally system, and once you've hit the appropriate number of tick marks, you'll vanish from Mom's life?"

"You're a lot like your father," he said, though it didn't sound like a compliment.

"In what way?" I pressed, eager for any connection to the man I missed.

"You never give up. Even when you should."

"He never gave up on you," I said softly. But I had. Not that I'd had a choice.

"Not many people have the unbridled, delusional optimism that Simon Walton brought to this world."

I sighed against Lucian's broad shoulder. I may have gotten my tenacity from my dad, but I had missed out on the delusional optimism gene. "He was one of a kind," I agreed.

We were silent for a long moment, both staring straight ahead at the frozen faces on the TV screen.

"I can't believe Ansel is dead," I said finally.

Lucian stiffened next to me like I'd just pushed the button where all his walls came up and the gate to his castle rolled down.

I put my hand on his thigh and gripped. "Wait. Before we jump into Lucian versus Sloane Round two million, let's call a temporary cease-fire and have some peace talks."

He looked down at me, his expression halfway between amusement and annoyance. "Peace talks? Why do women feel the need to talk everything to death?"

"If you'll shut up, I'll explain. Now, I'm not admitting to having wondered for a long time what sex with you would be like." His expression went wolfish, and I held up a finger. "No! We're still recovering. If we attack each other now, you'll sprain your penis or I'll lose feeling below the waist."

"I'm willing to take that chance."

I rose up on my knees and faced him. "Keep it zipped, Sir Fucks a Lot. What I'm suggesting is since we've appeased our curiosity with our one-night-only sexual shenanigans, why don't we apply the same consideration to all the questions we've always wanted answers to?"

"No."

I pouted. "You didn't even consider the offer. That's not very peace talky of you."

"Don't look at me like that."

Sensing impending victory, I deepened my pout, saddened my eyes, and straddled his lap. "Come on, big guy. We cleared the air sexually and survived. Why can't we drop a couple of truth bombs consequence-free before we go back to normal and never speak again?"

His handsome face with its poetic cheekbones and stormy eyes gave nothing away, but his cock was making its feelings known beneath me.

"I'm not above holding a pillow over your face until you stop annoying me, Pix," he warned.

"Yes, you are. Please?"

His hands came to my hips, and he dropped his head against the cushion. "If I say yes—" I wiggled

434

victoriously in his lap, and his hands gripped me tighter as his teeth clenched, deepening the hollows of his face. "Behave. I have conditions."

I slid my hands under his open shirt and rested them on the warm, firm flesh of his shoulders. "I'm all ears."

"You're never all ears. You're all agendas," he pointed out.

"Oh, come on. You're not the least bit curious about *anything?*" I prompted.

His eyes were steely on mine as he presumably tried to figure out my motive.

"I'm just thinking, we cleared the air sexually, why not clear it all the way? We end today baggage-free. Like lancing a boil."

"A very attractive metaphor," Lucian said dryly.

"Come on," I cajoled. "Admit it. It makes sense."

I knew how to build up a rapport with a suspect thanks to *Becoming Bulletproof* by former Secret Service Special Agent Evy Poumpouras. About a year ago, I'd started a secret, unofficial book club for a few local high schoolers who were going through tough times as unpopular misfits. We read a lot of self-help and nonfiction about interpersonal relationships, and I didn't mind deploying some psychological warfare when the scenario called for it.

"I don't like this," he said.

I bounced victoriously in his lap. "But you know I'm right. This could finally be our blank slate, big guy."

"Blank slates are for new beginnings."

"Ugh. Fine. This could be our 'the end.' "

"If I agree," he said, arresting my movements with his hands, "you have twenty minutes and then you're shutting up and I'm taking your clothes off."

I arched an eyebrow. "I thought we were done with each other."

"Do you have something better to do this afternoon?"

I grinned. "Nope."

"Twenty minutes," he repeated.

I scrambled off his lap and planted myself against the arm of the couch, hugging a pillow to my chest. "I'll go first. What kind of beard maintenance do you do? Or is it just rich guy magic where you wake up, look in the mirror, and command your facial hair to do what you want?"

His expression was priceless. "You can ask me anything and you want to know how I maintain my beard?"

I shrugged. "I'm warming you up before we get to the interesting stuff."

"I already regret this."

"Did you ever have feelings for Knox or Nash?"

Lucian's question caught me by surprise. We'd mostly lobbed softballs back and forth, participating in a delicate dance around the minefields of our past.

"Uh, yeah," I said emphatically.

"When?" he demanded, his grip on my feet in his lap tightening.

"Probably right around the time I hit fourteen and they suddenly got hot."

"Do Naomi and Lina know you lust after their men?"

"Yep. They're used to it. Anyone who enjoys looking at attractive men lusts after those two." I laughed when he looked downright grumpy. "Oh, come on. You're not left out of that equation. Women walk into glass doors trying to get a better look at you."

He grunted.

"My turn. Why won't you let me blow you?"

His laugh startled me.

"Do you find oral sex funny?" I demanded.

"On the contrary, I take it very seriously."

My lady parts knew this intimately. I nudged him with my foot. "Elaborate, Lucifer."

"I like being in control," he said as if that answered everything.

"You can be in control during a blow job."

His gaze slid to my mouth. "Not enough."

"Clearly, you haven't experienced the right kind of oral sex. I'll be happy to demonstrate in . . ." I checked the clock on the mantel. "Seven minutes."

"Pass."

"Party pooper. Since that was a lame answer, I get another question. Did you tattoo over all your scars?"

Lucian stared at me for a long beat. I wondered if I'd pushed too far.

"Yes," he said finally.

"Why?"

"Because I'd rather have marks on my body that I chose."

I nodded. It made sense. The man was literally rewriting his past on his own skin. He surprised me and reached for my wrist. He rolled it over and examined the silvery scars left behind. "A plastic surgeon could probably do something with this."

I smirked. "I dunno. I kinda think it makes me look like a badass. It reminds me of how brave I was once."

He cleared his throat and released my wrist. "Have you met your future husband yet?" he asked, changing the subject.

I closed my eyes. "I officially had my best date since I started this quest."

"And?" he prompted.

"Best doesn't mean much when it's stacked up against all the other catastrophes. Nice guy. Wants kids. Zero sparks. I almost fell asleep in my soup while he was talking about last season's fantasy football league. But maybe that's what marriage is? A sparkless partnership based on what you can accomplish together."

"Is that what you think our friends have? Sparkless partnerships?" Lucian asked, his lips curving ever so slightly.

I sighed. "No. They tamed the unicorn." At his

blank expression, I continued. "You know, they found the smoldering, I-wasn't-my-best-self-until-I-met-you, I-want-to-make-all-your-dreams-come-true kind of once-in-a-lifetime, I-still-watch-you-walk-out-of-the-room love."

"And you want the unicorn?" Lucian guessed.

"Who doesn't? Present company excluded, of course."

"Of course."

"Yeah. I want the unicorn," I admitted.

"Then you'll get it."

I glanced up at him, but there was no hint that he was making fun of me.

"You think so?"

He rolled his eyes. "Sloane, what have you ever worked for that you didn't end up getting?"

The man had a point. With the exception of my father's health, everything I set my sights on eventually came to fruition. Could I just will the perfect man into my life?

"Thanks," I said. "So tell me one of the things my mom was thanking you for at the funeral."

He remained silent.

"As per the rules, I'm not allowed to hold it against you or throw it back in your face ever," I reminded him.

He lifted my foot and applied a heavenly thumb to my arch. "Fine. I helped them find their condo."

The man was definitely withholding information. "That was nice of you. But in the pursuit of honesty, Mom was more thank-you-for-saving-the-life-of-our-favorite-child and less thanks-for-sending-me-a-real-estate-listing grateful."

He muttered something that sounded a lot like "tenacious pain in the ass" under his breath.

"Come on, big guy. This boil isn't going to lance itself."

"You are such a pain in the ass," he complained.

"Oh my God. Just tell me already," I said impatiently.

"Fine. I bought it for them."

I blinked. "Bought what?"

"If you're going to force me to talk, the least you can do is pretend to listen. I bought the condo for your parents."

That shut me up.

"Stop it," he said, dropping my feet and using my ankles to pull me closer.

"Stop what?" I managed.

"Stop trying to read anything into it. It wasn't heroic or thoughtful. I was just balancing the scales."

"Crap on a cracker, Lucian. What scales require a very expensive real estate transaction?"

"Sloane, your parents drove me to college and furnished my first shitty apartment. They helped me get a job. They fed me when I was hungry. They kept an eye on my mother until she moved. They took me out on my birthday every year since I turned eighteen. They showed up to my college graduation and stood up and cheered when I walked the stage. They invited me to be a part of their family when I couldn't be part of my own."

My eyes were starting to burn and blur. It had been a huge gift, finding the perfect "affordable" place just two blocks from Dad's oncologist. Lucian had given them that gift.

"That was very generous of you," I rasped.

This was not helping me. If I was going to get over the man, I needed to focus on his dark, stubborn side, not his hidden, microscopic heart of gold.

"Do not get emotional about this," he warned.

"I'm not getting emotional," I insisted even as my voice cracked.

"I should have just put the pillow over your face."

"Thank you," I said.

"For what? Not smothering you?"

I shook my head and then did something neither of us could have predicted twenty-four hours ago.

I hugged him.

My arms went around him, my face pressed into his neck, and I held on. "Thank you for what you did for my parents."

He tried to disentangle himself, but I refused to let go. Finally he stopped fighting it and gave me an awkward pat on the back. "I like it better when you hate me."

"Me too."

He tugged on my ponytail until I met his gaze. "Tell me the truth. Isn't there part of you that wishes you would have gotten that scholarship and gone into sports medicine? Is this life some kind of consolation prize?" He gestured around the family room.

Baffled, I sat up straighter. "Is that what you think?"

"You had bigger dreams than this, Sloane."

"Lucian, I was a *teenager*. I also wanted to marry Jerome Bettis from the Pittsburgh Steelers."

"Just because they were teenage dreams doesn't mean they weren't real," he said quietly, no longer meeting my eyes.

I wondered what teenage Lucian had dreamed of before he'd been forced to become the man of the family.

"This life is better than any I could have planned at sixteen. Or at twenty. Hell, even thirty. I love this town, this house. I love being close to my sister and my niece. All that time I got with my dad that I wouldn't have had if I'd moved across the country in pursuit of some crazy career. That time is priceless. I would have missed out on so many things. I wouldn't have the library. I wouldn't know Naomi and Lina. So no. I don't regret for one second that my teenage plans were derailed."

"Even though you don't have everything you want?" he pressed. "The husband. The kids."

"Yet. I don't have them yet. I built a life based on everything I wanted, and I fit them together one by one. That means the missing pieces of a partner and a family have an almost complete puzzle to fit into."

He let out a long breath, but it didn't sound like his usual exasperated sighs. It sounded like he'd let go of something heavy he'd carried for too long.

"What was it like?" I asked.

"What was what like?"

"The week Wylie had you locked up."

The silence was oppressive. It felt like a cold, wet blanket had descended on us both, smothering us with its damp weight.

I leaned into him and rested my face on his chest, listening to the steady thrum of his heart.

After a minute, his hands came to my back and began to stroke slowly.

"It was the worst six days of my life."

I absorbed the hurt, accepted it. I'd done that to him. I'd hand-delivered his worst moments. "How?" I asked softly.

"He was alone with her. There was no one to protect her. Officer Winslow knew, or at least he suspected, and he'd drive past the house a few times a shift. I know your parents were watching too. But there's a lot of damage that can still be done behind closed doors."

I swallowed around the lump in my throat.

"I knew it was only a matter of time before he ended up in the cell next to mine," he continued. "It didn't matter how friendly he was with the cops. Even Ogden wouldn't have helped him cover up a murder. But I knew my life was over. I turned eighteen in a cell, and I knew those bars and bunks were my future. I was going to have to become the kind of person who survived in a cage."

A tear scalded its way down my cheek.

"My safety, my well-being was at the mercy of all those badges. I wasn't even human to some of them."

I'm sorry. The words were there, in my throat, on my tongue, begging to be let loose. But they'd never be enough for either one of us. And I didn't know if that meant they weren't worth saying.

"What is that incessant buzzing noise?" Lucian demanded. He'd left his memories behind while I was still mired in them.

"Oh my God. It's my phone. I haven't looked at it since you showed up and whipped your dick out." I sprang off the couch and raced into the kitchen where I found my phone facedown next to Mary Louise's case files. "Twenty-four messages and two missed calls?"

Lucian appeared in the doorway, looking like debauchery personified. "Is there an emergency?"

"I can't tell yet," I said, scrolling to the top of the texts.

Naomi: Stefan Liao, did you really chicken out on telling Jeremiah you see a future with him and run back to New York this morning for a fake work excuse?
Stef: First of all, a board of directors meeting is not a fake work excuse. Second, yes. Yes I did.

Lina: Wow, Stef. I never pegged you as a coward.

Stef: Excuse me, Ms. Pit Stains on Her Wedding Dress!

Lina: I may have sweaty pits, but at least I'M STILL IN KNOCKEMOUT WITH THE MAN I LOVE!

Naomi: Normally I shy away from conflict and raise the de-escalation flag, however in this case I feel it's important to present a relevant case study: Knox Morgan.

Stef: I'm not pulling a Knox Morgan. I just had business to attend to so I'm attending to it.

Lina: You forgot to put quotes around "business."

"No emergency. Just busting on Stef for getting ready to make a grand gesture and then panicking and leaving town," I reported.

"What kind of grand gesture?" Lucian asked, opening a cabinet and helping himself to a glass.

"He wants to move here and live with his hot boyfriend, but he got cold feet about actually admitting it to Jeremiah," I said, still scrolling while Lucian got himself a drink of water.

Stef: Where's Sloane? She's always more fun to pick on than me.

Naomi: Sloane!

Lina: Yo, Sloane!

Stef: You don't think she snuck off for another date without telling us and got murdered, do you?

Lina: Well, I do now.

Naomi: She's not answering her phone. I'm worried.

Lina: Maybe she's in the shower?

Stef: Maybe she's in the shower with someone.

Naomi: She wouldn't be taking a ninety-minute shower.

Stef: Not alone at least.

Lina: She's probably working and left her phone in her office.

Naomi: I distinctly remember her saying she had today off. Chloe told Waylay Sloane had plans last night, but no one seems to know what they were.

Stef: Hopefully she's getting laid.

Lina: We haven't heard from her since 7:13 p.m. last night. Nobody gets laid for that long.

I smirked reading Lina's text. I turned the screen so Lucian could read it. "Well, *that's* not true," I said smugly.

"You'd better tell your friends that," he said, pointing to the next message.

Naomi: Maybe we should go to her house?

446

"Uh-oh," I said.

Lina: Nash and I are naked but we could be unnaked in about ten minutes. Try calling her again and we'll get dressed.

"Shit," I muttered, thumbs flying over the screen.

Me: No need for a welfare check. I'm alive and well. Just busy!

"They're going to know what you're busy doing," Lucian pointed out, running his hand down my ponytail.

"Damn it." He was right. "I'll tell them I'm cleaning the house."

"Naomi will be over here with a truckload of cleaning supplies in five minutes," he predicted. "Pick something they'll all find unpleasant."

"I'll go with the truth then. They'll be horrified," I joked.

His grip on my hair tightened. "Would you rather spend the afternoon being interrogated by your friends or letting me fuck you?"

Me: I'm having my septic tank pumped! The fumes are powerful! Anyone want to come over for game night?

25

I Will Not Apply a Chemical Peel to My Dick

Lucian

It was an exceptionally gray Monday. The invigorating February air was razor sharp as it hit my lungs. I felt awake, alive, ready to greet the day and destroy my enemies.

"Good morning, sir," my driver greeted me.

"Morning, Hank," I said, sliding into the back seat of the SUV. "How was your weekend?"

He blinked. "Um, fine, sir. Is everything all right?"

"Everything is excellent."

"That's . . . good." He closed the door with a look of concern.

I pulled out my phone and typed a text to Sloane.

Me: Good morning.

I frowned at the words. They seemed flat and inconsequential considering the sexual acrobatics we'd performed all weekend long.

Me: Good morning, beautiful.

No. Definitely not. That one made me sound like a lovesick Morgan brother. I immediately

448

deleted the text. What was the appropriate Monday morning greeting for the librarian who had fucked me into oblivion repeatedly?

Me: My cock is chafed.

Sloane: Good morning to you too. I think you sprained my vagina with too many orgasms.

Me: Is there some kind of balm or laser resurfacing treatment for this kind of situation?

Sloane: Repeat after me. "I will not apply a chemical peel to my dick."

Me: I had two charley horses in my calves last night.

Sloane: Poor baby. Drink some pickle juice and then tell me how I'm supposed to not think about our rabid fucking every time I sit down today.

Me: If I have to be haunted by our poor choices so do you.

Sloane: Good thing we wised up and won't be making the same mistake again. Our sex parts need time to heal.

Me: Glad we got it out of our systems. I haven't even thought about you naked at all in the last four seconds.

Sloane: Hold please. I need to get through a staff meeting today without thinking about your "staff."

She would think about me all day long, I decided with manly satisfaction as I pocketed my phone. Good. Not that I'd give her a second thought, of course.

"What happened?" Petula demanded the second I stepped off the elevator.

"With what?"

"You look cheerful. Did you unseat another senator?"

"I had a nice weekend," I said with as much dignity as I could muster.

Petula rattled off the morning's appointments while shooting me suspicious looks.

"What's with the face?" Lina asked, stepping out of the kitchen. I realized that for once, I wasn't the first person in the office. In fact, half of the staff was already here, gearing up for the day. I must have slept later than I thought thanks to She Who Shall Not Be Thought Of.

"Thank you, Petula. I'll take it from here," I said, dismissing her.

"If he starts to look feverish, I want to know," Petula told Lina. "I have a medical team on standby."

"There's nothing wrong with my face," I assured my newest employee.

"The mouth part is fighting its natural frown. You're almost smiling," she observed.

Nolan appeared behind her holding a cup of coffee and a stack of files. "Whoa. Someone got laid," he announced, taking one look at my face.

"Don't make me send you through HR's six-week sexual harassment training," I warned, telegraphing a message of dire consequences if he dared mention Sloane's name in front of Lina.

"He didn't even threaten to fire you," Lina stage-whispered. "It's official. Lucian Rollins has been abducted by aliens."

"Aliens that had a lot of sex with him. Initiate Protocol D, people," Nolan announced. Employees nearby grinned at him.

"You're both fired," I decided.

"You might want to hold off on that until I update you on that issue we discussed Saturday night," Nolan said, nodding in the direction of his office.

"This concerns you too," I told Lina.

Together the three of us trooped into Nolan's office. He closed the door and dumped the files on his desk. Lina took a seat and crossed one long leg over the other. I remained standing.

"I pulled Travers off the Rugulio background check and sent him sniffing around Felix Metzer's family this weekend."

"And?" I prompted.

"He was able to confirm that Tate Dilton was the one who showed up at the Metzer family barbecue. Three family members IDed him after Travers showed them a couple of photos of our mustachioed, deceased douchebag."

Lina was on her feet. "Tate Dilton. The son of a bitch who tried to murder my fiancé?"

"That's the one," Nolan said.

"Apparently he was connected to the man Anthony Hugo commissioned to create the list of law enforcement and informants," I explained.

"Did he put Nash's name on that list?" Lina demanded. Her fury was a controlled, icy blast.

"It looks that way," Nolan said.

"But why the hell would he put Nash's name on the list and then be the one to try to take him out?" she asked. "Why not just pull the trigger and forget the list?"

Nolan glanced at me. "The best we can figure it, Dilton was a dumbass."

"Well, that tracks," Lina said.

"He wanted Nash out of the picture but not enough to pull the trigger himself, until Duncan offered him cash. He could have been playing both sides, doing a little work for Anthony over here and a little something for Duncan over there. There's no loyalty in dipshit criminals," Nolan explained.

"It looks like that ties everything up in a nice neat bow," I said. "Dilton put Nash's name on the list. Dilton pulled the trigger twice. And Dilton ended up dead."

Lina's eyes narrowed. "I wish that asshole wasn't dead so I could knee him in the balls and wax his mustache."

"You, me, and the boss man," Nolan agreed.

"I'm telling Nash," Lina announced. "NDA or not, he deserves to know."

"I assumed you would." It worked in my favor, since then *she'd* have to listen to him bitch about civilians sticking their noses into law enforcement investigations instead of me.

She sighed. "Thanks for reading me in."

"Welcome to the team," Nolan said.

"Speaking of work," Lina said. "Morganstern Credit Corporation was just informed they're about to be hit with a lawsuit for skeezy debt collection practices. The attorney sends her thanks, by the way. She thinks this might turn into a class action suit."

"Good," I said, checking my phone for messages.

"You know, it sure is a small world," she mused. "Sloane went out with a guy from Morganstern who tried to scam her by faking his own death."

"Huh. No kidding," Nolan said, looking pointedly at me.

"Are we done here?" I asked.

"I've got a grumpy chief of police to call," Lina said. She was already pulling her phone out of her blazer pocket before she hit the hall.

"So not to be that guy, but now that we know who put Nash's name on that list, are we still planning on giving the FBI a hand with their case against Hugo?" Nolan asked.

I shoved my hands in my pockets. "It wasn't Duncan who had men tail Holly. Anthony made it personal."

"I'll move 'destroy the fucker' to the top of our to-do list," Nolan said amicably.

"What are you doing for your wife for Valentine's Day?" I asked suddenly.

Nolan's face lit up. "Callie's been working long hours lately, so I got a pair of massage therapists coming to the house for a couples massage in front of the fireplace. Then I'm gonna order her favorite pizza, and we're going to camp out on the couch watching rom-coms and drinking old-fashioneds until the frisky part of the festivities begins."

"Men shouldn't use words like frisky."

"So what about you? Big plans for the big V?"

"Why do I bother talking to you?"

Nolan grinned. "Because you secretly love me and think I'm delightful. So you and Sloane?"

I hated how much I'd wanted someone to say her name in front of me. "What about Sloane?"

"You walked in looking like your horse took the Triple Crown. Now you're standing in my office willingly making small talk. Somebody got under that prickly exterior. My money's on Blondie."

"As always, I regret our conversation," I said, heading for the door.

"Fine. But if you need relationship advice, you know where to find me," he called after me.

I presented him with my middle finger on my way out.

Nash: Lina is reporting that the head of the evil empire is walking around the office looking like he just got laid.

Knox: Hope this one didn't steal your watch and your robe.

Me: Running an evil empire takes significant focus. I don't have time for your girlish gossip. Especially now that I have to fire Lina.

Knox: He definitely got laid.

Nash: Let me know if you need to file a robbery report.

Knox: Wait a second. Weren't you in Knockemout this weekend? Neecey said you called in a pizza order Sunday.

Nash: Don't tell me you finally gave in to Mrs. Tweedy's advances.

Me: What Mrs. Tweedy and I do or don't do is none of your business.

Nash: I'm begging you. Please don't drive some poor, unsuspecting Knockemout woman crazy enough to start stalking you. I don't have the manpower to deal with it.

Sloane: I've had three patrons tell me I'm glowing. I had to start telling people I found a new foundation so they wouldn't know it was orgasmic. How's your day? Destroy the economies of any small countries yet?

Me: Petula has a medical team on standby because I smiled. Lina wants to know why I'm not frowning enough. And Nolan thinks that I secretly love him. I hate everything.

Sloane: On the bright side, your penis will have time to heal since you won't be shoving it inside me any time soon.

Me: Just to clarify for the official documents my lawyer is drawing up, we're no longer having sex, correct?

Sloane: I believe that is what was discussed somewhere between orgasms and your snoring when we took a nap on my couch.

Me: That was a coma, not a nap. So we're done then. Never to be mentioned again. You're off to focus on finding Mr. Perfect to build your gigantic, unruly family and I'm free to continue my capitalistic pillaging.

Sloane: Yep. Have fun pillaging!

Me: Have fun finding a husband who isn't incredibly disappointing in bed.

Sloane: It's going to take hours upon hours of exhaustive, naked research on my part.

Me: Are you sure your endurance is up for the task? Perhaps you should consider a training program to improve your cardiovascular baseline.

Sloane: Are you offering to sex coach me?

Me: Are you considering the offer?

Sloane: What about the official documents your lawyer is drawing up? I'd hate for you to waste all that money by having sex with me again.

Me: I can have the contract postdated. What are you doing Friday?

Sloane: Friday as in Valentine's Day?

Me: Friday as in Friday.

Sloane: I'm hosting an erotic author for a sexy, adults-only event at the library.

Me: And after?

Sloane: I guess after I'll be training on your very large penis.

Me: For science.

Emry: Sacha said yes to the symphony.

Me: Congratulations. You're one step closer to ending your bachelorhood.

Emry: I don't know how to date in this day and age. Do I bring her flowers or wine? Is a corsage acceptable? If she texts me should I respond with an emoji or a gif? How much body hair is acceptable on a man these days?

The image consultants on the screen on the wall above the conference table were annoying me with their inability to agree on how best to begin championing Sheila Chandra to the national media. I was about to tell them so when Petula signaled me from the door.

I gestured for Nolan to take over.

"Look, folks. We're not trying to turn her into a

completely different person and alienate her from the following she's already built," he began more politely than I would have.

"Grace from security needs a face-to-face," Petula explained when I joined her in the hallway.

That was never a good thing. Except for the time Grace told me she was pregnant with twins. One look at my head of security's face when I entered my office, and I knew this had nothing to do with maternity leave.

Grace wore a black suit, tactical boots, and a frown on her lovely face. Her black hair was tamed into its usual sleek bun that had been part of her uniform before I'd poached her from the Secret Service. "We've got a problem," she announced without preamble.

Petula shut the door and left us alone.

"What is it?"

"We found a tracking device on your vehicle during our weekly sweep."

"Which one?" I asked, aware that such a "rich guy" question would have Sloane rolling her eyes.

"The Escalade. I had the team sweep your personal vehicles as well, but they were all clear."

Relief coursed through me. I'd driven the Range Rover to Knockemout. I could have led Hugo straight to Sloane.

"Did you remove it?" I asked tersely.

Grace's lips curved. "Not yet. I figured you might want to take the opportunity to fuck with Hugo and his men, sir. My team is going over all the employee vehicles in the garage as we speak. Once we're satisfied, we'll do a bug sweep of your home and offices."

"Good. Increase security here at the office while I figure out how to use this against Hugo."

26

Dewey Decimal Justice

Sloane

A tiny groan escaped me as I maneuvered the cart into the reference section and pulled a volume at random off the shelf. My entire body hurt. It was distracting me from my Monday. And by "it," I meant Lucian Rollins. My nemesis. The man who had fucked me into oblivion, promised to never call, and then made a date with me for Valentine's Day.

I slid a dollar bill inside the cover and put the book back on the shelf.

It was official. I had lost my damn mind. It was why I'd abandoned my regularly scheduled to-do list to help Jamal set up for the monthly Kids Dewey Decimal Scavenger Hunt Extravaganza. I had to get away from my phone so I would stop checking it to see if the man I hated had texted me.

"There you are!" Naomi appeared in the stacks with a coffee in each hand.

I patted my chest. "Holy cheese and crackers, woman. Don't sneak up on me like that."

"Sorry. I would have called for you, but the Shushy Twins already shushed me twice this morning."

The Shushy Twins were elderly, widowed tattle-tales who spent every Monday morning on the first floor of the library working on their crossword puzzles and policing the behavior of all patrons and staff.

I shuddered. "They busted me for turning pages too loudly last week."

"Then it's a good thing we're meeting in one of the conference rooms upstairs, because the lawyer is here."

"She's early," I said, noting the time on my watch.

"I know. I like her already," Naomi said, taking a hit of coffee.

"Are those both yours?" I asked.

"Well, they weren't going to be, but it took me one entire cappuccino to find you, so unfortunately you have to acquire your own caffeine now."

Fran Vereen was a tall, boxy woman in her early sixties. She wore her blond hair cut bluntly at the shoulders, black pants, neon-green heels, and a pale-pink leather blazer emblazoned with lilies of the valley. I too liked her already.

"Thank you for battling the traffic to pay us a visit," I said, offering her my hand.

"It's nice to get out of the city every once in a while and play *Death Race* through northern Virginia," she said. "Shall we get started?"

Ten minutes later, Naomi and I shared a shell-shocked glance. Fran wasn't your run-of-the-mill attorney. She was the kind you called when you woke up next to a dead body. Lucian had hand-delivered the best of the best. And the most expensive of the expensive.

"So what you're saying is we should be mentally prepared for a very expensive, very long fight," I repeated.

"Like I said, things are incredibly difficult once a person is incarcerated. There's little incentive for a court to reopen a case they already invested in and won. But we have options."

My head was spinning.

"Okay. Let me try to summarize this," I said, reviewing my notes. "An appeal means taking the case to the appellate level and arguing the entire thing all over again. A commutation of sentence comes from the governor and could shorten Mary Louise's sentence, possibly to time served. But the Virginia judicial system is so confident in itself this is a slippery slope. Which also means a full pardon—also from the governor—is an even trickier quest. To make matters worse, the state abolished discretionary parole in 1995, which means all prisoners are required to serve at least eighty-five percent of their sentence."

"This doesn't sound . . . hopeful," Naomi said.

"It's a process that could take years," Fran explained.

Years meant expensive. Years meant Mary Louise wouldn't get to see Allen graduate law school.

"No offense, Fran, but I was feeling a lot more optimistic about this before I met you," I confessed.

Fran's grin was lightning quick. "It's my job to bring the doom and gloom to make sure you understand worst-case scenarios, which in this case means investing several boatloads of time, money, and energy. But . . ."

I perked up.

"I think we have a good shot at winning this," she continued.

"You're a roller coaster, Fran," I told her.

"I get that a lot. Here's what we do have going for us. The sentence is wildly disproportionate to similar charges in the state, which is reason enough to appeal. Given the fact that she's been through several public defenders, we can also argue that Ms. Upshaw did not receive proper representation."

"That sounds reasonable," Naomi said.

"We also have you," Fran said, looking at me.

I pointed at myself. "Me?"

"We need interest in the case, in Mary Louise. The more attention we can bring to this, the better. You've heard of convictions being overturned thanks to true crime podcasts and their rabid followings?"

"Sure, but I don't have a podcast."

"No, but you have a face and a story. We're sitting here today because your father passed away and you wanted to continue his legacy of championing the underdog. You, your dad, his connection to Mary Louise through her son, it's a story, and stories make people care."

"I get that. Believe me, I do," I said, sweeping my arm toward the window to indicate the book stacks. "But how am I going to help on that front?"

"You're the face," Fran answered. "We want people to know who Mary Louise is, why we're working to get her out, what they can do to help. And you're the one who is going to tell them."

"Uh, why can't you be the one to tell them?" I asked uneasily.

"Because nobody likes lawyers. You're a small-town librarian who believes in social justice. You're smart, you're pretty, and you're nonthreatening."

Naomi choked on her second cappuccino. "She's a little threatening."

"That works too," Fran said.

"Okay. So what do I have to do?" I asked.

Fran interlaced her fingers. "We'll start small. I'll set up an interview for you with some local media. I can put you in touch with some PR folks, give you some talking points. Once that article comes out and we get some interest drummed up, I'll see about an in-camera review with the sentencing judge."

"What's an in-camera review?" Naomi asked.

"Basically I'll ask for a private, in-chambers meet with the judge and district attorney. We can ask Judge Atkins to reconsider the sentence."

I straightened in my chair. "Wait, the judge could just decide to reduce the sentence?"

"It's a possibility. I haven't done any digging into him yet," Fran cautioned. "But this is an older conviction. The judge may have mellowed a little with time, or he might appreciate the PR boost that comes with criminal justice reform."

Naomi and I shared another look, a triumphant one.

"I'll give the best damn interview in the history of interviews," I promised.

Fran shook her head. "They're gonna love you."

"How does this work financially?" the ever-practical Naomi asked.

"My firm takes on a limited number of pro bono cases a year," Fran said, eyeing us both. "If this becomes a case that requires a significant time investment, we may ask you to pay reasonable court costs."

"Or we settle the whole thing in one visit with the judge," I pointed out. "So how do we move forward? Do we need to sign something to make it official?"

"I just so happen to have a retainer letter with me," Fran said, snapping open her sleek briefcase. "Once this is signed, I'll pay my new client a visit."

• • •

Me: Not that you care, but the attorney has been retained! And she's taking the case pro bono! She's on her way to meet Mary Louise!

465

Lucian: Congratulations, exclamation point abuser. Welcome to the nightmare of the justice system.

Me: Has anyone told you that you really need to tone down the over-the-top positivity? No? Weird.

Lucian: Has anyone told you that you're annoying? I'm the eleventh person today? Not surprising.

27

Special Delivery Electrosexolytes

Sloane

Valentine's Day rolled into Knockemout with four inches of snow and a wind chill that was best not mentioned. The library staff and I had decked the stacks with a variety of Valentine's Day decorations from handmade pink and red hearts with handwritten affirmations in the children's section to book displays of romance novels and the St. Valentine's Day massacre on the second floor complete with a tape outline of a body on the floor. We'd covered our bases for our patrons, both the romantic and the grumbly.

Things were pretty damn good. We were all set up for the evening's special event. My interview with the local paper about Mary Louise had been posted and had seen a positive reaction, which had led immediately to a second interview with the bigger, more important *Arlington Gazette*. And I had a sex date with Lucian Freaking Rollins.

"Just . . . one . . . more . . . inch," I groaned as I stretched as far as my muscles would allow.

"Get your ass down here right now, Sloaney Baloney," a familiar authority figure ordered.

I stopped what I was doing and glared down at Chief Nash Morgan. "Don't make me shush you.

You're on my home turf, buddy," I shot back from the top rung of the ladder.

"Your turf is about to be splattered with your pretty face when you fall," he admonished.

I climbed down the ladder and slapped a purple, glittery heart to the man's chest. "Since you're so manly, *you* finish hanging the heart garland."

Nash mounted the ladder in a warning-sticker-abiding kind of way and made quick work of the garland. I felt no shame in joining the rest of the female patrons in admiring his superior posterior.

"Did you come in here just to show up my decorating skills?" I asked when he climbed back down.

"I might have an ulterior motive," he said, scanning the folding chairs we'd arranged facing a podium. "What's going on here?"

"We've got a guest author coming in tonight. Cecelia Blatch. She writes dark and dirty paranormal romance. The book club has been obsessed with her since we picked up her series. We're hosting her for a book wining."

"A book whining?"

I grinned. "It's like a book signing but with wine."

"Nice. But shouldn't you have a Valentine's date?"

"Me? Why? What did you hear?" Did he know about Lucian? Had Lucian told him? Of course not. Lucian never told anyone anything.

Nash's gaze sharpened. "Now that's an odd reaction to me askin' you how your dating life is going. With all those dates you've been goin' on, I figured you'd have a hot date tonight."

Oh, *those* dates. Not the secret kind that involved my downtown being invaded by Lucian Rollins. Great. Now I was thinking about Lucian's penis. That wasn't good. Had I waited too long to respond to Nash? He was looking at me strangely. Was I being weird? Was Lucian's penis making me make things weird? Did every woman who ever slept with Lucian act like this?

I imagined a legion of penis-hypnotized women wandering like a herd of zombies behind Lucian as he went about his day.

"Ah. Yes. Well. I've had this event on the calendar for a while, and I didn't want to miss it, so no date for me," I said, sounding like I was being strangled.

Nash peered down at me. "You okay? You're turning red."

"It's, uh, hot in here." To illustrate my point, I whipped off my cardigan, accidentally dropping it on Ezra Abbott, the cherub-cheeked four-year-old ladies' man.

"Look! I'm a thuperhero," Ezra announced, lisping adorably through the space where his front teeth once had been. He zoomed off with my sweater flying behind him like a cape.

"I'll get that back later," I said, watching him disappear into the cushion fort. "Let's get back to talking about you. What are your plans for tonight?"

"That's one of the reasons why I'm here," Nash said, looking sheepish. "I got Lina a present, and I wanted to run it by someone first. It's our first Valentine's Day, and you know Angelina."

"She's not a candy and flowers kind of girl," I said.

He grinned. "Exactly."

If it was possible for a man to have cartoon hearts in his eyes, Nash Morgan looked as if he'd been struck by Cupid himself.

"I'm honored that you came to me," I said.

Nash got that funny, sheepish look on his handsome face again.

I planted my hands on my hips. "What?"

He winced. "I tried to get Stef, but Knox got to him first. No offense."

"None taken. Stef would have been my first choice too. So what did you get Lina?"

Nash looked over his shoulder. I did the same. In Knockemout, the gossip ran fast and loose. If the wrong set of ears overheard us, Lina would know what her gift was before Nash left the library.

He fished his phone out of his pocket and opened his photos. "These."

I took the phone from him and enlarged the picture of a pair of very sexy cowboy boots. "Shoes. Nicely done, Chief. You're definitely getting laid tonight."

Nash blew out a sigh of relief. "Thank God."

"Now, what else can I do for you?"

"I'd like to book one of the conference rooms

for some trainings over the next couple of weeks."

"Sure. What kind of trainings?" I asked.

"Autism awareness for first responders. We're starting off with my cops, then moving to fire, medical, and social workers. Figured the library would be a friendlier setting than the station."

Nash had been working his well-defined butt off on this initiative since the fall. The whole town had turned out for his BBQ fundraiser that earned enough to equip every first responder vehicle with noise-canceling headphones and weighted wearables. "Good for you, Chief. I'm proud of you."

Nash looked good and embarrassed. "Thanks, Sloaney."

"Sloane, sorry to interrupt. But I found something in the book drop," Jamal said, joining us.

I groaned. "Don't even tell me it's another squirrel."

"No, not this time, thank God. My lunch was still intact. It was this." He handed over a plain, white business envelope. "Probably one of the older folks mistook it for a mailbox."

My name was written in neat block letters across the back. We had seen our share of interesting items in the book drop. School books with homework stuffed in them, gloves, a retainer, a mangled loaf of bread that was supposed to feed the ducks in the park until little Boo Walkerson decided the book drop looked hungrier.

"Thanks, Jamal," I said, opening the envelope with my thumb. "Hey, can you let Belinda and

471

her friends know that Cecelia won't be here for a few more hours? They don't have to reserve their seats yet." I nodded to the crew of feisty, elderly readers who were claiming all the seats in the first two rows with whatever they could find in their oversize purses.

"Sure thing," he said and scampered off.

I unfolded the paper and frowned.

"Love letter?" Nash teased, peering over my shoulder. We both tensed at the same time. "What the hell?" He snatched it out of my hand.

I reached for it. "Excuse me, Chief Grabby Hands. That's mine."

Gone was the easygoing, lovestruck man worried about impressing his woman with footwear. In his place was a stone-faced cop who was definitely going to take this way too seriously.

"Is someone threatening you?" Nash demanded, rereading the note. It was written in the same block script as my name on the envelope.

Stop now before someone gets hurt.

"I'm sure it's nothing," I insisted. "Someone probably got their panties in a bunch over late fees."

"Have you had any issues with anyone lately? Besides Lucian," Nash asked.

Lucian. What if the note was from one of his former dicknotized lovers?

"Ha. Funny. Nothing out of the ordinary. I'm sure it's nothing," I insisted.

Nash held the note out of my reach. "All the same, a lot of my people found themselves in trouble these past few months. I'm not taking any chances. And I'm not letting you either."

"Nash, it's a note. A not very threatening one at that. What are you going to do? Fingerprint it and then run a handwriting analysis?"

Knockemout PD didn't have a big-city budget.

"I'm gonna at least follow procedure," he said stubbornly. "When was the book drop bin last emptied?"

I shoved my hands into the back pockets of my jeans. "It's supposed to be done before closing and midmorning. But we were busy with the setup today, so not since last night."

"I'll check the exterior cameras, see if we have a good angle," Nash said. "In the meantime, give a thought to anyone who might be extra pissed at you lately."

"Yes, Chief," I grumbled.

"And I wanna know if you get any other anonymous mail. Duncan Hugo is behind bars and Tate Dilton is in the ground, but that doesn't mean we should let our guard down."

"Fine. But can we at least agree not to say anything to anyone else? I don't want Naomi and Lina worrying about nothing."

"Nope."

"Seriously?" Nash had a habit of dropping truth bombs.

"You've got twenty-four hours to tell them your

own way. You don't, then I will. It's better for everyone to be in the know. I don't want anyone taking any chances."

"Okay. Now you're starting to freak me out. It's been months since Lina got abducted. You caught all the bad guys."

"Not all of them," he said evenly.

"Why would Anthony Hugo march into Knockemout to finish what his son started? And why focus on me? I had nothing to do with any of that. It doesn't make any sense." A creepy-crawly sensation prickled in my intestines as library life cheerfully bustled on around us.

"Until Anthony Hugo is behind bars, we can't afford to rest easy."

"Great. I'm definitely going to sleep like a baby tonight," I said dryly.

"I'm just saying, I want you to be careful. Be vigilant. If anything strikes you as off, I want to know about it."

"Fine. But that goes both ways. If something doesn't smell right to you, I want to know."

He studied me for a beat, then gave me a curt nod.

"Someone has a secret admirer," Naomi announced. She marched up to us, lugging a case of sports drinks with a gigantic red bow.

I snatched the card out of her hand, my cheeks warming.

For later.

"Who's that from?" Nash asked nosily.

"The card wasn't signed," Naomi said.

My face was the temperature of the surface of the sun as I stuffed the note in my pocket and grabbed the case. "Between the two of you, I'm starting to worry about my right to privacy," I complained.

"She's tomato red and deflecting," Nash observed.

Naomi eyed me shrewdly. "My guess is it's an inside joke gift from her date last week that she's been annoyingly tight-lipped about."

"Don't you both have work to do?" I asked them.

"What's this guy's name and home address? What kind of car does he drive?" Nash demanded.

"Oh my God. You're the worst. We went out. We had a nice time. It's nothing serious. Thank you and good day." I tried to dismiss them by taking my drinks and leaving.

But Naomi and Nash followed me.

"Are you going to see him again?" Naomi asked as we passed the reference section.

"Could he be the one who sent you the threat?" Nash added.

Naomi yelped. "Threat? What threat?"

I spun around and glared at him. "You said I had twenty-four hours!"

Nash grinned. "No time like the present. And you better update Angelina ASAP or she'll be pissed."

"You're the worst."

"Someone better tell me what's going on immediately," Naomi said, using her mom voice.

475

"Just for that, *you're* carrying these upstairs to my office," I said, shoving the case at Nash.

While the chief of police hauled my electro-sexolytes upstairs, I filled Naomi in on the completely innocuous note.

"I'm sure it's nothing to worry about. I get complaints all the time, and there's always weird stuff in the book drop. But Nash wants us to be on guard given everything that's happened in the past few months," I explained.

"If Nash says we should be careful, that's exactly what we should do," Naomi insisted dutifully.

I glanced over my shoulder to make sure Studly Do-Right wasn't within earshot. "Him being worried makes me worry," I confessed. "I'm concerned that he knows something he's not sharing. Maybe something about Lucian and the FBI's case."

Naomi pursed her lips. "I'll see what I can get out of Knox."

"Good idea. I'll talk to Lina and see if she can sexily wheedle anything out of Nash."

Naomi cleared her throat pointedly.

"Fine! I'll talk to her about sexy wheedling *when* I tell her about the dumb, not-very-threatening note," I agreed. "Even though I've had more creative and specific threats from the lady behind the deli counter at Grover's."

"Isn't it nice when we're all on the same page?" Naomi asked brightly.

"Yeah, yeah."

"Mith Thloane! Mith Thloane!" Ezra was back, still wearing my cardigan and now waving what looked like a scroll.

"Hey, buddy," I greeted.

"I made thith for you." He shoved the paper at me. It was tied in the middle with a red string.

Behind me, Naomi made an "aww" noise.

"For me? Wow, thanks, Ezra. That is so sweet of you," I said, carefully untying the string before unrolling the parchment paper.

"Thath you and thath me. We're piraths just like that book we read. And thath the library on our pirate thip. See all the bookth? And hereth the X for the treathure!" He pointed out each element of the three-foot-long crayon and marker drawing. Stick figure Ezra had one arm and four feet. My ponytail was green to match the hearts he'd sketched above and below the books.

"The. Cutest. I'm dying," Naomi whisper squealed.

"Do you like it?" Ezra asked hopefully.

"I love it," I said, unable to resist the urge to boop his nose. "It's amazing and so are you."

He flashed me a coy, tooth-deficient grin. "You could hang it up if you wanted."

"I'm going to hang it up in my office so I can see it every day," I promised.

"Awethome. Happy Valentineth Day!"

"Happy Valentine's Day, Ezra."

He launched himself into my arms for the kind of hard, sticky, heart-melting hug that only kids under the age of six gave, then made a beeline for the pillow fort again.

"My heart," Naomi said. "He's Gael and Isaac's new foster son, isn't he?"

"He is. I watched him here for half an hour when Gael had to leave for a pet store emergency the other day. We read two pirate books, and he drew pictures for his new big sister."

"It looks like you made quite the impression," Naomi said, tapping the drawing.

"Me or the pirates."

"You're going to be a great mom," she said.

Her words punched me right in the heart. "Thanks," I said. "You already are."

She leaned in and caught me in the kind of soft, spontaneous hug sisters exchanged. "We're going to raise our families together," she whispered in my ear.

"I was gone three minutes. What the hell has you two ready to bawl your eyes out?" Nash demanded, looking around the first floor of the library for obvious threats.

"Girl stuff," I insisted.

"Sloane's a pirate," Naomi said with a sniffle.

"I don't want to know," Nash decided.

Naomi released me with a watery smile. "I'm going to go do something library related." She gave Nash a peck on the cheek and headed for the stairs.

Nash pulled out his phone.

"What are you doing?" I asked nosily.

"Telling my brother that whatever he's buying Naomi, he'd better double it."

I chuckled.

Nash stowed his phone. "I better get back to work."

"Have a happy Valentine's Day," I told him.

His grin was a heartbreaker. "Will do."

He made it all of four feet toward the door.

"Oops. I seem to have dropped my necklace," announced Belinda, an elderly, busty patron who preferred her books steamy. She pointed at the huge crucifix that she'd just unfastened from her neck and tossed on the floor. "Be a dear and fetch it for me, Chief Morgan?"

Nash heaved a sigh and glanced my way.

I shrugged. "If you don't pick it up, they're just going to keep throwing things on the floor."

"I'm ordering new uniforms with tunics," he grumbled.

"The citizens who appreciate the male specimen would be devastated," I warned.

He bent at the waist and hastily plucked the necklace off the floor.

"You just made this old lady's day," Belinda said, smugly returning the crucifix to her more than ample bosom.

"Might want to get that clasp checked, Ms. Belinda, seein' as how it fell off in the grocery store last week and in the park the week before that."

"I'll do that," she lied glibly.

Shaking my head, I pulled out my phone.

479

Me: Did you send me a case of sports drinks or do I have a stalker who's concerned with my hydration?

Lucian: I thought it would be more appropriate than flowers and candy seeing as how I'm only using you for your body.

Me: You better be stretched and warmed up for go time. I'm not slowing down if you pull a hamstring.

The author event was a rousing success. Or "arousing" success, which was absolutely the pun I was going to make in the library newsletter for the week. The readers were excited, the author sold out of all the books she brought, and we ran out of wine before anyone got too tipsy.

"Go on home, Sloane. You've been here since opening. We'll handle the clean up," Blaze offered. As board members, she and her wife, Agatha, spent almost as much time here as the employees.

"Are you sure? I don't mind." I had another hour before Lucian would arrive to delight me with his penis.

"Positive. I'm sure you've got a handsome someone waiting for you."

She was fishing for information, and I wasn't biting. "What about you and Agatha?"

"We had our celebratory Valentine's brunch this morning, then changed the oil in the bikes."

"And they say romance is dead."

"Go on. Get out of here. We'll lock up," she said, shooing me away.

"If you're sure. I'll just run up and get my stuff."

I'd have time for a quick shower and another run at my legs with the razor before Lucian showed up. I could also spend some time overthinking the lingerie I'd picked out.

I was so deep in my head that I was halfway into my office before I realized there was someone sitting behind my desk.

"Cheese and crackers!"

Lucian Rollins, in disguise in a ball cap and a black hoodie, looked perfectly relaxed sitting behind my desk reading a book.

He raised an eyebrow at me. "Exactly what kind of defense is that?"

I looked down and realized I was holding my hands up in a cartoonish *Karate Kid* posture.

"What are you doing here? If someone sees you, the entire town is going to know that we're doing the horizontal mambo before we even get started! I've already had to deal with a Knockemout inquisition for the past week with everyone and their brother asking me who I'm sleeping with," I hissed.

"I got bored waiting. I thought this might speed things along."

From any other man, it would be a compliment, a statement about how much he missed me. But Lucian Rollins was accustomed to getting what he wanted when he wanted it. And he was using me for sex. Lucky for him I wasn't about to take the time required to teach him a lesson in delayed gratification, because I was *also* using him for sex.

"Blaze and Agatha are locking up. So we can leave as long as you stick to lurking in the shadows, because I do not want to deal with questions about whatever depraved thing this is between us," I explained.

"Get your things," he said, rising from my chair. He closed my copy of *The Midnight Library*. I noticed my bookmark was still in place . . . and he was several chapters beyond it.

"Are you actually reading that?" I asked.

"I do know how to read, Sloane," he said dryly. The amused yet dismissive way his voice caressed my name made me want to smack him in the face with the book. Conversely, it *also* made me want to take his pants off and use his cock until I couldn't walk.

I was still debating between the options when he rounded my desk, fisted a hand in my sweater, pulled me to my toes, and kissed the ever-living hell out of me.

There was nothing romantic or sweet about the way his tongue invaded my mouth. The way it conquered me, forcing me to follow its lead. My nipples budded, and my sex actually trembled. I lost the ability to breathe.

It was a kiss filled with carnal promises that I couldn't wait for him to fulfill.

He released me just as suddenly. "Let's go."

"Yeah. Let's do that."

It took us twenty minutes to make it to the parking lot. There were far too many patrons still lurking behind after the event. After I was stopped for the fourth time on the first floor, Lucian managed to slip behind the circulation desk and duck out the side door without being spotted. "Sorry," I said when I found him leaning against my Jeep.

"You're inconveniently popular," he said.

"Where's your car?" I asked.

"I had my driver drop me off."

I reached around him to unlock the passenger door. "That's awfully cocky of you to assume my blind hatred of you didn't overtake my need for you naked."

"I liked my odds." With that, he took the keys from my hand, opened the door, and tossed my tote inside. "I'm driving."

He had to push the seat the whole way back to accommodate his long legs, but he still managed to look comfortable, confident as he drove us back to my place. He asked me about the event and the author, and I did my best to answer, even though every sense seemed to be preoccupied with him. That full-body tingly awareness was even worse now that I knew what his body was capable of doing to mine. It felt like an electrical current charging my blood.

He pulled into my driveway, and I leaned over to punch the garage door opener. When we were officially alone and the door slid shut behind us, we exploded.

I released my seat belt half a second before he hooked me under the arms and dragged me over the console. I landed in his lap.

One inferno of a kiss and some dry humping later, he pulled back. "Go pack."

"What? Why?"

"We're not staying here."

I thought of the can of whipped cream in my refrigerator. The two new lingerie sets I'd bought. "Why the hell not?"

"Because if we stay here, someone is going to knock on your door or look through your windows or see me naked when they deliver dinner. You have off tomorrow. We're going to my place, where my neighbors know enough to mind their own business."

"Your place?" There were six million things that could and would go wrong with that. First, I couldn't kick him out of his own place when he inevitably pissed me off.

He didn't answer me. At least not with words. Instead he yanked the neckline of my sweater down and buried his face between my breasts.

"A very convincing argument. I'll pack."

28

Put It on My Tombstone

Lucian

I hate to admit it, but your place doesn't suck," Sloane mused over her pad thai.

We'd paused our sex marathon to refuel by eating Thai food naked in bed while watching *Brooklyn Nine-Nine* reruns. It was the most rom-com thing I'd ever done in my life.

I leaned over and stole some of her noodles. "I'm glad you approve."

She was naked except for her glasses. She'd piled her hair on top of her head with a few efficient twists of her wrists and a flimsy elastic tie. With my thousand-thread-count Italian sheets draped over her, she looked both adorable and sexy.

The women I dated—or more accurately took to bed—didn't do adorable. They were well-dressed, well-coiffed, and never seen in public in gym clothes. Sloane, on the other hand, had unironically packed pajamas with hearts. I couldn't wait to see her in them . . . and strip them off her.

She twirled her chopsticks in a circle to encompass my bedroom. "It doesn't feel like the lair of an evil villain. It's more like the bachelor pad of a hot wealthy guy with no personality."

The sly look she shot me did her in. We'd both gotten less insulting in the heat of the moment, which meant we had serious ground to make up when my cock wasn't inside her, making her scream my name.

I dumped the food cartons on the nightstand and snagged her by the ankle when she tried to escape.

"You'll pay for that."

I anchored her knee between mine, tightened my grip on her ankle, and tickled the bottom of her foot.

Sloane shrieked and tried to wriggle free.

"Apologize," I said mildly. It was a game we'd played when we were different people, and I probably should have left it in the past where it belonged.

"Okay! Okay! It's the bachelor pad of a hot, wealthy guy whose *designer* has no personality," she screeched.

My bedroom was done in rich browns. Large, dark furniture dominated the space and was softened by expensive ivory bedding and heavy curtains that currently blocked out the world.

"Try again."

"Agh! Okay! I'm sorry! You have a very nice place. I definitely don't hate it."

I gave her rounded ass a resounding slap and released her foot. "There. That wasn't so hard, was it?"

"That's what she said." Her voice was muffled by the pillow.

"That's not what she said twenty minutes ago," I reminded her, coasting my hand over her bare shoulders, down the silky skin of her back, drawing the sheet with me so I could memorize each notch in her spine.

Her body was a fascination. Generous curves packed in a tiny, feisty package. I never knew what was going to come out of her mouth next. An insult or a demand for me to defile her in a new way.

It had been a gamble, bringing her here. The less Anthony Hugo and his minions knew about my life, the better. But I'd laid enough false leads for them with the tracker on the company car this week before removing it. Besides, if his men spotted me with Sloane here, she would just look like some woman his enemy was fucking. In Knockemout, it would be clear she was much, much more.

I lowered myself over her and sank my teeth into one luscious curve of her ass.

"Did you just bite me?" Sloane demanded as I leaned back to admire my handiwork.

"I'm giving you a souvenir to remember our final weekend of debauchery," I said.

She clambered to her knees on the mattress and faced me, looking like a golden-haired goddess. I wanted her. Again and again and again. And each time I had her, I realized it still wasn't enough.

"In that case, I get to give you one too," she announced.

She pounced and I let her push me over backward, enjoying the feel of her warm, soft body in my arms. Her sleek thighs straddled my own, and when her hand gripped my already hard shaft, I had to grit my teeth to keep from groaning.

"Not there," I growled.

She pouted.

My phone rang from the bedside table.

"Does your admin usually call you at 10:00 p.m. on Valentine's Day?" Sloane asked, peeking at the screen.

"Neither one of us has a life," I explained before answering the phone. "Petula, you're on speakerphone and I'm not alone."

"Has the world ended and I'm unaware?" Petula demanded.

"Very funny. What do you want?"

"Representative Houser wants to move your lunch forward an hour tomorrow."

I glanced up at Sloane, who was releasing her hair from its knot. "Reschedule it. I'm busy this weekend."

"Does this have anything to do with your company tonight? You really should let me run a background check on her."

"You already did and it's just business," I lied.

A pillow hit me in the face. Sloane pointed at her bare breasts and mouthed, "Business"?

"I have to go, Petula. Something's come up."

Sloane smugly studied my hardening cock.

"Wait. While I have you, I need you to go to this address and take the man who lives there shopping for a new suit this week," I said, then rattled off

Emry's address. "Something that says eligible widower, not befuddled grandfather."

"Consider it done," Petula said. "One final thing. I confirmed your reservation for you and your lady friend next Thursday evening."

Sloane's eyes narrowed.

Shit.

"Thanks, Petula. Take the weekend off," I said quickly. I disconnected just as my blond bed partner vaulted off the bed.

"Sloane," I said sternly.

"Don't even try it," she said, grabbing something off the floor. It was the lacy corset I'd ripped off her. She threw it over her shoulder and bent again.

"Are you actually jealous?" I demanded, amused.

"Of course not," she huffed. "I just don't want to be cavorting with a penis that's cavorting with other vaginas. It's not hygienic."

Sloane Walton was unlike any other woman I'd ever taken to bed. "I'm not cavorting with other vaginas," I said dryly. "Where are you going?"

"If you think I'm just going to take your word for it, you're an idiot," she said, gathering her discarded clothing off the floor.

"I'd like to point out that of the two of us, you're the one actively pursuing men on a dating app."

"I'm not *sleeping* with any of them. Yet." Frowning, she whipped back the duvet cover and felt around under the sheets. "Have you seen my underwear? Never mind. I don't need them."

I reached for her, but she dodged me.

"I'm not sleeping with my Thursday date either."

"Yeah, okay." She gave an unladylike snort and bent for her bag.

It gave me the opening I needed. I grabbed her around the waist, lifted her in the air, and tipped us both onto the mattress.

"If you don't get off me right now, Lucifer, I'll knee you in the balls. And while it would be a destructive blow to women everywhere, I will do what I have to do," she said fiercely.

"You're jealous," I said again, thoroughly enjoying myself.

To be on the safe side, I rolled her and settled myself between her thighs before leaning down to kiss her mouth.

She softened instantaneously beneath me, but my victory was short lived when she bit my lower lip.

"Ow."

"Serves you right. Now, give me my pants, and we'll pretend this never happened."

That wasn't an option. "I don't have a date Thursday," I told her.

She flailed under me, which didn't help me forget about the raging hard-on I had nestled against her belly.

"I'm taking your mother out to dinner."

Sloane settled immediately. Her eyes were suspicious behind her now-crooked glasses. "You *do* realize that I can easily confirm that story."

I nuzzled my nose along her jawline and felt pride when goose bumps cropped up on her ivory skin. "We meet every week for coffee or a meal. I make sure she's not falling apart and hiding it from you and your sister. She makes sure I'm not working myself to death. We usually split a dessert. But I'm not sleeping with her."

She studied me for a long beat. "Okay. I believe you."

"You do?"

"You get irritated when you're hiding something. You just look annoyingly entertained right now."

"I find your jealousy annoyingly entertaining," I agreed.

"I'm *not* jealous," she insisted.

"I am," I said.

Her eyebrows shot up. "*You?* Why?"

"You're still dating. Any day now, you're going to meet Mr. Right, and then he'll be the one who gets to do this." I dipped my head and closed my lips over one pert nipple.

She arched under me, the added friction against my cock driving me wild.

I released her breast with an audible *pop*. "I don't want to be your Mr. Right, but I might actually miss this warm, willing body of yours when it's no longer at my disposal."

Sloane shivered. "Then I guess you'd better take advantage of me now."

I wasted no time rolling on a new condom and positioning myself between her legs.

Seeing her splayed out beneath me like a banquet to be enjoyed had me counting my lucky fucking stars. A few more fucks and a few more mind-blowing orgasms, and we'd finally be sated. But not yet.

I gritted my teeth and sheathed myself in her with one vicious thrust. Those green eyes slammed shut as every muscle in her body tensed around me, under me. Her body teased me by both welcoming me and trying to fight me.

I wanted to touch her everywhere. To memorize every inch of her. The full curves of her breasts and hips, the taut flesh of her belly. All that velvet-smooth skin that begged for my teeth.

"Tell me what you want," I rasped, withdrawing just far enough to slam back in, forcing the final inch inside her.

Her feet moved restlessly against the sheets. "So good," she rasped. "I hate that you're so damn good at this."

"Tell me what you want, Sloane," I insisted, punctuating each word with a hard thrust.

Her eyes were open now, hands reaching for me, drawing me down against her. "Just you. Give me you."

I lost myself inside her, in the grip and pull of those smooth muscles. In the emerald green of her eyes. In the way she breathed my name as I drove us both up. I couldn't stop. I couldn't pull back. Not with the way she was gripping me.

"You better get ready to come because I'm about to go off," I warned through clenched teeth.

"Shut up and fuck me harder."

I obliged, knowing that my orgasm would force hers. She hitched her thighs higher around my hips and took me even deeper. As her breasts bounced against my chest, she reached behind me and sank her fingers into my ass cheeks.

"Lucian," she whispered.

I came.

The churning in my balls fired up the shaft and erupted in a heart-stopping burst. And then she was gripping me, rippling and writhing. We were coming. Each wave all-consuming, each crest higher than the last as our bodies fought for every last drop of ecstasy.

Jesus, she was beautiful when she came.

It was perfect. *She* was perfect. The way she fit me, the way she begged for what I had to offer. The way she reacted to my basest needs. Every time we let this happen, I convinced myself it would be the last time. And every time we finished, I knew it wouldn't be.

Her arms came around my waist and held there.

"Good God, man. Do you have to register that thing as a weapon? Ugh. Where's my root beer? I'm dying. Valentine's Day sex killed me. You can put it on my tombstone." Sloane's muffled voice came from beneath me.

I smiled into her hair and decided I'd worry about what this seemingly never-ending need meant later.

29

Getting Stupid

Sloane

Honky Tonk was loud and crowded. There was a band occupying the small stage in the corner, and almost every table was taken. I spotted my friends at the corner of the bar and made my way toward them.

Naomi and Lina had their heads together, laughing over something. Knox and Nash stood guard behind them, beers hanging loosely from their hands, sharing wry smiles over something they both found amusing. Stef the Chicken had apparently returned to town and was two-stepping with Jeremiah on the dance floor in the middle of a crowd of burly bikers.

I felt like a big, dumb idiot at the wave of disappointment that smacked me right in the face.

Lucian hadn't said he was coming. It was silly to think that he'd make the drive on a Wednesday night. It was stupid to have even wanted him to. But that was me. Silly, stupid, and now downright disappointed. I'd dressed up for no reason, wasting a perfectly good matching bra and underwear set under the short skirt and tight sweater I thought would make his blood warm.

494

Of course, I hadn't actually *asked* him to come. We should be done. Finished. Finito. No more sex-o. Though we were still flirt fighting over text. But I sure as hell wasn't putting myself out there on a limb. Not with him. And not when I should be focusing on finding my future husband and father of my future children.

I tried to shake off my mood as I approached the bar. This was for the best. Lucian was nothing but a distraction from what I really wanted. It was time to forget about his gigantic dick and focus on my future.

"Lookin' hot tonight, Sloane," Sherry "Fi" Fiasco called from behind the bar where she was helping Silver the bartender sling drinks. She saluted me with her lollipop.

I fluffed my hair and blew her a kiss. And on the inside, I wished I'd gone with sweats.

No, I reminded myself. It wasn't a waste. I was hunting for a potential mate. Any guy in here could be the future Mr. Sloane. Like that one over there.

Mr. Michaels, Chloe and Waylay's handsome teacher, was sharing a beer with two other teachers and mechanic Tallulah St. John. He was good looking, had a great smile, loved kids, and wore glasses. And all I could think about was Lucian's tattooed naked body ranging over mine.

How was a girl supposed to meet a nice guy and settle for normal, non-mind-melting sex now? Was I going to be haunted by the ghost of all the orgasms he'd delivered? Would I compare every lover from now on to him, and would anyone come close to measuring up?

I was spiraling. Over Lucian's spectacular cock. I needed therapy and a drink.

I made a mental note to check out a book or two on hypnotherapy. I'd get over him . . . er, his sexual prowess if it killed me.

"There she is," Naomi said, hopping off her stool and hugging me despite the fact that we'd spent half the day working together.

"Sorry I'm late," I said. *I was busy fantasizing about my mortal enemy ripping my underwear off and making me scream his name,* I didn't say. I was absolutely going to swing by the library on my way home and grab whatever books I could find on breaking bad habits.

Knox gave my shoulder a squeeze. His wedding band caught the light, reminding me that if someone could come along and turn Knox Morgan into the marrying kind, I still had a chance at finding Mr. Right out there.

Lina flashed me a grin and a wave.

Nash leaned in over her. "What are you drinking, Sloaney?"

"I think I'll just have a root beer," I decided.

Disappointment called for sugar. I'd have one drink. Then I'd make my excuses, hit the library, and go home. And *then* I'd check the battery level on my vibrator.

Lina and Naomi boxed me in.

"Nash and I took Naomi and Knox to meet Mary Louise this afternoon."

I perked up. "How did it go?"

"We loved her," Lina said.

Naomi's smile lit up the bar. "Even Viking over there couldn't find anything to complain about."

"Now *that's* impressive," I admitted.

"Mary Louise is ecstatic that someone is taking an interest and your interviews have gotten good play," Lina said, her dark-red fingernails glittering against the bourbon in her glass.

"The library fielded six calls this week from people interested in the case," Naomi added.

"Fran called today. She said there's a podcast that wants to interview me, Mary Louise, and Allen. And she got on the judge's calendar for an informal meeting next week," I said.

"This is great progress," Naomi said, nudging me with her shoulder. "So why do you look like someone just tried to ban all the books?"

Damn my face.

"It was a long day. So did Stef tell Jeremiah he's ready to become a Knockemout resident yet?" I congratulated myself on my expert-level subject change as we all turned to study the happy couple on the dance floor.

Naomi shook her head and rolled her eyes heavenward. "He's convinced himself that Jeremiah is going to think he's a stalker."

"What an idiot," I said affectionately.

"Speaking of dating, how's your search going these days?" Lina asked.

Damn it.

"I haven't been on any dates in a week," I confessed. A week . . . ten days . . . ever since Lucian's penis invaded my vagina and my dreams . . .

"Hang in there. Mr. Sloane is out there," Naomi said, squeezing my hand.

"You can't get burnt out already. He's not going to stroll through that door," Lina said, pointing to the entrance.

The door swung open, and I damn near forgot to breathe when Lucifer himself stepped inside, his face serious, another insanely sexy, expensive coat flapping in the breeze. His eyes found me, and I felt . . . a lot of unholy things.

"Wow. That would have been pretty great if it had been a different tall, gorgeous, single guy," Naomi teased.

"Uh-oh, Angel. Looks like the boss is here," Nash warned Lina playfully.

"Here." Knox shoved a root beer in my face, forcing me to look away from the avenging angel of orgasms as he made his way through the crowd. I could hear my heartbeat over the music. Electricity crackled over my skin. Every cell in my body was acutely aware that Lucian was near.

"Thanks," I croaked.

"Lucy, what the hell are you doing here?" Knox demanded by way of greeting.

"I had business nearby. Thought I might find you here."

His voice, that low, velvety rasp, went straight to my lady parts.

While the Morgans took turns doing the manly, shoulder-clapping handshake greeting, I became fascinated by a crumpled dish towel on the back of the bar and tried to talk my body out of a full-blown anticipatory orgasm.

The band changed tunes, shifting into "H.O.L.Y." by Florida Georgia Line while I tried to calm the hell down.

"I love this song," Lina said to Nash.

He already had his fingers interlaced with hers and tugged her off her stool. "Let's go, Angel."

"Dance with me?" Naomi asked, sliding her palms up Knox's chest. He leaned down and whispered something in her ear that had her cheeks turning pink.

"Don't worry. I'll hold down the bar," I called after them, still ignoring Lucian.

The band's lights had dimmed, making our little corner dark as sin. Silver and Fi were busy on the opposite end. Lucian eased closer, still not saying a word.

I reached for my drink, determined to look bored and not at all horny. But my traitorous fingers bobbled the glass, and gravity did the rest.

"Shit!" I climbed onto the footrail and reached over the bar to grab a stack of napkins.

Warm fingertips ghosted up the back of my thigh, and I froze where I was.

Lucian took the napkins from my hand and efficiently tossed them on the spill.

His hand came around my stomach, and he lifted me off the footrail. I suppressed a yelp of surprise.

He slowly lowered me to the floor, and in doing so, I had the thrill of feeling his erection pressed intimately to my rear end.

Finding myself caged between his arms and the bar, I turned. "Hi," I said breathlessly. My nipples hardened to points sharp enough to cut through my practically useless bra.

He guided me into the dark corner where the bar met the wall and put a hand on either side of my head. "Hi," he said. His eyes were smoldering, his cock hard, and I was giddy.

I wanted to reach out and touch him, but I didn't trust myself to be able to stop.

"How was your day?" I asked.

"I don't feel like making small talk, Pixie," he said.

"What do you feel like doing?"

His lips curved into a wolfish facsimile of a smile. He hooked an index finger in the neckline of my sweater. The contact of his skin against mine had my lady parts celebrating. "You."

He'd touched me. That meant I got to return the favor, right?

I reached out and cupped the hard length of his erection with my palm.

He closed his eyes and pressed himself against my hand.

I gripped him *hard,* and those gray eyes opened. He returned the favor by cupping my breast and squeezing.

I was dizzy, breathless, so turned on I was afraid I was about to combust.

"I thought we were done," I said, even as I began to stroke him through his slacks.

"Do you want to be done?" His knee nudged my legs apart.

That hand kneading my breast was driving me to distraction.

Why did I have to be the one to say I wanted him again? Why couldn't he say it?

The beat of the music pulsed through me as our bodies inched closer in our dark corner of sinful secrets.

"Someone might see us," I said, ignoring his question.

His fingers slid inside the scoop of my sweater and dipped beneath the flirty edge of my bra to capture my needy nipple. My legs buckled, but I didn't fall. Not with his knee between my legs, his hard thigh making contact with my aching center.

I sucked in a breath.

"Tell me you want me again," he ordered as his fingers tugged at my nipple.

"What if I'm over it?" I breathed.

His grin was sinful. "I can feel how wet you are for me through my pants. You're not over it."

"Are you?" I asked.

"If I thought for a second I could get away with it, I'd have you bent over the bar with this tiny excuse for a skirt flipped up around your waist and my cock inside you."

My core spasmed recklessly at the image his words painted. Lucian could give a master class in dirty talk.

"Oh boy," I squeaked.

"Tell me," he insisted.

I swallowed hard. "I suppose I wouldn't be opposed to a few more orgasms. If you think you can deliver them." The rigid length of his penis pulsed under my grip.

He tugged harder on my nipple, sending ripples of sensation echoing through my body. "I think I can manage to wring a few more out of you. If you can find a way to keep your insults to yourself."

"I can't promise that."

It felt so good to be touched by him, to know that I was minutes away from being treated to his spectacular body.

"You two aren't fighting again, are you? 'Cause I can reattach those electrodes real fast," Knox said from behind Lucian's broad back.

I jolted and released my grip on Lucian's cock. He took his sweet time removing his hand from my shirt.

Apparently neither one of us had noticed that the song had changed and that our friends had returned. I ducked under his arm and stepped around him. I

502

felt his grip on the back of my skirt and understood what he wanted. I positioned myself between Lucian's bulging erection and everyone else's line of sight.

"They're definitely fighting," Lina said, taking a good look at my face. "She's all flushed and he's grinding his molars."

"We weren't fighting," I said. "We were . . ."

"Having a discussion we need to finish," Lucian filled in. He gave my ass a hard pinch under the hem of my skirt.

I took half a step back, grinding the heel of my boot into the fancy Italian leather of his shoe.

"I'll allow it as long as there's no bloodshed," Knox said.

"Call if you need backup," Nash told us.

"We'll be right back," I promised as Lucian steered me away from our friends. "Are you out of your damn mind?" I hissed as he marched us down the hall, past the restrooms and Fi's office. The second we turned the corner, his big hand wrapped possessively around my upper arm, and he pulled me against him.

His cock was rock-hard against my stomach, and then his mouth was molten lava against mine. He kissed the air out of my lungs, the thoughts out of my head, the warning bells out of my ears.

One hand fisted in my hair while the other slid down to cup my ass cheek with something that felt a lot like possession.

"Why do you look so pissed off?"

"Because I'm not inside you. Because I drove all the way up here and you weren't accommodating enough to be home alone."

"My apologies. I didn't realize I was supposed to be at your beck and call," I said, shoving a hand between our bodies and gripping his iron length.

He outdid me by dragging the neckline of my sweater down to reveal the spectacularly slutty lace bra I now had no regrets about harnessing my boobs into. His other hand found its way under my skirt to the apex of my thighs.

"My little tease."

My brain hooked on the "my." But all over-thinking ceased when Lucian's beard tickled my neck as his fingers traced the material over my sex.

"Someone could see us," I said, sucking in a breath. Anyone could take a wrong turn out of the restrooms and end up getting an eyeful of enemies in rut.

"Tell them you have to leave," he growled in my ear. The hand at my breast dove under the lace to palm me, to knead my flesh.

"We both just got here," I said breathlessly.

"Then quit stroking my cock." But even as he said the words, he pushed his erection harder against my hand.

His fingers found their way under the band of my underwear to my sex.

"So fucking wet for me. Every damn time," he murmured before thrusting into me.

I was spiraling out of control, and I wanted him

to fall with me. I wanted to drive him over the edge.

"Please," I whispered, knowing how me pleading set him off.

He went rigid against me. Every muscle in his spectacular body was waiting to hear what I wanted from him. "Please what?"

"Let me taste you."

He swore violently, but his erection betrayed him by swelling in my hand.

"Let me taste you, then we'll go back, finish our drinks, and get the hell out of here," I bargained.

He hesitated. But I felt the need in him. He needed to let me do this.

"Someone is going to come looking for us if we're gone too long," he said, sliding a single finger into my pulsating pussy.

"If you don't let me put my mouth on your cock right now, I don't know if I can go back out there. I just need to take the edge off."

"You're so close to coming," he said as my muscles rippled around his fingers.

"Please, Lucian," I whimpered. I'd come later. He'd make sure of that. But right now, I *needed* to feel him at the back of my throat. I needed to take him to the kind of place he took me.

He swore darkly and gave my breast another hard squeeze. Then he was releasing me.

I couldn't believe it. The man was giving me the one thing I wanted, even though it was the one thing he *didn't* want. As I worked his fly open, he brought two glistening fingers to his mouth and licked them.

My knees buckled, which was fine because the floor was where I had to be anyway.

I knelt on the cool concrete, feeling the heat from Lucian's attention as I freed his cock. From this angle, it was intimidatingly huge. The blunt tip was already wet with moisture that leaked from the slit.

"Thank you," I whispered. I looked up at him as I opened my lips and took him into my mouth. A shudder rolled through his body, and he pumped his hips convulsively against me.

"Jesus Christ," he hissed as I took him to the back of my throat and held him there.

Glancing up, I found his head tipped back, hands fisted against the wall.

I hummed and he looked down at me. Those gray eyes had fire in them. He reached out and stroked a finger over my cheek.

I took that as permission to continue. So I fisted my hand around the root of his shaft and began to move. Pulling, sucking him to the back of my throat, then dragging lips and tongue and fingers over him to the tip.

He was spewing profanity now as if I'd snapped nearly every tether of his control.

I loved this. The intimacy. The power. I was the one on my knees, but I was in control. He'd given me that.

"Stop."

I immediately froze at Lucian's rough command. He gripped my hair, wrapping it around his fist, and pulled me back until his erection slid free. We stared at each other, both breathing heavily in the relative silence of the hallway.

His eyes were half-mast, lips parted. He looked like he wanted more, and I wanted to give it to him.

Once again, he skimmed his knuckles over my cheek.

The moment was broken by high-pitched giggles and the swing of the restroom door.

Lucian scooped me up under the arms and set me on my feet. "We have to go back before they send out a search party," he said, tucking his monstrous cock back into his pants.

I was having trouble pulling myself together. The fog of lust had crowded out all my senses except for the ones Lucian currently occupied. I sagged against the wall.

"Stop looking at me like that," he ordered as he adjusted his raging hard-on.

"How am I looking at you?" I asked.

"Like you need me to fuck you."

"To be fair, that's exactly what I need."

He gritted his teeth and half turned away from me. Was I driving him as wild as he drove me?

As I shoved my boobs back into my sweater, I took inventory of him. His tie was crooked. His usually perfectly coiffed hair was standing up on one side. And his pants looked as if they were in danger of being destroyed by his very insistent erection.

"How can you still walk and talk with that thing?" I asked, gesturing at his penis region.

"Do *not* address my cock right now," Lucian growled. He was doing some kind of deep breathing exercise and looking everywhere but at me.

"It just seems like it gets harder every time. Is that normal? I mean, my boobs feel like they weigh a ton right now. I think my bra is cutting off my circulation."

Lucian closed his eyes. "Pixie, I can't get unhard when you're talking about your tits."

I grinned wickedly. The benefit of being a woman was that you could be turned on without pitching a tent in your pants. "They just feel so swollen. And my nipples are *so* sensitive."

He cursed and bent at the waist.

Struggling to Regain Control Lucian was downright endearing.

"Thirty minutes."

"What?" I asked.

"We're leaving in thirty minutes. You make up an excuse and I'll follow. Meet me in the parking lot."

A thrill zoomed through me. He wanted to fuck me. He needed to fuck me. I would have done a victory dance if I hadn't been so acutely aware of the wetness between my thighs.

"Deal," I agreed. "I'll go back first, and you take

a minute to try to stop thinking about taking my bra off and burying your face in my boobs."

His growl echoed after me as I danced past him, laughing.

We lasted twenty-two minutes. Twenty-two minutes of pure torture.

He stood behind me as I tried to focus on conversation with Naomi and Lina. But every time he touched me, his thigh crowding mine when he leaned in to order a drink, his finger tracing the bare skin between my skirt and sweater, I lost all train of thought.

Naomi finally gave me the perfect out and asked me if I was tired.

"I'm exhausted," I fibbed. "It's been a long couple of weeks, and I'm fantasizing about bed."

Neither of those things was a lie.

"You've been through a lot," she said with sympathy. "Go home. Get some sleep."

"You sure you guys don't mind?" I asked, stifling a fake yawn.

"I guess we'll just have to settle for the testosterone trio," Lina said. "Text me tomorrow."

"I will," I promised. "Good night, guys."

Knox and Nash said their goodbyes. Lucian pretended to ignore me.

I sauntered out of the bar, adding an extra swing to my hips, and I felt him watching me the whole way to the door.

I was just unlocking my Jeep when I sensed a

disturbance in the force. "Cheese and crackers! How did you get here so fast?"

"Long legs," he said, gripping me by the arm and steering me toward his Jaguar. "Get in," he said.

"What about my Jeep?"

"If you think I'm letting you out of my sight after that little stunt in the hallway, you're sorely mistaken. Get. In."

I got in.

30

I Have to See a Man about
a Pile of Frozen Rats

Sloane

"No touching," he ordered as he put the car in gear.

"Geez. Bossy much?" I pouted.

"If you so much as graze my dick with your pinkie finger, I'm pulling over on a public road, dragging you across this console, and fucking you into oblivion."

"That's not a convincing argument for why I shouldn't touch you."

"If you're a good girl and wait the four fucking minutes it takes to get home, I'll strip you naked and worship every inch of your beautiful body with my cock, mouth, and hands."

My hands fisted in my lap. Good enough for me. "Drive faster," I told him.

My breasts felt heavy and swollen. My clitoris was throbbing. And I was so wet, I was thinking about renaming my lady parts Costa Rican Rainy Season. He'd let me taste him. He'd let me take him in my mouth. My heart pounded at the near victory.

The tires squealed when he zipped past my

511

driveway and pulled into his. Neither of us said a word as the garage door rose in front of us. I didn't ask why he'd brought me here instead of my place. I didn't care. As long as he was about to touch me.

He pulled forward into the garage, and we were both out of the car in the span of a heartbeat. We met in front of the hood, and he took me by the hand and dragged me to the door. He slapped the garage door opener and manhandled me inside.

I was definitely not complaining that the touching moratorium was over.

Inside the ruthlessly organized laundry room, I shoved his jacket off his shoulders. It landed on the tile, followed by the coat he all but ripped off me.

"You drive me fucking crazy," he said between kisses as we exited the laundry room and entered the kitchen area.

"Good," I muttered, kicking off my boots. One landed under the dining room table; the other made it to the kitchen.

He grabbed me and kissed me until I couldn't think straight. The hot, hard pressure of his mouth, the dominating strokes of his tongue. I felt cool air and realized he'd stripped my skirt right off. My sweater came next, leaving me in nothing but thigh-highs, my bra, and my soaking wet underwear.

Lucian's gaze heated as he took a moment to sweep my body. "How am I supposed to not touch you when this is how you look?"

"Nothing's stopping you now," I said.

He opened his belt and I started to lose my mind. The zing of leather as he whipped it free made me tingle from head to toe.

He slid his thumbs in his slacks. I paid no attention to them as they pooled at his feet. I couldn't drag my eyes away from the black briefs that were failing to contain his cock.

I definitely lost my mind because instead of sexily unbuttoning his shirt, I yanked with both hands and sent buttons flying in every direction.

His smile was wicked. Evil. Like I'd just done something that had earned a punishment. I couldn't wait to find out what it was.

"I hope you don't expect me to pay for that," I told him.

"I can think of a few things I want besides money."

He hauled me against him and boosted me up with one hand on my ass. I wrapped my legs around his waist and plastered myself against him. Mouth to mouth, chest to chest.

We were moving. He was carrying me somewhere. I didn't care where as long as he stopped long enough to put that monumental dick inside me.

My back met drywall. He pinned me against the wall with his hips and opened the front closure of my bra with one deft flick. His growl made my blood simmer in my veins. I lived for that sound of approval. My nipples were hard, straining toward him like flowers following the sun.

513

He dipped his head and fastened his mouth over one lucky nipple.

"Gah!" I said as he applied the perfect amount of suction, drawing the pink nub deeper into his mouth.

I bucked against him, dangerously close to coming already.

I could feel the bare, wet head of his penis as it prodded my thigh.

He lavished my breast with attention until the ecstasy had my head thunking against the wall.

"You okay?" he asked, his voice rough and ragged.

"Yes," I breathed.

He moved on to the other breast, the other jealous nipple.

They felt so full and heavy. Every suck released a letdown of pure pleasure.

"Goddammit," he murmured, lips moving against my breast.

"What's wrong?" I asked, hissing as his chest hair teased my wet nipples.

"Every time, I think I'll take my time. That I'll spend an hour just on your perfect fucking breasts. I fucking lose it," he said.

"Wha—"

I didn't get any further than that. Because he plucked me off the wall and turned us.

I found myself on my knees, facedown on the upholstered ottoman in his living room. My ass was in the air, my face pressed into the blue linen.

Lucian hovered behind me, his erection nestled between my legs. I wanted him so damn much I was prepared to beg.

"You baited me at the bar," he accused, coasting a hand gently over the flowered silk of my underwear.

"How?" I asked, ready to lie.

"That sweater and little fucking skirt. Your fingers brushing my dick when it was already rock-hard for you. Those sexy little glances while you played with your straw. I should teach you a lesson."

His fingers curling in my panties, the drag of damp silk against my thighs was an exquisite kind of torture.

"As long as your lesson involves you fucking me, I'm all for it," I said breathlessly.

His hand resumed its gentle strokes over the slopes of my rear end. I peeked between my legs and watched his penis slide back and forth through my folds.

"I hate not being able to touch what's mine," he confessed.

I was about to point out that our arrangement definitely did not allow for "mine" talk outside bed. But the hot head of his erection branded me with every brush against my sex. I struggled against him, sliding my knees wider, begging with my body.

"Please, Lucian," I whispered.

"I don't have a condom on yet," he reminded me.

His tone sounded . . . different. Like there was something he wanted to ask for. Was it something I wanted too?

"I hit the gynecologist last month. All my tests were clear," I said. Then winced. "But I'm not on birth control."

"Vasectomy," he reminded me. "And I was tested six months ago."

His hands were still caressing my hips, the crown of his dick still nestled against my sex as if waiting for an invitation. My heart hammered in my chest.

He'd probably fucked his way through an entire professional cheerleading squad since then.

"I haven't been with anyone since," he added.

"Seriously?" No wonder he was so . . . explosive.

"Shut up."

"Okay," I said.

"Okay?" he repeated, prompting me for more.

"Put your bare cock in me and make me come, Lucian." I couldn't make it any more clear than that.

He tensed against me, and I wished I could see his face. But I forgot all about it as the broad crown notched into place. Yes! There! I shifted back against him, hoping he'd let me take him. But he stilled my hips with his hands.

"It's my turn to play, Pixie."

I'd never been so excited to be threatened before in my life.

"Then hurry up and get started," I groaned. "Please."

"Good girl," he purred. And then he gripped my hips and thrust himself home.

He felt hot and hard and smooth inside me.

My body tensed at the invasion. I was beyond wet, beyond ready, but he was so big and the angle was so deep it was still a shock. My head came up.

Lucian's palm landed with a stinging slap on my rear end.

I let out a yelp as a pleasant heat bloomed across my ass cheek.

"Hold still," he ordered through clenched teeth.

I let him guide me back down, feeling the length of him as it pulsed inside me. He stroked the sting away.

"You need to relax for me, baby. Relax so I can get all the way in."

My inner walls were quivering in anticipation of a muscle-pulling orgasm.

"Come on, Pixie. Breathe for me."

I wanted to do as he asked. I wanted to please him. Because then he'd please the hell out of me. I sucked in a weak breath and then forced it out like a teakettle.

He glided one hand from my neck all the way down my spine. "Good girl. Do it again."

This time, it was a real breath, and I felt my muscles relax a millimeter. Apparently so did he, because Lucian was withdrawing slowly and then thrusting in. Hard.

I took him all. I knew it even before his shout of triumph.

I was possessed by Lucian Rollins.

"I can feel you in my organs," I groaned.

He responded with a short, hard upthrust that had me moaning.

So full. So gloriously full I didn't remember what it felt like to be empty.

"You look so good taking my cock, Pix," he murmured, sliding his hands up my back and then around so he could massage my breasts as they hung heavily off the ottoman.

"Yeah, well, you feel pretty okay in there," I squeaked.

He gave my nipples a hard tweak that had my inner muscles clamping down on him. I could *feel* the dizzying pulse of blood in his shaft. With nothing between us finally, I reveled in the scorching heat of his body as it entered mine.

I was at his mercy and we both knew it.

And that was the realization that set me off. He was sheathed in me to the hilt, filling me in a way I'd never been filled before. The tension spiraled higher and higher, and all it took was a subtle widening of my knees and I was coming. I cried out as it rolled through me like a thunderstorm. Lucian held deep as it broke inside me in a spectacular thunderclap release.

His growl was feral as I milked his cock from the inside.

He let me have it, and then he was moving. Fast, slick drives, powering into my quivering core.

"More," he said, his fingers bruising my hips with their grip.

Sweat slicked our skin where it touched. He powered into me, through my climax, drawing it out until I wasn't sure if I was still coming or if he'd set off a new orgasm.

"Fuck, Sloane." There was a plea in his tone. His hands tightened on me, and then he was pulling me up, my back to his front, his hand holding my jaw so he could seal his mouth over mine.

I could feel it build for him, and I knew what he wanted but wasn't asking for.

I broke the kiss. "Yes, baby. Please come in me," I begged.

His grip on me tightened, and his mouth returned to mine. A second later, he went completely rigid, and I felt the first hot burst of his climax in the depths of my soul. It felt so good. So dirty. So right. Lucian Rollins was coming inside me.

His shout rang in my ears as another jet of release let loose inside me. "Sloane!"

I was coming again or still, triggered by his orgasm. He rode me, his thrusts slow and shallow as my body wrung every drop of his release free.

It was glorious. A fireworks show set off in my vagina, detonated by the obstinate man's obliging penis.

Lucian collapsed on top of me, flattening me to the ottoman. He was still inside me, still on top of me, still coming. I never wanted it to end.

"You make me feel like I have no control," he growled, still moving in me. It sounded like an accusation.

I took it as a compliment.

"This is ridiculous," Lucian said when I pulled his ball cap lower over his face. "We're adults, not teenagers. We shouldn't have to sneak around."

I zipped my coat all the way to my chin and covered my hair with the hood. "I'm hungry and all you have in your house are frozen, nutritious chef meals. Besides, do you really want Knockemout gossiping about us like we're some kind of grumpy-sunshine love story?"

"I'm the sunshine in that scenario," he said confidently.

"You're the delusional grump who never wants to settle down, especially not with the beautiful, charming, book nerd next door. I'm the perky, sunshiny heroine who believes in true love. Just not with you because I'm only using you for orgasms."

He shook his head. "You're going to miss those orgasms when you meet Mr. Right. There are some things only Mr. Wrong can deliver."

"We'll see about that."

We headed outside, cutting across his driveway and the strip of snow-covered grass to my place.

The lights were on across the street, but there were no errant dog walkers or couples out for a romantic, arctic stroll.

I blew out a sigh of relief and jogged up the walk to my front porch, pulling Lucian with me.

"I think I have some chocolate chips in the pantry," I said.

Suddenly, Lucian nabbed me around the waist and pulled me back.

"I take it chocolate chips make you horny?"

But he was positioning his body between me and the front door.

"Go back to my place," he said, his voice cold.

"What? Why? What's going on?"

I tried to peer around his broad back, but he spun and gripped me by the shoulders. "Do as I say."

I saw it then, the morbid, nauseating pile of matted fur and long, fleshy tails. "Oh my God."

On an oath, Lucian picked me up and marched me off the porch. He set me down on the walkway where I no longer had a clear view of the door.

"I don't suppose that's common behavior for rats," I said, fighting the rising nausea.

"No, it isn't," he said sternly.

"Damn it. You better go back. I have to see a man about a pile of frozen rats."

"No, you're going back to my place, and I'm calling Nash."

"If you call Nash, the chief of police will know that we were together tonight. Which means the rest of the town will know by morning. And they'll be speculating about these threats. And you don't live here anymore, but I do. I'm the one who's going to have to deal with the attention."

"Threats?" Lucian's voice was deadly calm.

"I still think the first one was a joke. This is clearly an escalation over some vague note." I was babbling. Apparently that was the effect a pile of dead rats had on me.

He didn't say another word. No, Lucian Rollins merely tossed me over his shoulder and marched me back to his house while placing a call.

"Why am I just now finding out that she's being threatened?" he snarled into the phone.

"Put me down, you big, gorgeous asshat!"

He ignored me.

"You'll want to see what someone left for her on her front porch. Bring the biggest evidence bags you have."

"Excuse me! This is kidnapping," I said, pummeling his back with my gloved hands.

"If you don't stop screeching, the entire neighborhood is going to come outside and witness this," Lucian said.

I was fairly certain he was talking to me.

"That's not relevant, and it's not anyone's business but my own," he continued.

That was definitely meant for Nash.

"Meet me at my place. I have to tie her to a chair," Lucian said.

"Nice going, Lucifer. Now Nash is going to tell Lina, and Lina's going to tell Naomi, and Waylay is going to eavesdrop and tell Chloe, and my niece can't keep her mouth shut if she's underwater trying to swim."

"Someone left a pile of dead rats on your porch, and your biggest concern is your niece telling everyone we're seeing each other?"

He unlocked his front door and carried me over the threshold.

"We're not seeing each other. We're seeing each other naked."

"I can explain," I said to the group before anyone else could begin. "It's just sex."

Lucian slapped a gloved hand over my mouth. "Shut up before you piss me off even more."

"Pay up," Lina said, holding her hand out to Nash. The chief of police had responded with his fiancée, his brother, *and* his sister-in-law.

The six of us stood in my driveway while we waited for Sergeant Grave Hopper to show up with an evidence bag big enough for a pile of rodents.

Nash and Knox exchanged annoyed looks, and both men reached for their wallets. Naomi and Lina grinned as crisp twenties were exchanged.

"A pleasure doing business with you," Lina said. "Don't ever doubt us again."

"And don't forget you owe Stef too," Naomi told Knox.

"What's going on?" I asked after prying Lucian's hand away.

"We knew," Lina explained. "Nolan told me he saw you at the hotel bar the other weekend and that the boss here went to 'deal with you.' Then both of you showed up to work with post-O face."

"Knox and I were skeptical until Honky Tonk," Nash admitted.

I smacked Lina in the shoulder. "Why didn't you say anything?"

"Why didn't *you* say anything?" she countered.

"*I* didn't say anything because I didn't think either of you would be fucking stupid enough to fuck around," Knox interjected.

"Lina said it was like approaching a skittish dog. You don't want to make any sudden moves or you'll scare it off," Naomi interjected.

"This is stupid. Can I please go back to my house?" I asked.

"Not until we make sure there aren't any other surprises waiting for you inside," Nash said.

I shivered.

"She's staying with me tonight," Lucian announced.

"Listen, Lucifer. Just because we've had sex a few times doesn't give you the right to tell me what to do."

At that moment, a police cruiser pulled up in the driveway behind Nash's truck. Grave and Officer Bertle got out.

"I'll leave you two to your bickering," Nash said and headed for his cops.

Lucian used the distraction to haul me several feet away. Lina and Naomi exchanged smug looks.

"What are you doing?" I hissed.

"You should have told me," he said coldly.

"Told you what? That someone left a lame

anonymous note in the book drop for me? Do you know how many weird things we find in there every week?"

"Someone is threatening you, and you *will* take it seriously," he announced.

"Ugh. Even after sex, you're infuriating."

"And you're still a pain in my ass that won't go away," he shot back.

We exchanged heated glares. But I caved first. "Look at us. Our friend would rather bag up dead rats than be around us."

"Listen carefully, Pixie. While my dick is in you, whatever you choose to call it, that makes you mine. And while you're mine, I get to know when someone is scaring you."

"I'm not scared. I'm annoyed. I really liked that welcome mat."

"You're not taking this seriously. Which is another reason I am."

"This is almost as bad as the mayor's snakes," Officer Bertle complained, stifling a gag as he stuffed a rat in the bag with a pair of tongs.

"Luce," Nash called.

"Take her inside," Lucian ordered, guiding me to Knox.

31

The Fuck Fest Is Over

Lucian

W ell? What did you find out?" I demanded, coming to my feet when Nash strolled into his office.

"Christ, Luce," he said, flicking on the lights. "It's 7:00 a.m. on a Thursday. At least let me have a cup of coffee before scaring the shit out of me with the lurking villain routine."

"Someone is threatening one of the people you're supposed to protect and serve, and *you* want a good night's sleep?"

I'd barely slept. We'd spent the night at my place, and while Sloane had curled comfortably into my side and passed out within seconds, I'd run through each and every probability and possible outcome. When I settled on the most obvious answer, I'd slipped out of bed, triple checked the alarm, and tried to sweat out my anger at the gym with Shania Twain in my ears.

I was still sweating and still furious.

She was acting as though it was just some practical joke played in poor taste. Clearly her ability to take dangerous situations seriously had not improved since she was a teenager.

Bad things happened. Good people got hurt. She knew this first-fucking-hand. Yet I seemed to be the only one taking this seriously.

Nash sighed as he shrugged out of his coat. "I won't waste my breath giving you the usual 'police business' speech since you never listen, and if some asshole was threatening Lina, I wouldn't be in the mood to mind my own business either."

I ignored the comparison. Sloane and I were fucking. That was the entire extent of our relationship. "Tell me what you've done so far."

Nash shoved a mug under the coffee maker and stabbed irritably at the buttons. "They were feeder rats. You buy them frozen at pet shops to feed to snakes. So far no leads on where they were purchased. Bannerjee will be knocking on doors in the neighborhood today to see if anyone saw anything suspicious. You want coffee?" he asked, looking me up and down.

I had enough adrenaline in my system. I didn't need a hit of caffeine. "I want answers."

The corner of my friend's mouth lifted.

"If you feel like doing something, talk Sloane into one of those video doorbells. Maybe a couple of those cameras. It'll deter anyone from trying something like this again."

"She's getting an entire security system, and I'm not about to waste time discussing it with her. What else do you have?"

Amusement flared in his eyes as he took his time settling in behind his desk.

527

"The way it looks, there's two theories. One, our little librarian pissed off someone who feels like letting her know about it. First the note, now this. They're warnings. Vague ones. It's not exactly like someone forced her into the trunk of a car or took a shot at her."

I knew Nash well enough to understand he wasn't insinuating that there was no actual threat. He knew better than any of us what kinds of darkness could fester beneath the surface.

"And your other theory?" I asked.

Nash leveled me with a cool gaze. "You two start spending time together, and suddenly someone has a problem with Sloane. Could be a coincidence. Could be related."

It was the same conclusion I'd drawn around the 5:00 a.m. mark.

"You make enemies faster than friends. Somebody could have been paying attention and seen you two together. An ex-lover, an old business partner, a crime boss you're going head-to-head with. And judging from your expression, you've already thought of that."

It was possible that I'd gotten careless and put Sloane in Anthony Hugo's sights.

I sat perfectly still, ignoring my mind screaming that I needed to get up and take action. At one time, I'd gone still to remain invisible. Now I did it because stillness reveals nothing to enemies.

I'd underestimated Hugo. While I'd been playing games with his tracking device and tails, I'd played right into the man's hands, serving up the perfect incentive for him to use against me.

"You're doing that stone-faced thing," Nash observed.

"What stone-faced thing?" I snapped.

"The thing where you look like you're constipated and really pissed off about it. You go all stone-faced when you're having feelings you don't want to have."

"I'm not having feelings," I insisted a little too loudly.

He put down his coffee mug. "Look, man. For what it's worth, I don't see Anthony Hugo driving up here and dumping a bunch of rat corpses on Sloane's doorstep. He doesn't go for subtle."

"We both know he's got an army of criminals eager to do his bidding."

"We don't know that Hugo has anything to do with this. It could have just as easily been Marjorie Ronsanto, who gives the library shit on a weekly basis. Or some idiot hormonal teenager who didn't want to pay his late fees."

"Or it could be Anthony Fucking Hugo. I'd expect you of all people to take this seriously."

No one seemed to be properly upset about this. When I'd gotten out of bed, Sloane had rolled over, buried her face in my pillow, and asked me to bring her back a doughnut. Now Nash was placating me like I was an overly concerned citizen.

"Look, Luce, I get it. You care and you're

worried. We'll keep her safe. Between you, me, and the rest of the department, no one's gonna get near her."

I shook my head. "I'm going back to the city," I decided.

If I was what had drawn Anthony Hugo's attention to Sloane, then I'd be the one to draw it away.

"You sure about that?" my friend asked.

"You don't need me here interfering in your investigation," I said flatly.

"As if that's ever stopped you before."

"Maybe I'm choosing to listen to reason this time."

His eyes narrowed. "Or maybe you're turning into a pile of chickenshit in my office."

"We're not in a relationship. We're fucking." Even saying it out loud had my muscles tightening.

"I love you like a brother, so hear me when I say don't fuck with Sloane," Nash warned.

"She knows the score," I said.

He shook his head. "You're an idiot."

"Why do people keep telling me that?"

"Because even I—an emotionally stunted Morgan man—can see that you've got feelings for her. You always have. And now that you're close to finding something real with her, you're gonna hightail it back to the city and pretend you're not scared shitless that she's in danger. If Lina were in trouble, there's *nothing* that would stop me from standing between her and that trouble."

530

"If Lina were in trouble, she'd kick it in the balls and sharpen her nails in its eye sockets."

"Sloane's not like Lina. She gets riled and she goes off half-cocked," he reminded me unnecessarily.

"That's not my problem." Hot acid was eating its way up my esophagus.

"It was once. I went through Ogden's old case files after dinner the other night. Sloane was the unnamed minor Ansel Rollins attacked, wasn't she? That's how she broke her wrist."

"She didn't fucking break it. He did," I said, getting to my feet. "And if you want details, you'll have to ask someone else, because I wasn't fucking there. I was in jail."

"Got sprung the very next morning though, didn't you?" he pressed. "Interesting coincidence, don't you think? That she's championing the cause of the wrongfully imprisoned."

"Keep her safe," I said coolly and headed for the door.

"I meant what I said," Nash called after me. "Don't fuck around with her."

"I won't," I muttered under my breath as I stormed out of the police station, already dialing my phone.

"Where's my doughnut?" Sloane pouted.

She was wearing my T-shirt, pouring coffee in my kitchen, and looking adorably disheveled. Something clenched awkwardly in my chest.

531

A wave of possession knocked me off balance. I wanted this. Her. And I couldn't have it. Not when being close to me made her a target.

"I didn't bring you one," I said flatly.

"Mean. What did Nash say? Did anyone report a rat heist?"

I took the mug out of her hand. "You should go."

"Why? What's wrong? Your face is all weird. Oh God. Did something happen to Meow Meow?"

There was only one button of Sloane's I knew how to push to make her walk away. "There's nothing wrong with your cat. I just don't want you here."

"That's not what you said last night," she said smugly.

"You can keep the shirt," I said, scanning her from head to toe, careful to keep my expression impassive.

"Oh no, Lucifer. I'm not going anywhere until you tell me why mere hours ago, you were begging me to make you come, and now you're Mr. Freeze."

"I remembered all the reasons I don't like you."

She snorted. "Nice try. You never forgot them in the first place."

"I spoke to Nash. He dug into my father's arrest record and connected some dots."

She remained silent.

"You jumped willingly into a dangerous situation."

"So did you every time your parents fought," she pointed out.

"That's different. It was my responsibility. You never should have been there. I never should have told you what was happening. It's bad enough that he ruined your plans. He could have ended your life. And you went over there willingly."

Sloane crossed her arms over her chest. "Because you loved her. Because you wanted to keep her safe. And because I couldn't stand another minute of you being locked up for a crime he committed." She spoke softly, firmly.

"He broke your wrist in three places. You had to have surgery. All your plans, your dreams, everything gone because you couldn't listen to me and do the right thing."

Snap.

My freedom wasn't worth that. My *life* wasn't worth that.

Snap.

"Lucian," she said carefully.

"What?" I realized I was yelling. I didn't raise my voice like him. I didn't have to. "What?" I repeated quietly.

"I'm sorry for not listening to you when you asked me not to call the police. I had no idea that would happen. But I'm not sorry for what I did to get you out."

I turned my back on her so I wouldn't be tempted to shake some sense into her, decades-old panic and anger rearing their ugly heads.

"I still feel sick about what happened that night, what I saw, what you must have lived with for so long," she continued. "I know how lucky I am that things didn't end differently. I've wasted a lot of time over the past several years thinking about the what-ifs. What if I'd gotten there too late? What if he hurt my dad? What if he'd gotten away with it? But I have never once regretted the way things worked out. He went to jail, and you got out. Justice was served."

I turned to face her even though I didn't want to look at her. "There's no such thing as justice," I spat.

"That sounds like a conversation neither one of us has time for."

"You have someone actively threatening you. Not only did you not think to mention it to me, you're also not taking it seriously. It's fucking selfish again."

She gasped and the fight in her eyes flared to life. "Selfish? You think me putting your father in jail so everyone would know who the real monster was is selfish?"

"You deciding you know what's best for everyone is selfish. You refusing to take the bare minimum of safety precautions once again is selfish. You putting yourself in danger is selfish."

She took a step toward me and laid her palms on my chest. "You're really starting to piss me off, and I don't like to be pissed off on Thursdays because it's Lunch Swap Thursday, and I like Lunch Swap

Thursdays. So I'm going to say this. I'm sorry for my part in all of it. I'm sorry for not doing what you needed me to do or not being what you needed me to be. I'm sorry for making it seem like I'm not taking these threats seriously, because I am. I'm freaking the fuck out that someone decided to throw a pile of dead rats on my front porch! *Now* can we talk about whatever this is like adults, or are you going to double down on shoving your head up your ass?"

She was yelling by the end of her tirade. Her chin jutted out as she glared up at me. I wanted to kiss her. To lock her in a bedroom and keep her safe. I wanted to shake her until her teeth rattled and she saw reason. That she never should have gotten involved. That once again, being close to me had brought her up against danger.

But this time, I could do something about it.

"I need to get back to the city, and you need to go home," I announced. "This little fuck fest is over."

"Doubling down, I see," she quipped. "Fine."

She gripped the hem of the T-shirt she wore and dragged it over her head. Sloane Walton was naked in my kitchen. I wasn't sure how many fantasies of mine had started that way, but it was at least a thousand.

"Keep the shirt," I insisted.

"I'd rather walk home naked," she snapped.

We'd spent too much time doing this. Fighting then finding our way back to each other only to blow up again. We were like magnets drawn together in one moment before we were reversed, repelling each other the next. But this time, it needed to be permanent. This time, I needed to blow it up forever.

I followed her to the coat rack. She snatched her parka off the hook and slid her arms into the sleeves in quick, jerky movements.

"Poor broody boy with his big cock and all that emotional baggage."

She hopped on one foot and yanked a snow boot over the other.

"You can at least get dressed," I said dryly.

"Thanks, but I'd rather burn it all than look at it again and think of you."

She was playing with fire. I was angry and she was pushing buttons like a toddler in an elevator. She was either oblivious to my anger or brashly confident in her nonexistent abilities to protect herself.

"I spent enough of my life with a woman who had no sense of self-preservation. I'm not doing it again. Not when I have a choice in the matter this time."

She stopped midhop and glared up at me. Fury snapped off her like sparks from a bonfire.

"Don't you *ever* compare me to your mother. And while you're at it, have fun spending the rest of your life alone because you're too fucking stubborn to learn to do better."

"As long as I don't have to deal with you on a

daily basis, I look forward to it. I pity your future husband."

Sloane's laugh was sharp and humorless. "I wouldn't waste any time thinking about me or my future husband if I were you. Because I'm going to forget you ever existed."

"Good luck with that."

But she didn't hear me because she'd already slammed the front door behind her.

I whipped it open and stepped outside. "A security company will be coming by this afternoon to install cameras at your place," I called as she stormed toward her house.

"If they have anything to do with you, then they're not getting anywhere near my property."

"Don't be a stubborn idiot."

"You already have the monopoly on that!"

She made it to her driveway and had just started for her front porch when she thought better of it and marched toward the garage door.

"If you see anything that feels off to you, call Nash. Immediately."

"Sell your damn house, assface!"

• • •

Emry: Does this suit make me look like I should have laid off the cookies a few decades ago?

537

32

Dead to Me

Sloane

Assface: To confirm, the security team will be at your house at one.

Assface: At least acknowledge that you'll be there to let them in.

Assface: The silent treatment. Very mature.

Assface: I'm not above getting the law involved.

Assface: I don't know what point you think you're proving by calling the cops on my team when they're just trying to keep you safe.

Assface: Just because we're not sneaking around having sex anymore doesn't mean I don't care.

Assface: I found your underwear behind the nightstand. Do you want it back?

The heyday of the Lawlerville courthouse looked as if it had occurred in the 1970s with its speckled tile floors, musty wood paneling, and ceiling tiles stained yellow from decades of cigarette smoke.

I shifted on the too-low, too-hard bench and stared at the door across from me.

The metal plaque on the wall read *Judge Dirk Atkins*. Behind that door were three people hopefully making Mary Louise's dreams come true. And I was stuck out here trying not to gnaw my fingernails down to the bone.

And trying not to think of He Who Shall Not Be Thought Of.

On cue, my phone buzzed on the bench next to me.

Assface: Lina says you're at the courthouse now. Good luck.

I glared at the text. It had been a week and a half since Lucian had kicked me out of his house. He hadn't been back to Knockemout since. Between the library, my family, Mary Louise's case, and my friends trying to oh-so-casually pump me for information about Lucian, I was staying busy. But not busy enough to forget that the assface existed.

I'd fallen into his trap twice now. If I fell a third time, I deserved to get mauled by the steel teeth of Lucian's perverse whims. He cared about me. He hated me. He wanted me. He wanted nothing to do with me.

That was a roller coaster I didn't need to get on again. I wanted stability, not volatility. A relationship, not a fuck buddy. A future, not a past.

I opened the dating app and, with a bracing inhale, started swiping.

The chamber door opened, and I bolted to my feet. My phone went flying.

Fran marched into the hallway, glaring at the district attorney, a man with wispy gray hair and thick glasses. He looked older than the forty-seven my internet search reported. But I supposed that was what the criminal justice system did to a person over time.

"Way to back me up in there, Lloyd," Fran snapped.

The attorney's shoulders hunched. "It's not a good look to have a magistrate reducing his own sentences."

"That sentence is out of line and you know it," she said, standing pink stiletto to scuffed loafer with the man.

"Is there a problem, ladies?" came honeyed southern sarcasm from the doorway.

Judge Dirk Atkins was a good-looking man in his late fifties. He had a head of thick silvery hair and a dignified posture, and the tie under his black robes looked like it was Lucian Rollins expensive.

Fran's face went from infuriated to impassive in half a second. The DA, on the other hand, looked as if he wanted the floor to swallow him up.

"No problem, Your Honor," Fran said smoothly.

Judge Atkins bent down and picked my phone up off the floor. He glanced at the screen.

"That's, uh, mine. Sir. I mean, Your Honor," I said, holding out my hand.

540

He looked up at me with pale-blue eyes and handed the phone back to me. "And you are?"

"This is my associate, Ms. Walton," Fran said.

"Well, Ms. Walton, I wouldn't swipe right on that one," the judge said, nodding at my screen. "He has a shifty look about him. A young lady like you can't be too careful these days."

"Uh, thanks?"

"We won't take up any more of your time," Fran announced, hooking her arm through mine.

"I take it it didn't go well," I said out of the corner of my mouth as she marched us toward the elevators.

"The judge didn't see anything wrong with the original sentence. Apparently he's made a career out of 'making an example' of the defendants who come through his courtroom."

"So he just doubled down?"

Fran stabbed the call button for the elevator. "Oh, he tripled down. He's seen your interviews and doesn't care for the 'one-sided storytelling,'" she said, adding air quotes. "He suggested we find a better use of our time rather than questioning his judgment."

The elevator doors slid open, and we stepped inside. I slumped against the back wall. "So what do we do now?"

"Now we start the appeal process. If Mary Louise is going to have a chance to get out, it's not going to come from this court."

I drummed my fingers against the handrail. "You

know, this makes me want to do more interviews just to piss him off."

Fran's smile was a little scary. "I was hoping you'd say that."

"I wish I had better news, Mary Louise," I said to my computer screen, feeling an uncomfortable combination of disappointed and pissed off.

"Honey, you've already done more for me than anyone else. I don't need any apologies," she said. Her beige jumpsuit blended in morosely with the industrial gray concrete block background.

"Don't give up hope," Fran said at my elbow. "This one was always a long shot. Now we can focus our resources on next steps."

"I just want you both to know how grateful I am that you're even taking an interest. It means the world to me and to Allen," Mary Louise said, tears glittering in her eyes.

"We'll be in touch soon," Fran promised.

"Stay positive, Mary Louise," I said, wishing we'd given her something to feel positive about.

The video feed cut off, and I slumped back in my chair. "Well, I feel like shit," I announced.

"Don't let it get you down," Fran advised, getting to her feet. "Otherwise, you'll be in the fetal position on the floor, and you'll miss out on celebrating the millimeters of forward progress."

Between my dad, the latest Lucian catastrophe, and now the disappointment Mary Louise tried hard to hide, the fetal position sounded pretty damn good to me.

I was wallowing, though at least not in the fetal position, when Naomi bounded into my office like an energetic golden retriever.

"Soooo. How are things?" she asked, perching on my visitor's chair. She'd been checking on me every hour since I updated her on the disastrous meeting with the judge.

I abandoned the newsletter template I was working on and dropped my head to my desk.

"That good, huh?"

"Everything sucks."

"I take it you saw it then," she said sympathetically.

"Saw what?" I asked my keyboard.

"The thing about Lucian."

I sat up. "What thing about Lucian?" I demanded.

Naomi winced and looked toward the door.

"What thing about Lucian?" I repeated darkly.

She brought her hands to her cheeks. "I'm sure it didn't mean anything. It was just some Capitol gossip blog."

My fingers raced across the keyboard as I typed "Lucian Rollins gossip blog" into the search engine.

I saw the pictures first. Lucian in a tux leading a stunning, statuesque woman by the hand into a hotel. Not just any hotel. *Our* hotel. Well, technically his hotel. She was beautiful in the kind of "I come from money and really good genes" kind of way. Her sleek, black hair was styled in a classic bun. Her ivory sheath dress contrasted beautifully with her rich, dark skin. And her tailored coat looked like it cost more than the one Lucian had given me.

There was another picture. Another woman on another night. Lucian had his hand resting intimately on a diminutive redhead's back as they exited a trendy restaurant. She was shorter, curvier, and somehow just as horribly gorgeous in a flirty cocktail dress designed to draw the eye.

I looked away from the screen and willed myself to forget Lucian Rollins and his penis ever existed.

I was no longer the one who drove him crazy, or maybe, as I'd fantasized in my darkest, drunkest moments over the years, the one who got away. Now, I was just one of the legions of women he'd left behind.

My head felt stuffy and full. I could feel my heartbeat at the base of my ponytail. I heard a snap and glanced down to find I'd broken the cap on the pen I held.

"Okay. I can fix this," Naomi said, pulling her phone out.

"What are you doing?"

"Calling Lina. We need alcohol and Silver Fox Joel."

"I'm fine. We weren't together. We were just having sex," I said robotically. "Oh, look at that.

544

His first date sits on the board of DC's largest food bank, and the second one is a freaking astrophysicist."

I wanted to reach through the screen and dump a very expensive cocktail over Lucian's beautiful head. I also wanted to ask his date where she shopped because her shoes were phenomenal. Not that small-town librarian me could pull off or afford that look.

He looked good with both women. Better than good. They looked like they belonged on his arm. Like they could sit next to him for longer than five minutes without bickering.

"You and Lucian have history. Unfortunately for you as a woman with strong feelings about everything, that means you can't *just* have sex with him."

"I can and I did," I insisted.

"You just broke your pen and crushed your paper cup. Iced coffee is literally running down your arm," she pointed out.

"Shit."

"Feels good to be on this side for once," Knox said, settling with satisfaction onto a sticky bar stool at Hellhound, a greasy, dingy dive bar outside Knockemout.

"This side of the bar?" Lina asked, angled into Nash, who stood next to her, his back to the bar, his gaze scanning the bikers gathered around rickety tables and arguing over pool games.

"Nope, this side of Men Suck, Let's Drink," Knox said.

"We are here purely for social reasons," I insisted. "There is no reason to participate in Men Suck, Let's Drink, because that would imply that I care what Lucian is doing when I don't because he means nothing to me. We had sex. Then we stopped having sex. End of story. Where is Joel? I need a drink."

"My bar is better," Knox said, giving no indication that he'd been listening to my convincing tirade.

Naomi beamed at him. "It is. But wait till you meet Silver Fox Joel." She pointed down the bar to where our favorite bartender poured shots of cheap whiskey in front of three morose-looking women in ripped denim and worn leather.

Lina waved at him, and Joel gave her the cool guy nod.

"Okay, I filled the jukebox with men suck songs and told the biker couple with matching tattoos that you're in a cult and looking to recruit members. That should buy you some time before anyone starts hitting on you," Stef said, grabbing the stool next to me.

I patted his knee. "Thanks, Stef. You're a good friend."

Knox and Nash moved closer to their women as the studly bartender approached. He stopped in front of me. "Hey there, blondie. What'll it be today? Shots? Spicy Bloody Mary?"

"Hi, Joel. I'd love a Bloody Mary for no other reason than that you make an excellent one. I'm not drinking away man problems or anything like that," I told him.

"Glad you cleared that up," he said with a half smile.

He took everyone's drink orders and went to work under Knox's watchful eye.

Naomi elbowed him in the ribs. "Stop staring and glaring."

"I'm not glaring, I'm judging him professionally," her husband insisted.

"I, for one, think since you two finally got each other out of your systems that it's time for you to tell us about that history," Lina announced.

"I agree. We're your friends," Naomi said, nodding her thanks as Joel handed her a very large glass of wine.

"For what it's worth, I think you should tell them," Nash said.

"How do you—" I closed my eyes. "You have access to sealed records."

Naomi and Lina shared a wide-eyed look. "What sealed records?" they demanded in unison.

"Is this like you insisting I burden everyone with a couple of anonymous threats?"

Nash shook his head. "No, Sloaney Baloney. This is different. Your personal safety is one thing. You don't get to hide dangerous things from the people who care about you. But you get to decide what stories you share."

Joel set a Bloody Mary in front of me with a resounding thump.

"For the record, if you don't tell us, I'll do whatever it takes to get the information out of hotshot here. And I can be *very* persuasive," Lina promised, a glint in her brown eyes.

Nash leaned in and pressed a hard kiss to her mouth. "Damn right, Angel."

I should have come here alone. Not that I needed to drink away my feelings or whatever. I just didn't need to be a fifth wheel in the happily ever after party. Especially not when all I wanted was my own happily ever after. And *especially* not when I'd just wasted weeks on Lucian Assface Rollins.

I took a sip of my drink. My eyebrows winged up at the spice level. "Nice one, Joel," I coughed.

Nash plucked his beer off the bar. "In accordance with man code, we're going to let you talk while we go hustle some bikers over pool."

"What if I wanna know what shit went down?" Knox asked.

"I'll give you the short version," his brother offered.

"I fuckin' love the short version," Knox decided. He looked at Joel. "You got 'em?"

"I got 'em," Joel agreed.

"We don't need babysitters," I insisted. "And I don't need to get anything off my chest."

But it was too late. Nash and Knox were already sauntering off, drinks in hand.

"I'll help you get something off your chest."

I turned on my stool and found a greasy, gold-toothed guy drowning in gold chains. He leered at my chest.

"Didn't you hear about the cult?" Stef asked him.

"I don't mind a girlie who's whacked in the head."

"Go away before I make you require an eye patch," Lina announced.

"Feisty filly," he said, licking his thin lips.

Joel leaned across the bar just as Nash and Knox started back toward us, but I held up a hand. "Listen, you unshowered, deodorant-avoiding dumbass. I'm in the market for a husband and kids. So unless you're willing to start showering, see a dentist, and learn to assemble nursery furniture, I suggest you move along."

"Nobody ever wants to just have a good time anymore," he grumbled and wandered off.

"That's because all good times must come to an end, as I recently discovered," I called after him.

"Okay. Spill it," Lina insisted, swirling her mediocre scotch around the glass.

"It's time," Naomi squeezed my hand.

"Or we're just going to speculate wildly," Stef added.

"It's not just my story," I said. Even though Lucian was a big, dumb, well-hung idiot, I couldn't share his part of the story.

"Then just tell us your part."

I took a bracing gulp of vodka and tomato juice.

549

· · ·

"They arrested Lucian?" Naomi gasped.

I'd told them a heavily redacted version that included no details of what Lucian's father had put him through. But even this edited version induced rage.

Lina slapped the bar. "Pardon my language but what in the fucking fuck?"

"I never liked that Wylie guy," Stef slurred.

My friends were a little bit tipsy, which made them an even more enthusiastic audience.

"Wylie Ogden was friends with Lucian's dad. Ansel told him that Lucian attacked them, and Lucian's mom backed up his version of the story."

I stared down at my second, mostly untouched Bloody Mary and decided I didn't want it anymore.

"That's horrible," Naomi said.

"He blamed me. I'd promised I wouldn't call the police, and then I did."

"Sometimes the right thing to do is also the wrong one," Stef said philosophically.

"You had your reasons," Lina said, reaching out and grasping my hand. Alcohol made her more affectionate.

"May I have some napkins, Joel?" Naomi asked, a tear sliding down her cheek.

Knox looked up from the pool table and glared. His husband radar was top notch. Naomi gave him a watery smile and a wave before blowing her nose on a cocktail napkin.

"What happened next?" Lina demanded.

550

"My dad went down to the station to try to get Lucian released, but Lucian's dad insisted on pressing charges. They were going to charge him as an adult. My dad kept fighting for him, but I felt so guilty. It was my fault he was in there in the first place. And I knew he'd be terrified that something was going to happen to his mom. So I decided to fix it."

"Uh-oh," Stef said.

Lina covered her eyes with her hand. "Oh God. What did you do?"

"I decided that I needed irrefutable evidence."

Naomi groaned. "This is going to go horribly wrong, isn't it?"

"Let's just say I achieved my objectives."

"At what cost?" Lina asked.

I looked down at my right hand and flexed my fingers. "Ansel Rollins caught me recording him at the window and broke my wrist in three places."

Stef held up his hand. "I think we're gonna need some shots here, Joel."

"It was fine," I assured them, even though bile rose in my throat. "Not only did I get him on camera, but a neighbor saw him come after me. No friendship could keep him out of jail with that kind of evidence. Lucian was released the next morning. But not before he missed his own high school graduation." I looked at Lina. "I think that was the moment Nash decided to become a cop. He saw how easily the bad ones could hurt good people and decided to fix it from the inside."

She sighed and looked moonily toward Nash, who

was bent over the pool table, his spectacular ass on display. "My fiancé is the most amazing man."

"With the most amazing ass," I added, admiring the view.

She snickered. "It's true. If I weren't me, I'd hate me."

"How did Lucian feel about . . . everything?" Naomi asked.

"You'd have to ask him. He got out of county lockup, we fought, and that's the way it's been ever since."

"What the hell did you fight about? He should have been worshipping the ground you walked on," Lina pointed out.

"You're not only beautiful, you're also incredibly astute," I told her.

"I know," she said with a wink.

"And you're stalling," Naomi pointed out.

"You guys are supposed to be too drunk to follow the story by this point," I complained.

"We had two drinks each," Lina said smugly.

"We just wanted you to feel safe opening up," Naomi added.

"Sucker," Stef teased.

"You sneaky, conniving, sober—"

"Compliment us later. What did you fight about when Lucian was released?" Lina said.

"He accused me of ruining his life and being selfish and stupid. I accused him of being ungrateful and stubborn. It went downhill from there."

"Well, you sure as hell didn't ruin his life. You're a goddamn hero," Lina said, tipping her glass in my direction.

"There's a fine line between bravery and stupidity," I admitted.

"So he goes all dick mode on you for the rest of your lives?" Stef asked.

"Not to side with the enemy, but I can see it from his perspective. A little. Even though he's very, very wrong," Naomi amended when Lina and I whipped around to pin her with twin glares.

"What's his perspective?" I asked, trying to sound casual.

She shrugged daintily. "He was a seventeen-year-old boy who felt responsible for keeping his mother safe. That's a heavy burden for a grown adult, let alone a teenager. I'd guess this was an escalating situation that he'd dealt with on his own for a long time, and that kind of long-term trauma can take a toll. He probably saw you and your parents as some kind of idealized version of a family he could never have."

I snorted. "That's just stupid."

"As stupid as deciding to make yourself the target of a raging alcoholic with a history of violence?" Lina pointed out.

"Hey!"

She held up her hands. "Don't get me wrong. Team Sloane all day every day. But Witty over here paints an empathetic picture."

I shook my head. "It doesn't matter. We're not

teenagers anymore. We're adults. It's our job to learn more and do better. But he hasn't changed. He gets all alpha over some pile of dead rats. You know the drill, 'You're not staying here alone' blah blah blah. Then the next morning, he says he wasted enough of his life with a woman who didn't care about self-preservation and that he's not going to do it again."

"Ouch," Naomi winced.

"He said what?" Knox sounded pissed off and baffled at the same time.

I hadn't noticed he and Nash return.

"Fucking idiot," Nash muttered.

"Where did he go that morning?" Lina asked, her eyes on her fiancé.

"He came to see me," Nash said evenly.

Knox slapped his brother in the chest. "Did you make him dump her?"

"Ow!" Nash rubbed his pectoral. "Watch the bullet hole."

"There was no one to dump because we weren't together," I said despite the fact that no one seemed to be listening.

"Hotshot, you've got some explaining to do," Lina said.

Nash sighed. "He wanted to know what we'd found about the threats. I told him what we had. Then he wanted to know my theories. So I told him."

"And what were those theories?" I demanded.

"That either you pissed someone off over late

554

fees or some shit, or maybe the timing meant there was a possibility you were being targeted because of your relationship with Lucian."

"Once again, I don't have a relationship with Lucifer. Second, we were sneaking around. No one knew we were not having a relationship. And third, I'm nothing to him. No one would try to manipulate him by threatening me because he literally doesn't care."

"That's bullshit," Knox said, tucking his wife under his arm.

Nash nodded. "Agreed."

"Gotta side with the testosterone twins," Stef said, hooking his thumb in their direction.

"They know something," Lina said, narrowing her eyes.

I crossed my arms. "Then they better say it."

The brothers shared a look.

"Uh-uh. None of that telepathic guy code," I insisted.

Nash cleared his throat. "Evidence suggests otherwise."

"What evidence specifically?" Naomi pressed.

"When you blew into town and needed money, Lucy coughed up half the cash to fund the grant that paid your salary," Knox announced.

"How do you know that?" Naomi asked him.

"Because I paid the other half," he said.

Naomi sighed. "Just when I think I couldn't love you any more than I already do."

I slapped the bar. "Hang on. You're saying I

didn't *earn* that grant? That you two bozos just *decided* to give the library the money?"

Knox shrugged. "We heard the funding you applied for wasn't gonna come through. So we made it happen another way."

"That's very generous of you," I said through gritted teeth.

"Uh-oh. Sloane's going to explode," Stef observed.

"No, I'm not." The effort to keep from shouting made my throat hurt. "Why would he do that? He's always hated me."

"No, he hasn't," Lina and Naomi insisted together.

"At the risk of breaking man code, let me tell you a story about Lucian's bike," Nash said.

"I don't care about Lucian's bike," I snapped. "I want to know why the guy who told me I wasn't worth his time because I'd ruined his life would dump money into a cause I care about."

"It's a metaphor," Nash promised. "Luce's aunt and uncle who lived in California got him this sweet mountain bike for his thirteenth birthday. He loved that thing. Rode it everywhere. Washed it every other day. Two weeks after he got it, Ansel got pissed at him for not taking the trash out or mowing the lawn crooked or some shit like that. He took the bike out of the garage, threw it in the driveway, and then backed over it with his truck."

I rolled my wrist. Apparently time didn't heal all wounds.

"That's horrible," Naomi said.

Knox handed her a fresh napkin. "Do *not* fucking cry, Daze."

"His aunt and uncle must have heard about it because they sent Lucian another bike. He hid it at our place in the shed. He only rode it when he came over. He never once took it into town or anywhere his dad might see him on it," Nash explained.

Knox frowned. "I remember that."

I didn't want to feel sorry for Lucian. Not right now.

"So he protected it by hiding it from his dad," Lina said. "That's a spot-on metaphor, hotshot."

"I do what I can," he said with a flirty wink.

I shook my head. "Yeah, okay. He was thirteen and living under the thumb of a god-awful monster. But what's his excuse now?"

"How the hell should we know?" Knox said.

"Sounds like the guy you're *not* worried about didn't grow up with any kind of emotional support to show him what it's like to be a real man in a real relationship," Joel said, magically appearing behind the bar. "A guy like that might think the only way he can keep something safe is by keeping his distance."

I didn't want a reason to empathize with the man who was currently fucking his way through the beautiful female philanthropic geniuses in the District of Columbia. I wanted to forget that Lucian Rollins existed.

I held up a finger in Nash's face. "First, you are hereby not allowed to discuss anything regarding

557

me, including any past, present, or future threats."

"Noted."

"Second, who the hell would be targeting me to get to Lucian? A discarded lover? Some politician he put into office?"

He shrugged. "Possibly. Or maybe someone like Anthony Hugo. An enemy with the resources to dig into exactly who and what Lucian is doing."

"Well, that puts a fucking damper on things," Stef said, breaking the ensuing silence.

"Look. Right now, we don't know who it is. So it's smarter to be vigilant," Nash explained.

"Then why the fuck isn't Luce being vigilant here?" Knox demanded.

Nash shrugged. "Because he's a dumbass? Did you at least install the new cameras you said you were going to get?"

"Waylay came over last weekend and helped me order everything," I told him. "Now can we please change the subject and start in on Stef for still not telling Jeremiah he's ready to move in together?"

Assface: How did it go with the judge?

Assface: Holly brought in gas station sushi to share. The entire office smells like listeria.

Assface: I'm making an effort here. You could at least pretend to have the maturity of an adult and respond.

33

Grumpy Bear

Lucian

How am I supposed to know the man's grandmother died?" I snapped in exasperation at Lina, who stuck to my heels like one of those annoying yappy dogs that wanted something from you.

I was marching down the hall when my employee lost her damn mind and committed a fireable offense by grabbing me by the back of the jacket and dragging me into an office.

"Carl, I'm sorry to do this to you, but it's for the good of everyone. Get out," Lina said.

Carl's eyes went wide behind his thick tortoise-shell glasses. Hastily he gathered his WORLD'S GREATEST DAD coffee mug, phone, and—inexplicably—the photo of his three bucktoothed children.

Petula needed to remind Carl that his benefits included dental insurance.

"You're definitely fired," I said to Lina when she shut and leaned against the door after Carl's hasty retreat.

"Good. Because I didn't sign on to work for a grumpy man bear. Broody man bear, yes. Grumpy, no. You're being a dick to everyone."

"Did it ever occur to you that everyone is too fucking sensitive?"

"Malik did two tours of duty in Afghanistan, and he was very close to his grandmother."

"I didn't know she died yesterday."

"You made Holly cry Monday."

I scoffed. "Holly cries when she watches Olive Garden commercials. And she rear-ended my security vehicle in the parking garage with the SUV I gave her," I reminded her.

"Holly is a lousy driver. She's rear-ended four people in the last month, but you're the only one who made her cry," Lina pointed out.

"Then either get someone to give her driving lessons or have security drive her to and from work. Or better yet, fire her," I said, crossing my arms over my chest.

"Yesterday, you told Nolan to get his ass out of your office until his presence wasn't a waste of oxygen."

In my defense, Nolan had taken it upon himself to question whether my mood had anything to do with Sloane.

"That statement stands for all employees," I said.

Lina squared up and put her hands on her hips. "Let me lay this out for you in language you'll understand. You're being a fucking asshole. People don't like working for fucking assholes. So unless you have time to deal with a mass exodus, unemployment claims, hiring a fresh team, *and* training them, I suggest you shut up and listen."

I sat on the corner of Carl's desk. "I'll listen for one minute, and then you're fired."

"You can tell a lot about a person by how they treat others when things aren't going well."

She let that hang in the air between us, meeting my eyes.

"You're going through a rough time, and that makes you feel out of control. But you don't get to take it out on other people."

Her words landed like hammers on my skull. "Leave. Now."

"Oh, I am. But just so you know, Nolan and Petula told everyone to spend the rest of the day working from home." She headed for the doorway. "Get your shit sorted out, Lucian."

"I don't recall asking for your opinion."

She paused in the doorway and batted her lashes condescendingly. "That's what friends are for. By the way, if you're this messed up in the head over her, maybe you're not as done as you think you are."

And with that, Lina strutted out the door.

Beyond her retreating back, the cubicles were a flurry of activity as employees put on coats and packed up, all while shooting nervous glances in my direction.

I ignored them and stormed to my own office. I'd run this company alone once. I could do it again if necessary.

I'd get more done without the distraction of needy employees lurking about, I decided, slamming my door, then cursing the soft close mechanism. I wasn't upset about Sloane, the stubborn pain in the ass. It wasn't like I saw her face every fucking time I closed my eyes.

I was behind my desk, scowling through the latest vague report from the FBI, when I was interrupted by a knock at my door.

"Unless the building is actively on fire, I suggest you leave," I barked.

Petula flung my door open. "If you don't lighten up, IT is going to have to replace your down arrow key again."

I pettily stabbed the key again with excessive force.

"Do you have a reason for annoying me, or are you hoping to get fired too?"

"You'd never find someone else less annoying to deal with your temper tantrums. Now if you're done being a gigantic toddler, your mother is here, *sir*."

Behind her in the doorway stood my mother, who looked like she was desperate for an escape. *Shit.*

Kayla Rollins was a lovely woman by anyone's estimation. She was tall and delicate. Everything about her seemed ethereal, fragile. She wore her thick, dark hair swept back in a sleek twist. Simple gold hoops adorned her ears. Her dress was ivory, her coat a knee-length camel. Her face looked younger, fresher, and I guessed she'd paid another visit to Dr. Reynolds. Something I should have

562

noticed if I'd bothered paying attention to her bank accounts lately.

She'd never remarried after my father. And except for a brief stint in Grover's Groceries the summer after his arrest, she'd never held down a job. I'd gotten "creative" in college, supporting myself and my mother with some legal and not strictly legal employment, selling test scores and fake IDs.

"I can come back another time," my mother said, her dark eyes darting for an exit.

I rose and used the walk from desk to door to rein in my dickishness. "Go home, Petula. After you've given security instructions," I said, nodding toward my mother. I didn't need Anthony Hugo targeting her too.

"Gladly," she snapped.

"What can I do for you, Mom?" I asked more gently.

"It's really not that important," she said to her Jimmy Choo wedges as she inched for the door.

"It's fine," I insisted as gently as possible. "What do you need?"

I looked like him. I assumed it was this reminder of old ghosts that always made her behave so tentatively toward me.

"Well, I just came from a meeting with the event coordinator at the hotel. There was a problem sourcing some of the menu items, and the budget is . . . no longer adequate," she finished quickly as if ripping off some invisible bandage.

I drew on the last reserves of my patience.

"That's fine. I'll allocate more funds if you think the changes are necessary."

"I think it's a good idea?"

Most of her statements sounded like questions, as if she were asking someone else to constantly tell her what she thought and wanted.

"I'm fine with it."

She cleared her throat. "So how are things with you?"

"Fine," I said gruffly. "I've decided to sell the house in Knockemout."

"Oh. That's . . . nice."

We never discussed what had happened in that house. We never mentioned his name. We hadn't even discussed the fact that he was dead. We were both satisfied with sweeping it under the rug and then avoiding the gigantic lump in the middle.

"How are you?" I asked.

"Oh, fine." She hesitated, then glanced down again. "Actually, I'm seeing someone."

"You are?" I'd missed that too. I blamed Sloane for distracting me from keeping a closer eye on my mother. Another item on the long list of things I blamed her for. My anger welled up again like lava from a volcano. Anger and a stupid longing that felt like a knife to the gut.

"It's nothing serious," she said quickly. "We just met."

"Good for you, Mom." I meant it too. There was no reason both of us should be paying penance for my father's actions.

"Well, I'll let you get back to it," she said, waving her slim hand in the direction of my desk.

"We'll have dinner soon," I decided.

"I'd like that," she said.

"Security will see you home."

Her eyes widened. "Is something wrong?"

"Not at all," I lied.

"Oh, all right. Well, goodbye, Lucian."

"Bye, Mom."

We managed to meet in the middle for an awkward hug, and then she was gone.

My phone vibrated in my pocket.

Nash: Hey, fuckface. Did you just seriously fire my woman?

Christ.

"What's wrong with you?" I demanded.

My friend Emry was slouched in his chair, rubbing both eyes with the heels of his hands.

"Is everything all right with Sacha? The family?"

I'd come here so Emry could tell me I was right and I could finally put all thoughts of Sloane to rest.

"The symphony was wonderful. Sacha is wonderful. My family is wonderful. You, my migraine-inducing friend, are what's wrong with me," he said, picking up his glasses and polishing them violently.

"I don't think a therapist is supposed to talk to his patients like that. Especially not ones whose fees helped buy that beach house you're so fond of," I reminded him.

"You can lead a horse to water, but some animals are so dense you have to half drown them before they'll drink."

"That's not how that particular metaphor goes. Am I the horse or are you?"

"You're the man whose identity is so tightly bound to how he sees his father that you sabotage your own chances for happiness. He didn't deserve to be happy, so by default, neither do you."

"I don't have the time for happiness." *Or the capacity,* I added silently.

"Lucian, you love her," he said simply.

"Don't be ridiculous," I scoffed even as my gut twisted sharply.

"You love this girl turned woman who placed herself between you and your abuser. Who fought the injustice you faced because of it. Yet you keep pushing her away, pretending that you're some kind of emotionless artificial intelligence distracted by eradicating the world of abusers of power and she's just another enemy, when in reality, you feel unworthy of her. But you're never going to *feel* worthy until you stop pushing love away. The second you get anything good in your life, you do your damnedest to rid yourself of it. So you keep engaging in this profoundly annoying self-destruct cycle."

I sat there for a beat. "How long have you been holding that in?"

Emry rose abruptly and rounded his desk. He jerked open the bottom drawer and produced a bottle of scotch. "Too long." He poured two glasses and handed one to me before flopping back down in his chair.

"This has nothing to do with me feeling worthy."

He cracked a smile, then shook his head. "The infuriating part is you *know* this. Yet you keep making the same choices. Well, I've got news for you, Lucian. *No one* feels worthy. Everyone feels like an imposter. It doesn't matter what family you come from, your net worth, or how many powerful friends owe you favors. None of that is going to make you feel like you deserve to be here."

"Everyone? I find that hard to believe."

"The ones who don't? The ones who think they deserve it all? Those are the ones you have to watch out for. Those are the ones who inflict the real damage. They're the ones who don't spend years in therapy trying to better themselves. They're the ones who don't bother asking themselves if they're the good guy or the bad guy."

I wasn't a good guy worried about being a bad guy. I was a self-aware villain. There was a distinct difference.

"Let's change the subject," Emry suggested. "You seem to be playing the field quite aggressively."

I sighed. Frankly, I was exhausted. Between redoubling my efforts to nail Hugo to the wall, I now had to carve time out of my packed schedule to go out to dinner and parties I didn't want to go to with women I had no interest in.

If Hugo had targeted Sloane because of me, he was going to get the message loud and clear. Sloane Walton meant nothing to me. She was just one woman in a long line of meaningless conquests.

"It's not what it looks like," I admitted. "Hugo is looking a little too closely at me. I'm doing what I can to confuse him."

I automatically flipped my phone over and checked for new messages. There were none from *her*. Not that I would expect it. I'd had to burn that bridge to keep us both safe. But now that I'd had her, now that I knew how my name sounded from that mouth when she came, this surgical excision of me from her life was driving me insane.

She couldn't just cut me out completely. Not when we shared our small circle of friends and a property line. Not that I wanted anything to do with her, I reminded myself.

"I worry about you, Lucian," Emry announced.

I looked up, baffled. "Why?"

"I worry that you prioritize winning over happiness, and I don't know if you'll be satisfied with winning at the expense of everything else."

34

A Good Old-Fashioned Ass Kicking

Lucian

L ife's fuckin' funny sometimes," Knox mused.
We were occupying the corner of Honky
Tonk's bar on an unseasonably warm March night.
I'd been summoned to Knockemout by Nash and
Knox, who seemed unnecessarily concerned that I
was in the midst of some midlife crisis. Stef and
Jeremiah had tagged along for the Shiraz.

Lina's firing had been reversed—as soon as I
realized I couldn't actually handle the workload
alone—and I'd been reasonably polite to everyone
at work today. They had nothing to worry about.

"In what way?" I asked, not particularly caring.

Spring was in the air. It made me want to drink
until I couldn't see straight. It was my first time
back in town since my last time with Sloane, and
every damn thing in this fucking place reminded
me of her.

"The three of us growin' up, raisin' hell. Gettin'
in trouble. Now look at us."

"Three grown men still raising hell?" Stef
guessed.

"You should have seen them in high school,"
Jeremiah teased. "It's a miracle this town is still
standing."

569

Nash's mouth quirked. "Now we're almost respectable."

"And we've got women too good for us." Knox shot me a pointed look. "Well, two outta three."

"Way too damn good for us," Nash agreed.

Knox raised his glass. "May they never come to their senses."

I ignored the toast. But I couldn't ignore the train of thoughts it ignited.

My life was now divided cleanly. Before Sloane and After Sloane. I should have felt better by now. I was keeping her safe by keeping my distance. Something I should have done from the beginning. Something I always seemed to be incapable of. But I'd done the right damn thing. So why the fuck did I feel so damn knotted up inside?

Even now, I was watching the door, willing her to appear. And then what? Would she continue to freeze me out? Or would she direct her fiery temper at me?

"Where are these way too good for you women tonight?" I asked.

"If you're trying to get information on Sloane's whereabouts, it's not coming from us," Nash said.

The bearded Morgan brother shrugged. "You fucked it up, you fix it. And since you didn't come to us before you fucked it up, we sure as shit aren't helping you fix it."

"There's nothing to fix," I insisted. "We had a good time. We're done having a good time."

Stef snorted into his wineglass and exchanged what-an-idiot looks with Jeremiah.

Nash set his bottle down on the bar. "I'm just gonna throw this out there before one of us does or says something stupider. Do *not* talk about Sloane like she's one of the model scientist one-night stands you've been burning up the sheets with lately."

"Things just got interesting," Stef sang and nodded toward the door.

There she was. In a short black turtleneck dress that showed off the curves I'd so thoroughly explored. Her hair hung in a straight, sleek curtain down her back. Every muscle in my body tensed. My cock went rock-hard. It was too soon. I shouldn't have come here. I wasn't ready to see her and not feel things.

"Looks like someone isn't waiting around for you to call," Nash observed.

It was then that I realized she wasn't alone. She was on a date with Kurt Michaels, the kid-loving teacher. He looked exactly like the kind of guy who would have kids. He'd buy a minivan and coach baseball, and every Christmas Eve, he'd stay up late, putting together toys.

Fuck.

"Man, that's gotta sting," Knox said smugly.

"Gotta admire our guy Luce here," Nash said. "If Angelina had shown up on a date, I would have gone in swinging and not stopped until I carried her out over my shoulder. Not Rollins though."

571

"Luce could give a shit that the girl he pushed away because he was too chickenshit to have feelings just showed up on a date," Knox said, picking up the thread.

"Fuck you both," I said into my bourbon.

"You could at least stop staring at them like you want to rip his arms off prior to carrying her off like a caveman," Stef suggested.

"Fuck you too," I shot back.

Jeremiah held up his hands and grinned. "Don't look at me, man. You live your life the way you want."

What I wanted was to turn away, to at least look in another direction. But I was riveted. The silver tips in her hair were gone. In their place was a single lavender streak.

"Now, I'm a straight man," Knox mused at my elbow. "As such, I'm not the greatest judge of male attractiveness. But that guy is hot."

"Agreed," Stef, Jeremiah, and Silver the bartender said in unison.

"I hate all of you," I announced.

Knox grinned. Silver smirked and slid me another bourbon.

The conversation shifted to weddings, family, and small-town gossip, none of which I could contribute to. Not that I was listening anyway, since Sloane had leaned in and put her hand on the teacher's arm as they shared a laugh about something.

My insides coiled into an icy knot as a torrent

of delusional thoughts raced through my mind.

Her hand should be on *my* arm. I should be the one sitting across the table from her. I should be the one taking her home, waking up next to her. Reading what she was reading. Yelling at the evil cat. It should be *me* in her life.

Sloane released the teacher's arm and got up from the table. Without even glancing in my direction, she made a beeline for the restroom. I poured the bourbon down my throat, set the glass on the bar, and followed her.

"Oh, no. Not today, Satan," Sloane announced, shaking her head when she exited the restroom three minutes later and found me lurking like a felon.

"I just want to talk," I assured her.

"There's nothing to talk about."

She'd frozen me out for nearly two weeks and now tossed casual disdain in my face like I was some petty annoyance.

"How's your date going?" I asked acidly.

"Great. Thanks for asking," she snarled.

"You're welcome. I'm so fucking happy for you," I shot back.

"I'm surprised you didn't bring your parade of women out with you tonight."

"Jealous?" I asked, hoping.

"You're the one who cornered me outside the bathroom while I'm on a date with a sweet, smart, *hot* guy who is excited about starting a family, Lucifer."

"Come over tonight," I said, hating myself even as I said the words.

"Gee, I can't. I'm busy having the case of whiplash you caused," she snapped.

"Now you're being dramatic."

If fire could explode from a woman's eyeballs and incinerate a man, I would have been nothing more than a pile of ashes.

"Do you really not get it? We had sex. You decided to stop having sex with me. The end."

There was never going to be an end to us. "It was more than sex, Sloane. We've always been more."

"Yeah? Well, even if we *were* more at one point, you not only walked away, you pushed me away, burnt the bridge, and ran like hell. But that doesn't matter."

"I beg to differ."

"Ugh. Still annoying as hell, I see. Get this through your mercurial head, Lucifer. I want a husband, a family, a man I can count on to be there, especially when things get tough. I'm not ever going to settle for someone who runs just when things are getting good."

"You admit they were good." I held on to that with both hands like it was a lifeline.

"You're an idiot."

"You drive me insane. I don't want to be with you, but all you have to do is walk into a room and I can't help myself. I didn't want to talk to you. I didn't want to hunt you down and force you to look at me just so I can get close enough to see the green smudge in your left eye. I sure as hell didn't want to beg you to leave your date so you could come home with me tonight."

There was fire blazing in Sloane's eyes now. I just wanted to touch her, to let that fire burn me. "You arrogant pain in my ass," she hissed. "He's a *nice guy*. I'm sure your incredibly good-looking astronaut is nice too. You wanted our sexcapades to be over, so you ended them. You don't get to whine to me about your choices."

I couldn't help myself. My hands found her hips and I buried my face in her hair, breathing in the familiar smell of her shampoo. She let out a breathy moan that drove me mad and relaxed infinitesimally against me. I could feel her resolve melting. The physical attraction was too much for either one of us to deny, and I wasn't above using it to my advantage.

I'd been hard since the second she walked in, but now my cock turned to stone. Pressing my luck, I thrust against her, letting her feel my erection. "It wasn't a mistake. We're no good for each other."

Her breath was coming faster now, and the hard outlines of her nipples under her dress made my mouth water.

"Agreed," she breathed.

"I missed touching you," I said, pressing my mouth to her neck. If she did go back to her date, I wanted my mark on her. It was an asinine, caveman-like desire. I let one hand trail over her shoulder to her breast. She gasped when I cupped it, kneading the flesh until I could feel the hard point of her nipple against my palm.

"Lucian."

My name from those red lips had me losing my fucking mind. This was another mistake in a long line of them where Sloane Walton was concerned. I shouldn't have gotten so close. I couldn't control myself when I was this close to her.

"Let me touch you. Let me taste you," I whispered, thrusting against her again.

"Ugh! No." She growled the word even as her hand shot out to cup my erection.

I was so close to release I didn't dare draw a breath.

"Goddammit, Lucian," she muttered. "I can't believe I almost let you do this again. Do you have industrial-strength pheromones or something? God. I really hate you. You suck."

"I hate to point this out given the situation, but *your* hand is on *my* dick, Pixie. And if you move a muscle or take a deep breath or even make eye contact with me, I'm going to come."

I realized the mistake a second too late.

Because she didn't take her hand off my cock. No, the woman deliberately licked her bottom lip, shoved my hand into the top of her dress, and then gave my dick one hard jerk.

"Fuck," I rasped as she held my aching hard-on in a death grip.

"Did you get what you wanted?" she whispered in my ear as her nipple taunted my palm. "Then go the hell home and forget I ever existed."

As if that were physically possible.

"This isn't what I wanted," I said through clenched teeth.

She raised an eyebrow and gave my shaft another squeeze. She was so fucking beautiful when she was being diabolical. "Bullshit."

"Shit. Fine. Okay. Of *course* this is what I wanted. You know how good it was between us," I reminded her.

"I'm fully aware of how good the sex was. It was everything else that was subpar. I'm not settling for being someone's weekend fuck buddy anymore. And I'm sure as hell not allowing some overgrown man-child to cast me aside like I'm nothing because he can't deal with feelings. I'm out of your league, Lucifer. This was your last freebie."

I wanted to kiss her. And judging from the look in those heavily lidded green eyes, Sloane was having similar thoughts. I wasn't above taking advantage of that.

"There a problem?" I didn't need to look up to know the Morgans had entered the hallway.

"I love you two like brothers, but if you don't leave now, I'm going to rearrange your faces," I threatened.

Sloane rolled her eyes and removed her hand from my throbbing dick. "Man-child."

"Sloaney, which of us do you want to leave? Me and Knox or Rollins?" Nash asked.

She locked eyes with me, and I found that dark

577

smudge in all that green. "I want Lucian to go," she said firmly.

"Pix," I whispered.

But she shook her head. "No more, Lucian. It's time for you to go."

My heart, if I actually had one, fell out of my chest onto the floor and was crushed under her boot as she turned and walked away from me.

"Let's go outside, Luce," Nash said in his cop voice. "You look like you could use a smoke break."

Each brother grabbed an arm and hauled me through the kitchen and out the side door into the parking lot. For once, they were united, and perhaps for the first time ever, it was against me.

"You don't get to treat her like that, Luce," Nash announced when the door slammed shut behind us.

"I really wanna introduce my fist to his face," Knox said through clenched teeth as his boots scuffed at the gravel.

"I get it, believe me. But we can't," Nash insisted.

"I hate not getting to punch people."

"There's nothing stopping you," I said, deliberately taunting him. A fist to my face would feel better than the raw, jagged hole in my chest.

Knox's fist relaxed, and then he was pushing a finger in my shoulder. "You're lucky your dad was an abusive asshole. Otherwise, I'd be mopping the floor with your dumbass face."

We'd scuffled as young boys always did. Thrown

rocks at each other. Wrestled in the creek. But somewhere along the line, Knox and Nash had continued their pummeling of each other and I'd been left behind. They'd fought over toys, then bikes, then women.

"What does my father have to do with this?"

Knox looked to his brother for help.

Nash looked at his feet. "Why don't we go get ourselves another round? Save ourselves the trouble," he suggested.

"Not until you tell me why you make each other bleed on a weekly basis but you're acting like I'm some delicate flower." Using Sloane's exact words made me miss the taste of her even more.

"Gettin' hit doesn't mean the same thing to us as it does you," Knox said finally. "If I punch my pain-in-the-ass brother in the mouth, it's because I love him and he pissed me off."

"Expound," I demanded.

"Fuck," Nash muttered.

"Finish it," I ordered, growing impatient.

"We don't hit you because you got hit at home. Your dad wailing on you was all kinds of fucked up. Maybe we didn't know exactly what was going on, but we weren't stupid. Least not *that* stupid," Knox amended.

"You two don't fight with me because you think I don't know the difference? That I can't handle it?"

They glanced at each other, then shrugged. "Basically," Nash said.

579

"Yup," Knox agreed. "Besides, you're more likely to throw some fancy lawyer than a punch."

I took off my jacket and draped it over the tailgate of the nearest pickup.

Knox hooted. The side door of the bar opened, and Stef and Jeremiah stepped outside, holding their drinks.

"Told you we didn't want to miss this," Jeremiah said.

"Can't we just have one night that doesn't end in someone getting punched in the face?" Nash grumbled.

"Not tonight," I decided.

"You sure about this?" Stef called to me. "There's two of them and one of you."

"You're here," I pointed out as I rolled up one sleeve.

"I am. But in this case, I'm Team Sloane. You dicked over a great girl—for reasons that probably made sense to you at the time but in reality are total shit. I gotta cast my vote with the Morgans here."

His morals annoyed me.

"Same here," Jeremiah agreed.

I turned my attention to my other sleeve, unbuttoning the cuff and beginning to roll it up. "I hate all of you. What the hell are you doing?"

Knox was pacing back and forth, rolling his neck and taking turns stretching each arm across his chest.

"Clearly this guy hasn't been in a fight over

the age of thirty," Knox said conversationally to his brother.

"You gotta warm up," Nash instructed, dropping into a squat.

Knox rolled his neck again and started performing shoulder circles.

"What happened to the days of sucker punching some unsuspecting asshole in a bar?" I asked.

"Throw a punch and pull a muscle in your back so bad you can't wipe your own ass, then we'll talk," Nash advised, circling his arms backward, then forward.

"This is more anticlimactic than I thought," I complained.

A fist shot out and rammed into my jaw, snapping my head back.

"*That's* what happened to sucker punching, unsuspecting asshole," Knox said cheerily as my head rang like the inside of a church bell. "Do better. Don't treat women like shit. Especially not Sloane."

"Christ." I bent at the waist, rubbing my jaw and biding my time. "I didn't treat her like shit. We agreed it was nothing, and then we ended the nothing."

"That's bullshit and you know it. Besides, you can't be done already. Nash didn't even get a shot yet," Knox insisted, slapping me on the shoulder.

"Let's go back in and drink," Nash suggested, sounding disappointed.

"You didn't get to hit him yet. It's pretty fuckin' satisfying," Knox said.

581

"Guess I'll just insult him and call him names for being a coward who's afraid of a little blond librarian," Nash said.

That little blond librarian was more terrifying than any of us, and we all knew it.

Knox was half turned to look at his brother and didn't see me coming. My fist plowed into the side of his face with satisfying force. He stumbled sideways before recovering with a grin. "Now *that's* more like it."

"My turn," Nash said, moving into position. "You don't get to treat Sloane like she's some one-night fuck. Doesn't matter what went down between you two or how things end, you treat her with respect."

"What are you two? Her big brothers?"

I feigned a punch and Nash ducked. He caught me with an uppercut to the solar plexus that knocked the breath right out of me. I swung again, glancing a shot off his jaw.

My friend, the goddamn chief of police, grinned wickedly and drew back his arm. I blocked, but not well enough. His blue-collar, law-abiding fist caught me on the bridge of the nose.

"Didn't hear a crunch," Knox said.

"I'm holding back, okay?" Nash muttered. He grunted as my left fist connected with his bad shoulder. "Oh, somebody's here to play dirty," he teased.

"I'm here to beat some sense into you two. Sloane means nothing to me."

"Bull. Shit." Nash punctuated each word with a fast jab. "I saw you climbing out of her bedroom window in high school. I see the way you look at her like she's the goddamn sun and you're not supposed to stare directly at her but you can't help yourself."

"None of us can, fucking idiot," Knox added, shoving his brother out of the way and landing a punch to my eye.

"I'm not you. I'm not cut out for a relationship. Especially not one that neither of us wanted in the first fucking place," I argued.

"Just 'cause you say you don't want it don't mean you don't want it," Knox said, ducking my fist.

Nash took a swig from a water bottle. "He's the idiot who fake dated Naomi and then tried to real dump her."

"Where the hell did you get a bottle of water?" I panted and slapped Knox across the face to change things up.

He was unfazed.

"I'm not in love with her, assholes." The words tasted strange in my mouth. I chalked it up to blood.

"He's a delusional idiot," Stef assessed.

"Agreed," Nash said, tagging back in.

"I feel sorry for him," Jeremiah said.

"Are you enjoying yourself?" I asked Stef as he pulled out his phone and started taking pictures.

"Immensely."

Nash and I continued trading blows in a dignified, well-paced fistfight. It was so dignified that even the patrons just arriving in the parking lot didn't bother hanging around to watch.

"Evenin', folks," Harvey Lithgow, a bear of a man in leather chaps, said as he wandered toward the front.

"Evenin', Harvey," we said in unison.

"You're still holding back," I complained when Knox jumped in to land a shot to my gut. My entire upper body already felt like I'd been backed over by a truck.

"Yep," he said easily.

"You keep holding back, I'm gonna take advantage," I warned, throwing an elbow that caught him squarely on the chin, followed by a shot to the gut.

He spat blood into the gravel and grinned. "Fuck around and find out."

Melee wasn't the right word for what proceeded. Without any real hatred driving us, we mostly just used our lifetime of history to sneak past each other's defenses to land cheap shots.

"You give up yet?" Nash grunted.

We were all on the ground. I had Nash on his knees in a headlock. But he was making an admirable effort to dislocate my pinkie finger. Knox had my left arm pulled behind my back, and I had my foot in his groin.

"Everyone smile and say 'dumbass,' " Stef said,

stepping in front of us. Jeremiah stepped in front of us and flashed a cheesy smile and thumbs-up as his boyfriend snapped another photo.

"Don't make us beat your ass," I warned him.

I released Nash, who mercifully let go of my pinkie, and gave Knox a half-assed kick to the thigh. The three of us flopped over in the gravel, bruised and bleeding.

"Sloane is gonna kick your asses for kicking my ass," I said, snapping my fingers for Stef to throw me my jacket. He hit me in the face with it.

"No fuckin' way," Knox said, swiping Nash's water. "Girl hates your guts. She'll probably give us trophies."

I shook my head and produced my cigarette and lighter. "She'll be pissed you didn't let her have any of the fun."

"Why can't you just take a shot with her?" Nash asked.

I savored the first sweet sting of tobacco, then exhaled toward the night sky. "Because she's too good for me."

The brothers guffawed.

"What?" I demanded.

"You think I was good enough for Angelina?" Nash asked with a smirk.

Knox grinned. "I *know* none of you think I was anywhere near Daisy's league."

"This is true," Stef agreed. "They're both a thousand times too good for you."

"Aren't relationships supposed to make you feel

worthy?" I asked. It sounded like something my therapist would have said.

"Pretty sure the only dumbass who can make you feel worthy is you," Nash said.

"The second you think you're as good as or better than your woman is the second it all starts goin' to hell," Knox said.

I swiped my bleeding mouth across my sleeve and took another drag. "So you're just supposed to what? Drag them down to your level?"

Knox threw a pea-sized piece of gravel at me. "No, you fucking moron. You're supposed to spend the rest of your lucky-ass life trying to live up to them."

"That sounds exhausting."

"It sure ain't for the faint of heart," Jeremiah said.

I rubbed my jaw. My face and fists hurt like a bitch. But that tightness in my chest seemed just a little looser.

"You comin' back in?" Knox asked, gesturing toward Honky Tonk.

I shook my head. I needed to be alone.

Stef and Jeremiah hauled the Morgan brothers to their feet.

Nash reached down and clapped a hand on my shoulder. "You're not a bad guy, Luce. You're just an idiot."

"Thanks," I said dryly and watched the brothers limp back to the bar together. Jeremiah followed with a wink at Stef.

Stef held out a hand to me, and I took it.

"You know, I've spent the last few weeks second-, third-, and fourth-guessing myself," he said.

"About what?" My left eye was swelling, making it hard to see him.

"About everything. Moving here. Making things official with Jeremiah. Committing."

"There's nothing wrong with being wary of commitment," I pointed out, testing my aching jaw.

"There's wary and there's chickenshit."

"Bite me," I muttered.

"Listen, I'm the last guy to give relationship advice," Stef admitted. "But the way you look at her, it wasn't just a good time."

"Everyone in this fucking town thinks there's a goddamn happily ever after for everyone. You know nothing about our situation," I reminded him.

"No, but you're making me wonder if it's not better to at least take a chance. Maybe getting my heart ripped out and stomped on is better than being too afraid to try in the first place."

"Love makes men stupid," I quipped.

"Yes, it does. But does denying it make us stupider?"

35

You Love Me, You Idiot

Sloane

W hat goes better with intermittent crying jags? Grilled chicken salads or cheesesteaks?" my mother asked, holding up two takeout menus.

It was Monday, and my mom and I had taken the day off to go through some of Dad's things. We were in my parents' bedroom, working our way through his collection of books, deciding what to keep, what to donate, and what to sell.

"Tears make cheesesteaks too soggy. What about grilled cheese?"

"Perfect! There's a gourmet grilled cheese place right around the corner. I'll order," Mom said.

Frankly, I wasn't hungry. A statement I rarely got to make since it usually only signified the onset of a stomach bug. But this was no stomach bug. This was shame. After my run-in with Lucian—and his cock—at Honky Tonk Friday night, I'd been feeling furious with myself and more than a little guilty.

I'd been on a date with another man—a perfect one on paper—yet I still couldn't keep my hands to myself. I'd been a willing participant in the hallway second base ambush. Then I'd forced

588

Lucian's friends to police him, when I was just as much at fault. And judging from their bruised and bleeding faces when Knox and Nash returned to the bar, there had been a *lot* of policing.

I was embarrassed and disappointed in myself.

Mom returned and gracefully sank back to the floor.

"This sucks," I said as tears escaped my burning eyes. "I miss Dad."

"I know you do, honey. I do too. So much."

"Damn it!" I wailed. "I thought I'd be done crying by now."

"Ah, to be so stupidly naïve," Mom teased, cupping my damp face in her hand. "Let's get a few more piles done before the food arrives."

We both took a moment to blow our noses and compose ourselves.

"How about this one?" I asked, holding up a thick tome on Virginia tax law.

"Donate. Oh! Do you remember this one?" She held up a worn law book. "Your father used to quiz Maeve on the legal precedents in family law when she told him she wanted to be a lawyer at ten."

The memory floated over me like a soft blanket. Dad and Maeve cozied up in the breakfast nook with legal pads and law books while Mom helped me with my homework at the kitchen island.

Dad had been so proud and excited that his oldest daughter wanted to follow in his steps. Teenage Maeve was fierce and determined to be the best.

"Definitely a keeper. Put it in the Maeve box."

"So I need to ask you something that's probably going to upset you," Mom announced, dropping the book in the box.

"Is this what it feels like to be a parent?" I joked.

"Lucian," she said.

I went still. "What about him?" She couldn't know about our brief, ill-advised fling. Could she? She would have said something. Unless she was saying something now.

Mom pushed a tall stack of alumni magazines into the recycle pile with her feet. "I know you two don't really talk, but I was wondering if you'd heard anything about him lately. He canceled our dinner two weeks in a row and hasn't been returning my calls since. It's highly unlike him, and I'm worried."

It appeared as though Lucian had dumped two out of three Walton women. "You two sure seem to spend a lot of time together," I ventured.

"Don't get all snooty about it. Your father and I adore Lucian. He's been part of our lives since he snuck into your room that first time. It was our greatest disappointment that you two didn't fall in love and make a bunch of beautiful grandbabies for us."

My mother was joking, but given my current life goals and Lucian's recent occupation of my vagina, it felt like a personal attack.

"You're more likely to end up with Michael B. Jordan as a son-in-law than Lucian Rollins," I said dryly.

"Cute and talented. I wouldn't be upset having to stare at that gorgeous face every Thanksgiving," Mom teased. "So you haven't heard anything? I'm worried. It's not like him to ghost me, as the young people say. He's done a lot for your father and me, especially since we moved down here, and I miss him."

I wanted to quiz her on all the ways the emotionally stunted stallion had supported my parents, but I heard the sadness in her tone and felt like an ass. A guilty ass. If my nonbreakup with Lucian had cost my mother her relationship with him, that meant now she was missing two men instead of receiving all the support she deserved. And I was going to let Lucian know that was unacceptable at the first possible moment.

"I'm sure he's just busy," I fibbed. "I bet he'll be calling you up for lunch next week." I would rain hellfire down on him to make sure of it.

"I hope so," Mom said. She dumped the remaining law books on the carpet and sprayed down the bookshelf with a thick layer of lemon Pledge. "Enough about me. How's the husband hunt going?"

"It's . . . going. I had a first date with Kurt Michaels Friday night." I did not add that I'd all but jerked off Lucian in the hallway during said date. My mother didn't need to know she'd raised a trollop.

Mom abandoned her dusting. "And?" she prompted.

"And he's nice. He's smart. Cute. Obviously great with kids. He's looking to settle down. And unlike everyone else I've dated, he isn't married, lying, or running from the law."

She raised a motherly eyebrow. "But?"

"How do you know there's a but?" I demanded.

"Mother's intuition. Just like I knew you were planning to sneak out to Sherry Salama's sweet sixteen when you were grounded."

I sighed. "On paper, he's perfect. Hell, in person, he's perfect. But there's no . . ."

Engulfing flames of desire? All-consuming need to tear his pants off? Off-the-charts chemical reaction?

"Spark?" Mom supplied.

Spark seemed too tame in comparison to what I'd experienced with Lucian.

I shrugged. "Maybe I just want too much. Maybe I can't have it all in a partner. I mean, who gets to have a husband who changes diapers, respects your work, and performs like a romance novel hero between the sheets?"

Mom threw her arm over my shoulder. "You'd be surprised."

"If you're going to use this as a segue to tell me about your sex life with Dad, I will send you the bill for therapy."

"I'll get my checkbook."

I groaned and slumped against her. "Why does it have to be such a pain-in-the-ass process?"

"Nothing worthwhile is easy. Finding a partner

isn't about ticking all the boxes. No one is perfect, not even you, Sloaney Baloney. Falling in love is about discovering someone who makes you better than you are alone and vice versa."

I plucked at the carpet. "What if they hurt you?"

"People make mistakes. A lot of them. You get to decide which ones are forgivable."

"What kind of mistakes did Dad make?"

"He was always late. He brought his work home with him. When he was working on a case that was particularly important to him, he was in his head and not present with us. He had terrible taste in fashion. He was always sneaking junk food into the grocery cart."

I chuckled.

"But the good always outweighed the bad. Your father and I had a very robust sex life, you know," Mom added with a wicked gleam.

"Mom!"

She collapsed on the floor laughing. "Ah, that never gets old."

"You drive me to drink," I said, joining her on the carpet and staring up at the ceiling.

"I'm just returning the favor."

"Mom? I don't know if I ever really told you, but thank you for being such a great mom. You and Dad never once made me feel like I couldn't . . ."

Mom sat up and grabbed a tissue from the box between us and held it to her eyes. "Sloane, I appreciate your heartfelt sentiments, but if you want me to stop crying anytime soon, you'd better insult me in the next ten seconds."

"Your pot roast is dry, and I think your obsession with teeth is creepy."

We were still half crying, half laughing when the doorbell rang.

Mom got to her feet. "I'll get the food." I heard her blowing her nose noisily through the condo.

I hefted the million-pound box of gardening books and lugged it over to the writing desk. I slid it onto the surface and accidentally sent a stack of paperwork flying.

"Crap," I muttered. I knelt on the floor and began collecting papers, creating a sloppy pile of death certificate copies, greeting cards, and medical bills.

"Floor picnic or should we eat at the table like civilized people?" Mom called.

"Floor," I yelled back, spotting one last paper that landed between the wall and the leg of the desk. I crawled over and retrieved it.

A name caught my eye as I transferred it to the top of the stack.

Frowning, I skimmed the document.

Lichtfield Laboratories.

Paid in full.

Lucian Rollins.

I felt an icy rush of shock sweep through me.

Mom stuck her head in the door. "Do you want more wine, a sparkling water, or should we switch to Bloody Marys since I forgot to order tomato soup?"

"What's this?" I asked, holding up the statement.

She glanced at it, and I saw the flash of guilt followed by an involuntary softening. "That's what I wasn't supposed to tell you about."

"What the hell is *wrong* with you?" I demanded, bursting into Lucian's office waving the statement like I was leading a marching band.

Behind his desk, he looked at me with that cool, flat mask, but there was heat in his eyes. And bruises on his face. He looked like some heart-throbby heroic boxer who'd lost a title fight.

"Sorry, sir," Petula huffed, screeching to a halt in the doorway behind me. "She's faster than I thought."

"It's fine," Lucian said, making it sound like it was anything but fine.

"Kick his ass," Petula said to me under her breath and disappeared.

"You may go, Nallana," Lucian told the woman in the chair across from him.

Her hands were tucked in the pocket of a Nine Inch Nails sweatshirt. She looked amused. "But I wanna stay and watch the show," she said.

"Go away," Lucian said, eyes still on me.

On a sigh, she hopped out of the chair, shot me a wink, and left.

I slapped the paper down on his desk. Then just to be a jerk, I dragged my fingertips across the spotless glass top. "Explain."

"I owe you zero explanations. You need to leave."

"Not until you explain this," I said, drilling my finger into the paper.

He glanced down at it, then reached into his desk drawer and did something I didn't expect. The son of a bitch put on a sexy pair of reading glasses.

It was like the universe was mocking me. The hot guy who rocked my world between the sheets and wore reading glasses was the one man I didn't want.

"This looks like an invoice that's been satisfied," he said as though I was the dumbest human on the planet. "Now if you don't mind, I don't want you here."

"I *know* that, you insufferable oaf. It's a medical invoice for an experimental cancer treatment not covered by health insurance. Why is *your* name on it?"

"My name is on a lot of things," he said. He took off his readers, then fed the paper through the shredder at his feet. "If that's all, I'll have security escort you out."

There was a tension in him, a nervousness that I'd never seen before.

"I'm not leaving without answers. The faster you give them to me, the sooner I'll be gone."

He snatched up his desk phone and dialed. "Ms. Walton will be requiring an escort back to her mother's place in five minutes."

I crossed my arms and glared at him as he listened to whoever was on the other end of the phone call.

"Yes. Have her vehicle swept and post a guard." He hung up abruptly and leveled me with an icy look. "Ask your questions, and then you need to go."

I was hanging on by sheer will. I closed my eyes and took a calming breath. "Lucian, why is your name on an astronomically expensive cancer treatment for my father? A treatment I was told was a clinical trial? A treatment that gave him six more weeks with us." My voice broke pathetically.

The tension between us ratcheted up to unbearable heights. We stared each other down even as my eyes dampened.

"Don't do this, Sloane," he said quietly. "Please."

"For once in your life, just tell me," I begged.

"You should discuss this with your mother."

"She told me to talk to you."

He was silent for a long beat. "He wanted one more Christmas with you."

I took a step back and hid my face behind my hands.

"You're not going to cry, are you?" he demanded gruffly.

"I'm having a lot of feelings right now, and I'm not sure which one is going to win out," I said from behind my hands.

"You're angry with me," he surmised.

"I'm not angry that you spent seven figures giving me a few more weeks with my father, assface. I'm beyond grateful for that, and I have no idea how to handle it. But why would you do something like this without telling me? Why hide this?"

"Perhaps you should try taking deep breaths? Outside. Far away from my office."

"What else?" I demanded.

"I'm not following you," he said, gaze darting toward the door.

I closed the distance between us, gripped his damn tie, and looked him in the eye. "I'm giving you this one, last opportunity to be honest with me. What else have you paid for or donated or created for my benefit without ever telling me while still treating me like I'd ruined your life?"

"I don't know what you're talking about."

I inhaled sharply. "So Yoshino Holdings, the Stella Partnership, and the Bing Group aren't ringing any bells?"

His face hardened.

"I'm in the middle of a very busy day—"

I gave his tie a yank. "I don't care if you're in the middle of your own lifesaving appendectomy, Lucifer. We are having this conversation."

His silence was stony, and it damned him.

"The Yoshino Holdings Foundation funded a $100,000 grant that allowed the library to upgrade our computer system and start the tablet and laptop lending programs. The Stella Partnership awarded the library a $75,000 grant to extend our community program offerings including creating a position for Naomi. And the Bing Group funded a generous donation to cover the rest of the building costs of the Knox Morgan Municipal Building, which coincidentally houses my library."

"If you're finished—"

"Lucian, all those organizations are named after cherry tree varieties. And all of them are owned by *you*." It was all coming together into one unimaginable picture in my head.

He scoffed. "I don't know where you get your information, but I can assure you—"

"I'm a *librarian,* you hulking pain in the ass. It's my job to know things! What I don't know is why you would be funding *my* dreams with *your* money when, as you so eloquently put it, you can barely stand the sight of me."

"I don't need to explain my tax write-offs to you."

"I don't know if I want to throw your stapler through your window or at your head," I muttered, stepping away from him and starting to pace.

"I'd prefer the window," he said behind me.

I glanced down as I passed his desk and spotted something familiar in the still open top drawer. "Oh my God," I said, snatching up a pair of broken glasses. *My* broken glasses. They'd fallen off during a Halloween skirmish in Knockemout, and I hadn't been able to find them.

"Stay out of my things," Lucian said, starting for me.

I held up the glasses. "If I mean nothing to you, why did you give me more time with my dad? Why did you donate so much money to my causes? And why the hell are you keeping *my* glasses that I lost at Book or Treat last fall in *your* top desk drawer?"

"Lower your voice, or security is going to carry you out of here," he growled.

"Say the words, Lucian."

"If you're going to waste my time speaking in riddles, you might as well sit down and drink some damn water," he said gruffly, heading for the crystal decanter on the conference table.

"You love me, you idiot. You've loved me since we were kids. You loved me even when I broke your trust. You loved me after I fixed it. You *still* love me."

He stopped midstride and turned to glower at me. "You didn't fix anything. You nearly got yourself killed. And if he had gotten out for even an hour, he would have made sure to end you. That's what he did to things I cared about. There is no court order that would have protected you from him."

"So you protected me by keeping our friendship a secret. And you continued to protect me by pushing me away. I was just some crazy, nosy neighbor girl."

"He would have found a way to hurt you. He *did* find a way to hurt you."

"He's gone now, Lucian. He's dead. What's your excuse now?"

"I don't know where this narrative is coming from, but you're embarrassing yourself. I don't love you," he insisted.

His tone was even and chilly, his face stony. But

I could see the truth, the yearning in his eyes.

"Are you sure that's the answer you want to stick with?" I whispered.

"I don't love you," he insisted stubbornly.

I let out a shaky breath. "After all those years, all the things we've been through together, you still can't even be honest with me."

"I'm being honest," he said, not quite meeting my eyes.

"You love me," I repeated. Twin tears escaped, sliding hotly down my cheeks. "You love me, and yet you're content to never try. That's not sad. That's pathetic."

"You need to leave, Sloane," he said sharply.

My heart felt like it had been tossed into a wood chipper. Everything hurt.

"I will." I headed for the door and then stopped. "I'll never be able to repay you for those last months with my father."

"I don't want you to repay me," he muttered, shoving a hand through his hair. "You can't come here again. It's not safe."

"Fine. But you can't give me anything again. No more secret donations. No more keeping an eye on me. Thank you for your baffling generosity, but understand this. I can't accept anything else from you. Ever."

"Why?"

"Because, after all this, I think we both deserve a clean break."

He was still a long moment as his eyes roamed

my face, looking for something that he wasn't going to find. "There was never going to be an us, Sloane. He made sure of that."

I shook my head. "Your father is dead, Lucian. You're the one who made sure there would never be an us."

I headed for the door again, hoping to hold it together long enough to get out of the office. Two burly security guys were waiting for me in the hall. I paused in the doorway and turned around one last time. "I loved you. You know? When we were kids, I loved you. And I think I could have again."

His eyes went stormy, but he stayed where he was and said absolutely nothing.

"By the way," I continued. "Just because you're done with me doesn't mean you get to dump my mother too. She misses you, so pick up your goddamn phone and call her."

"That's not a good idea right now," he hedged.

"Take her to lunch or dinner or whatever the hell you two do, and do it now or I will find new and creative ways to torture you for hurting her when she's already grieving. Do not abandon my mother."

"This a good time, boss?" Nolan said, strolling between the two guards. He looked up from the fat file in his hands. "Nope. Never mind. Very not good time. Good to see you, Blondie."

36

Too Many Whammies

Sloane

"Your podcast interview about Mary Louise is getting a lot of hits."

"Really?" I asked, stirring my ice cream in a clockwise motion.

Kurt Michaels was smart, charming, and handsome. He told dad jokes and wore sexy cardigans and hot nerd glasses. Total dad material. Unlike *some others* who were just "daddy" material.

He held my hand. He opened doors for me. He listened carefully. He took an interest in things that were important to me, like Mary Louise's case. And on our previous two dates, I had never once felt the need to fake an emergency or climb out a bathroom window. Also, he bore a striking resemblance to Michael B. Jordan.

But this was our third date, and I was having heart palpitations over the idea of sex. Not the good kind either. It wasn't that I assumed Kurt was going to be bad in bed. I'd scoped out his dance moves from the Christmas concert video on the school's Facebook page. The man knew how hips worked. Plus, we'd shared two perfectly pleasant kisses at the end of each previous date.

But I knew deep down—in the vagina region—

that Lucian Rollins had ruined me. And I wasn't mentally ready to accept just how badly.

Kurt's dark, smooth hand reached across the table and squeezed mine. I jumped.

"Sloane," he said expectantly.

"What?" I tried to remember if he'd asked me a question.

"I get the feeling that you're somewhere else. Possibly with someone else?"

I winced, my single-girl-on-a-hot-date facade crumbling like a toy block tower. "It's not exactly like that. I really like you," I insisted.

"I'm pretty likable," he agreed amicably.

"You'd make a great husband and father. And you don't have any obvious red flags or impossible-to-overcome emotional baggage."

He flashed me one of those sexy smiles. "What can I say? I'm a catch. Why don't you skip ahead to the 'it's not you, it's me' part?"

I groaned and stared at the half-eaten cup of rocky road. "I know everyone says this, but in this case, it's true. It really isn't you. It's all me."

He cocked his head like the hella-good listener he was. "You have feelings for someone else," he stated.

"How did you—never mind. It's not *those* kinds of feelings. More like I'm filled with rage and annoyance and frustration toward someone else. But also, seriously, how did you know?"

He blew out a breath. "I'm getting over someone else too. Or trying. She wasn't ready for a relationship. So I'm attempting to move on."

"Same, dude," I admitted, slumping in my chair with relief. "Except I don't want to get over him. I want to exorcise him. If never seeing him again isn't an option, then I want to figure out a way to feel nothing."

"That sounds like there are some very strong feelings still in play," Kurt observed.

"Homicidal feelings," I insisted. "He's all wrong for me. He wants nothing I want. Hell, he doesn't even want me. And I don't even want him. We just have this physical connection that . . . And I shouldn't be talking about this on a date with another man."

He shrugged. "Maybe you just need some kind of closure before you can move on."

"Believe me. I got all the closure any normal, sane person would need. But there's this dumb sliver of idiotic romantic in me that wonders how a physical attraction can be so powerful, so good, when the rest is just hot garbage." I winced. "Sorry. Tell me about your situation before I humiliate myself further."

Kurt grimaced. "You might feel homicidal toward *me* if I tell you."

I perked up. "Trust me. You can't be any worse than I am."

"You're going to regret saying that," he predicted.

He looked so earnest and concerned.

"This is going nowhere between us, right?" I confirmed.

"Unfortunately, that's how it appears," he agreed.

"Okay then. This should make you feel better. I ran into the guy I was seeing on our first date at Honky Tonk. He stupidly asked me to come back to his place, even though he made it clear he wanted nothing to do with me besides sex. Like a hormonal tramp, I stupidly let him get too close, ran a couple of bases with him in the hallway on our date, then told him to never speak to me again."

He leaned back in his chair. "That actually does make me feel better."

My eyebrows shot up. "Really? Lay it on me. It can't be worse than my confession." Feeling relieved and unburdened, I shoved a heaping spoonful of ice cream into my mouth.

"I'm in love with your sister."

I choked on my rocky road, unprepared for the whammy. "Excuse me?" I rasped.

"Here," he said, pushing a glass of water toward me. "You can drink it or throw it in my face."

"Maeve?" I rasped.

He nodded, then swiped his hand over his face. "It started last summer. We met at the end of school assembly, hit it off, then had a summer fling. It was just supposed to be fun. She was busy. I'd just landed a job here. Obviously it was a terrible idea. She's the mother of one of my students."

"I can't believe it," I said.

"I know. I'm a monster," he said.

"No! That you two were able to keep a secret like that in Knockemout."

"You're not mad?"

I shook my head. "I'm impressed. Keeping secrets in Knockemout is like training an army of cats to do your bidding. It's just not possible. So why did you let my friends hook us up?"

He looked sheepish. "Part of me—a pathetic part—thought that if Maeve didn't want to be with me, at least I could stay in her life. The incredibly stupid part of me thought maybe it wouldn't be the worst thing in the world if Maeve was a little . . . jealous."

"Wow."

"I'm not proud of it. And I was going to tell you tonight that I wasn't over Maeve, right after I told you I wasn't going to be able to have sex with you."

"I wore granny underwear and didn't shave my legs," I confessed.

He grinned.

We were still laughing when we entered the parking lot ten minutes later. It was dark, and I'd chosen the café in Lawlerville to avoid another potential run-in with Lucian in Knockemout.

"So what are we going to do?" I asked him.

"Well, the obvious hijinks choice would be to fake date each other until our exes are overcome with jealousy. But seeing as how we're adults and I'd hate to do any damage to your relationship with your sister, maybe we should go with option B."

"Friends?"

"Friends," he agreed. "You know, I really wanted

to be there for Maeve when your dad passed. I tried reaching out a couple of times. But she made it clear it was something she wanted to deal with alone."

"She pushed you away. I'm familiar with that feeling," I said.

Kurt nudged my shoulder as we approached my Jeep. "For what it's worth, Lucian is a simpleton if he doesn't recognize his feelings for you."

My feet skidded to a halt on the asphalt. "How did you know—"

"Knockemout doesn't keep secrets. I saw the way he looked at you when we walked into Honky Tonk. That's not nothing. And it sure isn't hate."

The moon was rising behind him. The trees had thousands of buds. Spring was coming. New beginnings. But all I could think about was the most recent ending.

"I had a really good time tonight," I told Kurt.

"I did too."

I rose on tiptoe and pressed a kiss to his cheek.

He wrapped me in a warm hug. He was going to make an excellent brother-in-law someday, I decided.

"Maybe we can make one of those pacts where if we're not married by the time we're fifty, we'll take the plunge."

I grinned. "Sounds like a plan to me."

I got in my Jeep and watched him cross the parking lot to his car. I waited until he pulled out before grabbing my phone and opening my texts. Maeve and I were in for a very interesting conversation.

I yelped when my door was yanked open. A big, gloved fist gripped my sweater and pinned me to my seat. Another one covered my mouth, muffling my scream.

I couldn't breathe. My attacker had sealed his hand over my mouth, and one of his fingers covered my nostrils. I immediately felt dizzy with panic as I stared at the black ski mask where a face should be. What did he want? Money? My Jeep? I hoped it wasn't me.

I flailed against his grip and opened my mouth.

"Stop trying to bite me," my attacker complained. "I got a message for you."

Adrenaline dumped into my system. My free hand dove into my tote, feeling around for my pepper spray while I tried to memorize important details. Height? Taller than me. Weight? How the hell should I know? He was dressed all in black, and the dashboard light did nothing to illuminate any details. Was he familiar? Did I recognize his voice? His smell?

Was that cinnamon? Was my attacker chewing gum?

"Leave Upshaw where she belongs," the man said.

"Mary Louise?" My words were smothered by the thick glove. This wasn't a random mugging or carjacking. Someone had followed me here and waited for me.

"Leave it alone or you *will* get hurt," he said.

Then the hand on my chest disappeared for a second before returning to slap something that sounded like paper over my heart.

"This is your final warning. Heed it. Please."

It sounded like a genuine plea. Was it possible that my assailant didn't actually *want* to hurt me? Or maybe I was hallucinating. The lack of oxygen and the blood thundering in my ears could be distorting everything.

Then he was gone just as suddenly as he'd appeared.

This was too many whammies in one night.

With shaking hands, I reached for the door handle and yanked it shut. It took me four tries to find and press the lock button. By the time I had, my attacker was nowhere to be seen.

With shaking hands, I found my phone on the floor and dialed.

"N-Nash?"

I wasn't a nail biter, but I'd nibbled my way through my left hand and was about to start on the right.

On the surface, Nash looked calm, but his leg was bouncing under the table. After giving my statement to the Lawlerville police, I had begged Nash to take me to see Mary Louise. I had an awful feeling in the pit of my stomach.

He'd put up a fight, seeing as how I was ready to disobey direct orders from an anonymous bad guy.

But I needed to see with my own eyes that she was okay, and Nash wasn't ready to let me out of his sight.

"Are all prisons this awful?" I asked Nash.

He glanced around at the cracked ceiling tiles, the flickering fluorescent lights, the peeling vinyl floor. "No. The place Tina Witt's in looks like a country club in comparison."

I frowned. "What's the difference?"

"This place is privately owned. Which means the owners can funnel the profits into their bank accounts. There's no real incentive to improve the facilities if you get to pocket what's left over after expenses."

The door opened, and I jumped out of my chair. Mary Louise entered.

"Oh my God. Are you okay?"

Her face was bruised and swollen, and her left arm was cradled against her chest in a sling. But what made it all worse was the fear in her eyes.

I wanted to hug her, but she looked as if she were about to collapse in on herself. "Do you need a doctor?"

"I'm fine," she assured me.

"What happened?" Nash asked.

"A little altercation in the cafeteria," she said dully. "It happens."

"We need to get you out of here. I'm calling Fran," I decided.

"Don't," Mary Louise said, her voice suddenly sharp. She shook her head. "No more calls.

No more petitions. No more meetings. I'm done."

"What are you saying?" I whispered, sinking back into my chair.

"Did someone threaten you, Mary Louise?" Nash asked.

Her gaze shifted to the door. "I'm saying it's best for everyone if I serve out the rest of my sentence."

"No," I said firmly. "We're so close, Mary Louise. Don't you want to see Allen graduate?"

She shook her head again, tears welling in her eyes. "It was foolish of me to hope. There are better ways for you to spend your money. Other people you can help. I can do another nine years."

She said it like she was trying to convince herself.

I looked at Nash with desperation.

But he shook his head at me, his eyes all cop.

"Listen to me, Mary Louise," I tried again. "We'll figure this out. I'll do whatever I can to keep you safe. Just don't make any decisions yet until I see what I can do."

"You don't understand. I *need* to stay here. I *need* you to stop helping."

"We can't just leave her in there," I said, jogging to keep up with Nash as we headed toward his SUV.

"Just let me think, Sloaney."

"She's obviously being threatened. Someone attacked her, and now all of a sudden, she doesn't want us to help?"

"I know. Calm down and shut up so I can think."

"We don't have time to think!"

Nash stopped, and I ran into his broad back. He turned to face me. "Honey, I know. But you need to understand, you getting attacked the same day that Mary Louise gets jumped is not a coincidence. They might be focusing their threats on the two of you, but that doesn't mean you're the only two targets."

"Allen," I said, realization dawning.

He nodded. "And Lina. And Naomi. And Maeve. And anyone else involved in this case."

I closed my eyes. "Damn it. She'd never risk Allen, let alone anyone else."

"You call Fran," Nash said, unlocking the doors and pulling out his phone.

"Who are you calling?" I demanded.

He looked me dead in the eyes. "Who do you think?"

"What the hell is Lucian going to do?"

"He's the only one I can think of with the strings to pull to get her and Allen the protection they need immediately."

He was right.

I put my hand on his arm. "Don't tell him about me. Please."

"Sloane, you're in fucking danger. You were threatened tonight."

"I am aware, *Chief*. But it's none of his damn business. Besides, I have you. Lucian needs to focus his evil powers on protecting Mary Louise and Allen."

37

It's Getting Hot in Here

Sloane

The only thing I liked more than a closed library was an open one. Surrounded by all those books, all those worlds waiting to be explored on the page. The ASMR-like buzz of whispers, keyboards, and turning pages. But I usually enjoyed the after-hours silence almost as much.

Except now it gave me too much time to think.

I'd worked open to close today. Not because it was necessary but because I didn't know what else to do.

It had been two weeks since the threats against me and Mary Louise. Lucian had worked his dark magic and got Mary Louise transferred to a new prison—the one Naomi's sister, Tina, was serving time in—the morning after. But even though Allen was now protected by full-time security, she was still refusing to move forward with her own case.

Naomi and Lina had slowly relinquished their obsessive need to check in with me. After five successive nights of sleepovers, we'd all agreed that I was probably safe enough in my house with its locks, new basic security cameras that Waylay helped me install, and hourly police drive-bys.

And being the excellent friends they were, they'd agreed not to mention the inciting incident to Lucian.

My personal life was nonexistent thanks to the near-constant presence of the Knockemout PD, who were "keeping an eye on me" and looking into who would want to keep Mary Louise behind bars. Even if I'd wanted to date, it would have been too awkward with a uniformed, armed babysitter tagging along.

To make matters worse, I was under strict orders from Nash to leave the investigations to the professionals. I could have used the distraction of some interesting research to dig into. But Nash had used his scary cop voice and threatened to tell Lucian I'd been targeted if I didn't agree. So I'd mostly acquiesced.

Sure. Maybe I took a peek at Mary Louise's case files from her trial every night until I was too bleary-eyed to see straight. I wasn't hurting anyone. And if I found something, it would be better for everyone in the long run, considering the police investigation consisted of a series of dead ends. Not only were there no fingerprints or other identifiable evidence left from my attacker, but by all accounts, the attack on Mary Louise appeared to be random and unprovoked.

A soft thump from the children's section had me bobbling two John Sandford novels.

I blew out a frustrated breath, fluffing my hair away from my face and fogging my glasses. Ever since the man with the cinnamon breath had scared the shit out of me, I'd been an anxiety-ridden hot mess.

"Get a grip," I muttered to myself.

I was disappointed in myself. I'd always thought I'd react to a dangerous situation with the quick wit and backbone of a feisty heroine. Or at least like an adorably bumbling Stephanie Plum. Instead, I was waiting for a hero to save me. And not even my own hero. Nope. I was waiting for my friend's fiancé, the chief of police, to save my ass.

It was a sobering, humbling thought.

I finished scanning in the evening's book returns, then turned out the lights on the first floor before heading upstairs to my office. There were a few more admin tasks I wanted to see to. Not that they needed to be done tonight. But what else did I have to do?

Besides, the library was the only place the cops felt comfortable leaving me the hell alone since it was attached to the station and all. Someone would have to be quite the idiot to try to do harm next to an entire police department.

Upstairs, I settled in behind my desk with a fresh root beer and cranked my Get Shit Done playlist. By the time Joan Jett's "I Hate Myself for Loving You" came on, I'd scheduled out three weeks of social media posts for the library's Facebook and Instagram pages, drafted the next two weeks' worth of newsletters, and ordered several new indie novels for circulation.

I'd never been so far ahead on my to-do list in my entire life.

There was only one person to blame.

I took out my phone and scrolled through my messages. Despite the fact that I hadn't answered him, Lucian had continued to text me daily.

Assface: I had dinner with your mother.
Assface: I think she needs a pet to keep her company.
Assface: Cat or dog?
Assface: Small, condo-sized pony?
Assface: It doesn't have to be this way, Pixie. We could find a way to be friends.

Friends? Ha. Friends trusted each other. Friends were honest with each other. I'd wasted enough of my life on a man who was never going to admit to having feelings for me. I didn't need anything else from Lucian Rollins.

I had more important things to do. Probably.

How was I supposed to find a man, allow him the space and time to prove to me that he was trustworthy, and then convince him to get married while my eggs were still viable? That seemed like a decades-long project.

What if my eggs weren't actually viable?

What if I wasn't going to find a Simon Walton?

What if that wasn't part of my story?

"Oh my God, I'm annoying myself," I complained over my music. "Stop moping and fucking do something."

But what? My heart and vagina just weren't into the dating scene. But that didn't mean I had no other options. I thought of Knox and Naomi and Waylay, then, chewing on my lower lip, I navigated to the county's foster care system page and started scrolling.

Icona Pop was in the middle of the chorus of "I Love It" when a faraway noise dragged me out of research mode. I turned down the music to listen, only to be startled by the ancient printer spitting out the foster care and adoption brochures.

I snatched the papers out of the tray and strained my ears. Nothing. It was probably a book tumbling off a shelf or one of the heavy poster boards in the children's section finally winning its war against the tape.

I returned the music to its original volume and launched my inbox to take care of a few remaining tasks.

This time, it wasn't a sound that caught my attention. It was a smell. A faint, bitter, chemical scent. Almost like melting plastic or old, stale coffee that had cooked to the bottom of the pot.

I'd turned off the coffee makers. Hadn't I?

Yes. I always remembered to do it after seeing the news special about a family's house that had burned down on Christmas Eve due to a faulty air fryer.

I pushed away from my desk with a frown. The smell was getting stronger now. The lights in the library were still out, but there appeared to be a sort of eerie glow through my office window. Was it getting hotter in here? Maybe the furnace was on the fritz.

I opened my office door, and the sharp tang of smoke hit me.

"What the . . ."

It couldn't be a fire. The entire building had been equipped with a state-of-the-art sprinkler system when it had been built.

But there was no mistaking that orange, undulating glow coming from the first floor or the punch of heat that enveloped my body.

I raced back to my desk and picked up the phone to call for help. But there was no dial tone. The line was dead.

"Damn it! Okay. Think, Sloane. Do not fucking panic."

With shaking hands, I found my cell phone and managed to dial 911. As it rang, I gathered my tote, indiscriminately shoving books and personal items inside. I yanked Ezra Abbott's Valentine's Day pirate drawing off the window and rolled it up.

"911. What is your emergency?"

"This is Sloane Walton calling from the Knockemout Public Library," I said as I raced back to the door. "There's a fire. In the library. At least I think it's a fire." The air felt thick and hot, and it burned the back of my throat.

A coughing fit overtook me, and I bent at the waist, trying to suck in a breath.

"Calm down, ma'am. Please tell me your location."

"Don't tell me to calm down, Sharice. And don't ma'am me either. The library is on fire," I rasped as I left my office. Sharice was a recent graduate of Knockemout High School and had been a library summer camp counselor for the last three years.

It was getting hotter by the second, as if I'd relinquished thermostat control to the always cold Barbara during book club.

Fires required fire extinguishers. I embraced the thought with relief. I remembered the big, red one hanging on the wall in the kitchen.

Ducking low to see through dark, fetid smoke, I headed away from the stairs and toward the kitchen. I was sweating freely.

"Sorry, Sloane. Do you know where the fire is located?"

"I think it's on the first floor. I'm upstairs." I cradled the phone against my shoulder and blindly felt along the wall, bending over as far as I could in search of fresh air.

My fingers found the protrusion of the doorframe, and I hurriedly reached for the handle. It was warmer than it should be against my palm.

"I'm putting out a call to the fire department now. Can you get out of the building safely?"

"I'm getting a fire extinguisher from the kitchen."

"Ma'am—er, Sloane, I need you to tell me if you have a way to exit the building," she said crisply.

"I'll tell you after I find the damn extinguisher."
I was not about to go into battle unarmed. I felt inside the door for the light switch, but nothing happened when I flicked it.

Shit. No lights.

I stumbled into the kitchen, ignoring the muffled conversation on the other end of the call.

"I have police offers responding to the scene now."

"I would hope so, considering they're literally in the same building."

"You are to evacuate with them immediately. The fire department is on their way."

My shin met something hard, and I went down with a yelp.

My phone and tote went flying.

The goddamn trash can. The dark and smoke made a familiar place a disorienting maze of danger.

"Damn you, Marjorie Ronsanto!" I muttered, climbing onto my hands and knees. It was a little cooler and a lot less smoky down here. I crawled forward, feeling around for the phone. "If you're still there, Sharice, could you yell really loud or push some buttons?" I asked the dark.

But I realized the roaring wasn't just in my ears. It was coming from beneath me.

"Why the fuck aren't the sprinklers working, and where the fuck is the extinguisher?" I demanded.

Miraculously, I found my way to the cabinets and followed them to the far wall. I composed a staff-wide memo in my head as I crawled. Fire extinguishers will now be mounted inside the door, not all the way across the goddamn room. And Marjorie's trash can was officially being retired to the dumpster.

My throat and lungs burned. I was sweating so profusely I wondered if it was possible to turn into a human raisin.

Finally, I ran forehead first into the far wall. "Ouch!"

Scrambling to my feet, I skimmed my hands in wide arcs over the drywall. My pinkie finger smashed into the metal canister, and I cried out in pain and triumph.

Blindly, I yanked the extinguisher off the wall.

"I got the extinguisher from the kitchen," I yelled in case the call was still connected. I shuffled back toward the door as quickly as I dared. "I'm going to try to get down the stairs. If I can't, I'll go to one of the windows on the side—"

My foot met something unexpected, and I fell sideways awkwardly. My ribs met something hard and unmoving, knocking the wind out of me. The damn table I sat at every damn day.

"I won't have a chance to die of smoke inhalation at this rate," I wheezed. "I'm going to clumsy myself to death."

The immovable thing on the floor turned out to be my tote bag. I shouldered it, tucked the extinguisher under my arm, and crawled out the door.

"Sloane!"

Sergeant Grave Hopper was calling for me from somewhere, and he sounded *pissed.*

I sucked in a breath to call back, but another coughing fit overtook me.

I was the worst firefighter ever, I decided as tears streaked down my face. I stayed as low as I could, crawling with only one arm, and made my way toward the stairs.

"Sloane!" another voice called.

"Here." It came out as more of a croak than a shout, but it was enough.

"She's on the second floor."

"There's no exit up there."

"I'm coming down," I barked. "I have a fire extinguisher."

"Drop the fucking extinguisher and get your ass to the stairs," Grave ordered.

Drop the extinguisher? There were books to save. But I heard them then. The sirens. They would save the books.

I was so tired. My lungs hurt. My head rang. It was so dark. I just needed to rest for a minute.

38

Stupid Pills

Lucian

As the helicopter banked to the east over Knockemout, the sight of emergency vehicle lights slashing through the dark churned an anger I wasn't sure I could control.

Sloane had been alone inside when the fire started. And I'd been miles away on a conference call with the West Coast.

While she blindly crawled down the stairs through smoke and flame, I'd been handling a minor PR crisis for a California state representative. A minor crisis that I could have easily handed over to someone else.

While Sloane was helped from the building by a cop and the firefighter who took her to her senior prom, while she was looked over by a paramedic who happened to be a member of the library's book club, I had been pulling strings and smoothing ruffled feathers for virtual strangers.

"Preparing for landing, sir." The pilot's voice sounded flat and distant in my headset.

I had the door open and was climbing out by the time the skids kissed the ground at the private airfield just east of Knockemout. In less than a minute, I was behind the wheel of the waiting SUV and speeding toward town. I turned off my mind and focused on the road, the familiar scenery as it flashed by.

I didn't let myself think about Sloane. Alone. Unprotected. I didn't let myself consider the fact that I'd left her that way, believing she'd be safer.

The echo of Knox's voice rang in my ear. *"Nice of you to finally pick up, asshole. The fuckin' library's on fire, and Sloane was inside."*

It felt like an eternity before the flashing lights filled the windshield as I drove into the heart of Knockemout.

I got out and strode into chaos. The smell of acrid smoke burned my throat as I pushed through the gathered crowd. The two-story redbrick building still stood. The gold lettering that read THE KNOX MORGAN MUNICIPAL BUILDING was tarnished but still there. The front doors were propped open. Windows on the library side were broken, allowing black, billowing smoke to escape, tainting the night air.

I grabbed the closest first responder I could find, a tall, grizzled woman with soot streaking her gear and an axe slung over her shoulder. "Chief Morgan," I snapped.

"Over there." She pointed toward the police station parking lot where a tent was set up and a dozen first responders clumped.

No one tried to stop me as I made my way over. It was one of the many privileges of being Lucian

Fucking Rollins. Most rules didn't apply to me because there wasn't anyone willing to stand up and enforce them.

"Nash," my voice cracked like a whip over everything.

My friend looked up from his conference with Sergeant Grave Hopper, who was covered head to toe in soot, the fire chief, and Mayor Hilly Swanson. Nash looked grim, and I felt that anger inside me expand exponentially.

He excused himself from the others and put a hand to my chest. "She's okay."

I closed my eyes and let that permeate the panic.

"Where is she?" I rasped.

"I had Bannerjee drive her home about ten minutes ago."

I wanted to go to her. I needed to see her. To see for myself that she was okay. But first I needed answers.

"You let her go home by herself? What the fuck is wrong with you? Why isn't Knox with her? Where are Naomi and Lina?"

"It's almost two in the fucking morning on a school night. Sloane sent them all home about an hour ago. Bannerjee checked the house, including all doors and windows, before she left."

"What the hell happened here?"

Nash's face pokered up. "We don't know yet. Fire department seems to think it originated on the first floor. Sloane was upstairs in her office, working late. She was the only one on this side of the building. The alarms and the sprinkler system didn't go off like they were supposed to, but she smelled the smoke, opened her door, and immediately called 911. Grave evacuated our side and went running into the library like an untrained idiot. He found Sloane on the stairs, and they were making their way out when the fire department showed."

I wanted the names of every person who installed the alarm and sprinkler system because I was going to systematically ruin their lives. Then I was going to buy Grave a penthouse in whatever vacation town he wanted.

"How bad is the damage?" I asked. I'd rebuild it brick by brick for her. Whatever she wanted. She couldn't stop me.

"We'll know more in the morning. The structure seems stable, but . . ." Nash swiped a hand over his face. "Those books went up like fucking kindling."

I absorbed it like a gut punch. Sloane would be devastated.

"I'm going to her," I announced.

He shook his head. "Man, that's not the smartest idea. She's not going to want to see you. Not after the bullshit you pulled."

"I'll unpull it."

"You're either overestimating your charm or underestimating her stubbornness. Either way, you're probably the last person she wants to see tonight."

He didn't understand. No one did. When things

turned to ruins, Sloane and I were there for each other. Always. It was time we both remembered that. Because I wasn't walking away. Not this time. Not ever again.

"She's not going to have a choice. She'll listen to reason."

Nash stared at me like I'd just invited him to a poker game with Bigfoot and the late Sammy Davis Jr. "Did you take stupid pills this morning?"

I glared at him. "I'm going to fix this."

"Listen, Luce. I get that you have complicated feelings for Sloane. But I love that girl like a little sister. Always have. Knox too. If you fuck with her, if you upset her more than she already is, I'm not gonna be gentle with you. And we both know Knox won't want to be left out of the ass kicking."

I squared off with Nash and looked him dead in the eyes. "If you or Knox or anyone else in this fucking town tries to keep me away from Sloane, I will destroy you."

His mouth curved up in the corner. "Looking forward to it, brother. Good luck."

"Open the goddamn door, Sloane," I bellowed, hammering my fist against her front door.

She hadn't responded to any of my calls and texts since I'd kicked her out of my house, certainly none of the dozens since I'd shown up on her doorstep. But she *had* made the deadly mistake of turning the porch light out on me five minutes ago.

The first floor was dark. And I guessed she

was either sitting in the dark enjoying my temper tantrum, or she'd gone upstairs to ignore me.

"I'm not going anywhere, so you might as well let me in," I called.

The curtain in the front window closest to me twitched, and I lunged for the glass only to find the cat watching me dispassionately like she was some kind of guardian gargoyle. Could cats smirk? Because that was exactly what this tubby tabby appeared to be doing at my expense.

"You're name is Meow Meow. You have no room to judge," I told the cat through the glass.

The fur ball ignored me and focused her attention on the paw she was cleaning.

I gave up on the knocking and sought a new plan of attack.

The key.

I remembered Simon and Karen used to keep their spare key under the red planter they filled with ferns every spring and evergreen boughs every winter. Eagerly, I tipped it back and felt around the floorboards under it. Nothing.

Damn it. I guess some things did change. I moved the entire planter a foot to the right, then looked under Sloane's whimsical welcome mat. I scoured every inch of the porch around the front door, then expanded my methodical search, pausing every minute or two to text her.

Me: I'm not leaving. Let me in.
Me: Are you okay?

Me: If you don't at least respond, then I'm going to have to call Nash and have him do a welfare check.
Sloane: I'm fine.

Relief immediately gave way to suspicion. No insults. No accusations about shouldn't I be drinking the blood of unicorns and leaving her alone. No hurling my past actions in my face.

The panic was back.

I checked the underside of the entire length of the railing. No key. When I got inside, I was going to bully her into giving me a spare key. Then I was going to have my security team install a state-of-the-art system to keep her safe. I paced to the end of the house where the porch wrapped around the side. The flashlight from my phone panned over the thick, flaky bark of the tree trunk.

For the first time in weeks, I grinned.

I vaulted over the railing and landed in the flower bed between a budding rhododendron and an azalea. I shoved my phone in my pocket, then wrapped my hands around the trunk. With one confident hop, I sacrificed my leather Brioni loafers against the rough tree bark.

The trick with climbing a cherry tree was to keep all the force pressing in a downward motion so the bark didn't peel away from the tree. I shuffle hopped my way up the trunk until I reached the first branch. The first cherry blossoms had already started to bloom, filling my head with their familiar scent. It fueled me, fed me, and I climbed faster.

I chose an aggressive trek, and when I reached my foot for a higher branch, I heard the telltale rip of fabric. The rip was followed immediately by a flow of fresh air over my balls. The tree was a few decades older than the first time I'd climbed it, and I was out of practice, but I managed to land on the porch roof with only a few more scrapes and tears.

Sloane's bedside lamp was on, I noted as I scrambled up the gentle incline over the shingles to the window.

My heart stopped.

Her light was on, but she wasn't in bed. Sloane. *My* Sloane was sitting on the floor, arms wrapped around her knees as she rocked back and forth. Tears washed clean trails as they cut through the soot on her beautiful face. Her clothing was dirty. Even her hair had lost its brilliant shine. Her ponytail drooped with the heavy weight of smoke residue.

The middle window was open a few inches. It always had been. So I did what I'd always done. I pushed it up and let myself in.

I could only imagine the picture I made, slinging one leg over the sill onto the cushion of the window seat. But Sloane didn't laugh. Or yell. Or tell me to go fuck myself and leave her alone.

She looked directly at me, then covered her face with her hands and cried harder.

"Fuck," I muttered, clambering into the room and racing to her side. "Sloane. Baby." My hands searched her arms and torso for injuries. Because only the worst injuries could break her like this. The worst injuries and the worst heartbreaks.

Finding nothing, I shifted her into my arms. Panic was a living breathing thing in my chest when she didn't fight me. She should be telling me what an asshole I was. She should be throwing me out. Not collapsing against me.

I picked her up and held her cradled against my chest, and when she didn't start throwing punches and insults, I marched us to the head of her bed. I dragged the covers back, kicked off my ruined shoes, and sat against the pile of pillows, still holding her.

Silent sobs racked her body, forming wounds in my cold, black heart. A bottomless well of tears soaked my shirt as I held her tighter to me and let one hand stroke down her ponytail. Over and over again. She smelled like the kind of smoke that destroyed dreams, and I could hardly bear it.

Yet even though it carved me up to see her pain, I realized what a gift this was. To be here when she broke. To pick up the pieces and help her put them back together again.

I didn't tell her it would be okay. I didn't beg her to stop crying. I just held on tight as my pathetic, cowardly heart broke.

I thought I'd been doing the right thing by keeping her at a distance. She was supposed to have been safer that way. But by leaving her alone, I'd left her vulnerable to a danger I hadn't anticipated. I wanted to protect her from me, from the dark shadow that was my past, from the danger that was my present. But I'd left her open and vulnerable to something else. Something that had almost stolen her from me.

If my distance couldn't protect her, my proximity would. From now on, I would be Sloane's shadow.

The tears stopped sometime later. They were replaced by full-body shivers. She still hadn't spoken a word to me. And I was eager to do whatever I could before she regained her voice and tried to kick me out. Without a warning, I gathered her up and carried her into the bathroom.

"What are you doing?" Her usually husky voice was a painful rasp.

"You're shivering," I said, leaning down to turn on the water to the tub. It was a deep, jetted tub built into a tile surround under a stained glass window.

"N-no, I'm n-not," she whispered through chattering teeth.

It took two tries before I could put her down. Terrified that she'd run, I didn't take my eyes off her as I closed the tub drain. She had candles on the tile surrounding the tub. I pulled the lighter out of my pocket and lit them. Still not trusting her to stay, I closed my hand gently around her wrist and pulled her with me as I gathered fluffy, sage-green towels and stacked them next to the tub. She came with me willingly as I pulled her toward the shower where I collected her shampoo, conditioner, and soap.

I arranged the haul and adjusted the water temperature, all with my grip still firm on her.

When I finally turned to face her, she was staring blankly at the water as it poured forth. Tears had carved paths through the filth marring her lovely face. There was no light, no fight in those beautiful green eyes. No emerald flames warning me of my imminent verbal evisceration.

"We need to take off your clothes, Pixie."

She gave no sign of having heard me, so I saw to it myself. I reached out and dragged the ruined sweater over her head. I sucked in a vicious breath when I saw the bruises already forming on her arms and ribs. Still she made no move to stop me or help. So I continued.

There was a tender vulnerability in the way she let me undress her like she was a doll. As the tub filled, I took my time, peeling away the layers and discarding them until she stood there shaking and naked. Dirt and soot streaked her face, hands, and hair. Bruises painted her ivory skin as if her body was a canvas.

Fury burned inside me. I wouldn't rest until I knew who was responsible for those bruises and made them pay.

Her beauty was so exquisitely fragile I couldn't catch my breath.

I'd almost lost her. Really lost her. Not pushed her away, but lost her. I could have already seen her for the last time and not known it. That thought sunk in on a razor-edged moment of clarity.

I could have been standing inside a morgue tonight instead of Sloane's bathroom because I was a stupid, selfish coward. I hadn't trusted myself to protect her before. But now I had no other choice.

I nudged her chin up until those green eyes found mine, and I knew. I was never leaving her again. We'd parted ways for the last time. She just didn't know it yet.

"Ready?" I asked her.

She said nothing, just stared emptily up at me. My chest constricted tighter. Her pain was my pain. And for the first time in my life, I realized what she must have felt at sixteen, her window open, the whispers of my own pain carried to her on the night breeze.

Fuck.

I shut off the water and guided her to sit on the tile next to the tub. When I was certain she was stable, I stripped off my own shirt and pants.

"W-what are you doing?" she asked, each word coming out hesitantly as if she'd forgotten how to say them.

"We're taking a bath," I said, removing my underwear and socks and adding them to the pile of clothing I was going to throw away at my earliest convenience. I never wanted to see her ruined pink sweater again. I'd buy her a new one. A dozen new ones. I'd rebuild her library brick by brick, book by book. And I would never let her face danger alone again.

Something loosened in my chest. Something old and rusted. Like an ancient lock finally forced open. Fresh air swept inside, blowing aside the cobwebs, lighting the hearth. She'd always been mine. I was just now accepting that fact. Once something was mine, I never gave it up.

Feeling lighter than I had in years, I swung one leg followed by the other into the tub. "Come on, Pix. I've got you." I hooked her under the arms and lifted her into the water. I lowered us both and stretched my legs out in front of me before settling her against my front, her back to my chest, her head tucked under my chin. Wrapping my arms around her, I leaned back.

I was taking my first-ever bath with a woman. Not just any woman. Sloane.

That looseness in my chest warmed. I was going to have so many firsts with this woman.

We rested like that, in steam and flickering candlelight, as the water warmed us for several long minutes. When she let out a small, broken sigh, I picked up a sponge and a bottle of soap and went to work gently cleaning the soot and dirt from her skin. My beautiful broken girl didn't help me or fight me. But she *did* relax against me. She *did* press her damp face to my neck. And for the first time in my life, I felt like the hero instead of the villain.

I was hard. It was a biological impossibility to

not get hard around her, let alone when she was wet and naked against me. But what was happening between us was so much deeper than sex I barely gave my arousal a second thought.

"Here, baby," I said, my hands moving under the water to cup her hips. I pushed her forward and bent my knees before settling her back against my shins. "Let me wash your hair."

Sloane said nothing as I worked the tie free. Her hair tumbled down in a silky, thick curtain that hung over my thighs, the ends kissing the water.

I grabbed an empty wineglass next to the tub and filled it with water. "Lean back," I urged, gathering her hair around my free hand and tugging gently until her head rested on my knees. "Good girl."

I poured water over those blond tresses and refilled the glass, repeating the process until I was satisfied that her hair was thoroughly wet. Then I went to work, massaging the shampoo into her roots and down the silky lengths. I worked slowly, using my fingers to rub gentle circles against her scalp.

She let out another sigh, and her body loosened as it melted against me. I took my time soaping and rinsing, then repeating the same with her conditioner until every smudge and shadow had been washed clean.

When we were both finally clean, I picked her up out of the cooling water, bundled her in too many towels, and led her into the bedroom. "Stay here," I ordered, nudging her onto the window seat.

"What are you doing?" she asked sleepily.

"Changing the sheets. Don't move."

I found fresh sheets in her closet and made another mental note to contact my organizer in the morning. I'd make room here for me and at my place for her.

I made quick work of changing the bed linens while shooting nervous glances in Sloane's direction. She wasn't watching me. She was staring dully down at her feet on the carpet.

As I arranged her legion of pillows in the right formation, I swore whoever was responsible for this would pay. I'd make sure of it.

When the bed was ready, I returned to Sloane and tugged her to her feet. "Time for bed," I said.

She followed docilely, making me wish she'd put up a fight. Show me a glimpse of the real Sloane Walton.

She paused, staring at the mound of pillows I'd arranged in a U.

"You remembered," she said softly.

"I remember every second of us."

39

Who Has the Head Wound

Lucian

I woke to a warm, vibrating weight on my chest. It felt comforting. Until the weight shifted and something sharp prodded me in the face.

I opened my eyes and found yellow ones glaring back. The cat apparently had an opinion about me sharing Sloane's bed. The woman in question was sleeping soundly, her back glued to my side, her head resting in the crook of my arm.

The moment felt so fucking right. Like earning my first million. Only this was terrifyingly better. Money could be made and lost. It could be replaced. Sloane couldn't.

I savored the moment . . . until it was ruined by another stab of claws. Silently, I glared at the stupidly named feline. She returned the look, tail flicking against my bare chest. Then, with a glance in Sloane's direction, she opened her mouth and released a feral-sounding yowl.

"Shut. Up," I hissed at the cat.

Sloane grumbled in her sleep and shifted against me.

I saw the gleam in the cat's eyes, the shift of her weight, and caught her just before she pounced on Sloane's sleeping form.

"Absolutely not, you demon fur ball from hell."

I dumped the cat on the floor and carefully slid my arm out from under my exhausted librarian. Meow Meow must have felt I was taking too long rearranging the pillows behind Sloane because I received another puncture wound. This one to the calf.

"Christ, cat. I'll feed you. Just give me a minute to find clothes."

I was naked, and yesterday's suit was not an option. Between the tree climbing and cradling the soot-streaked Sloane, my suit had met its maker.

With the cat obstinately threading her way between my feet, I poked through Sloane's closet until I discovered a pair of pale pink sweatpants that would have to do. I dragged them over my thighs, seams straining, then unearthed the sweatshirt she'd offered me when I'd chased her home.

The ex-boyfriend sweatshirt. I was going to take it with me and conveniently lose it in a trash bin.

"Fuck," I muttered, looking at my reflection in the full-length mirror.

The pants barely covered the top of my ass crack in the back. In the front, the thin, tight fabric did everything it could to accentuate the outline of my cock.

"Meow," the cat said, sounding smugly amused.

"Let's never speak of this again."

Together, we quietly headed downstairs where the cat went into full meltdown mode, yowling at me like she was a spoiled heiress and I was an incompetent waiter.

"I want to make Sloane breakfast, not you."

Meow Meow was unimpressed and narrowed her yellow eyes at me.

"Fine. I'll feed you. Then you'll stay out of my way, and I'll stay out of yours. Deal?"

I took the slow blink as a binding contract and went in search of cat food. I poured a medium-sized mound of dry food into the cat face-shaped dish on the floor and then headed to the coffee maker.

Coffee started, I was ten minutes into a recipe for pancakes and texting Petula a list of necessities that I was going to need here since I'd be staying for the foreseeable future when the door-bell rang.

Cursing, I pulled the pan off the burner and made the quietest, fastest run possible to the front door. I nearly took a header into the door when the cat appeared out of nowhere and cut in front of me at full gallop.

"You furry little fucker," I snarled as I threw open the door.

Nash and Lina stood on the doorstep, gawking.

"If you woke her up, I'll be kicking your ass," I warned Nash.

"Uhhh." Lina's mouth was open, her eyes wide and riveted to an area below my belt.

Nash covered his fiancée's eyes and choked out a laugh. "What the fuck are you wearing?"

"The only thing that fucking fit."

"No, you're not," Lina said, her voice tinged with hysteria.

"Wardrobe opinions aside, what the hell are you doing here?" I demanded.

Nash pokered up immediately. "It's about the fire."

Ice formed in my gut. "You know the cause?"

"Can we talk about this inside?" he hedged.

"Fine. But if either of you wakes her, you're fired and you're getting your ass kicked," I said, pointing first at Lina and then at Nash.

"Fair enough," Nash agreed.

They followed me inside and into the kitchen.

"It's just as bad from the back," Lina whispered.

I tried to hitch the pants higher but only succeeded in nearly spraining my balls.

She gave a strangled laugh.

"Jesus, man. Have some dignity," Nash said, throwing a dish towel at me.

"I have clothes being sent," I said testily. "Tell me about the fire."

"Wait a second. Why are you answering Sloane's door dressed like that?" Lina demanded, recovering from the hilarity.

"I spent the night."

She shot Nash a long, meaningful look. He rolled his eyes.

"Man, how many times are you going to fuck this up?" he asked me. "Didn't we beat some sense into you last time?"

642

I crossed my arms over my chest. "Apparently not. Talk."

"I'll be honest. I need to talk to Sloane. You can be here if she says it's all right, but I'm not talking directly to you about this."

"It was arson, wasn't it?" I demanded. The thought had kept me up through the entire night. It was the only thing that made sense.

"Arson?" We all turned to see Sloane standing at the foot of the back stairs. She was wearing knee socks and an oversize long-sleeve shirt that I wished I had seen when I was raiding her wardrobe. Her hair was exploding out of a knot on the top of her head. The bruise on her forehead was more vicious-looking today. She looked so fragile and so beautiful I forgot how to breathe.

"Hey there, Sloaney," Nash said gently. "How ya feelin' today?"

"Sore. You said arson," she repeated.

"That was Mr. Fashionista here," he said, hooking his thumb at me. "But yeah. Investigators found evidence that someone set the fire in the back of the first floor near the kids' section."

Sloane's face remained impassive as she crossed the kitchen and walked directly to the coffee maker. "Do you guys want coffee? I want coffee."

Lina, Nash, and I exchanged a look. "Sure, honey. I'll take some coffee," Lina said and headed in her direction.

With the women occupied with coffee, I punched Nash in the arm and then shoved him into the dining room. "What. The. Fuck?" I demanded.

"What what the fuck?" he asked, rubbing his bicep.

"She almost died last night. You think you could break the news a little more gently, asshole?"

His eyebrows winged up. "You're the asshole who said 'arson,' not me."

"Who did this? I want names."

"We don't have any suspects at this time," Nash said snootily.

"Bull fucking shit."

"I do."

I turned and found Sloane standing in the doorway holding a mug of coffee. Lina was behind her.

"Who?" I demanded.

She shook her head, making the bun on her head wobble precariously. "Uh-uh. First, tell me how extensive the damage is and how long it'll be before we can open again."

I bared my teeth and Nash elbowed me. "Humor her," he hissed under his breath.

"Why don't we talk over those pancakes Lucian was making when we interrupted him?" Lina suggested.

I sucked in an irritable breath. "Fine," I growled.

"Maybe don't clench so many ass muscles, Lucy. You might owe Sloane a new pair of pants," Nash said, slapping me on the back.

She blinked, then her eyes widened behind her glasses as if she noticed what I was wearing for the first time. "Those are my pants."

"I'm not sure you're going to want them back. He's commando underneath," Lina warned cheerily as we all trooped toward kitchen.

I snagged Sloane's hand and pulled her around to face me. She was staring at my crotch, so I nudged her chin up. "How do you feel?"

"Tired. Sore. And very, very mad."

Mad was good. Mad was better than shattered.

"I'll find whoever did this and make them pay," I vowed.

"Not if I find them first," she said.

She didn't get it. Not yet. But she would understand soon. I would make sure of it. I reached out and tucked an errant strand of hair behind her ear. She looked vulnerable yet so fierce. A pixie ready to do battle.

I leaned down, intending to brush my mouth to hers, but she pulled back. "Why didn't you go next door to change?" she asked.

"Because I'm not leaving you."

Not now, not ever again.

She rolled those green eyes at me. "You're so weird. And don't think for one second just because we took a bath and you made me pancakes that we're back on, bucko."

"Bucko?" I repeated, trying hard not to smile. Sloane Walton was back, and she was ready to kick some ass.

"Oh, no, big guy. You better get that idea out of your thick head real fast. We're as done as done can be. Last night meant nothing."

645

"You're wrong, Pix. It meant everything. And I'm going to prove it."

She glared up at me. "Go away."

"Do you all want us to eat these pancakes by ourselves while you fight, or can we talk like adults?" Nash asked, gesturing with a spatula.

"Let's talk fast. I have to get to the library. See what can be salvaged and start the conversation with the insurance company," Sloane said when we were all settled in at the dining room table with plates of pancakes.

The cat perched at the foot of the table, regally cleaning her ass.

"Now, Sloane, it's an active crime scene. I can't have you Nancy Drewing your way around. Especially not before we have the okay from the structural engineers," Nash insisted.

Her jaw tightened.

"You said you know who did it," I said, drawing her attention. "Let's start there."

"It was clearly either the guy who attacked me in the parking lot or the one who gave the orders to have Mary Louise roughed up," she said, dumping the better part of a bottle of syrup on her stack of pancakes.

My knife and fork clattered onto the plate, startling the cat, who hit the floor like a bowling ball before stampeding out of the room.

"What did you say?"

"Uh-oh. He's using his scary voice," Lina noted.

"It's none of your business," Sloane said crisply.

"I'd like to speak with you outside, Morgan," I said to Nash, ignoring her.

My friend shook his head. "Uh-uh. You don't get to punch me in the face until *after* breakfast."

"Then talk. Now," I ordered.

"I was leaving a date, and some guy in a ski mask opened my car door, pinned me to the seat, and told me to leave Mary Louise alone. Does anyone else want more coffee?" Sloane asked.

"What?" I roared. This whole time, I'd assumed I was the one who'd put her in danger. But in reality, it had come from a different direction, and I could have been there to stop it. I should have been there to stop it.

"He's gonna hulk his way right out of those pants," Lina warned.

"Please," Sloane scoffed. "Do us all a favor and drop the overprotective act."

"You were attacked?" I said, looking at her.

"It was only a little attack," she said with a shrug. "More of a warning than anything else."

"And you didn't tell me?" I said, pointing at Nash.

"Still no face punching until after breakfast," he reminded me.

"Leave his face alone," Sloane said. "I asked him not to tell you."

"Technically, she blackmailed me into it. She said if I told you, she'd stick her nose into the investigation and make herself even more of a target," Nash said.

"Let's not forget that it's none of your business," Sloane pointed out irritably.

"You are always my business. You always have been, and you always will be. The only difference is now you know it," I said icily.

Sloane snorted and looked at Lina. "I'm the one who gets a head wound in a burning building, and he ends up with the hallucinations."

"We'll discuss this later," I assured Nash.

"Oh, I have no doubt."

"Let's get back to the arson," Lina suggested with feigned cheer.

"Right. The back door was jimmied open, and the inspector found two gas cans under what used to be the pillow fort in the children's section. Grave corroborated that the first floor smelled like gasoline when he got inside looking for you. The alarm system, sprinkler system, and phone lines had all been disabled."

"Did he know she was inside?" I demanded.

Nash leveled me with a look. "We don't know that yet. But her Jeep was in the parking lot."

I would find the man responsible, and I would personally destroy him.

"We haven't identified any persons of interest yet, but it's early in the investigation," he continued, cutting another bite from his plate.

The doorbell rang again.

"Stay here," I ordered when Sloane made a move to stand.

I stalked from the dining room into the living

room and yanked the door open. Knox and Naomi stood on the front porch holding a carrier of to-go cups and a bag of bagels.

"What the fuck are you wearing, man?" Knox asked, staring at my pants.

Naomi elbowed him. "Hi. We thought Sloane might want some breakfast."

"Might as well join the party," I said, hooking a thumb in the direction of the dining room.

There were hugs and platitudes and more than one skeptical look thrown in my direction.

"Can we get back to the topic at hand?" I demanded.

Knox smirked. "Now who's the sweatpants-wearing whiner?"

"How long is it going to take to rebuild?" Sloane asked.

"Levi from Benderson Builders already stopped by this morning," Nash explained.

"I talked to him too. Levi thinks he can get the work done in three or four months. He's willing to start now so you don't have to wait out the inevitable fucking around of the insurance company," Knox said.

"You talked to him?" Nash repeated.

Knox shrugged. "Building's got my fuckin' name on it. I'm invested."

"Three or four *months?*" Sloane looked pale. I reached out and gripped her hand in mine. Those green eyes swung in my direction. "What am I going to do?"

"Baby, we'll figure something out," I assured her. "We'll find a temporary location. We'll save what can be saved and buy new of everything that was lost."

"Baby?" Knox muttered.

"That was a lot of wes," Lina pointed out.

"You're gonna be hearing a lot of both, so I'd advise you get used to it," I warned them.

"Don't mind Lucian. He's suffered some kind of break with reality," Sloane said, slathering a bagel with cream cheese.

"That's it," I said. I pushed my chair back and stood up. "If you'll all excuse us for a minute, I need to have a word with Sloane."

"I'm not going anywhere," she sniffed, cramming a bite of bagel into her mouth.

I dragged her chair backward and tossed her over my shoulder.

"This is not gonna end well," Knox predicted as I carried the shrieking Sloane out of the room, through the kitchen, and out the back door.

Outside on the porch, we were met with the perfect spring morning. Warm sunshine, chirping birds, and a thousand new blooms brought her backyard to life.

Spring. A new beginning. A fresh start.

Just what we both needed.

"Put me down, you gigantic assface!" Sloane shouted.

I set her on her feet, noting that she'd managed to keep hold of her bagel.

"You need to understand something," I told her calmly. "I'm not going anywhere, and you are my business because we're together."

Her gasp was one of outrage. "You can't just *tell* me we're in a relationship." Her feistiness was back in full force. I took credit for that.

"I'm merely stating a fact."

She shook her head vehemently from side to side. "No. You've clearly suffered some sort of head wound and are experiencing an alternate reality."

"Sloane, we're together. End of story. The sooner you accept that—"

"You expect me to be all like 'okey-dokey!' when you've dumped me twice now?"

"I was trying to protect you. I thought Anthony Hugo connected you to me and was going to hurt you! When you showed up at my office, I was fucking terrified that he'd see you there."

"And instead of telling me that and coming up with a solution together, you kicked me out of your house, had me escorted from your office, and then proceeded to date an army of the most beautiful and talented women in the DC area?"

"I didn't want Hugo to be able to connect you to me. If you were just one of many, he'd leave you alone. But it was someone else who wanted to hurt you, and I'm not going to let that happen."

She was still shaking her head. "I want *kids,* Lucian. Actual children. I want a big, loud, messy family."

"Then we'll have one." I meant it. Anything Sloane wanted was now my job to procure.

She blinked rapidly. "I'm sorry. Did you say . . ." She brought a hand to her head and starting prodding the bruise on her forehead. "Maybe I did give myself a concussion. I could have sworn you said—"

"If you want kids, we'll start today," I said, leaning against the porch post.

She was back to shaking her head. "You don't understand. I want to live here. I want to raise a family here."

"No, Pixie, you don't understand. I could have lost you last night. I'm not going to let that happen again. Ever. If you want ten kids, we'll have them. If you want a six-story library full of medieval first editions, I'll buy every book for you. If you want to raise a family here, I'll move back and feed your asshole cat every morning. If you decide you want to throw it all away and move to a tasteful hut on a tropical beach, I'll build the fucking hut."

"You've lost your damn mind. We're incompatible. We have nothing in common. We make each other miserable. We can't stop insulting each other, you sweatpants-stealing lunatic," she added.

"We'll work on it. I happen to know an excellent therapist."

"That's not how any of this works. I'm sorry you freaked out about the fire. But I'm not getting into a relationship with you again. I've learned my lesson on multiple occasions now."

"Sloane, I don't think you understand what I'm saying. There's no discussion necessary. We are in a committed relationship. You mean something to me, and I'm not letting you go again. Not now, not ever. Everything else is just details."

"Having a family is *not* just details. I want a husband and a partner, not someone who's going to hire a fleet of nannies."

"I don't think that's the correct term. And if you don't want a fleet of nannies, I'll hire a small infantry of nannies."

She threw the bagel at me, and I caught it with one hand.

"Fine. No nannies. You just tell me what you want, and I'll make it happen."

"I want you to go away. Immediately and forever."

"No, you don't," I said smugly, remembering the way she'd cuddled closer to me in bed.

Sloane let out an exasperated groan. "This is *not* happening," she decided, back to shaking her head. "I'm probably in a hospital bed right now, loopy from smoke inhalation."

I closed the distance between us and took her wrists. "If you were, I'd be next to you."

"That sounds like a threat."

"A threat, a promise, whichever you prefer." I could feel the racing flutter of her pulse beneath my fingers.

"Why are you smiling? You don't smile. You glower. You brood. You . . . fester!" she said.

"I've never once festered," I argued.

"Oh, shut up."

I took her gently by the shoulders. "Sloane, listen to me. There will be no more hiding. No more pretending we can't stand each other."

"I think I'm going to be sick," she murmured.

"You're mine and I'm yours. For better or worse."

She sagged against me for a moment. "Only Lucian Fucking Rollins would think he could order a woman into a committed relationship."

"I'm just cutting through the bullshit."

She pushed away from me and started pacing while she resumed her yelling about all the reasons we wouldn't work. I found it adorable. I had never felt better about a decision in my entire life.

40

A Face Full of Chardonnay

Sloane

"T hank you for your time," I said and disconnected the call with the sandpaper-voiced
insurance adjuster lady. "Which is absolutely
worthless, you paper-pushing pain in my ass. As if
I'd burn down my own library."

Naomi grinned at me from behind my dad's desk.
We were in the study, which had become library
command central. It had been two days since the
fire, and I was deep in the weeds of bureaucratic
red tape.

"Apparently the insurance company isn't comfortable paying out until they can be sure I wasn't
the one who started the fire," I complained loud
enough to be heard over the squealing drills outside.

Naomi flashed me a pitying look while efficiently
finishing an email on her laptop. "I happen to have
an in with the chief of police. I'm sure we can get
Nash to convince the insurance company you had
nothing to do with the fire," she said.

I hopped up from the chair and marched to the
window overlooking the front porch. Besides
the team of security experts on ladders, it looked

like a going out of business sale at a bookstore. The fire department had gone through the building and brought every book that looked rescuable to the only place I could think of: my house.

Now I had a few thousand books airing out in the spring breeze on the wraparound porch.

Thanks to backup servers, our collection of ebooks and audiobooks was still available for patrons to download. But as a community library, we were so much more than just the books we provided.

People depended on us. We were part of daily life in Knockemout. I wasn't about to let a little arson change that.

The drilling started again, and I glared at the team installing the James Bond–level security system outside. My six-foot-four shadow, Lucian, had deemed my Wi-Fi cameras "inadequate" and stubbornly insisted on upgrading the technology. I still wasn't sure how I'd lost that argument. I also wasn't sure how the man was still here. Or how he'd gotten a closet organizer named Miguel past me.

Jamal poked his head in the doorway, waving his phone. "Good news. The GoFundMe to replace the children's books just hit $30,000."

"Seriously?" I asked, momentarily forgetting my frustration. That *was* good news.

"In more good news, the synagogue and Unitarian church volunteered to join forces and cover all the June free breakfasts for the kids.

They're willing to cover July as well if we're not open by then," Naomi said chipperly.

"I love this town," Jamal sang as he headed back to his workstation in my dining room.

The thump and scrape of chairs came from above.

"Are they still up there?" Naomi asked.

"Yes," I said grimly. "They" were Lucian and several of his employees. The man hadn't left my side since he'd climbed through my bedroom window the night of the fire. He also hadn't dropped the charade of being committed to a relationship with me. My patience was wearing thin.

The doorbell rang, and I ignored Lucian's distant "I'll get it."

I opened my front door to find Lucian's driver holding several dry-cleaning bags in each hand. "Morning, Ms. Sloane. Where can I put these?" Hank asked.

"If you were your employer, I'd be happy to tell you where you can put them, Hank. But I'm not mad at you."

"You can put them upstairs in the last bedroom to the right," Lucian said, appearing behind me. I turned to glare at him. He looked the way he always did, unfairly gorgeous. He was keeping things casual around here, sticking to tailored trousers and well-fitting button-downs rather than an entire suit. Meanwhile I was still wearing my cat pajamas.

"I don't have room for you in my bedroom," I insisted, crossing my arms as Hank marched across the threshold.

"That's why I hired Miguel. Ah, here come the groceries," Lucian observed as yet another vehicle pulled into my driveway.

"Groceries?"

"I invited your family to dinner tonight. We're cooking."

"Have you lost your damn mind?" I demanded.

"On the contrary, I finally came to my senses," he said before kissing me on the top of the head.

"Maybe I'm losing mine," I muttered to myself as he met the grocery delivery guy on the walkway.

"Or maybe he's just showing you how he really feels for the first time," Naomi said, joining me in the doorway. "By the way, he invited Knox and Waylay and me for dinner next week."

"I don't know what game you're playing, but I am not lying to my family and telling them we're in a relationship," I said as I violently massaged the kale. We were in the kitchen working around Meow Meow, who decided the island was the perfect place to sprawl out for a nap. Candles were lit, music was playing, and whatever we were making smelled good enough to make my stomach growl.

Lucian drowned out the rest of my concerns by turning on the blender and smoldering at me until I closed my mouth.

"I'm not playing any games, Pix," he said, abandoning the blender to open a bottle of wine.

Still grumbling, I handed him two glasses. "You can't just pretend your way into a relationship."

"You're the one who's pretending," he said, setting a glass of wine in front of the bowl of kale. "By the way, the instructions say massage, not murder."

"I'm pretending it's your face."

"You'll get used to the idea sooner or later," he said confidently.

I abandoned the kale. "That's it. Give me your cigarette. I know you didn't smoke yet today, so hand it over."

He looked up from the shredded chicken he was plating. "I quit."

"You quit?" I repeated.

"You don't date smokers," he reminded me.

"You quit your one and only dirty habit for me?"

He slid the plate of chicken across the island next to the lump of cat. She raised her head and sniffed skeptically.

"Why should you find that so hard to believe?" he asked, arching an eyebrow.

"Stop trying to bribe my cat into liking you. She's not going to fall for your pandering. And stop trying to convince me you've had some change of heart. Just days ago, you were dating anything that moved."

The cat flopped back down, pretending like she had no interest in the juicy chicken.

"They were decoys," he said.

"Decoys?" I parroted.

"If Anthony Hugo wanted to come after something that mattered to me, I wasn't going to take any chances that that something would be you."

I snorted even though I was secretly pleased with his answer. "You could have put them in danger."

"Not if I only saw them once. If it was clear there was no attachment."

Lucian Rollins was in my kitchen, cooking dinner for my family and willingly answering questions. This was an opportunity I didn't want to pass up no matter how pissed I was at him.

"So why did you end things with me then?" I asked, taking what I hoped was a casual sip of wine.

He looked away.

"Aha! See?" I slapped the counter triumphantly. "I can't be in a relationship with someone who refuses to be honest with me."

Lucian rounded the corner and boxed me in. "You are in a relationship with me whether you like it or not. And if you want my honesty, it's going to require some patience on your part."

"What are you talking about?" I said as he leaned into me. My hands automatically went to his chest. Everything about him felt so solid, so good, so right. Except I knew better than to trust that feeling.

"You're asking questions that involve answers

I've never put into words before. I don't know how to explain to you why I am the way I am or why I'm trying to change that now. Yet. But I will find a way."

"Do you maybe have a timeline on that?" His mouth was hovering just above mine. I hadn't kissed him in so long. My entire body wanted to be reminded of what his lips felt like against mine. My entire body except for my brain, which was sending me SOS signals.

"I'll let you know after my next therapy appointment," he said huskily.

"I can't tell if you're joking," I whispered.

The doorbell rang, jolting me out of my stupor. Lucian grinned down at me and kissed the tip of my nose. "I'll get it."

I sagged against the counter and watched him leave. Meow Meow did the same. The second he disappeared from the room, she hefted her fluffy bulk onto her feet and gobbled up the bribery chicken like it was laced with catnip.

"Traitor."

"Thank you again for joining us," Lucian said, topping off my mother's glass of wine.

I'd cleared off the dining room table and massaged some kale, but Lucian Freaking Rollins had arranged blossoms off my cherry tree, cued up music, lit candles, and made an epically delicious meal for my family.

Mom looked like she was happy enough to shoot

rainbows out of her eyes *and* her butt. Maeve looked properly suspicious. Meanwhile, Chloe sipped her chocolate milk and stared at Lucian like she was trying to figure out how to weasel a new wardrobe out of the man.

"It's our pleasure. And I have to say it's really nice to see the two of you together," Mom said sunnily from the opposite side of the table. I didn't know if it was a conscious or subconscious decision, but we'd left Dad's place at the head of the table empty.

"We're not together. He just won't take the hint and get out of my house," I said.

"And it does a mother's heart good to know that you're keeping my daughter safe," Mom continued, ignoring me.

"With Sloane being an obvious target, I thought it wouldn't hurt to show whoever's watching that she's protected." Lucian's eyes slid to me. "By me," he added firmly.

Maeve kicked me under the table.

"Ouch!" I reached down and rubbed my shin.

"Is everything all right?" Lucian asked.

My sister looked at me pointedly.

"Yeah. Fine. The cat just stabbed me in the leg," I lied.

Meow Meow chose that moment to wander into the dining room from the kitchen.

"So, Mr. Lucian, you look like you have good taste. Where do you think a tween could get some reasonably priced cashmere?" Chloe asked.

"Maeve, can you help me get more . . . uh . . . kale in the kitchen?" I said.

My sister vaulted out of her chair and grabbed her wineglass. I took the cue and my wineglass and followed her into the kitchen.

"So you two are just playing house now?" Maeve said, whirling around to face me.

With a sharp *shush,* I dragged her through the kitchen and into the family room. "I'm not playing anything. He won't leave!"

"Yeah, okay," she scoffed.

"Have you ever tried to make Lucian Rollins do something he didn't want to do?"

"No, but I know you're probably the only person on the planet who could," she shot back.

"What's that supposed to mean?"

"It means you two have been something to each other since the beginning of time. And if you really wanted him gone, he'd be gone. So maybe you're thinking he deserves a second chance."

"He already had one of those," I reminded her.

"Fine. A last chance."

I cocked my head. "Who are you and what have you done with my sister?"

"What? I'm not saying I think you *should* give him another chance. I'm just suggesting that the two of you bonded over a traumatic incident and now appear to be living together."

I held up my palms in defense. "Listen, I'm too busy to even consider getting into a relationship with him. Hell, I'm too busy to kick him out properly."

"Believe me, I get it. But maybe at a certain point, you start wondering if being busy is keeping you from having a real life," Maeve said.

"Okay, now I'm actually worried about you," I decided. After the attacker cornered me in my Jeep and Mary Louise told me to stop pursuing an appeal, my intentions to confront my sister about her secret relationship and ensuing breakup with Kurt Michaels had fallen to the back burner.

Once again, I'd let circumstances distract me from what was a top priority: family.

"Lucian told me he'd have a family with me." I timed the announcement poorly and ended up with a face full of chardonnay.

"Shit, I'm sorry," Maeve said, gasping and choking.

She handed me a box of tissues from the end table, and I mopped up the spit wine. "I basically had the same reaction, only slightly less damp," I assured her.

Chloe's high-pitched giggles carried to us from the dining room along with the low baritone roll of Lucian's laughter.

Maeve took another hit of wine. "Shit. Well, hold on to something, because I'm going to give you some very not me-like advice."

Theatrically, I gripped a floor lamp.

"At least hear him out," she instructed. "If a guy is offering you everything you've dreamed of, maybe you owe it to yourself to find out if he's serious."

"You really miss him, don't you?" I asked.

"Who?"

"The guy you were secretly seeing but broke up with because you were too busy to let yourself fall in love."

"Little sisters are so annoying," Maeve complained. Another round of laughter echoed out of the dining room. "Mom and Chloe sure seem to like him."

"Yeah, well, they haven't been subjected to his whims yet. Tonight he's charming Lucian. Tomorrow he could morph into sulky, solitary Lucian again."

The doorbell cut off any further conversation.

"I'll get it," I yelled even as I heard the scrape of a chair from the dining room.

Lucian and I got to the front door at the same time. "I told you I don't want you answering the door," he growled.

"And I told you that *I'm* the one who lives here," I shot back.

We wrestled for the handle and managed to open the door, revealing a determined-looking Kurt Michaels holding a huge bouquet of lilies.

"Uh-oh," I said.

"Sloane is busy. With me. And for future reference, she's allergic to lilies," Lucian said.

"He's not here for me, Lucifer," I said, stopping him from slamming the door in Kurt's face.

665

"I'm going big," Kurt said, nodding at me.

"Good luck," I whispered. "She's in the dining room."

He squared his shoulders and walked past us into the house.

"What the hell is going on?" Lucian demanded.

I sneezed twice. "He's in love with my sister."

"Then why in the hell was he dating you?"

I shrugged and sniffled as I closed the front door. "Love makes people do stupid things." I sneezed again, then blew my nose in the chardonnay tissues.

"You're damn right it does," he muttered.

"Shh!" I hissed.

"Mr. Michaels, what are you doing here? Is it because I got four talking warnings during the math test today? I told you I like to verbalize the numbers," Chloe said.

"Mom, please excuse me. I need to deal with something," Maeve announced. Seconds later, she appeared in the hallway, dragging Kurt and the flowers.

I opened the front door and grinned. "Why don't you two talk on the porch? And remember, hear him out. If a guy is offering you everything you've dreamed of, maybe you owe it to yourself to find out if he's serious."

"Bite me, Sloane," my sister snarled.

41

The Butter Knife Defense

Lucian

"Why am I finding this folded up under a tote of Christmas decorations in the second spare room?" Sloane demanded, bursting into the umbrella-wallpapered guest room I'd commandeered as my office, waving her ex's sweatshirt like it was a flag.

I turned away from the command center of screens my IT team had set up for me and gave her my full attention. "Because I was smart enough not to actually throw it out," I said mildly.

It had been five days of us sharing a house, a bed, like an actual couple, and Sloane was showing no signs of cracking. The only reason she let me sleep in bed with her was because she was so exhausted at the end of each day that she fell asleep midargument.

Those long nights were both the sweetest reward and a newfound torture since she'd made it clear that sex was off the table. But I'd gone most of my life without knowing what her body felt like under mine. I could tough it out until I changed her mind.

Sooner or later, she had to acknowledge that those feelings she'd had for me hadn't just vanished into thin air.

Unfortunately, that day was not today. She'd thrown a toasted bagel half at my head in the kitchen this morning.

It didn't matter. I had infinite patience. I would simply wait her out until she accepted the fact that we were together.

"You don't get to have a problem with me keeping an ex-boyfriend's sweatshirt, Lucifer," Sloane said, stomping into the room. She was barefoot and wearing holey jeans and a tight long-sleeve T-shirt the color of raspberries. All that blond hair was piled on her head in a messy knot. She'd gone with the purple-framed glasses today and a bold red lipstick. Every morning, I couldn't wait to see what lipstick she chose. The bolder the color, the feistier her attitude.

I fucking loved being this close to her. At the same time, I hated the sliver of distance she managed to wedge between us. I wanted it all. I wanted all of her, and I wasn't going to back down until she found me worthy enough to have her.

"I don't like the idea of my girlfriend, the woman I'm going to marry and have a family with, cuddling up in an old boyfriend's disgusting sweat rag and reminiscing about the good old days."

"You don't want to marry anyone, and you've made it abundantly clear *with a vasectomy* that you don't want kids. So why don't you save us both a lot of time and *get out of my house!*"

She ended on a shrill screech that had Meow

Meow abandoning the heated cat bed I'd installed in the window.

"And another thing," Sloane said, pointing at the retreating feline. "Stop making friends with my cat!"

"I take it your meeting with the board didn't go well," I guessed.

She'd spent an hour and a half locked in the dining room with the entire library board for an emergency planning session.

Sloane flounced over to the periwinkle wingback chair next to my desk and sat, hugging a throw pillow to her chest. "They actually voted not to open a temporary location and focus on getting the building back in usable shape. Can you believe that?"

"I don't think you want me to answer that," I said diplomatically.

"I can't just sit around doing nothing for three to four *months*."

"Fine. Pack a bag."

"Uh. Excuse me?"

I stood and began loading accessories into a sleek leather bag. "I have business in the District. I'm not leaving you alone here. So you're coming with me."

She took a deep breath and prepared to launch another argument. "I can't just pick up and leave—"

"Your board voted. They're not going to let you proceed with anything right now, and I don't know about you, but I'm sick of staring at the same wallpapered walls. We'll go to DC. I'll set you up with a workspace in my office. You come up with the services that are a priority, and then we'll figure out how to continue offering them in the interim. Then when we come back, you can present the solutions to the board."

Those green eyes behind the lenses of her glasses blinked once in surprise. "You'd do that for me?"

I crossed to her and put my hands on the arms of the chair. "I'd do anything for you."

Those green eyes rolled to the ceiling. "Oh, please," she muttered.

"Especially if it stops you from whining," I added, dropping a lightning-quick kiss on the tip of her nose.

The corners of those red lips curved up.

"We're going out for dinner," I announced as we entered my condo after a long afternoon. "Can you be ready in an hour?"

Sloane had spent most of the day complaining, first about her workstation being in my office, then about me refusing to let her out of my sight in a city where "probably no one" wanted to murder her. But I'd held firm. Until my investigators or Nash's found the person responsible, I wasn't leaving her side.

After an unnecessarily loud coffee catch-up with Lina, Petula, and Holly in my office while I'd stupidly attempted to take care of actual business, she'd finally settled in and gotten to work creating a priority list of services the library could continue to offer even without a physical location. We'd managed to work surprisingly well together in the shared space. Her energy was infectious, and I found myself tackling my own to-do list with more enthusiasm than usual.

"It better be some place with a drive-thru, because I only packed jeans and sweats," she said, toeing off her sneakers and stripping her shirt off to reveal a sexy lace camisole that was working valiantly to contain her impressive breasts.

"What are you doing?" I demanded as my mouth went dry. The need to touch her was driving me mad.

"This is what actual humans do when they come home from work."

I picked up the shirt she'd discarded and folded it. "They strip naked in their foyer?"

"They put on comfy clothes," she instructed, eyeing my suit with what felt like judgment.

"I'm perfectly comfortable as I am. Besides, it would be a waste of time to change now when I'd just have to change back into a suit for dinner."

She shook her head, which sent her hair dancing over her shoulder. "Sad. Just plain sad."

I watched her disappear into the kitchen, wondering what was happening to my face. When I realized it was a smile, I shook it off, loosened my tie, and turned my attention to the mail on the foyer table.

Sloane reappeared, looking suspicious. "Why is there root beer and junk food in here?" She was holding a bottle of soda in one hand and an already open bag of potato chips in the other.

"I just told you we're going to dinner, and you make yourself a snack?"

She crunched into a chip with enthusiasm. "Dinner's a whole hour away. And what if the restaurant's busy or we don't order an appetizer? That's serious hangry territory. I'm doing you a favor."

She was insufferably adorable. Fucking beautiful. And excruciatingly untouchable. My nerves were fraying at an alarming rate now that I had her to myself.

The doorbell rang, and I sprang for it.

"Are you expecting someone?" Sloane asked warily.

"As a matter of fact, I am."

She muttered something that sounded like "It better not be the astrophysicist."

I was still smiling stupidly when I opened the door.

Grace, my head of security, strolled inside, pulling a dress rack behind her. "These just arrived. For the record, I'm a fan of the red," she said.

Sloane looked at me and frowned. "I take it there's no drive-thru?"

"No drive-thru. But my mother will be there."

Her eyes widened. "Interesting. Grace, you have impeccable taste. Got any shoes on this magic rack of fashion?"

"If the food here is too snooty, you're definitely taking me for a burger afterward," Sloane said as I towed her through the restaurant. It was one of those fine dining venues with muted neutrals and small, artfully arranged portions of gourmet specialties.

More than a few sets of eyes followed us to our table, though I was certain the attention was equally divided between my scowling visage and Sloane, who looked like a breathtaking, curvy goddess in the red dress.

I didn't like parading her out in public when there was still a threat at large, but it was the most efficient way to spread the word. Sloane Walton was under my protection.

To ensure her safety, I had a security team on-site and a second car parked in the alley. I was taking no chances.

I spied my mother already seated at the table, looking cool and lovely in an ivory cocktail dress.

"Mother," I said when we arrived. I leaned down to kiss the cheek she offered. "You remember Sloane."

"Hello, Mrs. Rollins," Sloane said, offering up her best we-don't-have-to-acknowledge-the-past smile.

For just a second, I caught a flicker of something on my mother's face. Dismay? Shame? Embarrassment? But it disappeared just as quickly.

"How lovely to see you again," she said, offering Sloane a careful smile.

I didn't get the feeling she meant it. I couldn't blame her. It wasn't often she was invited to dinner with the woman who'd personally witnessed her violent attack and landed her husband in jail.

"Please, call me Kayla," Mom said, recovering her social graces.

I pulled Sloane's chair out for her and scanned the restaurant as she sat. It was the usual crowd of new and old money, each trying to subtly outdo the other. I suddenly wished we had gone for fast food.

"Sloane and I are seeing each other," I said, taking my seat.

Mom's eyes widened. Sloane choked on her water. Loudly.

"It's serious," I continued matter-of-factly as I patted Sloane on the back.

"Actually—" Sloane began, but my less-than-gentle grip on her shoulder gave her second thoughts.

"How wonderful," Mom said, quickly recovering. "Lucian's never brought a girlfriend to meet me before. And it seems I have a surprise of my own." She nodded toward a man headed in our direction.

He moved like a shark in a too-shiny suit. There was a predatory gleam in his eyes as he sized up each table he passed. He carried extra weight around the middle, and his gray hair was distinguished but thinning. A pinkie ring adorned his left hand. I didn't have to see it up close to know tasteful diamonds spelled out the initials AH.

Anthony Hugo sat down next to my mother with a look of triumph.

"We finally meet in person," he said to me as he took my mother's hand with a sense of ownership.

My hands balled into fists under the table.

"Lucian, this is my date, Anthony," Mom announced breathily.

"Oh, shit," Sloane murmured. She snatched up her butter knife.

My hand clamped down on her thigh.

"I've heard a lot about you, Mr. Hugo," I said.

Anthony Hugo, crime boss and bad dresser, was sitting across from me with his arm around my mother.

"Not as much as I've heard about you," he said, showing too many teeth.

"Anthony and I met at a charity auction recently," Mom said, blushing like a boy-crazy teenager. "He asked for my number, and it's been a bit of a whirlwind ever since."

"And who might this lady in red be?" Anthony asked, turning that mean, toothy smile on Sloane.

It was Sloane's turn to clamp her hand on my leg, and it was the only thing that kept me from vaulting out of my chair and murdering Anthony Hugo with a lobster tail in the middle of a crowded restaurant.

"None of your business," Lucian said.

My mother giggled awkwardly. "That's Sloane. My son's date. It seems they're childhood sweethearts."

"I don't think I've had the pleasure yet," Anthony said, letting his gaze linger on Sloane's chest.

"And you never will," she said sunnily.

My mother gave a dismayed gasp. "Lucian, your date is being horrendously rude."

"And your date is a homicidal, drug-dealing criminal," I shot back.

"Come now," Anthony said. His tone was friendly, but he had the eyes of a sociopath. "We can all still be friends. We're practically family. I think you know my son, don't you, Lucian?"

"I don't understand what's happening," Mom said.

"Why don't you and I go to the ladies' room?" Sloane suggested, reaching for my mother.

I tightened my grip on Sloane to hold her in place. There was no way the biggest crime boss in the Washington/Baltimore areas came here alone.

"Nobody is making a fucking move," Anthony said, dropping all vestiges of social niceties. "Not until Rollins and I have had a little talk."

"Can I interest anyone in an appetizer?" The unlucky server chose the wrong break in conversation to return.

"I'll tell you what. Don't fuckin' come back here unless you want to be pickin' your fuckin' teeth off the carpet," Anthony snarled.

Mom gasped and cowered under his grip, a reaction so painfully familiar to both of us.

"There's no need for violence," I said, doing my best to sound bored despite the fact that Sloane and I had each other in a stranglehold beneath the table.

"Oh, but I think there is. You and your fuck buddy feds have had your fun. It's time to put it to rest, or I'll put everyone you care about in the ground. Starting with these two lovely ladies."

"Fuck. You," Sloane said, wielding the butter knife at him.

My mother's lower lip began to tremble, and she looked as if she were trying to melt into the back of her chair.

Anthony smirked. "Little girl's got a big mouth to go with those tits. Heard about the arson. Thought that woulda taught her to mind her own fucking business."

I was halfway out of my chair, but Sloane was faster. She leapt to her feet and wielded the useless knife at him, drawing audible gasps from the tables nearby.

"I'm a librarian, asshole," she said. "Everything is my fucking business. Because of you and your dysfunctional relationship with your son, I almost lost friends. So if you think for one second that I'm going to let you sit there and threaten us, then you're an even bigger idiot than your son."

"Thank you for your input, Sloane," I said, removing the knife from her hand and setting it on the tablecloth. "You've been warned by my woman. Now you'll listen to me. Take your hands off my mother, and get the fuck out of here. If I ever see you anywhere near me or anyone I care about, I'll drop you where you stand."

Anthony stood and smoothed a hand over his jacket. "You might have cash and class, but I got something you never will."

"Questionable fashion sense?" Sloane guessed.

"Killer instinct. I know when someone's outlived their purpose, and I ain't never once been afraid to end their journey. You have forty-eight hours to give me everything the feds have on me along with a few million in reparations, or I'm gonna start ending journeys," he said menacingly.

My mother was crying silently. Sloane was vibrating with rage next to me.

"You have that same forty-eight hours to get your affairs in order, because by the time I'm done with you, there will be no journey left to end. I will dismantle your business, your life, your family, your fucking face. And I'm going to enjoy doing it," I said.

My mother reached for her water glass with shaking hands. Sloane, however, was looking at me like I'd just rescued a litter of puppies from a flood, shirtless.

"Dunno. From where I sit, you're the one at this table with the most to lose," he said with an insipid smirk.

"When you have everything to lose, you'll do anything to keep it," I said darkly.

Anthony snorted, then slapped the table like it was a bongo drum. "Forty-eight hours. Can't fuckin' wait." He turned to my mother. "I'll be seein' you soon, doll." Then his gaze centered on Sloane. "But I think I'll be seein' you first."

"Gee, that'll be tough after I claw your eyes out," she said with a feral smile.

Anthony pointed his fingers at me like a gun and mimed pulling the trigger.

Sloane lunged, knocking over a water glass and sending several sets of utensils to the floor.

I hauled her back into my side. "Easy, Pix."

Together we watched Anthony Hugo slither his way out of the restaurant. With the snap of a finger, four men in suits followed him out.

Sloane breathed a sigh of relief. Meanwhile, my mother was slumped in her chair, one hand covering her face. Everyone in the entire restaurant was staring.

"I didn't know we were getting dinner and a show." The amused comment came from none other than Maureen Fitzgerald, who looked both angelic and sinful in a glittery cocktail dress the color of champagne.

"Wow. Killer dress," Sloane said.

"Now is not the time, Maureen," I told her.

"Oh my God. You're Maureen Fitzgerald?" Sloane whispered.

"The one and only," she said, winking at Sloane. "After witnessing Anthony's little hissy fit, I thought I'd stop by your table and offer my services."

"What services might those be?" I asked, holding

679

Sloane by the wrist and texting my security team with the other hand.

"I might have some information that can help you with your problem." She nodded toward the door Anthony had exited.

"Not here," I said.

"Of course not. Tonight. Your place."

"Be careful," I cautioned.

"I'm a woman. I'm always careful." Her gaze skipped my mother and landed on Sloane. Her smile warmed. "It looks as though Lucian's tastes have significantly improved."

"Your skin is flawless," Sloane whispered.

I rolled my eyes. But Maureen patted one cheek with feminine pride. "Thank you. She's a keeper, Lucian. Try not to ruin it."

I grunted and nodded at Grace when she entered the restaurant. "Let's go."

Grace led us through the kitchen to a service elevator in the back. The staff didn't even blink as we made our way past prep stations and fiery grills.

My mother sagged against the elevator wall when the doors closed.

"I don't understand what happened," she said, bringing her hands to her cheeks. "All I know is I was humiliated."

"I apologize for embarrassing you by preventing you from being the pawn of a madman. Anthony Hugo is a criminal who would have no qualms about making you disappear just to get to me."

"It's always about you. Every man who shows any interest in me is just trying to get something out of you," Mom whispered bitterly.

"That man is a thug. He's had people killed for far less than what I'm doing. And you think that's all right because he treats you like some kind of trophy?"

"Your father wanted to hide me away. He never wanted anyone to acknowledge that I existed."

"This isn't about the past. This is about your safety right now."

She fluttered her delicate, birdlike hands in front of her face. "I can't discuss this with you right now."

"We'll discuss this now. Do not answer his calls. Do not go anywhere with him. If you see him anywhere, leave immediately. Grace, I need you to—"

"Beef up the security detail on your mom. Got it," she said grimly.

"And now you're telling me where to be and who to see. Controlling everything. What I do, where I go, what I spend. You're just like him," Mom whimpered.

"Right now, I don't give a fuck, Mother." I saw the flash of pain and the blur of movement. The crack of her hand against my face rang out.

Grace made a move, but Sloane got there first and shoved her way between us. "Excuse me, *Kayla!*" Fury was a fire that lit her up from the inside. She put her finger in my mother's pale, dignified face.

681

"You do not ever, *ever* lay a hand on him like that again. After everything that you two have been through, you hit your son for protecting you from a certifiable sociopath? That's insane."

"That's enough, Sloane," I said, resting a hand on her shoulder.

She was vibrating against me.

"It's not nearly enough. You have the worst taste in men. Anthony Hugo is a walking red flag, and you *invited him to dinner*. Oh, and if you want to spend your money on whatever you want, then get a fucking job, lady. You only get to be a victim for so long before you have to evolve into a survivor," Sloane continued.

"You don't understand what it's like," Mom said with a tearful whisper.

"I wanted to be nice to you, to have empathy for poor, victimized Kayla. But that was two decades ago. You've had twenty-plus years to grow up. Yet here you are, all those years later, still perfectly comfortable playing the victim. Still accepting your son's checks because you're too fragile to stand on your own two feet. He doesn't owe you, lady. *You* owe *him*. For every time he stepped between you and the man you chose over him. For every time you made him responsible for your choices. I'm trying not to blame you for that, but you're making it really fucking hard."

Sloane was shouting now. My head of security was nodding in agreement.

"You are not to have any contact with Lucian

until you can apologize for every shitty thing you've done to him," Sloane announced.

The elevator doors opened into a parking garage. Both my cars were waiting, engines running, and half a dozen of my security team were stationed outside.

My mother gasped and hurried out of the elevator.

"Enough," I said quietly.

But Sloane wasn't finished. "And another thing. Go to therapy!" she called after her.

I grabbed Sloane around the waist. "Take my mother home," I ordered Grace, nodding at the first SUV.

I half carried Sloane to the second one and deposited her in the back seat before sliding in next to her. The door slammed shut, casting us into darkness.

"Hey! You promised me din—"

I cut off her accusation by crushing my mouth to hers.

42

A Volcano of Lust

Sloane

We barely made it home.

I knew Lucian had important, vital things to take care of. Like destroying a crime boss who had just threatened our lives. I trusted him to handle it, I realized.

I didn't trust the man not to crush my heart into a pancake, but I trusted him with my life.

All that was very important. But there was one thing that trumped them all. It had been weeks since we'd been together—orgasmically—and crime boss or no crime boss, I was a volcano of lust.

"That was so fucking hot," I murmured against his mouth as he carried me over the threshold and kicked the door shut behind us. My legs were locked around his waist, my hands fisting in his hair, holding him to me.

I knew what had gotten into me, but I wasn't sure why Lucian had turned ravenous beast the second he'd pushed me into the back seat after I'd gone all "shrew" on his mother. At the moment, I didn't particularly care.

"What was?" he demanded, yanking the straps of my dress down.

"You being all 'ho-hum, I'm so bored by your pathetic threats,'" I said, kissing and biting my way down his neck.

He growled, and the vibrations rippled through my nipples that were plastered against him. "You have two seconds to help me get you out of this dress, or I'm going to destroy it."

I didn't move fast enough for his liking and found myself perched on the cold marble of the entryway table. The man had the top of my dress wrestled to my waist in seconds with only one or two horrendous ripping noises.

"This doesn't mean anything," I reminded him over the hammering of my heart.

"You're right. It means everything," he countered.

"Agree to disagree," I decided. It wasn't an argument worth having right this second.

He removed my strapless bra deftly with one hand and let out another low growl before diving for me face-first.

I let out a strangled laugh. "Why are you so obsessed with my boobs?"

"For the same reason you're obsessed with my dick. Because they're fucking perfect," he said as his mouth found its way to the first sensitive peak.

Well, he wasn't the only one who was going to play. It felt too good, being spread so wide in front of him, his mouth working its magic on my sensitive peak.

I reached between us and found his erection

straining beneath the fabric of his pants. I gripped him hard.

"Goddammit," he hissed against me.

A shudder ran through me. I could feel the pulls of his mouth echo inside me.

Without breaking contact with my breast, Lucian reached between my legs and dragged the sheer pink crotch of my underwear to the side. "Need to feel you."

I was good with that. So good with it I barely flailed at all when he gripped me by the hips and scooted me to the very edge of the table.

"Hold still, Pix," he ordered, batting my hand away from his crotch. I was about to argue until I heard the sound of his zipper.

"Oh God," I groaned as he angled the plush head of his penis against my clitoris, parting the lips of my sex.

Lucian released my sensitized nipple with a pop. The cool air made the wet tip even more pronounced.

"Don't stop working my cock, baby," he ordered before moving to my other nipple.

I obliged and gripped the velvet-smooth shaft.

He groaned and whispered, "Such a good girl," against my breast.

I let out a pathetic, gasping moan as he laved my ignored nipple with his magical tongue. I was so wet, and every suck from his mouth, every nudge from the head of his cock made my insides spasm emptily.

My grip on him had to be painful, but the noises he made at my breast were ones of ecstasy. I grabbed the back of his head with my free hand and held him against me. My breasts felt heavy and swollen from his attention.

Without warning, he reached between us and speared two fingers into my opening. We moaned together as if sharing the pleasure.

His fingers worked me mercilessly as I rode his hand and stroked his cock with borderline violence.

It felt like magic. We were magic.

He braced a hand under my rear end, angling me until my back was on the table. And then I felt the probing finger. First it dipped between my legs where I had turned to Aquawoman. Then it slid higher, dancing up the cleft between my cheeks. It stopped and probed gently at the puckered entrance.

He pulled back from my breast, leaving my nipple damp and distended. There was a question in his eyes. He was asking for permission.

I didn't trust my words. So I answered him the best way I could, by shifting my hips and pushing back against that finger.

With a possessive growl, Lucian speared one finger into my rear end just as his other fingers curled inside my sex. His cock released a surge of precum onto my fingers. He liked possessing my body, craved it even.

I was hanging on by one teeny, tiny, tensile

thread. I was spread open and filled up. My entire body was taut with the need to orgasm. And when his mouth found my breast once again, when he gave one, deep suck, I came apart.

The orgasm slammed into me, wrecking me. My inner walls clamped down on his fingers as he worked them inside me.

I kept working his cock with my hand, kept riding his fingers, kept pressing back against that single digit that filled me in a brand-new way.

"That's my girl," he muttered. "You're so fucking beautiful when you come."

I clung to his cock like it was an anchor in the storm while my orgasm ravaged us both.

"Let me come on you," he demanded roughly.

But I had other ideas.

I released his erection and pushed against his chest. He backed off immediately. "Tell me what you need," he said, his voice husky.

I slipped off the edge of the table and sank to my knees in front of him.

"This," I said, reaching out to encircle the root of his shaft with my hand. "Please."

Fire blazed to life in those gray eyes when he realized what I was asking for.

His cock surged in my hand, wanting what I was asking for. Needing it.

"I trust you to take care of Hugo. I want you to trust me to take care of you," I told him.

Lucian swallowed hard, his cheeks hollowing above the groomed edge of his beard. Then he nodded. My heart climbed into my throat. It was acquiescence enough. He was going to let me give him this.

I leaned forward and danced my tongue over him from root to tip. His convulsive shudder and whispered oath gave me the confidence of an oral sex superhero.

I parted my lips and, with no warning, took him to the back of my throat.

Lucian's fist came down on the tabletop behind me. "Christ!" he barked as I worked him with mouth and fist. I took as much of him as I could, wanting to systematically seduce him, to reduce him to the need to come.

I cupped his velvety sack and squeezed.

A finger gently slid over my cheek. I looked up at him from my knees. He was a king, a titan, but I was in control. Then that finger was gone and he was shoving his hand roughly into my hair. "Dammit, Sloane. You're the only one," he muttered.

I let him guide my head with his hand, setting a new rougher, faster pace. The last vestiges of his control had vanished. I had done that to him.

He said it again and again as he filled my mouth over and over again. "You're the only one."

My fingers tightened on his heavy sack, and Lucian froze and held at the back of my throat. There was a sudden hot burst of precum.

"Fuck. Fuck. Fuck," he said. Dragging my mouth off his cock, he tackled me to the cold tile. "Say yes," he said, notching the head of his erection between my legs with jerky movements.

"Yes!"

He held me in place with one hand on my shoulder and, with one surge, entered me. "Take me. All of me," he ordered, his beard abrading my neck.

I was dizzyingly full. It felt so good. It was too much and yet somehow exactly right. There was nothing between us. I was fully possessed by him.

It was raw, real, and God help me, I wanted more. And Lucian gave it to me. When he released the first hot rope of come inside me, I obediently followed him, careening over the edge. I had no other choice.

"God. Yes, Sloane. My Sloane." He groaned as he came and came inside me, detonating a release like no other.

• • •

Maeve: So Party Crasher Kurt and I talked and we're going to try again.

Me: Hallelujah! I can't wait to tell your kids about how Auntie Sloane made out with Daddy Kurt once when Mommy Maeve was being a dumbass.

Maeve: Maybe it's best to leave that out of the conversation.

Me: Aha! You didn't automatically dismiss the idea of having kids with Kurt! I knew you LIKED him liked him!

Maeve: Your little sister colors are showing.

Me: I can't help it. Your happiness makes me happy. Also, I just had a bunch of orgasms . . . so . . .

Maeve: Same, girl. Same.

Me: High five.

43

The Takedown

Lucian

N o one leaves here until we have a game plan," I announced.

Sloane sat contentedly in my home office, dressed in pajamas, eating the burger and fries I'd had delivered. She'd tamed her "sex hair" into a long, loose braid that she wore draped over one shoulder. With her legs tossed over the arm of the chair and her bare feet wiggling, she was the picture of relaxed.

Meanwhile, behind my desk, I was a roiling cauldron of rage.

The team I'd assembled wasn't helping my mood.

"This'll be fun," Nolan said, plowing into a platter of chicken fingers.

"Speak for yourself," Lina complained. "My fiancé had just invited me to join him in the shower when I got the summons."

"So what kind of dirt are we looking for?" Nallana the private investigator demanded, shoveling two pieces of pizza onto her plate. She was dressed in a cocktail dress and leather jacket. I realized I had no idea if this was her off-the-clock look or another undercover getup.

"Yeah. It would help to know what we're looking for," the only member of the cybersecurity team who'd bothered answering her phone asked around the mouthful of Twizzlers she'd just shoved into her face. She had platinum hair worn long on top and shaved on the sides. Her name was something like Pasture or Great Plains.

"Anything that will force the FBI to move on Hugo now. Not a month from now or a week from now or even forty-eight hours from now. I want him in custody by noon tomorrow."

Nallana let out a low whistle. "That's a tall order. Prairie's right. We need some kind of direction."

Prairie. So close.

"Your 'direction' is to do whatever it takes to get me something we can use. I don't care if you get arrested in the process. Find me something," I said on a near snarl.

The doorbell rang.

"Want me to get that?" Sloane asked tentatively.

I shook my head. "Grace will get it."

I wasn't letting Sloane out of my sight until Anthony Hugo and his entire organization were nothing but rubble. And then I was going to force her down the aisle. The woman had defended me not just to a crime boss who threatened our lives but to my own mother. And when this was all over, I was going to show her exactly what that had meant to me.

The door to my office opened, and in walked Maureen Fitzgerald, still in her dress from earlier.

693

"Well, this looks like an interesting party," she observed.

"Is that . . ." Prairie began.

"The most successful, notorious madam in Washington, DC?" Lina filled in. "Yep. I like your shoes."

"Thank you," Maureen said with a feline smile. "Here's a little party favor for your team." She dropped a two-inch-thick folder on top of the pizza box. Nolan reached for it, but Maureen laid a manicured hand on top of the folder. "I trust I can count on your discretion."

"Oh yes, ma'am. Absolutely nothing but discrete around here," Nolan promised.

"Good," she said, removing her hand and sliding her arms free of her wool coat. "Are there any chicken fingers left?"

"So we've got three more shell corporations nailed down thanks to Maureen's girls' intel," Nolan summarized, stifling a yawn. "First two have about $2 million apiece scattered in offshore accounts. Prairie is digging into the third now."

"Keep digging." A few million dollars wasn't enough to have the FBI knocking on Hugo's door in the morning.

Lina joined us. "Update time?"

"What have you got?" I asked her.

"Security has informed everyone the offices are closed for the next two days. Petula is rescheduling all in-person meetings and shifting what she can to virtual. Grace beefed up security everywhere, including your mother's and Sloane's mom's. Nash and the Knockemout PD are on high alert and keeping an eye on things back home. Nallana called. She's squeezing a few street-level sources, looking for intel. Rumor has it he's got a big shipment due in from South America by the weekend."

"That's too far out," I reminded her.

"Maybe Hugo was just yanking your chain about the forty-eight hours?" Nolan suggested, yawning again.

"Is this crisis interrupting your beauty sleep?" I asked dryly.

"A, it's four in the fucking morning. And B, the wife got me up for a 6:00 a.m. yoga class today . . . Yesterday. Not all of us run on no sleep and the tears of frightened children," he pointed out.

"You got up before dawn because your wife asked you to. Hugo said I had forty-eight hours to deliver everything the feds had on him or he'd start with Sloane."

"Start with as in . . ." Lina trailed off, and we all turned to look at the little librarian who was sitting on the floor frowning over fanned-out paperwork.

"I'm not letting that happen," I said.

"Does Blondie believe you're in it for the long haul yet?" Nolan asked as Sloane shoved her glasses up her nose.

"Not yet. But if it takes killing a man in cold blood to prove it, I'll do it."

"Let's keep that as option B," Lina said. "I hear they're not as lenient with conjugal visits anymore, and judging from Sloane's sex hair, you two have a lot of ground to make up."

I left them and crossed the room to her.

She looked up at me as I crouched down. "You have that line between your eyebrows you get when you're concentrating," I observed, running my finger over the spot in question. "You should get some sleep."

"And miss all the fun?"

"When this is over, I'm taking you to a private island where we can drink piña coladas naked on a beach so I can teach you what fun is," I decided.

Sloane grinned at me. "Since when is Lucian Rollins an expert on fun?"

"Since he almost came in your mouth when you were on your knees."

"Very flattering. But I need you to put away your party hat for a second and get out your broody-master-of-the-business-and-political-universe beret for a second, Lucifer."

"What do you need?"

She wet her lips and glanced down at the papers in front of her. "Something Hugo said tonight has been bothering me."

"Everything the asshole said should have bothered you."

She shook her head. "The thing about the fire. About me not learning my lesson from the arson. At first I thought it was just him letting us know he'd been watching me. But I started thinking what if he was connected somehow?"

I sat next to her and helped myself to a swig of her lukewarm root beer. "Connected in what way?"

"We think the fire was retaliation for me working on Mary Louise's case, right? I was threatened by Cinnamon Man, who specifically mentioned her name on the same day Mary Louise was attacked. Mary Louise dropped it, but I kept pushing. You got her moved to a new facility where she'd be safer and got Allen protection. I kept digging. So someone decided to let us know they weren't happy by setting fire to the library while I was in it."

Her recap of the situation was raising my already dangerously high blood pressure. "What's the connection? Why would a sociopath crime boss in DC care about a wrongfully convicted female prisoner?"

Sloane bit her lip. "What if it's the prison?" She handed me a sheet of paper. "Fraus Correctional Center is a private prison owned by a corporation called Civic Group, which is owned by two other corporations. Which then made me think about all your sneaky underhandedness hiding grants and donations in entities named after cherry trees. And while I was thinking about your sneakiness, this one caught my eye." She tapped the page above the words Rex Management. "Rex is Latin for king," she explained.

"Which Hugo fancies himself to be," I mused, following her drift.

"Exactly," Sloane said, beaming at me. "So I did a search for other private prisons in Virginia, Maryland, and North Carolina and found three more facilities owned by Civic Group. All rundown. All with overcrowding and understaffing complaints. But all providing profits to Civic Group and its owners. I can't tell what kind of profit we're talking, but each place has a contract with the government providing them money for each inmate housed. The more people in the facility, the higher the profits."

"When I threatened to have Duncan Hugo moved to another facility, he panicked," I recalled, scanning Sloane's research. "He said he wouldn't be safe."

"Was it one of these three?" she asked, rising to her knees in excitement.

I pointed to Lucrum. "That's the one."

Sloane threw her arms around my neck. "I knew it! I did good, didn't I? Two-time convicted felon Anthony Freaking Hugo is part owner of four private correctional facilities. That's got to be seriously illegal."

"Not to mention the fact that he can have anyone in one of those prisons eliminated if necessary," I pointed out.

Sloane pulled back, looking horrified. "Holy shit."

"This is good, Pix. Really good," I said, giving her a squeeze.

She cupped my face in her hands. "Take him down, big guy."

I gave her a hard kiss on the mouth and deposited her on top of her research. "Pasture!" I snapped at the hacker.

She looked up and pointed at herself. "Me?"

Sloane leaned in. "I think you mean Prairie."

"Right. Prairie. That's what I said. Stop what you're doing, and give me everything you can on Rex Management and Civic Group."

I gave Sloane's shoulder a squeeze as I dialed Special Agent Idler.

"It's 4:00 a.m. This better be fucking good," she rasped.

"How soon can you put a team together to drag Hugo into the nearest cell?"

I hadn't slept or showered in thirty-six hours, but Anthony Hugo looked worse than I did, I thought smugly as I took the chair across from him.

Gone were the slick suit and the diamond pinkie ring, and in their place, he wore a baggy orange jumpsuit that only made him look more sallow.

"You come here to gloat?" he demanded as the guard cuffed him to the table with a satisfying snap. "Because I'll be out of here within a day. They can't keep me."

"Ah, but they can," I said, leaning back on the metal chair. "I just came from Special Agent Idler's office."

"That bitch will be the first to go." He sneered

cagily. "Well, maybe the second after your little blond girlfriend."

"Here's the thing about that, Anthony. These are just the beginning of your charges. The other officers in your little Rex Management have all been arrested. Coincidentally, they're also most of your inner circle. And they're singing like their lives depend on it. The feds have already talked to a dozen of your crew serving sentences in your facilities, and they've confessed to an astonishing number of crimes, including assaults and murder. Most of them weren't afraid of pointing the finger at who gave the orders now that you're behind bars, especially after they were promised deals and sentence reductions."

Anthony went even paler.

"You listen to me, you son of a fucking bitch—"

"No," I said stonily. "It's your turn to listen. In less than two days, I've dismantled every piece of your business. Everything you worked for your entire life. It's all gone. Your assets are frozen. Your men are sitting in interrogation rooms around the city. Including the ones you had dump Felix Metzer in the Potomac. You have nothing left. Do you know why that is?"

"Fuck you."

"Wrong answer. I took everything from you because you tried to take from me. You threatened my family. No one walks away from that."

"I'll get to you. And when I do, I'll finish the job I started with that list your police chief friend was on. I'll take out every single one of the people you love, and then I'll make you bleed."

I smirked. "Good luck with that."

"You think seein' your friend pumped full of lead and that library fire were bad? I'm just getting started. I'll come for you personally. I got guys watching you and that FBI bitch. One call from me and you're both dead like Metzer. No one crosses me."

I stood up and buttoned my suit jacket. "I wouldn't be so sure of that. That FBI bitch had your 'guys' arrested yesterday. Third strike for quite a few of them, which made them surprisingly cooperative. Now, if you'll excuse me, I have someplace I need to be."

I strolled out of the room and left his snarled threats behind me.

"Tell me everything!" Sloane pounced the second I opened my front door. "Does he know he's cooked? Did he threaten you? Did you laugh in his face? Is there surveillance footage of him freaking out that I could watch?"

She was wearing pajama pants with palm fronds on them and a tight black tank top. Her hair was damp from a shower, and her eyes were sparkling.

Something warm and bright expanded in my chest. It felt like I'd swallowed the sun.

I gripped her wrist, bent at the waist, and tossed her neatly over my shoulder.

"You two are free to go," I said to Lina and

Grace, who had been on Sloane guard duty for the last twenty-four hours.

"Woo-hoo!" Grace said.

"Have fun, kids," Lina called as I carried Sloane down the hall to the bedroom.

I tossed her on the bed, making her laugh. "You're awfully frisky for a man who hasn't slept in two days."

"Ruining the life of a bad guy does that to me," I teased, stripping off my jacket and tie.

"My hero."

The words from her did strange things to my insides. And I knew I'd treasure them just like every "attaboy" I'd earned from her father.

Sloane crawled higher up the bed and propped herself on the new mound of pillows I'd had delivered. She patted the spot next to her. "Come tell me all about it, big guy, and then we'll get naked and do naughty things to each other."

I made it a quarter of my way through my retelling of Hugo's arrest before I passed out with Sloane in my arms and proceeded to sleep the sleep of a hero for the next ten hours.

44

It's Not about Drawer Space

Sloane

Stef: Flowers and champagne are too cliché, right?

Me: Too cliché for what?

Stef: For asking a man to move in with me.

Me: I'm honored that you'd come to me for your grand gesture advice.

Stef: Naomi is too much of a romantic, and Lina wouldn't know romance if it bit her in her delectable ass. So I'm asking you. Advise me already. Too much or not enough?

Me: It depends on the rest of the setup. Is this an intimate-conversation-over-wine-and-homemade-pasta-or-whatever-your-talented-gay-hands-make thing? Or is this an announcement-with-fireworks-and-a-marching-band-in-front-of-the-entire-town thing?

Stef: I see I've come to the wrong person. I should have asked a straight dude.

Me: Have you thought about tattooing "Will you move in with me?" on your ass?

703

Or turning a kid's birthday/petting zoo into a surprise proposal?

Stef: I need to go back to the drawing board. Everything has to be perfect, meticulously planned. It's got to be romantic and on-brand. A story we'll tell our kids. My God. What if he doesn't want kids? Do I want kids?

Me: You're spiraling. Go eat some chocolate.

Aha! There you are," I said, triumphantly digging the bra I'd been looking for out of my overnight bag. I shoved the rest of the contents back inside and zipped it shut.

The very naked, very sinful-looking Lucian cast a baleful look in my direction from his position on the bed.

"What? You said we were going out for dinner. I can't go braless in public. These babies unleashed have been known to cause stampedes," I said over my shoulder as I headed into the man's massive spa-like bathroom. Hexagonal charcoal tiles were warm and toasty under my bare feet. The double vanity had enough space between the high-end onyx sinks to play a round of shuffleboard. And the shower. Oh, the shower.

It was the main reason I hadn't yet demanded that Lucian take me home to Knockemout.

Anthony Hugo had been in custody for four days. The danger was officially over. But I was still here, enjoying four days of dinners out and walks under the cherry blossoms. Four days of working out of the same office together, sharing the same bed. Four days of having an astronomical amount of sex with Lucian Rollins.

I unpacked my toiletries from the bag I kept hanging on the linen closet door and finagled the settings on the shower's touch screen.

"I can program your preferences into the system," Lucian offered from behind me.

I eyed him as he prowled into the bathroom naked. "Nah. I like pushing buttons," I said as I took in the obscenely fine view. He looked like a moving statue. A marble ode to perfection come to life.

I stepped into the tiled shower and let the rain head faucet pelt me from above. I groaned. "Ugh. This makes me want to renovate my bathroom."

Lucian joined me, his hands immediately finding the curves of my hips.

We showered in silence, luxuriating in the hot water and each other's bodies. But I could feel a tension in him that hadn't been there before.

"What's wrong? Is there a problem with the Hugo case?" I asked as Lucian watched me pensively in the mirror while I towel dried my shampoo and conditioner bottles before slipping them back in the bag.

"My problem is you," he said, turning to face me.

"Me? Now what did I do?" I demanded, trying

not to be dazzled by the water droplets sprinkled across his chest.

"I gave you drawers and closet space. I gave you vanity space," he announced, yanking open one of the empty drawers next to the sink he'd designated as mine. "I made room for you in my shower, *in my home.*"

"And I told you I don't need any of that."

He stuck a finger in my face. "That *is* my problem. How are we going to share a life together when you won't even unpack your shit, Sloane?"

"Seriously?" I scoffed. "You're mad because I'm not taking up enough of your storage?"

"You won't unpack here. You didn't make space for me in your place. I had to bring in a closet company just to make room for myself. You're not committing to us."

"Lucian, we haven't even talked about being an 'us' beyond you stubbornly announcing that we were a couple."

His scowl darkened. "You want to talk? Fine. We'll talk."

"You could have at least let me dry my hair," I grumbled as Lucian stabbed the bell on a swanky three-story brick home on a tree-lined street in Georgetown. Every vehicle at the curb looked as though it cost somewhere in the six-figure range.

The door opened, and a white-bearded, bespec-

706

tacled man peered out at us. "You're early," he announced. He wore a white apron over a black, orange, and neon yellow speckled cardigan.

"Emry, meet Sloane. Sloane, Emry," Lucian said as he towed me across the threshold and toward a stately study.

"Sorry about Lucifer. I think he's hangry," I explained over my shoulder.

"Well, this should be fun," Emry announced, rubbing his palms together and following us inside.

It was the office of a man with means, intellect, and great taste, I decided, scanning the titles on the dark mahogany bookshelves.

"Work your therapy magic and fix her," Lucian announced, taking a stance near the fireplace.

"I thought we were going to dinner at your friend's?" I pointed out.

"We are friends. He forgets that from time to time," Emry added, crossing to a cabinet and producing a bottle of wine. He gestured toward one of two leather armchairs in front of the bookshelves. I sat.

"I don't need your friendly advice. I need a therapist to talk some sense into this woman," Lucian announced, crossing his arms and glaring at me.

I glared back. "Seriously?"

"This is highly unusual. Even for you," Emry said to Lucian.

"Don't look at me," I said with a shrug. "One second, I'm enjoying the shower of the gods, and the next, he's yelling about drawer space and closet organizers."

Lucian pushed away from the fireplace and began to pace. "Do you see what I have to deal with?"

Emry looked amused. "I take it this is not about drawer space? Though if it is, I'm happy to call Sacha. She's the expert in home organization. You should see her pantry."

"She won't commit," Lucian announced, then winced. "Sloane, not Sacha. But you should burn that sweater before Sacha sees it."

"I think it's a lovely sweater," I insisted.

"I'm trying to integrate our lives both here and in Knockemout, and Sloane is refusing to participate. The woman repacks her toiletries after every shower!" Lucian bellowed.

Emry looked as if he were trying very hard not to laugh as he poured three glasses of wine. "I see."

I got out of my chair and stalked toward Lucian, interrupting his pacing. "And *I* told *you,* you don't just get to order me into a relationship. A couple of drawers are not going to make me feel secure enough to even entertain the idea of dating you."

"We're not dating," Lucian said. "We're living together. We're having sex. We're *getting married.*"

"If that's your proposal, it needs work," I shot back.

I heard a crunching sound and found Emry settled in the chair I'd vacated, snacking on pistachios and watching us gleefully.

"Why can't you just accept that I mean what I say?" Lucian demanded. He shoved both hands through his hair. His movements were jerky and frenetic, so unlike his usual animallike grace.

"Because past experience dictates I should run screaming into the night! You've cut me out of your life twice now—once for two decades—and you just expect me to forget about that? To trust you?" I was shouting now too. I definitely wasn't winning any dinner guest of the year awards.

"Tell me what you want, and I'll give it to you," Lucian said, frustration bleeding into his tone.

"I want everything you're promising, but I don't believe you're going to deliver! Happy now?"

Silence descended between us as we stared at each other. Emry cleared his throat and brushed the pistachio crumbs from his hands. "It sounds as if you two have never really had the opportunity to deal with the issues that kept you apart in the first place."

"I always thought that I needed to forgive you," Lucian said suddenly. He took a breath and stared down at me, his gray eyes stormy. "You broke my trust. You deliberately disobeyed me, and because of you, I went to jail. Because of you, my mother was left completely vulnerable to him. I missed my eighteenth birthday, my high school graduation. Because of you, my past cemented my future."

I winced as the truth he'd kept bottled up for all these years hit its target. It was a wound that had never fully healed in either of us.

"But . . ." Emry prompted, reaching for another handful of pistachios.

"But you put yourself between my mother and father to protect her, to protect me. You did it again this week. Trying to stand between me and a madman threatening us both and then once more with own my mother," he rasped.

"If you're pissed off about that, you're wasting your time, because I'm not apologizing. Anthony Hugo is a dickless slug, and your mother doesn't get to raise a hand to you *ever*," I told him, my voice shaking with emotion.

He reached out and took my wrists, his thumb sliding over the old scar. "I don't want an apology. I don't need one. I never did. You are the only person in the world to ever stand up for me like that."

I opened my mouth, but he shook his head.

"Yes, Knox and Nash would if given the chance. But I've never asked. I never had to ask you either. You simply did it. Because that's the kind of person you are. Stupidly brave. Dangerously headstrong."

"Your proposals and your compliments really suck," I said.

But he didn't smile. Instead he squeezed my wrists again. "Broken men break women, Sloane."

I went still. "Lucian," I whispered.

"My father broke my mother to the point that even years later, she's still a victim," he continued. "She might never be whole or healthy because of him. I didn't want to chance that with you. I didn't

710

want you anywhere near me where men like my father or Anthony Hugo could hurt you to hurt me."

I gripped his forearms, unsure of what to say. I felt dizzy and off-kilter, as if his words were enough to shake the very foundations I'd built my life on.

"I can still hear the snap of your bones in my head," he confessed. "I wasn't even there, but it still echoes. It's the first thing I hear when I wake up in the morning. It's what I hear every time you walk out of a room and I want to go after you. It's been my reminder to leave you alone. He could have killed you, and I couldn't protect you because I was behind bars. I couldn't protect her. I couldn't protect you."

My eyes welled with tears. I reached up and cupped his face in my hands. His beard was rough against my palms. "Lucian, honey. It was never your job to protect your mom. It was never your job to keep the world safe from your dad."

"For the record, that's what I've been saying for years," Emry cut in.

"Go burn a casserole," Lucian said without any heat to his words.

Emry chuckled.

"I broke your trust. I'll admit that," I said. "I was young and impulsive, and I couldn't stand the thought of him hurting you. You hear my wrist breaking in your head? I hear him screaming and hitting you that night. It still haunts me."

Lucian closed his eyes. "Sloane—"

"No. Now it's my turn. I was scared. Too scared to go outside and stop him. And too afraid he'd hurt my dad if I told him. Maybe if I had, things would have been different. But we'll never know because I called 911 just like you asked me not to. And I watched Wylie Ogden march you out in handcuffs just like you knew he would. And I will never, ever get over that. If I had made a different decision that day, you wouldn't know what the inside of a cell looks like."

"I would have. Eventually. Because there was only one way he was going to stop."

"That's why I called. Because you wouldn't have recovered from that. You would have spent your life thinking you were just like him. Which, by the way, means you're nothing like him."

He drew in a shaky breath, his eyes burning into mine.

"But thinking about all the what-ifs is a waste of what we both know is precious time," I continued. "I'm so sorry you've spent your life believing that you're tainted. That you don't deserve happiness. That breaks my heart, Lucian, because you're the most stupidly generous person I've ever met. You see a need to be filled, and you quietly go about filling it. You don't require an audience or accolades. You've spent your life righting wrongs at the highest level. And that's heroic. *You're* heroic."

"I don't see it that way." His words were quiet,

but his hands had moved to my hips and were holding me gently.

"I know. And I'm so sorry you've been battling with that by yourself. You aren't to blame for a single thing your father ever did."

"According to him, I was to blame for everything. My room wasn't clean enough. My grades weren't good enough. I didn't call him sir loud enough. Everything I did was wrong."

My heart wasn't just cracking open now. It was shattering into a million shards.

I held on tighter to him. "You did nothing wrong, Lucian. That was all on him. He was a broken man who tried to break you, but he failed. On his best day, he would never be able to hold a candle to you. I'm so proud of the boy you were, the man you became. You took back your family name, and made it mean something good. You don't have him in you. I see more of my father than yours in you."

"I have a temper. But I'm working on it. I've been working on it." He gestured to Emry, who was still devouring pistachios like a chipmunk.

I snorted indelicately. "Who doesn't have a temper? It's what we choose to do with it that matters. Your self-control is annoyingly impressive. And that's coming from someone who dedicated most of her adult life to trying to drive you nuts."

Lucian shook his head. "All this time, I thought I needed to forgive you for what you did."

713

"How about now?" I prompted.

"And just like it wasn't your fight to win, it was never your apology to make."

"I feel like you're gearing up to apologize to me. Are you hangry or dehydrated?" I asked.

He traced his knuckles over my cheek. "You don't need to apologize to me, Pix. Because I don't need to forgive you."

"Do you want, like, a Snickers or something?"

He shook his head. "I'm sorry, Sloane. Sorry for blaming you. Sorry for putting you in the position where you felt you had no choice. Sorry for never communicating what I really wanted or needed until now."

"What do you need now?" I asked breathily.

"You. Only you. Always you."

Now I was downright terrified.

He was closing the distance between us. His breath was hot against my face, and I was already anticipating the feel of his lips on mine.

"I think you've both done some excellent work here tonight," Emry said, wrecking the moment like a human record scratch. "I'd like to suggest that you take some time to get to know each other on a deeper, more intimate level before you make any decisions."

"Time?" Lucian repeated, like the word tasted bitter on his tongue.

"There's a lot of undoing to be done. This is real life. It's not like the movies where one grand gesture will convince Sloane that you aren't going to close down and abandon her again," Emry explained.

I'd seen that look before on Lucian's handsome face. A challenge had been laid, and he was compelled to meet it.

"Now, who's ready for some wine?" Emry asked.

"Me," I said with more than a hint of desperation.

• • •

Naomi: How are things with Lucian?

Lina: Has he let you out of his bedroom/ sight yet?

Me: Things are . . . complicated. Well, not in the bedroom, just everywhere else. He says he's committed to this. That he's not going to change his mind. He's saying all the right stuff. Everything I've spent years wishing he'd say. But I still feel like I'd be an addled idiot to just happily believe he's going to stick around and make a family with me.

Lina: What if he buys you a castle or something as a symbol of your happily ever after?

Me: I wouldn't hate that.

Naomi: Or maybe his grand gesture will be listening to the therapist and proving himself to you over time?

Me: Great. We'll play "getting to know you" while my eggs shrivel into raisins. I just don't think there's anything he could do that would undo twenty-plus years of distrust. At least not before I'm a barren wasteland of fertility.

Naomi: There are other ways to be a parent.

Lina: Yeah. You just have to wait for your evil twin to abandon the child you didn't know about.

Naomi: I was thinking more along the lines of adoption. But I can confirm that the evil twin thing works!

Lina: Hey guys, not to steal the spotlight, but I'm getting married next week!

Me: Has Nash thrown a Morgan hissy fit over baby's breath yet?

Naomi: There will be no fit throwing of any kind. Only bridal perfection!

45

Snippity-Doo-Dah

Lucian

Nash: Good luck today. Make sure you can still walk down the aisle next week.
Knox: Oh fuck. Today's the day our boy becomes a man?
Me: Fuck you both very much.
Nash: I'm feeling unloved and used.
Knox: Yeah. Maybe we shouldn't hold up our end of the deal until Lucy learns to play nice.
Me: I hate you both and plan to kick your asses at my earliest convenience.

I took a deep breath and straightened my tie in the mirror. On the outside, I looked cool, calm, perhaps a touch pissed off. On the inside, I was a roiling mess of . . . something. I narrowed my eyes at my reflection.

I was Lucian Fucking Rollins. I didn't get anxious about shit. I made shit anxious about me.

I adjusted my cuffs one final time, nodded to the mirror, and headed out of the room to kick-start my future.

My future was sitting at the breakfast bar,

polishing off an omelet, looking both adorable and sexy in tight jeans and a red sweater with strawberry elbow patches.

"Let's go," I said, spinning the keys for the Jag on my index finger.

Sloane looked up, and I caught her quick grin. For years, her first reaction on seeing me was a scowl. I wasn't about to take that smile for granted.

"You didn't have breakfast," she pointed out, glancing at her watch. "And it's not even 7:30 yet."

I pressed a kiss to her wrinkled brow. "We're not going to the office this morning."

"Where are we going?" she asked, looping her arms around my neck.

"It's a surprise."

She frowned. "You didn't buy a castle, did you?"

"A castle?" I asked, ushering her toward the door. "No. Do you want one?"

"I'm not sure."

Fifteen minutes later, Sloane looked even more concerned.

"The urologist? Listen, big guy, I'm great at peeing after sex. I swear I don't have a UTI," she said, eyeing the building in front of us as I locked the car.

"We're here for me, not you," I said dryly.

"Oh God. Did I break your penis with that spinning maneuver?"

"Not yet. But I'm sure it's only a matter of time," I said, handing her the keys.

"Are you sick? Is something wrong?" Her eyes were wide and worried behind her glasses.

"I'm fine," I assured her as I held the glass door open for her. The waiting room was all marble and leather and chrome. There were half a dozen men my age, most looking nervously toward the exit, with unread magazines in their laps.

Sloane trailed me to the check-in desk where I gave the nurse my name and accepted the clipboard she handed over.

"Lucian, what the hell are we doing here?" Sloane hissed.

I turned to face her. "I'm getting my vasectomy reversed."

What came out of her mouth wasn't a sentence. It wasn't even words. It was the garbled tongue of an ancient civilization.

"That was not the reaction I was expecting. That wasn't even English."

"Oh my God. You're willing to have penis surgery just to make babies with me?" Sloane announced to the entire waiting room. She looked like she was about to faint.

I reached for her arm, determined to keep her upright.

"It's more in the testicles," a stranger in a golf shirt said, pointing to a helpful 3D model of a ball sack.

I waved a hand in front of Sloane's face. "Pix? You in there?"

"I think she's in shock," the guy's wife observed

as she got out of her chair. "Come here, sweetheart. Let's get you a drink of water."

"Vasectomy. Babies," Sloane murmured. "He's going to unsnip whatever they snipped just because I want to have a family."

The woman led her to the beverage center and pressed a paper cup of water into Sloane's shaking hands. "Well, honey, some men surprise their wives with jewelry. Other men surprise them with surgery on their genitals."

"Don't be scared, buddy," the husband said to me. "It's in and out, bingo bango. You get to sit on the couch for the rest of the day icing the boys. Nothing to it."

"Take it from him. This is his second vasectomy. Snippity-doo-dah," his wife said, returning Sloane to me. "He's a pro."

"Say something, Sloane," I ordered.

She was staring at me with glassy eyes and a dazed expression. I had never in my life seen her make that face before.

"If you don't say something in the next ten seconds, I'm going to drag the nearest medical professional away from the nearest set of testicles to examine you."

She bent at the waist and sucked in a dramatic breath.

"Well, hell, Lucian. I didn't know you were *serious* about this. I don't know how to handle this." She straightened and scrunched up her nose at me. "What if *I* don't want to have kids with *you?*"

"You do," I assured her smugly.

"Fair point. But if we have kids, we're going to have to get married. Not that you have to be married to have kids, but because I want to. I want a partner. I don't want to be a single mom with a baby daddy who sends a check."

"Judging from the suit, it would be one hell of a check," the wife mused in not quite a whisper.

"We're getting married, Sloane. I already told you that."

"Heh. He thinks he can tell her shit like that," the husband wheezed in amusement.

"I–I–I just don't know what's happening right now," Sloane said, pacing two steps away from me before returning to pinch me. "You feel real. You look real. Am I real? Did I slip into some kind of alternate dimension? Oh my God, am I the main character from *The Midnight Library*?"

"You're not dying," I said.

"You read *The Midnight Library*?" Her voice rose a full octave.

"I read all your book club picks," I told her.

"But why?"

"Why? Jesus, Sloane. Why do you think? Because I love you. I'm *in* love with you. I've had the last twenty-some years to obsess over you from afar."

The wife elbowed her husband. "You never obsessed over me from afar."

"That's because the farthest afar you go is your sister's book club meetings. Maybe if you went

721

farther, I'd have some room to obsess," he shot back.

Sloane brought her hands to her face. "Shit. I don't know what to do or say. Last night, Emry told us to take some time. This isn't time. This isn't even a day later! Not that I wanted time because my fertility is probably dropping by the second. But I was so sure there was nothing you could do to prove to me that you meant everything you said. And now . . ." She trailed off and gestured at my crotch.

"Pixie."

"Don't laugh at me. I'm allowed to freak out over this. Damn it," she muttered, rubbing her forehead. "I would have handled a castle better."

"I'll keep that in mind next time."

"I still don't see why you couldn't recover at home," Sloane said, marching me up the walkway to her front porch.

"I thought you'd like driving the Jag, and I *am* recovering at home," I said. It was the truth. The Waltons' house was the only real home I'd ever known.

"Rest. And ice. That's what the doctor said," Sloane reminded me.

"I had minor outpatient surgery. I'm fine," I insisted as she walked backward up the porch steps, holding me by the biceps. I was sore and hungry, but mostly I was nervous as fuck about this next part.

She was so intent on helping me up the porch steps that she was ankle deep in cherry blossoms before she bothered to look down. "What the . . ."

I made a mental note to kick Knox's and Nash's asses. The Morgan brothers had outdone themselves to the point of insanity. The entire front porch was buried under four inches of cherry blossoms. It looked as if a florist shop had exploded.

"Sloane—" I began.

"Okay. This is weirder than a pile of dead rats," she decided, still holding on to me and frowning at her own blossom-laden cherry tree. "Where did this come from?"

"From two possibly well-meaning idiots who are about to meet their maker. Come here." We waded through the avalanche of pink petals to the porch swing. There, on a table at least, was the champagne I'd ordered. Next to it was a bottle of bourbon that I hadn't, and in front of both bottles was a greasy Dino's pizza box.

I knew I should have called Stef, not Knox and Nash. But Stef was busy with his own grand gesture.

"Lucian, what the hell is going on?" Sloane demanded, opening the pizza box with suspicion.

A movement in the shrubbery caught my eye. Knox Morgan, wearing camouflage and green face paint, rose out of a rhododendron with his phone. He gave me the thumbs-up.

"What. The. Fuck?" I mouthed to him.

"Video, asshole," he mouthed back, pointing at his phone.

I leaned over the railing and shoved him back into the bush.

"Lucian?" Sloane repeated.

"There's something I want to talk to you about," I said, returning to her side.

My heart was in my throat. I could feel my heartbeat in my head as I closed the distance between us.

I had almost reached her when the opening bars of Shania Twain's "You're Still the One" sounded from a fat spruce on the opposite side of the porch steps. I spotted the torso of Nash's uniform peeking out from behind the evergreen. He was holding the speaker of his phone up to a bullhorn.

This was why people hired professionals.

"Why is there booze and pizza and a half ton of cherry blossom on my front porch?" Sloane asked nervously.

I took a deep breath. "Loving you has been a touchstone for more than half my life. But being loved by you? That's a fucking miracle. You, Pixie, are my fucking miracle."

Sloane took a shuddery inhale and shook her head. "I'm not mentally ready for this, Lucian," she whispered.

"Yes, you are. And so am I. Marry me, Sloane."

She brought her hands to her eyes, still shaking her head. "What?" she croaked.

"You heard me. I'd get down on one knee, but I

don't know if I'd be able to get back up right now. Marry me. Be my wife. Remind me every day that I'm better than I think I am. Show me what it's like to be loved by you. Because that's all I ever wanted. To be good enough for you."

I skimmed my hand over her cheek, then threaded my fingers into her hair.

She let out a choked sob.

"Don't cry, Pixie," I begged, brushing my lips to her forehead. "It kills me when you cry."

"Don't be so sweet then," she said accusingly.

"Just hold on a little bit longer and we can go back to hurling insults," I promised.

"Okay," she said on a hiccupping little sigh.

"Sloane Walton, I have loved you for so long I don't remember what my life was like before my heart was yours. It's changed over the years. But I've loved you as a friend, an enemy, a lover. It would be my greatest honor in this lifetime if you would let me love you as my wife."

Tears slid down her cheeks one after the other.

"Marry me, Sloane. Be my wife. Let me share your life up close. Let me protect you and love you like I'm ready to."

I let go of her to retrieve the box from my pocket. It opened with a quiet snick.

The noise that came out of her mouth was a wheezing, keening moan that sounded like a bag-pipe running full speed into an accordion.

A second later, she hurled herself into my arms, knocking me back a step.

"I'm taking this as a yes?" I said between the kisses she landed on my cheeks and mouth.

She pulled back and cupped my face in her hands. "Yes!" she shouted.

I chuckled softly. "Let me put the ring on you, Pix."

"God, I wish you hadn't just had a penisectomy," she said, holding out one shaking hand.

We would be editing that out of the engagement video, I decided as I slid the cool, smooth band onto her finger.

"Jesus. It weighs, like, five pounds," she said, reverently holding her hand up so the greedy diamond could catch the spring sunlight.

"I'll get you another one to wear on the other hand so you'll be even," I promised as a joy I'd never known bloomed inside my chest.

"Lucian?" she said, her voice breaking.

"You're not having second thoughts already, are you? I thought the whole vasectomy reversal thing would buy me until at least tomorrow before you started panicking."

She shook her head, fresh tears falling. "There's something you need to know."

I held her by the upper arms. "What? I'll fix it or buy it or destroy it."

"I love you."

Her words, the sincerity behind them, had my stomach throwing itself off a cliff.

"Say it again," I ordered gruffly.

Her smile was a sunbeam that warmed the darkest corners of my heart.

"I love you, Lucian Freaking Rollins. I always have. I always will."

I kissed her. Hard. I crushed my mouth to hers as I yanked her body to mine.

"Chief, we've got a 10–91A of the rooster variety at the Pop 'N Stop again." The static-filled radio announcement drowned out Shania.

"Shit, sorry, Lucy," Nash said through the bull-horn.

Sloane grinned up at me, and once again, I basked in the feeling of being the hero instead of the villain. "Your smile makes me love you even more," I confessed.

"Back at you, big guy."

"I can't wait to wake up tomorrow and remember this," I admitted.

"I love you, Lucian. Even if you wear suits to bed and are snooty about peanut butter brands."

"And I love you, Sloane. Even if you drive me absolutely insane twenty-four hours a day for the rest of my life."

"I really wish we could have sex right now," she said. "But I appreciate the long game."

"I'll make up for it the second the doctor or Google gives the okay. Whichever is first."

I kissed her again, long and hard.

"Naomi is gonna kick my ass for not telling her about this," I heard Knox mutter distantly.

"Just tell her it was man code," Nash advised.

"My mom is going to freak out," Sloane pre-dicted.

727

Karen: Welcome to the family, my favorite soon-to-be son-in-law!

Maeve: Don't fuck things up.

Chloe: Uncle Lucian, as junior bridesmaid, here are a few of the designer dresses I think I would look best in for the ceremony and reception.

46

Books Save Lives

Sloane

"S top jiggling your leg," Jeremiah ordered Lina, who looked as if she were about to bolt from his salon chair.

It was the perfect spring afternoon, and we were at Whiskey Clipper, Knockemout's hip barber shop/salon, getting glammed for Lina and Nash's wedding rehearsal that evening. The cool barber shop/salon was hopping on a Friday afternoon. Knox's basset hound, Waylon, flattened himself on the floor with a chew bone while Knox was giving Vernon Quigg's lustrous mustache a trim. Naomi was oohing and aahing over the sleek updo stylist Anastasia was assembling.

Knox's business manager and Jeremiah's sister, Fi, was huddled behind the front desk's computer with Waylay as the twelve-year-old walked her through the new scheduling software.

Stef and I were on the leather couch under the front window, watching the chaos. My hair was done in a high, flirty ponytail that I gleefully knew my fiancé, Lucian Freaking Rollins, would wrap around his fist before the night was over.

The bride glared in the mirror at Jeremiah as he

ruffled her short dark hair this way and that. "I'm not jiggling. *You're* jiggling."

"It's kind of fun watching the calm, collected Lina tiptoe into a meltdown," I mused.

Stef took a pensive sip of his whiskey and continued to frown.

"I'm not having a meltdown," Lina said, taking obvious offense.

"Yeah, you are," everyone in the shop except for Stef chorused.

"All of you can bite me," she grumbled, crossing her arms under the cape.

"Are you okay?" I asked Stef. He was staring at Jeremiah and looking downright miserable.

"I'm great." He got up, looking anything but great, and refilled his whiskey from one of the decanters on the shelf.

"Psst!"

I looked up.

Waylay nodded in Stef's direction. "What's his problem?" she mouthed.

I shrugged and made a face.

Jeremiah spun Lina's chair around to face him. "Listen up, you fierce, beautiful badass. I don't think you're nervous about getting married. I think you're nervous about the wedding."

"Is there a difference?" Lina asked dryly.

"I've seen you with Nash. You're excited about *being* married. About starting your lives together. Don't let wedding day jitters make you doubt that."

730

Lina opened her mouth, then shut it again. "Huh," she said.

Naomi tiptoed her chair around to face the bride. "He's right. Not everyone is excited about being a bride, the center of attention all day. But I know you. And I know you're thrilled to be a wife."

Lina's shoulders relaxed. "Oh, thank God. I thought there was something wrong with me."

"No, but there's something wrong with me," Stef said, knocking back the fresh whiskey and slamming the glass down.

Fi took the lollipop out of her mouth. "Uh, what's happening here?"

Waylon dropped his chew bone and tip-tapped over to Stef's feet.

Stef marched over to Jeremiah. "Your apartment is gross," he announced.

I pressed my lips together to keep from laughing.

"It really is," Fi agreed. "Who disassembles a motorcycle in their living room?"

"Okay," Jeremiah said cautiously.

"It's gross, and there isn't enough closet space. But I think we should move in together," Stef blurted out.

"Oh, shit," Fi whispered, grabbing Waylay in a headlock hug.

"I know we haven't talked about the future, and I know that it's probably stupid crazy of me to move here, but you're here," he said, looking at Jeremiah. He turned to Naomi. "And you're here. You're *all* here. I have family here, and the more

731

I think about it, the crazier it would be to stay away."

Jeremiah tipped his head down and studied the toes of his boots.

Lina and I shared a wide-eyed look.

"Guess you won't be selling your half of the business after all," Knox said to his partner.

All heads whipped back to Jeremiah, who was grinning now. "Guess not."

"You were going to sell?" Stef repeated. "Why in the hell would you do that? You love this place."

"I love you more." Jeremiah said it simply, without fuss.

The words had tears prickling at the backs of my eyes.

"This is why communication is fucking important," Knox said, crossing his muscly arms.

"Seriously?" Lina said with a smirk. "You of all people."

"Fuck off. I've evolved and shit," Knox said.

Vernon pulled the hot towel off of his eyes. "What the hell is goin' on here? This mustache ain't gonna shape itself."

Naomi beamed at her husband. Waylay rolled her eyes.

"Hang on," Stef said, waving his hands. "I had a lot of whiskey in a very short period of time. Are you saying you're okay with us moving in together even if I make you move out of your apartment that smells like diesel fumes?"

Jeremiah began to approach slowly. "I'm saying

732

let's buy a house or a farm or an estate or whatever you want."

Stef was nodding and swallowing. "Yeah. Okay. That sounds . . . fine."

Jeremiah took Stef's hands. "I'm saying let's be a family . . . with our families."

"Oh my God," I breathed and pulled out my phone to record the moment.

"What are you saying, Jer?" Stef demanded.

"I'm saying, let's move in. Let's get married. Let's do the whole damn thing. I've been waiting a long damn time for you. Let's get started already."

Naomi brought her hands to her cheeks.

"Don't you dare start cryin', Daze," Knox ordered gruffly. He abandoned Vernon and crossed to his wife.

"Oh brother. Now they're gonna make out," Waylay predicted, returning her focus to the software update with an exaggerated eye roll. "I'm chargin' extra for this."

"Yes," Stef said, sounding dazed. "Yes, to all those things."

Naomi let out a loud sniffle. Knox swore.

Fi bolted out of her chair, and her lollipop went flying. "My baby brother is getting married and moving out of that poor excuse for an apartment!"

Waylon sauntered over and slurped up the discarded candy.

"Drop it, Way," Knox barked.

"He means you," Waylay said to the dog without looking away from the monitor.

733

"Bust out the champagne," Vernon decreed, offering up aftershave-scented high fives.

I got in line to offer my congratulations. "We're all going to raise our families together," Naomi said with a trembling voice.

"Do *not* make me cry, Witty. I'm a puffy crier, and I have to look stunning tonight," Lina groused.

Family. Just a few short months ago, I'd realized it was what I wanted more than anything. Now, thanks to Lucian and these women, there would be new life in my home. More parties. More holidays. More love. More laughter.

I felt the pang. My dad would have loved this. He would have been over the moon, planning engagement parties, writing funny toasts, practicing our father-daughter dance. I missed him so much it hurt to breathe.

I love you, Dad, I said silently. *Thank you for everything.*

As if reading my mind, Naomi squeezed my wrist. The one a monster had broken all those years ago. That monster's son had managed to put his own broken pieces together again and heal my broken heart in the process.

"We're getting married," Stef yelled, holding up Jeremiah's hand.

We converged on the happy couple. Even Knox and Waylay got in on the hugging.

My phone rang as I drove home with great hair and a full heart.

734

"You are *not* going to believe what happened today, big guy," I announced when I answered the call.

"As it turns out, I have news for you too," Lucian's buttery smooth voice said through the Jeep speakers. "You go first."

"Stef asked Jeremiah to move in with him, and Jeremiah asked him to marry him!"

"That escalated quickly," he quipped.

"I can't wait for their wedding. Queer weddings are the best," I said happily as I turned onto my street. "Now, tell me your news. Is it good or bad?"

"It's very good news. I just got out of a briefing with Special Agent Idler. It appears that Hugo's shell corporation was bribing officials to assign prisoners to his private prisons. They've only just begun quietly digging, and it looks as though several judges, district attorneys, even some local law enforcement were also on the receiving end of some highly illegal kickbacks. The higher the sentence, the bigger the kickback."

"Wow," I said.

"The preliminary list includes the Not So Honorable Judge Dirk Atkins."

"As in the Dirk Atkins who refused to reconsider Mary Louise's sentence?"

"One and the same," Lucian said smugly. "Idler promised me she'd personally look into Mary Louise's case. There's a very good chance that an investigation will result in many of his sentences being overturned."

"Overturned?" I squeaked. "As in *get out of jail overturned?*"

"It will take some time, but I'll do what I can to speed things along. We should have her out before Allen's graduation," Lucian continued.

My response was a choked sob.

"Sloane." Lucian's voice was an affectionate rasp over my name.

"I'm so happy," I whispered through tears.

"Yes, I can tell," he said dryly.

"God, I love you."

"Get ready to really mean it, because I arranged for you and Fran to call Mary Louise to tell her the good news in five minutes."

"Geez Louise, Lucian," I said, whipping into my driveway. "I'm running out of room on the blow-jobs-when-the-doctor-clears-you tally sheet."

"I'm confident you'll make room," he said. "Now go call Mary Louise."

"I appreciate the call, but like I said before, I'm not going to change my mind about this. I'm not going to endanger my son by telling my story," Mary Louise announced as soon as the greetings were exchanged.

"Why don't you share the news?" Fran said to me from the screen of my laptop. She was wearing a canary-yellow knit blazer with sparkly threads.

I was all but bouncing out of my chair. "Mary Louise, you don't have to tell your story, and we don't have to appeal. But you're still going to go home soon."

Her face froze and then her eyes started to go wide. "I'm sorry. I think there's something wrong with our connection. It sounded like you said . . ."

"It's true," Fran verified. "The judge has been implicated in some hinky dealings, and once the investigation is underway, they're going to be taking a hard look at his cases. Starting with yours."

"The judge and everyone else connected is going down. Not only won't you have to do anything about it, you also won't have to worry about retaliation anymore," I promised her, knowing Lucian would help me keep that promise.

Mary Louise brought her hands to her face, covering her eyes. "I don't believe it. I just can't believe it."

"Believe it," Fran advised with a rare smile. "Now here's what I think we can expect . . ."

As the lawyer walked Mary Louise through the next steps, I absentmindedly paged through Mary Louise's case file. All those years lost. All that time stolen. It could have easily been Lucian all those years ago.

All because greedy men wanted to line their pockets. I hoped they'd pay. Every last one of them. Lucian and I would make sure that they did, even as we figured out this new normal and began to build a life together.

And Mary Louise would get her life back.

Tears clouded my vision again. I blinked them back and stared down at the papers on the desk. A familiar name on the page caught my eye, and I frowned. It was a copy of Mary Louise's arrest record. *Arresting Officer: Chief Wylie Ogden.*

My heart stuttered in my chest.

Lucian had mentioned local law enforcement had been on Hugo's prison scheme payroll. Was Wylie one of them? He sure as hell hadn't played by the book when he was chief of police, letting his friends off the hook and cracking down on citizens he didn't feel any loyalty toward.

Another thought struck me like a brick to the face. He'd been friends with Tate Dilton, who had been up to his eyeballs in involvement with the Hugo crime family. What if Wylie had been the one to make the introduction?

My heartbeat was echoing in my skull. I needed to call Lucian. And Nash.

"We'll be in touch as soon as we know more, but we wanted you to know that your days in that place are officially numbered," Fran was saying, drawing my attention back to my laptop.

Mary Louise's shoulders shook as she cried silently. She dropped her hands suddenly. "My baby. Does Allen know?"

I shook off my stupor and pasted a smile on my face. "Not yet. We thought he'd like to hear the news from you—"

The video feed and everything else in the house cut off abruptly.

"Damn it," I muttered. Power outages never happened at convenient times.

I snatched up the arrest report and was just scrolling for Lucian's number on my phone when the doorbell rang.

I raced to the front door, hoping it was Nash on official wedding business, and yanked it open.

But it wasn't Nash. No, standing with dirty boots on my new welcome mat was Wylie Ogden. He was holding a box of books. A red toothpick dangled from his lower lip.

Fuckity fuck fuck.

Relax, I told myself. *He doesn't know I know. Hell, I don't know if I know.*

"Hi, Wylie," I said, sounding suspicious as hell. "What can I do for you?"

"Picked these up at an estate sale and thought you might want them for the library. Shame about the fire."

The fire that he could have easily set. The fire. The note. The rats on my porch. Oh God. Something tickled my nose. Was it . . .

"Your toothpick smells like cinnamon," I said in a strangled voice.

"Family habit," he said. "My dad always had cinnamon toothpicks on him when I was growing up. I wanted to be just like him from the time I could walk."

I wasn't sure what a normal person would say in response to that. So I just gave him my best fake smile. "Well, thank you for your generosity. I'll be

739

happy to take those books off your hands," I said, reaching for the box.

"It's a heavy one, and I'm a gentleman. I insist."

Short of shoving him out the door and slamming it in his face, I didn't know what my next move should be. If I did that, he'd know that I knew.

"You can set them down just here on the floor. I'll get to them after Nash's wedding. In fact, he should be here any minute to pick me up," I lied brightly.

"She knows."

The husky southern drawl behind me had the blood draining out of my face.

I spun around on my stockinged feet only to find Judge Atkins standing in the hallway, wielding a gun with what appeared to be a silencer screwed to the barrel.

"Uh, that's not a gavel," I joked stupidly.

"Shut the door, Ogden," Atkins ordered.

Wylie set the books down, then obediently closed and locked the front door. "Don't get your robes in a knot," Wylie complained. He was nervous, shifting his weight from foot to foot, his eyes darting around. It made me even more nervous.

"She knows enough to be scared half to death of you knockin' on her door, now doesn't she?" the judge said, wiggling the gun in my direction.

I glanced around me, trying to come up with a plan of action. If I ran, I guessed the judge would have no qualms about shooting me in the back. If I tried to fight him like the rabid weasel he was, well, I'd end up with the holes in my front, and I really liked this dress. I didn't have shoes on, so traction and kicking were problems.

I needed to at least stash the arrest report somewhere that Lucian would find it. He'd put two and two together.

My gaze snagged on one of the nearly hidden security cameras Lucian had installed in the living room. But the light wasn't on. They'd cut the power and the Wi-Fi, I realized with a sinking sensation in my gut.

I dropped the arrest report and slowly put my hands on my head to show them I was no threat. "What's the plan here, guys? It's a small town. Odds are someone saw you on my porch or climbing my fence."

"I was just donating books," Wylie reminded me, producing a gun of his own from the waistband of his old-man pants. Great. Now two gun-wielding bad guys were making a Sloane sandwich. "And you were fine when I left."

I was going to throw up. Everywhere.

"And I'm not here. I'm with my wife enjoying a romantic anniversary dinner," Atkins said with a mean smile. "And any evidence will be burned up in the fire."

The man intended to shoot me and set fire to my house. I almost felt sorry for him because Lucian wouldn't stop until he'd destroyed everything Atkins held sacred.

"Look, I don't know why you think you have

to do this. Is it really necessary? I mean, so you took some kickbacks from a prison and set fire to a public library. It's not like you murdered someone."

"I'm not letting some little blond destroy my legacy over a few dollars," the judge announced. "I've made my life's work putting criminals behind bars."

Yeah, the asshole was a goddamn hero.

"You should have listened to the warnings," Wylie said sadly. "It shouldn't have come to this."

I debated sharing the news that the FBI would be closing in on both them, then rejected it. They wanted me dead to protect themselves. Having absolutely nothing left to lose probably wouldn't make them any more amenable to letting me stay alive.

"Where are we doing this?" Wylie asked.

"Do I look like I give a good goddamn where we kill the girl?" Atkins demanded.

"How about the front yard?" I suggested weakly.

"We'll take her in the back of the house," Wylie decided and waved his gun at me. But there was something in his stare. Something pointed. His gaze slid to the library cart just inside the living room doorway, then back to me. It was stacked high with several thick thriller novels.

He lowered his chin at me, and I nodded once.

"Let's go," he said, gesturing me to walk into the living room.

I stepped into the room, the wall briefly hiding

me from the judge's view. Praying I hadn't misread the signal, I grabbed the end of the cart and shoved it with all my might just as Atkins rounded the corner.

There was a crunch, a groan, and a muffled shot followed by three louder, rapid shots.

I patted down my torso and was exceptionally relieved to find no holes in me or my dress.

"Son of a bitch," Atkins gurgled as he lost copious amounts of blood on my hardwood floor from wounds in his neck, chest, and torso.

"Oh my God. Oh my God," I chanted as Wylie picked up Atkins's gun. "What do we do now?"

"I really hate to do this to you, Sloane, but you gotta understand," Wylie said, pointing both weapons at me.

"Seriously, Wylie? Why the fuck do you *still* want to shoot me?" I screeched.

"Tying up loose ends. With you and the judge gone, there's no one left to point a finger at me. The money I got from Hugo was nothing compared to what Atkins got. A few thousand here and there. I never even cared about it. I only cared about the job."

The job he'd abused. The job Nash had taken from him.

"So what if I made a little money on the side? A police chief's salary ain't nothin' to write home about. I was proud of my work. And Nash Morgan took that away from me. I'm sure as hell not gonna let his little friend take my reputation too."

743

I closed my eyes for a second as the realization sunk in. "You put Nash's name on that list, didn't you?"

"Didn't want to miss out on the opportunity. Metzer was makin' a list. I helped him out. My fee was adding one more name."

I shook my head. "So you set it all in motion."

He shrugged. "I have a legacy to protect. It's all I have left."

"That's not a legacy. That's a pattern of bad behavior."

"You don't know what it takes to protect an entire town."

"Yeah? Well, obviously neither do you. You put a seventeen-year-old boy in jail and let his abusive father nearly kill his mother because *you were fishing buddies*."

"Say what you want because it don't matter. Only one of us is walking out of here tonight, and it ain't gonna be you."

"What are you going to do? Shoot me with the judge's gun?"

"Seems like a good plan to me."

I heard a squeal of tires on the road out front and prayed that help was on the way.

"No one is going to believe that you just happened to come upon a district judge threatening me and shot him," I told him.

He shot me a crooked grin. "They believed it once already."

His words sank in slowly. "Jesus! You didn't kill

Tate because you were protecting Nash. You killed him because you were protecting yourself."

"I waited till he pulled the trigger, thinking either he would take care of Nash for me or he was out of bullets. Son of a bitch never did learn to count his rounds. I hated to do it. He was my friend, but Tate was a loose fucking cannon. He would have run his mouth to the wrong guy eventually."

"So you killed your own friend."

"According to the official report, I shot a man defending an officer of the law," he corrected.

"And what's the official report going to say this time?"

He shrugged. "I was just returning my library books."

He was going to do it. He was going to shoot me and ruin Nash and Lina's rehearsal night. I grabbed a hefty hardback off the side table and hurled it at Wylie's head. Both guns went off as I launched myself over the couch.

I landed hard, catching my jaw on the sharp edge of the console table leg. More bullets flew, this time through my couch. I rolled, gained my feet, and sprinted low through the dining room, pulling chairs down after me.

He was close, but I knew every inch of this house. I darted through the kitchen and backtracked into the hallway where I took the stairs two at a time.

The sirens were getting louder now.

"You can't run from me," Wylie shouted from the foot of the stairs.

"And you can't expect me to stand still so you can shoot me!"

His boots hit the stairs.

A streak of fur passed me on the landing as I hustled for the second floor, I heard a thump and muffled swearing.

Thank God for asshole cats. Meow Meow had just bought me precious seconds.

I heaved myself up the last steps and ran face-first into a hard, male body. I was just getting ready to kick the shit out of him when a hand clamped over my mouth and I was lifted off the floor.

47

Wrongs Righted

Lucian

S top kicking, Pix," I hissed as I shut and locked her bedroom door behind us.

I released my flailing fiancée, and she spun around to face me. She was wearing the pink cocktail dress that I'd personally picked out because it clung to her curves in all the right places. Her hair was secured in a high, platinum ponytail with strands escaping everywhere. Her glasses were a spring green that only served to make her eyes look brighter. There was a bloody gash on her jawline.

"I'm going to fucking kill him," I announced. Rage bloomed inside me like a deadly flower.

Sloane lunged for me and held on tight. "You can't. It's Wylie."

"I know. I saw the security footage just before it cut off."

"He made me think he was going to help me. Then he shot the judge. Oh yeah. The judge was here too, but I think he's dead in the foyer. And then he tried to shoot me. Wylie, not the dead judge. And he's the one who put Nash's name on the list, not Dilton. Oh my God, and he murdered

Dilton to keep him quiet, not to save Nash. I am so pissed! Do you know how long it's going to take to get bloodstains out of hardwood? And they burned my library!"

The words came out in a deluge of indignation, but her explanation only served to light a match inside me.

"You can't hide from me long enough to stay alive, Sloane. I'll drop you where I find you before the cops get here," Wylie announced from the hallway. We heard the clomp of his boots and the creak of doors as he started checking rooms.

In the distance, I heard sirens. I'd just pulled into the driveway when I heard the gunshots. It had taken years off my life.

I grabbed a clean handkerchief from the dresser and pressed it to Sloane's face.

"Ow!"

"Come on, baby." I half dragged, half carried her to the window seat.

She eagerly climbed onto the cushion and swung a leg over the sill of the window I'd left open. "Let's go," she said.

I shook my head. "You go first. I'll make sure he doesn't see you on the roof."

She flinched. "Lucian."

"Sloane. Go!"

The footsteps were getting closer, and that lock on the door wouldn't hold back an overly excited golden retriever.

"I'm not leaving you," she said stubbornly.

I cupped her face in my hands. "Pixie, I need you to trust me this time. Trust me to handle this. I'm asking you, but in a second, I'm going to be telling you. I need to deal with this, and I can't do it if I'm worried that he has a clear shot at you. Trust me to do this."

The doorknob rattled, followed by Wylie's raspy cackle. "I know you're in there, girl."

"Ugh. Fine. But I'm also trusting you not to murder him," Sloane said.

"I'm not promising that."

She swung her leg over the windowsill. "Don't let me down."

Women.

"Oh, also, he has two guns. His and the judge's. He was going to make it look like he caught the judge murdering me."

The sirens were screaming down the street now, and an anger unlike any other I'd ever known tinged everything a bloody-murder red.

I shoved her out the window onto the roof. "I love you. Now get the fuck out."

"I love you too. Don't end up in jail," she whispered.

I shut the curtains on her just as a boot landed a hard kick to the door. It flew open on the second kick, rebounding off the wall as I hurried across the room and flattened myself against the wall.

The barrel of a gun with a silencer came into view. "Come out, come out, wherever you—"

I brought my arm down on his in a fast, sweeping

arc. My forearm connected with his. I grabbed him and dragged him farther into the room.

"Son of a bitch!"

"More like son of a bastard," I snarled back as we wrestled for the gun.

"Your dad was a good man. You were just a no-good brat who thought he was better than everybody."

"I was better than him. You took everything from me once. I won't let it happen again, old man." I threw an elbow to his jaw, and he howled in pain. The gun tumbled to the floor, and I kicked it toward the bed. "You hurt her. You threatened her, burned down her library, and you made her bleed," I roared over the sirens.

His eyes were a bloodshot blue and desperate. "You should have stayed out of this. Neither one of you needed to get involved."

"And you should have gone to fucking jail instead of me, asshole. I'm going to make sure everyone who's ever heard your name knows exactly what kind of man you are."

He pushed me back two steps, and I let him. I heard feet pounding on the stairs. But this was between him and me.

"Better get those hands up so the chief can cuff you. I've been looking forward to this perp walk," I taunted.

In a move impressively fast for an asshole of his age, Wylie reached behind him and pulled the second gun. But I was already on the move.

He pulled the trigger just as the first cop hit the second floor. I dodged to the side and kept coming like a freight train.

I drew my fist back and let it fly. It connected with his jaw, and Wylie Ogden crumpled like he was made of paper.

The gun was right there. I could pick it up and put an end to him, to all the pain he'd caused over the course of his lifetime. But I was better than that. I was better than men like Ogden and my father. I had Sloane to prove it. I had a lifetime with her ahead of me, and nothing was going to endanger that.

Nash entered the room, weapon drawn, vest on over what looked like a decent suit. "Suspect is down," he reported into his radio as he eyed me. "We good?"

I nodded curtly. "Yeah."

"Thank Christ. I didn't want the paperwork on this."

"You might want to let him wake up before you personally slap the cuffs on him. He put your name on the list, not Dilton."

"Fucker," Nash muttered. "He's lucky Lina's not here. Hey, you're bleeding."

"Fuck."

"Lucian!" A blond and pink blur flew at me, and Sloane launched herself into my arms.

"Go easy on him, Sloaney," Nash instructed. "He's shot."

"He shot you?" She tried to wriggle free.

"Where do you think you're going?" I demanded.

"I'm going to kill him," she announced, heading for the door.

I nipped her around the waist and pulled her back.

"No, you're not. I don't want our first time post-vasectomy reversal to be in a conjugal trailer."

She growled in response. Laughing, I carried her to the porch swing where EMTs converged on us.

"She wouldn't let us fix her up until you came out," the first explained as he began to clean Sloane's wound. She winced and I anchored her to my side.

"Are you okay? Does it hurt?" I asked gruffly.

"Only when I smile, which is going to suck for tomorrow when two of our best friends get married."

"I hate when you hurt," I confessed.

"I'm not too fond of you having a gunshot wound, big guy."

I dropped a kiss on the top of her head.

"I have bad news," Sloane said, plucking at the skirt of her dress.

"What?"

"Besides my dress being ruined, it looks like one of the shots went through the window in Dad's study and hit the lower branch of the cherry tree. It broke when I climbed down."

It looked as though we all would be carrying the scars from this day.

"We'll fix it," I promised her. If I had to call in a team of fucking tree surgeons, there was no way I was going to let evil and greed destroy something so precious to me.

"This is a clean through-and-through," said the other EMT as she examined my wound. "An inch or two higher and we'd have had a real problem."

Sloane clung to my hand in silence as they patched us up.

The street was blocked by emergency vehicles, but a crowd of bystanders was already gathering.

Knox, Naomi, Waylay, Lina, Stef, and Jeremiah were crowded together on the other side of the police barricades in their rehearsal dinner finery. Most of the rest of Knockemout had shown up too and watched as a groggy Wylie Ogden was led down the driveway into the back seat of a waiting patrol car.

A circle closed along with the car door, I thought with satisfaction.

"You two stay here. Bannerjee will be back to take your statements," Sergeant Hopper instructed us.

I expected to feel a sense of victory as the man who'd nearly ruined my life faced humiliation and the end of his life as he knew it. Instead, I felt a wave of frustration at the pointlessness of it all. Greed didn't just destroy the greedy. No. The quest for power corrupted, ruining all it touched. Men like my father, like Hugo and Ogden and Atkins, left a path of destruction behind them. For what? Money? Power? Respect?

They'd been the things I'd chased too. But no dollar amount could compare to the woman in my arms.

A squealing of tires drew my attention, and I watched as Nolan drove right up onto the sidewalk and vaulted out of an SUV. He hustled up the porch steps two at a time, then froze when he saw me. "Thank fucking, Christ!" he said, slapping a hand over his heart, and then he proceeded to tackle hug me on the swing.

Sloane's laughter was music to my ears.

"Ouch! I'm shot, not dead, and you're not a golden retriever. Get the hell off me," I complained.

Nolan winced, still holding on to me. "I'd let go if I could, but I got airsick in that fucking whirlybird. I don't know if I'm gonna puke or pass out."

"I don't care which one you do. Just don't do it on me."

"I've got this," Sloane said, rising from the swing and putting an arm around Nolan. "Come on. Let's see if Naomi has any snacks in her purse. That'll make you feel better."

Nolan looked back at me. "Glad you're not dead, boss."

"That makes two of us," I agreed.

I watched my fiancée lead Nolan to the barricades and deliver him to our friends. Sloane was immediately engulfed in worried hugs but valiantly fought her way out of them and returned to me.

I held out my arms, and she dropped into my lap, resting her bandaged face on my chest as chaos reigned around us. I pushed off with my foot and set the swing in gentle motion.

She held up her hand and studied her engagement ring. "Thanks for not going all homicidal on Wylie."

"Thank you for trusting me . . . and for warning me about the second gun."

She snuggled closer to my side and let out a satisfied sigh. "You don't think this whole gunshot wound thing is going to push back sexy time even further, do you?"

"If we didn't have law enforcement crawling all over our house and a wedding rehearsal to attend, I'd have you naked right now."

48

The Happy Couples

Sloane

The flap of the bridal tent opened, and my gorgeous fiancé strolled inside, looking like all seven of the deadly sins in his tuxedo.

Naomi looked up from where she was patting Lina on the back while Lina hyperventilated into a paper bag. Naomi smiled. Lina waved.

"Everything all right, ladies?" Lucian asked.

"I'm deeply in love with my husband, but my goodness, Lucian. You look like sex in a suit," Naomi said, wide-eyed.

Lina dropped the paper bag. "Just tell me Nash is here and still wants to go through with this, Suit Daddy."

Lucian's grin was panty-incinerating. "Your almost husband is wearing a trench in the ground, muttering about how he can't wait to see you."

"Oh, thank God," Lina said, collapsing back in her chair.

"For what it's worth, he'll go weak in the knees when he sees you in that dress," he predicted.

"Thanks, boss," she said weakly.

He turned his attention to me, and I felt like a flower blooming in the spring sunshine. "May

I borrow my fiancée for a moment?" he asked.

"Sure," the bride said.

"Bring back more champagne," Naomi suggested, nodding at the empty bottle in the grass.

I all but skipped to the door.

Outside, it was a stunning spring day. Warm, sunny, blue skies. Birdsong and the babbling of the creek provided the perfect backdrop to the slow country songs the band was playing. Nash and Lina had decided to start their journey together on the grassy expanse of land they would build their house on.

The ceremony and reception would take place under a large white tent next to the creek. It looked as though all of Knockemout had been invited.

Lucian led me away from the tents and pulled me behind an oak tree.

"What's going—"

I didn't get any further in my question because Lucian's mouth found mine in a knee-weakening, breath-stealing kiss.

"Holy crap," I managed to gasp when he pulled back.

"That was the first order of business. Now on to the next," he said. "Give me a date."

"You want to go on a date?" My brain was still scrambled from the kiss.

"I want to *set* a date. For *our* wedding." He glanced around us at the chaotic merriment. "I don't want to wait. I already wasted enough time. And watching you walk down that aisle today, knowing it's for someone else, is driving me insane."

"Christmas Eve."

He went still and tense. All his attention was on me. His face was all hard angles and planes, but there was an exquisite softness in his expression.

"Christmas Eve," he repeated.

I nodded. "Last Christmas was rough. Why not make this one for the record books?"

Lucian swallowed hard, then nodded. "Christmas Eve," he said again, his voice barely a rasp.

I wrapped my arms around his neck and beamed up at him. "I love you, big guy. So stupidly much."

He crushed me to him, then winced.

"Poor baby. Bullet hole or testicle surgery?" I teased.

"Both."

Lina didn't float down the aisle, she marched. Her father nearly had to jog to keep up with those long, purposeful strides. Her gaze never left Nash's face. And when the happy couple joined hands and stared into each other's eyes with a blinding joy, there were tears from the entire bridal party. Well, okay. There were tears from Naomi and me. Knox and Lucian were mostly stoic and manly.

Lucian watched me with that hellfire intensity of his throughout the entire ceremony. And when we met in the middle to walk back down the aisle together, he handed me a fresh handkerchief.

We danced, we laughed, and we cried some

more, christening with love the very spot that Nash and Lina's house would be built.

I barely left Lucian's arms the entire evening. I was safe there. I belonged there. After yesterday's terrifying chaos, I suddenly felt . . . free. Like the last of the shadows that had been looming over our group, our town, had finally dissipated. With Anthony Hugo and Wylie Ogden in jail and Judge Atkins in the morgue, we'd finally made it through the dark forest and come out on the other side.

This was the beginning of our happily ever after.

As night fell, the festivities continued. Liza J cut a rug with the handsome biker Wraith. Next to them on the dance floor, Maeve and Kurt swayed side to side, staring deeply into each other's eyes. Nolan and his soon-to-be wife again, Callie, were holding court with my mother, her friends, and several empty bottles of wine. Naomi's parents were in the middle of a hotly contested game of cornhole with Lina's parents. Chloe and Waylay were sitting at the abandoned head table, devouring dessert.

Half of Knockemout appeared to be shit-faced on the dance floor. The other half—including the entire police department—was lined up at the bar. Lawlerville had kindly lent Nash some officers so his cops could celebrate with him.

As Lucian and I swayed to a Chris Stapleton song, a grinning Stef and Jeremiah appeared, each holding two bottles of champagne.

"Shall we?" Stef asked, nodding toward the night.

"We'll get the glasses," I volunteered.

Lucian and I collected the bride and groom, who were saying good night to Nash's father. Duke's sobriety was still a new, fresh thing in the family. We helped ourselves to eight champagne glasses and found our way in the dark to a quiet spot in the meadow where Stef, Jeremiah, Knox, and Naomi were already waiting.

"To the happy couple," Stef volunteered after Jeremiah filled my glass.

Lina shook her head, brilliantly beautiful as a bride. "To the happy couples," she amended.

"May we all live happily ever after," I added.

"Cheers!"

We sat in the grass, drinking champagne and listening to the night symphony of laughter, music, and spring peepers.

Lucian pulled me into his lap and nuzzled my neck.

"Married, married, engaged, engaged," Knox said, pointing at each couple in our little circle. "Shit sure happens fast round here."

"Have you two set a date?" I asked Stef and Jeremiah.

"Stef wants at least a year to plan 'the wedding of the century,'" Jeremiah teased.

"Hey! Naomi and I have been dreaming about our weddings since we were infants," Stef said defensively.

"Just don't get married on Christmas Eve," Lucian said, picking up my hand and kissing my engagement ring. "That date's taken."

Lina and Naomi squealed. "You set a date!"

"None of you are invited," Lucian teased.

"You're *all* invited," I corrected.

Lucian "Lucifer" Rollins was going to be my husband. And I was going to be his wife. We were going to spend the rest of our lives building a family . . . and driving each other absolutely insane.

Maybe it was the champagne or the happy tears, or maybe it was my dad working a little heavenly miracle, but I'd never seen the stars so bright.

"I love you, Pixie," Lucian whispered against my hair, his thumb brushing the scar on my wrist.

Epilogue

A Christmas Wedding

Sloane

December 24th dawned crisp and cold with an accommodating amount of snow that had fallen earlier in the week. Perfect for the Christmas effect but without impeding guest travel, according to the wedding coordinator Lucian had hired, what with Naomi and Knox being distracted with fertility specialist appointments.

Wedding coordinator Tiffany had coordinated us to within an inch of our lives.

Our house was full. Even now, laughter rose up from the first floor as the people I loved most in this world got ready to celebrate with us. Lina was probably comparing pregnant bellies with Nolan's wife, Callie, while everyone else broke into the champagne.

We'd decided to get married at home where Lucian had spared no expense on decking our halls for our first Christmas together. The ceremony would take place inside, and then the reception was in the backyard. Lucian had somehow managed to get the entire yard under a large, heated tent filled with all the glamorous fixings for an event to remember. The aisle was blanketed in cherry blossoms, which were so far out of season I didn't even want to know how much Lucian had spent arranging it. The man had probably paid scientists to clone our tree.

Tiffany had been in wedding coordinator heaven with an unlimited budget and a groom who wanted the best of everything. She was terrifying in her detail management and time schedules, which was why I was hiding in our bedroom.

I'd sent my half of the bridal party and my mother downstairs to welcome Mary Louise and Allen, who had just arrived, while I took a private moment to freak the fuck out.

I was dressed, made-up, shoes on, ready to go. And starting to panic.

Not seeing Lucian since the—thankfully drama-free—rehearsal dinner had stirred up my nerves.

I paced in the most romantic, perfect wedding dress in the history of wedding dresses and thought about how far we'd come in the past several months.

Lucian had set his sights on making every wish I'd ever had come true, starting with renovating our bathroom and installing not one but two rain showerheads and a platoon of body jets and continuing to complete the library in record time with new bells and whistles the entire town was still swooning over.

I nervously smoothed my hand over the ball gown satin skirt as I wandered our room.

As happy as I was for this particular occasion, I

still felt the hole of my father's absence. Knowing how proud he would have been to walk me down the aisle, how he would have loved quizzing Kurt, now Maeve's fiancé, about his curriculum for the year, how he would have danced with Mom until their feet hurt, my heart was still just a little bit broken.

"Shit. Don't freaking cry now and wreck the eye makeup," I warned myself.

Tiffany would kill me if the makeup artist had to come back.

I fanned my hands in front of my eyes and thought about not sad things. Like the fact that Wylie Ogden was in prison and would never have the opportunity to hurt anyone I loved ever again. And Lucian was working from home two days a week and commuting—often by helicopter—on the other days. And about how the entire town had turned out for the grand reopening of the library.

Crap. I was back to teary again. I wished Lucian was here. He always knew how to calm me down . . . or rile me up, depending on the situation.

I thought about texting him and then remembered that Naomi had my phone to document the big day without me having to do the documenting.

A tap at the window startled me. I spun in a voluminous pool of taffeta and satin to find Lucian Freaking Rollins crouched on the porch roof in a tuxedo.

I ran to the window as he opened it.

"I thought it was bad luck to see the bride before

the wedding," I said even as I half dragged him through the window.

He stood staring at me, then slowly shook his head. "I don't believe in bad luck. Not anymore." His smile was devastating.

"What do you think?" I asked, twirling in front of him.

"I think you're the most beautiful bride I've ever seen and I'm the luckiest man on earth."

It was the boob-highlighting corset top, I decided.

I stopped twirling and fell into his arms. "Good answer."

"Are you still sure about everything?" he asked, tipping my chin up to look into my eyes.

"Marrying you?"

"Marrying me. Two weeks in Fiji. Fostering. All of it."

When we returned from our excessively sexy honeymoon, we would be beginning the application process to become foster parents. Traditional baby-making efforts were still ongoing and very, very enjoyable, but neither of us wanted to wait to start our family.

"Absolutely," I promised. The tears were welling up dangerously fast this time. "Thank you for making all my dreams come true, big guy."

Lucian ran a thumb under my eye, catching a tear as it spilled free.

"It's all I've ever wanted to do," he said earnestly.

"Nope! No! Stop it right now," I ordered as I stepped out of his arms. "No more sweetness or I'll cry and ruin my entire face, and Tiffany scares the hell out of me. She might call off the wedding."

"Tell me what you need," he said, a faint smile curving his lips.

"I need one of your insulting pep talks. Don't hold back," I insisted, gesturing for him to bring it on.

His smile was wicked. "Get your shit together, Sloane. Do you want to look like Alice Cooper in our wedding photos that are going to be splashed all over publications across the country? I thought you were tougher than that."

"Good. That's good. Keep it coming."

"If I so much as see one single tear on that beautiful fucking face of yours before you walk down that aisle to me, I'll tell Tiffany we want her to plan every anniversary party for the rest of our lives."

I gasped. "Mean!"

"Don't be a fucking baby."

"*Me?* You better keep it together since you're the one who's been dreaming about this since the first time you climbed that damn cherry tree," I shot back.

"You'll be happy to know that 'that damn cherry tree' is weight-bearing again. The tree surgeons did an excellent job."

"Good. Keep distracting me," I said.

"I have something for you."

"Damn it, Lucifer!"

"Suck it up and deal with it," he said, handing over a thick, rich-guy envelope.

"Where do you even buy stationery like this? Wealthy Person Mart?" I demanded, waving the linen envelope under his nose.

"Don't be ridiculous. We shop at Riches R Us."

Rolling my eyes, I opened the snooty envelope and pulled out the papers. "This is a lot of legalese. Did you just *gift* me a prenup? I told you I'd sign one."

With a roll of his eyes, Lucian flipped through the pages and tapped one. "It's not a prenup, Pix. It's an endowment and paperwork to make the Simon Walton Foundation official."

"Well, shit, big guy." My eyes went right to the number. "Is that a phone number? Or is that an incredibly well-endowed endowment?"

"You did good work. This will allow it to continue. Maybe with a few full-time employees."

I looked up at him, stunned. "Like Mary Louise?"

"Who better to handle the day-to-day? And I thought Allen might be interested in officially joining the fight now that he's passed the bar. I also thought, though the decision is yours, my mother might be a good addition."

Shortly after their fight, Kayla had started seeing a therapist. She and Lucian had quickly reconciled, and Kayla had finally started to take her independence seriously. In the process, she and my mother had managed to become friends.

I stared down at the page as words and numbers swam before my eyes.

"You're going to cry again, aren't you?"

"No, I'm not, assface. God, why do you have to give such thoughtful gifts? You're such a jerk," I sniffled.

"Suck it up, or I'll be forced to unleash Tiffany."

Blinking back tears, I crossed the room to my nightstand and found the wrapped package I'd tucked into the drawer.

"This is for you," I said, thrusting it at him.

While he carefully undid the wrapping, I resumed the fanning of my eyes.

"What is it?" he asked, flipping over the frame.

He went statue still, looking like he'd been carved from marble by a besotted sculptor.

It was a picture from this summer of me, Maeve, Mom, and Chloe on the front porch. Lucian was grinning in the middle, his arms around us protectively. Beneath the photo was a slip of paper. The last text my dad had sent him.

If I could have chosen a son in this lifetime, it would have been you. Take care of my girls.

Lucian swallowed hard. He opened his mouth, but no words came. And when he covered his eyes with his free hand, I knew I'd hit the mark.

"This is . . ." His voice was raspy. And when he looked up at me, those gray eyes were red-rimmed and filled with so much love it took my breath away.

I waved a hand between us. "Don't you dare. You need to get your shit together, Lucifer, because if you break, I break."

He reached for me and hauled me into his chest.

"He'd be so proud of you, Lucian," I said on a broken whisper. "I can feel it. He'd be bursting with pride, and he'd be so happy for us."

A silent shudder rolled through the man I loved, the man who'd taken a bullet for me, the man who'd rebuilt my dreams for me.

"I love you so damn much, Lucian. I always have."

He pulled back and peered down at me, holding my wrists in his strong hands. "Everything I did was for you, Sloane. Because it was always you."

"This is everything I've ever wanted, Lucian," I confessed. "You're everything I ever wanted."

"You saying that, in my arms, wearing my ring, is everything I've ever wanted."

The ceremony was performed by Emry, who needed to pause several times to blow his nose noisily into a billowy handkerchief.

Sloane didn't walk down the aisle. She ran and jumped into Lucian's arms. They said their vows locked in an embrace.

When the officiant asked "Who gives this woman to this man?" Karen Walton stood and said, "Her father and I do." There wasn't a dry eye for the rest of the ceremony.

Nolan cried and wrapped Lucian in a bear hug. Nolan's wife documented the hug with her camera, and Petula framed it for the office.

Sloane and Lucian danced their first dance as man and wife to Shania Twain's "From This Moment On."

Lina took Sloane and Naomi aside to whisper the word "twins" to them on the dance floor.

Knox, Nash, and their father shared a hug on the dance floor.

The family was surprised to find the front porch Christmas tree sporting a new angel that bore a striking resemblance to Simon Walton. No one knows where it came from, but everyone agrees that it looks like he's winking.

Bonus Epilogue

Happily Ever After

Lucian

A decade or so later

Christmas Eve was always chaos in our house. It was tradition that our family gathered here every year for an over-the-top holiday/anniversary dinner. Over the years, our family had grown considerably.

In the immediate family, we had two dogs, the now elderly and still judgmental Meow Meow, and a very expensive saltwater aquarium with one bad-tempered fish that had proceeded to eat every other fish until a pretty little clown fish kicked his ass. Sloane named him Lucian.

Despite my annual offering to hire a caterer, the women—and Stef—commandeered the kitchen, drinking wine, laughing, and cooking for hours while the men ran herd on the younger kids.

There were so many traditions and so many people observing them. It should have been overwhelming, but every time the front door opened and a familiar face wandered in carrying gifts, bundled up against the cold, another broken piece inside me knit itself back together.

Not that I'd ever admit it. I was, after all, Lucian

771

Fucking Rollins. And even though I'd gone part-time in my own company, I was still a scary motherfucker.

Except to my family, of course.

I wandered into the kitchen, holding my first grandbaby. Amara was a tiny, bald little peanut in a too-big Christmas onesie. I hadn't put her down since she got here. Sloane swooped by and delivered a kiss to Amara's cheek and then mine.

"Lookin' good, Grandpa," she teased.

Our oldest son, Caden, was twenty-five. We'd finalized his and his sister Caitlin's adoption from foster care when Sloane was pregnant with our first baby, a boy we named Simon. In the course of four months, we'd gone from zero children to three. And we'd added a fourth, Juliana, just one year later.

I shot my wife a smoldering look, a promise of things to come.

She winked, then asked, "When will Nolan's family get here?"

"They'll be here tomorrow night in time for Stef and Jeremiah's Christmas party." Stef had purchased the foreclosed Red Dog Horse Farm on the outskirts of town and turned it into a luxury spa. Every year, we gathered there for a catered feast.

Knox marched through the kitchen with his youngest daughter tossed over his shoulder. He paused long enough for Gilly to reach down and snag two cookies off the platter.

"Viking and Mini Viking, you're both in trouble!" Naomi called after them.

"Does anyone need anything in here? A beverage? A clean dish towel? Some sanity?" I offered, admiring the platters of food.

"Wine," everyone chorused at the same time.

"Lou, the kitchen needs wine," I bellowed at Naomi's father who, with Lina's father, was manning the bar we'd added in the dining room. Amara looked up at me wide-eyed and then belly laughed.

"How's my little one?" Waylay asked, cooing at her daughter nestled in my arms.

In a twist of fate, Caden and Waylay had officially joined our families by overcoming years of friendship and falling in love in college. I still thought they were terrifyingly young to have jumped into that kind of commitment, but Sloane made me promise to keep my concerns to myself.

As my beautiful wife pointed out, if we'd done our job right, Caden would be a well-adjusted, productive adult who knew what he wanted. So far, her prediction appeared to be accurate. Even Emry, who was in the family room with his wife, Sacha, wearing a Hanukkah sweater and explaining the dreidel to Nash's twins, assured me that they seemed like a happy, healthy couple.

"Knock knock!" a cheery voice called from the front door.

"Let's go see who it is," I told Amara. We arrived in time to see my mother-in-law, Karen, stroll through the door with my mother, their boyfriends, and their suitcases. I was still withholding judgment on both men. Even though the barrel-chested Max, who charmed Karen through salsa dancing, and the Purple Heart recipient veteran José looked at my mother as if she'd given birth to the sun, the moon, and everything in between, I wasn't ready to trust either of them any further than I could throw them.

The great-grandmothers dissolved into delighted squeals, and Amara was wrestled from me.

My flour-covered wife appeared and started doling out hugs and cheek kisses. "Your rooms are ready upstairs. Dinner is in an hour. And wine is now," she said.

"We'll take the bags," Jose offered, using his good arm to heft my mother's overnight bag. As an above-the-elbow amputee, the man was annoyingly good at everything. Which only served to make me want to find his weakness even more.

Karen sighed as she watched Max head for the staircase. "Tell me the truth. Am I too old for this?"

"Too old for what?" Sloane asked, slipping her arm around my waist.

"To be so . . . infatuated."

"We're never too old," my mother assured her emphatically, winking at me as she jiggled Amara on her hip. I was still getting used to this new, confident Mom. And she was still getting used to Lucian the family man. But we were making it work.

"Mom, it's like Dad picked him out personally for you. He's lovely," Sloane said.

"He is, isn't he? Speaking of lovely, when are Maeve and Kurt getting here?" Karen asked.

"Maeve just texted. Chloe and her girlfriend just arrived so they'll be here in a few minutes," Sloane reported.

"I can't wait to meet the woman who got Chloe to stop talking long enough to fall in love," Karen said with a grin.

A twitch of fur caught my eye, and I spotted Meow Meow hidden behind the drapes in the front window.

Knox growled theatrically from the living room and lunged on hands and knees. Two kids screamed and streaked down the hallway, three dogs yapping at their heels. Knox laughed, until he had to get to his feet.

"Goddammit, this middle-aged thing sucks," he groaned.

We were all older. More things hurt getting out of bed in the morning. But I'd never felt better in my life. Being part of this circus of a family had healed so many scars I didn't even know I carried. I'd stopped tattooing over the physical ones after watching my wife wear hers like a badge of honor.

"Ho! Ho! Ho!" Duke Morgan, Knox and Nash's father, appeared in the open doorway. The man was dressed as Santa, and his wife was dressed as Mrs. Claus. On the porch was a red velvet sack overflowing with presents.

"Grandpa Santa's here," Nash, in uniform because he was on call, yelled. Lina was tucked into his side, her arms around his waist. Kids from all corners of the house ran to greet the newcomers.

Taking advantage of the distraction, I grabbed Sloane by the wrist and nodded toward the front door.

She grinned at me. We snuck our coats out of the closet and ducked outside onto the porch.

"There's too many damn people in there," I complained as she led me to the swing.

"You love it, and you know it, Lucifer."

I did, and there was no hiding it despite my best efforts.

I pulled my wife into my side and covered us with the fleece blanket we kept on the porch for such escapes.

Sloane snuggled against me and let out a sigh of contentment. "Every year just keeps getting better," she said.

I stroked my hand over her hair, currently a silver blond. It really did. My semiretirement hadn't been the bump I'd expected it to be. Nolan and Lina had been promoted. The unbearably chipper Holly had moved in next door to us in my old house with her new husband to work with Sloane's foundation. Between the library and her foundation, Sloane continued to amaze me with her generosity and tenacity.

We'd kept my place in the city, but it had taken buying a monstrous place in the Outer Banks to get Sloane to truly slow down. Every year, we wrangled the entire extended brood into a two-week beach vacation. The kind I'd always dreamed of as a kid. With bonfires and fireworks and lazy days spent getting too much sun.

The life we'd built was the stuff of dreams.

Sloane sat up and looked at me with eager eyes. "I got you something."

"You got me everything."

"Said the rich guy who literally showers me with gifts on a daily basis. Do you think you can handle your anniversary present?"

I sighed. "Of course, but do it quickly before someone finds us out here."

It had become yet another little tradition between just the two of us, sentimental gifts exchanged privately on our anniversary. This morning, I'd given Sloane hers, a custom-made dress by the same designer who had made her wedding gown. She was wearing it now, and every time I looked directly at her, my heart beat just a little faster.

Smugly, she lifted a pillow from the end of the swing to reveal a package wrapped in red-and-green-plaid paper.

I unearthed an acrylic frame from beneath the paper and lifted it free.

It was a single, perfect cherry blossom.

"It's from our tree. I figured since you gave each kid a cutting that you should have something from it that you can enjoy all year-round."

I traced my fingers over the blossom that had symbolized so much for me for so long.

Hope. Love. Family.

All of it I'd earned. All of it Sloane had given me.

"It's . . . uh . . . It's . . . nice." I managed to get the words out around the lump in my throat.

Sloane grinned, bouncing on the cushion. "I knew you'd love it!" She paused her victory dance as the sound of breaking glass, a chorus of "uh-ohs," and raucous barking sounded from inside. "Now, get your shit together before we go back in there."

I chuckled and looked up to catch the winking angel on top of the porch tree. "He would have loved this," I said.

"You know what else he would have loved? The dad and grandpa you are."

I pulled her into my lap and framed her face with my hands. "All for you. Always."

Dear Reader,

I never type The End. Not even on the happiest of happily ever afters. It's a superstition of mine because I'm never quite ready to say goodbye. To me, these characters that have occupied my brain all live on long after the book or the series ends.

But Knockemout has come to a close, and I don't know what to do with myself now. These characters have been part of my life for more than two years. Two years of drastic change and wild dreams and tragic losses.

Not only am I a better writer because of Knockemout (write nearly half a million words about anything and you're bound to improve), but I feel like I'm a better person. I learned so much about love and loss and everything in between thanks to Naomi and Knox, Lina and Nash, and Sloane and Lucian. And I remembered the magical properties of laughter (that "shocking" dinner scene).

Thank you for being on this journey with me. I appreciate you more than you'll ever know!

Xoxo,
Lucy

Acknowledgments

Joyce and Tammy for all of the things ever, especially the reminders to shower.

Kari March Designs for the trifecta of perfect covers.

Victoria Morrone for your generous donation to the LIFT 4 Autism auction.

The teams from That's What She Said, Bloom Books, and Hodder Books for . . . well, literally everything. Special shout-out to Tim, Dan, Deb, Christa, Pam, and Kimberley.

My agent, Flavia, and my attorney, Eric, for preventing me from doing many stupid things. *So many.*

ELOE, Tiki, and the TWSS authors for making the hard part about writing easier.

All the readers I got to meet in person on tour.

All the readers I haven't got to meet yet.

Taco Bell forever and always.

About the Author

Lucy Score is an instant #1 *New York Times* bestselling author. She grew up in a literary family who insisted that the dinner table was for reading and earned a degree in journalism. She writes fulltime from the Pennsylvania home she and Mr. Lucy share with their obnoxious cat, Cleo. When not spending hours crafting heartbreaker heroes and kick-ass heroines, Lucy can be found on the couch, in the kitchen, or at the gym. She hopes to someday write from a sailboat, oceanfront condo, or tropical island with reliable Wi-Fi.

Sign up for her newsletter and stay up on all the latest Lucy book news. And follow her on:

Website: lucyscore.com
Facebook: lucyscorewrites
Instagram: @scorelucy
TikTok: @lucyferscore
Binge Books: bingebooks.com/author /lucy-score
Readers Group: facebook.com/groups /BingeReaders Anonymous
Newsletter signup:

Center Point Large Print
600 Brooks Road / PO Box 1
Thorndike, ME 04986-0001 USA

(207) 568-3717

US & Canada:
1 800 929-9108
www.centerpointlargeprint.com

DUE DATE	MCN	11/23	39.95